T0326011

PRAISE FOR MICHAEL J. MALONE

'A tense, creepy page-turner' Ian Rankin

'A terrific read … I read it in one sitting' Martina Cole

'Beautiful, lyrical prose takes the reader through a perfectly constructed, often harrowing tale' Denzil Meyrick

'A fine, atmospheric chiller couched in Malone's customary elegant prose' Douglas Skelton

'A dark and unnerving psychological thriller that draws you deep into the lives of the characters and refuses to let go' Caroline Mitchell

'Poetic and beautifully crafted, this is a chilling and compelling read' Caro Ramsay

'A master storyteller at the very top of his game … weaves the most exquisite tale … mesmeric and suspenseful' Marion Todd

'Tense, pacy and lyrical … cements Malone in the firmament of Tartan Noir, marrying McIlvanney and Banks to a modern domestic noir' Ed James

'A chilling tale of the unexpected that journeys right into the dark heart of domesticity' Marnie Riches

'Once again, I closed a Michael Malone book sad that it had ended, excited for the next one, and in admiration of his beautiful writing' Louise Beech

'A beautifully written tale, original, engrossing and scary … a dark joy' *The Times*

'With each turn of the page, a more shocking detail is revealed … There is barely enough time to catch your breath' *Scotsman*

'A gothic ghost story and psychological thriller all rolled into one. Brilliantly creepy … a spine-tingling treat' *Daily Record*

'Malone is the master of twists, turns and the unexpected, with the skill to keep things grounded ... Superb storytelling from a master of his craft' *Herald Scotland*

'A deeply satisfying read' *Sunday Times*

'Prepare to have your marrow well and truly chilled by this deeply creepy Scottish horror' *Sunday Mirror*

'A complex and multilayered story – perfect for a wintry night' *Sunday Express*

'A fine, page-turning thriller' *Daily Mail*

'Unsettling, multi-layered and expertly paced' *CultureFly*

'Michael J. Malone is a master of literary gothic imaginings ... If you like your stories beautifully crafted, with a hint of witchcraft and the unexpected, then *The Murmurs* will be for you' Jen Med's Book Reviews

'Subtle, sensitivity written, wrought with emotion and has to be one of my most captivating, heart-breaking reads EVER' The Book Review Café

'With an immense sense of place ... a curse, a psychic ability, generations of witches, *The Murmurs* is the perfect Halloween read. If you like your thrillers on the mysterious side, with a bit of family drama and a supernatural angle, it should be at the top of your list!' From Belgium with Booklove

'Mesmerising, beautifully written and it's just made me so much more of a member of #TeamMalone. Just incredible!' The Reading Closet

'Truly intriguing and addictive ... *The Murmurs* is not to be missed if you love novels about curses and secrets' Sally Boocock

'A complex, nuanced story that is utterly compelling ... I ask again, why is he not more seriously lauded?' Live & Deadly

'Compelling, provocative, emotive and, as always, beautifully written' Hair Past a Freckle

'It is affecting. It is dark. It is disturbing' Swirl and Thread

'Every single word in this book has more than earned its place on the page' Chapter in My Life

Other titles by Michael J. Malone
available from Orenda Books

A Suitable Lie
House of Spines
After He Died
In the Absence of Miracles
A Song of Isolation
Quicksand of Memory

The Annie Jackson Mysteries
The Murmurs

ABOUT THE AUTHOR

Michael Malone is a prize-winning poet and author who was born and brought up in the heart of Burns Country. *Blood Tears*, his bestselling debut novel, won the Pitlochry Prize from the Scottish Association of Writers. His psychological thriller, *A Suitable Lie*, was a number-one bestseller, and the critically acclaimed *House of Spines* and *After He Died* soon followed suit. After three further thought-provoking, exquisitely written psychological thrillers, *In the Absence of Miracles*, *A Song of Isolation* and *Quicksand of Memory*, cemented his position as a key proponent of Tartan Noir, Michael began his first series, the Annie Jackson Mysteries, with the highly acclaimed *The Murmurs*.

A former Regional Sales Manager (Faber & Faber) he has also worked as an IFA and a bookseller. Michael lives in Ayr.

Follow him on X/Twitter @michaelJmalone1, facebook.com/themichaeljmalonepage and Instagram @1michaeljmalone.

THE TORMENTS
MICHAEL J. MALONE

ORENDA
BOOKS

Orenda Books
16 Carson Road
West Dulwich
London SE21 8HU
www.orendabooks.co.uk

First published in the UK by Orenda Books, 2024
Copyright © Michael J. Malone, 2024

Michael J. Malone has asserted his moral right to be identified as the author of
this work in accordance with the Copyright, Designs and Patents Act, 1988.

All Rights Reserved. No part of this publication may be reproduced in any form
or by any means without the written permission of the publishers.

*This is a work of fiction. Names, characters, places and incidents are either products of
the author's imagination or are used fictitiously. Any resemblance to actual events,
locales or persons, living or dead, is entirely coincidental.*

A catalogue record for this book is available from the British Library.

B-format paperback ISBN 978-1-916788-28-2
eISBN 978-1-916788-29-9

Typeset in Garamond by typesetter.org.uk
Printed and bound by Clays Ltd, Elcograf S.p.A

For sales and distribution, please contact *info@orendabooks.co.uk* or visit
www.orendabooks.co.uk.

THE TORMENTS

Prologue

She has watched over and preyed on the inhabitants of this cloud- and mist-covered land for an age, several ages, truth be told – before the Norse, before even the armies of Rome. She remembers little before the time when she crawled out of the bracken and heather, dressed only in thin garments that took on the colours of the moss and trees, and made it up onto her knees, then her feet, trudging through heavy peat and moor, driven on by a hunger so strong and harsh it all but drove reason from her mind.

She was born of the elements – wind, air and rain. She was bound by greed and lust, and by hope. And guided by beliefs so ancient they were issued to the air long before wretched iron was torn from rock.

Succubus, some called her, but she wanted more than men's seed, it was their life blood and their soul she was after. And she had the wiles, the teeth and claws to get what she needed from them.

And what did they get from her? A tainted dream? A torment of last moments?

Let the legend of one of the earliest men to call her offer some form of explanation.

He was a poor sheep farmer and after his first wife died in labour, he spent weeks alone in the hills tending to his sheep. He was bone-tired, heart-sore, and aching in the ways men ache for a woman.

Not many know the call, but he did, and as he sat in his tumbledown bothy, smoke from the fire stinging his eyes, the smell of the damp hair of his pony and his dog teasing his nostrils, he put the whistle to his lips and blew. He played the tune as if it were the last time music would find his ears, for he knew the moment he stopped playing the spell would be broken. And as he blew he made his wish – for a woman of tender heart and warm loins. Someone to bear him a son and work on this patch of earth he called home while he ranged over the moors, tending to his herd.

On he played, and on. The sun rose, and fell again, the wind whistled through the thatch of his roof, rain dampened the earthen floor, and then as he was thinking he might need to moisten his lips before his tune faltered, a shadow entered.

Her beauty sank him into silence. She was everything he could have wished for, and more. Large, dark eyes, wide-hipped and strong of limb. And possessing of the grace of queens.

She nodded, reading the strength of his longing, and accepted a beaker of whisky he offered with a stammer.

The woman hid her smile and sharp teeth behind the cup, and her cloven hoofs within the folds of her dress. She smiled because she knew that a God-fearing Scotsman should only make such a wish during the hours of darkness if he also invoked God's protection. Without it, his wish would be granted, but in the most terrible of fashions.

This fellow, however, was so in thrall to his desires that he failed to claim the protection of the Lord – and in that failure he had sealed his doom.

They kissed, and she silently noted his tremble of desire and longing, hearing his thoughts as if they were her own. She closed her eyes. Savoured his need and ache for her, knowing he would die in mere moments, his stare wide and his terror distilled into the liquid of his eyes.

She put a hand on his chest, held him off. 'Patience,' she whispered, her half-smile and raised eyebrows, her nearness, her promise of love and loving pushing him into a torment of yearning.

He was found several days later – his faithful hound's ceaseless barking drawing the neighbours' attention. The man's body was as cold as a mountain top in winter, his throat ripped out, his flesh entirely empty of blood, but, mysteriously, naught but the foot-prints of animals around him.

Throughout the ages many, many more victims fell to her hunger.

But that was then.

Now, as old beliefs die, religions fall, and people numb themselves to the lack of purpose and meaning in their lives with a sugared potion, or smoking stick in one hand, and a small box of flickering light and stuttering sound in the other, She has found a new way to prey, for down the centuries her hunger for man-flesh has only grown.

She has waited. Shown the patience of the ages.

And She will not be denied, for She is cunning. She is chaos. She is torments untold.

She is legend.

She is the Baobhan Sith.

Chapter 1

Annie

Annie reached for her car keys on the little kitchen table and felt a surge of anxiety twist at her heart and shorten her breath. The minute, the *second*, she sat in her car, the murmurs could awaken and harass her until the moment she stepped back inside her little stone cottage.

There was just no pattern to them. Often they would leave her alone for hours, sometimes days, but then they would populate every waking and sleeping moment, making her feel constantly on edge.

Inside the cottage, though, in the garden, or by the little beach that edged the loch, they were much quieter.

Sometimes she was able to deal with them, but there were

moments when the hateful, accusatory voices became too much and she just wanted to curl up into a ball and rock herself to sleep.

For the millionth time she sent a prayer of thanks to her Aunt Sheila for leaving her this place – a woman she had only met a couple of times in her life, while only a girl. How she had known the little building would offer Annie sanctuary from the curse that had haunted her family for centuries Annie didn't know, but she would be forever grateful.

Annie looked out of the window, at the still surface of the loch and the heathered hills beyond, and felt the soothing they always offered.

The only way *to*, is *through*, she told herself; the little mantra that had helped her face her troubles over the years. Just one of the nuggets she'd been taught by her adoptive mother, Mandy McEvoy.

With that thought tight in the forefront of her mind she gripped her keys. Felt the metal dig into the soft flesh of her palm.

You can't lock yourself away up in Ardlochard forever, Lewis's voice sounded in her ear. Her twin brother had phoned her just that morning from his office in Glasgow, like he did almost every day.

'Watch me, brother,' she'd replied.

Being isolated from the rest of society not only muted the voices but it also offered relief from knowing how someone was about to die – another part of the family curse. She did appreciate, however, that being almost entirely on her own, without another human within a ten-mile radius, was not a good way to live. And might well lead to quite a different form of madness.

All she needed was a brood of cats and she was set, she thought ruefully.

Steeling herself, she walked to the door. Lewis was right. Besides, it was time to go to work. It was only four afternoons a week. And importantly, without the income she earned at the little café in Lochaline, she wouldn't be able to afford to live here, so there really wasn't much of an argument to be had.

Another step closer to the door.

She set her jaw. Listened.

The voices were there, but were low, like a distant hum.

The last time she went to work they'd started up the moment she turned the key in the car. With the surge of the engine came the build-up of aural insanity, and by the time she'd reached the road-end she was close to being a sobbing wreck.

Right.

Just go.

Leave.

Chapter 2

Annie

Happily, the murmurs were fairly quiet during Annie's shift at the café. And she was kept busy enough that she was distracted from their constant drone. But there was one man who set off that other part of her curse – the *knowing* how someone was about to die.

The crew of the local lifeboat were running a practice drill out in the waters of Loch Aline, and when they finished, they berthed just by the café and popped in for bacon rolls and cups of tea.

One young lad caught her attention. His blue eyes shone with the pleasure at being included in the team, and he soaked up the words of the experienced men and women around him

That familiar sick taste bloomed in her mouth. Lights sparked in the periphery of her vision, his face blurred, the skin on it peeled away and she could see the bone beneath. A flash of noise and movement, and in her mind's eye Annie saw a small, dark-blue car all but wrapped around the trunk of a tree.

A voice of insistent horror filled her ears. A mass of unintelligible words, murmuring and sibilant, and woven through that the sound of flames and of wood sap boiling and cracking in the heat.

These feelings of dread and sickness rose in her every time she received one of these premonitions. She battled against them, as she always did.

'You alright, hen?' a man she was about to serve asked. She realised she'd paused in the action of setting down a cup of coffee in front of him.

She looked around. Out of the café window she saw a little blue car, fully intact. The car in her premonition.

She coughed. 'Whose is the wee Corsa?' she asked, wondering how she might avert a disaster, knowing at the same time that whenever she'd tried to warn someone about how they were going to die, it always ended badly for her, and more importantly, didn't stop the death from happening.

Someone at the table said, 'That's your wee heap of shit, Lachlan.'

The young man with the blue eyes held his hand up.

Everyone laughed. Annie read the strong camaraderie, and realised the young man's death would affect the whole team.

'The shaggin' wagon,' one older man shouted.

Lachlan joined the laughter, good nature on show, and shot the speaker a finger. Then he turned to Annie and winked.

'Why? Want to buy it?' he asked with a cheeky grin.

'Be careful, hen,' one of the older members of the team counselled. 'He'll be after your phone number next.'

More laughter.

'Maybe once you get that slow puncture fixed, mate,' Annie replied.

Everyone chuckled as their young friend's attempt at banter with the waitress backfired, and Annie could see that none of them knew who she was: the infamous Annie Jackson who'd uncovered the truth of the 'Bodies in the Glen'. As far as they were concerned, as far as *everyone* in the local area was concerned, she was Annie Bennett. She'd decided to adopt her birth mother's surname as part of her attempt to blend in to the local population as just another incomer.

Moments later she returned to the table with Lachlan's roll and bacon. As she placed his food down she leaned forward and urged quietly, 'Get your tyres seen to, eh?' He looked up in surprise, but before he could respond, she quickly walked away, her heart thumping.

The rest of her shift passed without any further dramas – the lifeboat crew leaving just before she did.

As one of the older members walked past he said, 'Best rolls and bacon in the area.' Annie knew him. Geordie Harrison. She had come across him several times. He owned the local hotel and bar, and was prominent at any community gatherings. Geordie was a small, lean man with a shoulder-length mane of grey-and-black hair. Something told her that there was money behind many of his dealings with the locals, that they were performative rather than coming from any wish to develop a sense of meaning in his life.

She was sorely tempted to offer young Lachlan another warning via Geordie, but fear stilled her tongue. Her warnings never had the desired effect – no one ever listened, and all that happened was at best, strange looks, and at worse, a mouthful of abuse. It was, Annie determined, another way for this curse to punish her – she knew the details of someone's demise while being aware there was absolutely nothing she could do to change the situation. She smiled at Geordie and he went on his way.

Throughout the morning Annie had become aware of the stares of a woman in the corner, and her studied indifference when Annie looked over. She was middle-aged and slim with chin-length white hair, wearing sturdy shoes and what looked like a quality waterproof jacket. At first sight, Annie thought she might be a walker, but she could feel the woman's eyes on her back wherever she came out of the kitchen, and she realised there was more to her.

Periodically, ever since she had been in the news, people would seek her out. Mostly it was by letter – addressed to her by name, often only with the word 'Ardnamurchan' as the address – and mostly these letters would end up unread in the bin. When they first started arriving she read them out of guilt, but the distress she invariably picked up from them became too much. Occasionally, people would find their way to Lochaline or Mossgow, hang about with her photo on their phone for heaven knows how long, and pounce the moment they saw her. They would then plead with her to help them find their lost relatives or friends.

It was heartbreaking. The weight of their loss was stitched into their expressions and the shape of their bodies. But that pain often turned to anger or disgust when she declined to help them.

Seeing this woman, Annie groaned, sure it was going to happen again. And on top of the guilt she was already feeling over Lachlan, it was too much. A quick look at her watch and she saw that her shift was about to end, so she ducked into the kitchen, whipped off her apron and told her boss, Jan, she had to leave straight away. But before she reached the door, the woman intercepted her, placing a hand on her arm.

'I don't want to disturb you,' the woman said quickly, the eagerness in her eyes betraying the lie. 'But if I could just talk to you...'

Playing out in Annie's mind, as clear as the woman barring her exit, Lachlan's car surged forward, hit a tree. His scream of fear and fright sounded in her ear. Then, she saw his bloodied and crushed head against the steering wheel before he was engulfed in flames. And in the background her murmurs crowed their terrible tune of demented pleasure at her pain.

'Please God, no,' Annie shouted. 'Leave me alone. Enough.' In desperation she moved to the door. Perhaps she could catch up with Lachlan. Wave down one of his friends? In her haste she collided with the woman, and knocked her back onto the corner of a table.

The woman groaned. Corrected herself. Grimaced. Held a hand to her back. 'But you must read this,' she insisted. 'And then get in touch. We need to talk.'

Annie took the letter automatically. But then anger surged. Even after Annie's rudeness and their accidental collision, this woman wasn't deviating from her plan.

'Jesus,' Annie said, and slammed the envelope down on to a table. 'Just give up, will you?' Then she pushed past the woman and left the café before she said something truly nasty.

Sadly, there was no one from the lifeboat crew still in the car park, so she couldn't deliver her warning. So she made her way back home, dropped her car keys onto the kitchen table, took a seat, and with a mind full of images of the dying Lachlan and the desperate woman in the café, she waited for her heart beat to slow to a normal rate and for the murmurs to drop to a quiet hum.

Going out of the house was worth it, she told herself. Besides, she had no other option, despite how difficult it was, and if she moved back to the city, it would be ten times worse. There she wouldn't have the almost-quiet she experienced whenever she walked inside the cottage.

If only there was a way to bottle that and take it everywhere she went.

Annie made herself a cup of tea and a sandwich, and after she had finished and washed up her dishes, she settled down by the unlit fire with a book and tried to savour the silence.

Apart from Annie herself, and the very occasional visitor, the only people who used the road to her cottage were forestry workers. This really was a quiet, unpopulated place to live. The nearest houses were around five miles away down the single-track road, where it joined the B-road. Left took you to Lochaline, and right to Mossgow, and at this junction was a terrace of four white cottages, built, she guessed, to house estate workers. Most of the area, she knew, was owned by Conor Jenkins' family, but the local gossip was that Conor would inherit none of it now his involvement in the Bodies in the Glen case, as the gutter-press named it, had become clear.

The part of the track she could see out of her living-room window led upward a good two hundred yards to the brow of a hill. During the darker months, the first sign of someone's approach was the sweep of car lights breaching the summit moments before a car appeared. Today, it was late summer, so it wouldn't be dark for a good few hours yet.

She put her book down, struggling to concentrate.

The young Lachlan's face appeared in her mind. The good-humoured shine in his eyes as he accepted the jokes at his expense from his lifeboat colleagues. Then she saw him in his car. He was approaching a bend too fast. He lost control. Ploughed into a tree.

Annie felt sickness surge up from her stomach. She made it to the toilet just in time.

After, trembling, she stood at the sink, washed her face and looked at her tired eyes in the mirror. Maybe she was wrong. Maybe her warning about his tyres would fall on listening ears and he'd do something about them.

She shook her head. She knew this was a false hope.

A knock at her front door made her jump. Rapid. Heavy. Insistent.

Who could that be? she wondered, thinking they must have driven in while she was being sick, as she hadn't heard a car engine.

'Coming,' she shouted.

When she pulled the door open it was to find Geordie Harrison, and judging by his white face, clenched fists and his mouth in a pale line of fury, he wasn't happy.

'Geordie...' she began.

'What did you do?' he demanded.

Annie stepped back, shocked at this display of anger. 'I don't—'

'Lachlan...' he choked. His eyes were red. Puffy. 'He died at the scene. Went off the road.'

'Oh my God.' Annie's hand shot up to cover her mouth.

'You're that woman, aren't you?' he demanded. 'The one who Chris Jenkins tried to kill up by?' He cocked his head in the direction of the lost settlement. 'The psychic who uncovered all those dead bodies?'

'Geordie, what happened?'

'You knew and you did nothing.' He shook his head. 'Your wee jokey comment about the tyres. Why didn't you say more?' His eyes were pleading now. 'Why didn't you stop him? You as good as killed that boy. If I ever see you in the village again I won't be responsible for my actions.' He spat at her feet. 'Fucking witch.'

Chapter 3

Sylvia
1958

Whenever Sylvia cast her eyes to the side she caught sight of something. A shadow. If she was quick enough. If she tried to look directly at ... whatever it was, there was nothing there. But she wasn't scared. Indeed, she took comfort from it, and would speak to it, and play with it during breaktime. Of course, it didn't reply, or do anything really, it was just there in the corner of her eye, like an absence of light.

Sylvia would always remember the first time. She was sure someone was by her side – but when she turned she was on her own. Then, inexplicably, she had an urge to proffer her hand for someone to hold. And then came the knowledge that the shadow would always be by her side. Occasionally afterwards a warmth enveloped her hand – fingers clasping hers with a touch as light as a single feather. Like a gentle validation.

She tried, once, to talk about this with her grandmother, but such was the look of disgust on her face, Sylvia never mentioned it again.

Sylvia was a trust-fund child, and an orphan. Her parents died in a plane crash on the way home from a second honeymoon in

Africa. They'd been on safari at the famous Treetops Hotel in Kenya just a few months after Queen Elizabeth spent time there. A place that Sylvia's mother dreamt about going to, apparently, from the moment she read about the Queen's travels in all of the popular magazines of the time.

Sylvia was only a matter of months old when her parents took that holiday. The legend was her parents decided to leave her at home, fearing the Mau Mau rebellion that was causing all kinds of 'upset' at that time in the British colony of Kenya.

This was all relayed to Sylvia by her grandmother, Maude Purbeck, related to the grand Villiers family of Buckingham fame, who was so fraught at the loss of her only child that she took to holding regular seances in order to speak with her dead daughter whenever a decision was to be made.

Of her dead son-in-law, Maude said little. When she did it was prefaced by 'that boy'. And even if she never articulated it to her, Sylvia sensed her grandmother blamed Sylvia's father for her mother's death.

The Mau Mau mentions passed Sylvia by, but the seances were a feature of her life that she prayed would continue even though she was soon going away to school.

Later in life she would recall that the gravity of those moments was difficult to translate at the time, but when her grandmother closed the heavy damask curtains and they sat face to face at the little highly polished table she remembered excitement bubbling under her skin. She loved the ceremony of it all, and the fact that she was deemed to be central to the seances' success. And of course, she loved that she would get to hear the words of her dead parents.

That these words could be heard only in the mind of her grandmother mattered little. The young Sylvia received them from her grandmother's lips without question.

So it was that, at age five years and three months she was deemed to be ready to attend Clevelland School, as all the young of her family had, going back several generations. And it was there that she found herself at a desk, sitting beside a solid and strange little boy who whispered to her, 'I'm going to make you cry.'

Chapter 4

Annie

It had been two weeks since Lachlan's crash; two weeks in which Annie barely went out of her front door, avoided work altogether and refused to answer the landline. Until the day she received three calls in quick succession. Mandy, her adoptive mother. It had to be.

'Hi,' Annie replied.

'Annie?' Mandy asked instantly. 'Have you been avoiding your phone? I ran three times last night as well, you know. I hate you being up there and so out of touch.'

It was an ongoing argument and one Annie struggled to continue. 'I'm just not getting wi-fi, Mrs Mac, and there's not much I can do about the crappy signal on my mobile up here.'

'Well, at least answer your house phone when it rings.'

'Sorry,' Annie roused herself from her poor mood. 'What's up?'

'What's up with you, more like? I left a couple of messages. Your dad and I are really worried. What's going on?'

Annie thought about lying, and decided against it. Mandy could read her like a book. 'Just having a tough few days, that's all.' She didn't want to get into the whole Lachlan thing because Mandy would fuss for two hours straight and then get in the car with her husband to drive north to see her.

'Oh. Right.' Mandy was good at understanding Annie's state of mind. But she didn't delve further, which suggested she had an issue of her own that was distracting her.

Annie exhaled. 'Anyway, enough about me.' She huffed a short self-deprecatory laugh. 'What's up? Why have you been ringing me non-stop?'

There was a pause.

Annie filled it. 'You okay, Mrs Mac?'

'My sister, Chrissie's been on the phone,' Mandy began.

'Right.'

'You remember her son, Damien, the one that was in prison?'

Annie only vaguely knew Mandy's side of the family, but was aware that, despite her solid and loving nature, she had always been at odds with her only sister. Annie had met Damien plenty of times when they were younger, but from their teens and beyond, they'd led very different lives. Damien, she remembered, was a footballing prodigy as a teen. All the large Scottish clubs were after him, and a few English, until he signed for one of the big Glasgow teams. He had an injury, or something happened that Annie couldn't quite recall, and thereafter he fell into the anti-social deep end. Fighting, booze, and drugs, until he ended up on the street – Mandy reported that with a rueful smile about the tough love meted out by her sister and her husband. In the end, Damien seriously injured another man in a street brawl and was given time in prison. Last Annie heard, he was out, trying to rebuild his life, and working to earn a relationship with his little boy, Bodie.

'He has a kid now, right?'

'That's why Chrissie is so worried,' Mandy replied.

'Why? What happened?'

'You know I wouldn't ordinarily ask you this, dear,' Mandy said, and Annie could see Mandy in her mind's eye, fidgeting with the little gold pendant she wore round her neck.

God. No, Annie thought. Please don't ask.

'He's gone missing. Chrissie's desperate. She needs your help. This is so unlike Damien. He really has turned his life around.' Mandy's tone managed to be apologetic and pleading at the same time.

The murmurs surged. Sibilant consonants and long vowels in an unintelligible cacophony. Growling. Pleading. Mocking. Urging. Raging. Fury given sound.

Mandy didn't know the scale of what she was asking her to do, Annie thought – to seek out those voices deliberately when for the best part of a year she'd been almost constantly fighting them off?

'I know what I'm asking you is tough,' Mandy said. 'But she has no one else. The police aren't even vaguely interested.'

Annie released a tremulous breath, aware only then that she had been holding it in.

'How does she know?' Annie asked, realising she sounded defensive, and knowing that Mandy should never be the target of her bad mood. 'About me, I mean?'

'I didn't tell her,' Mandy replied quickly. 'She saw it on the telly along with everyone else in the country.'

Stupid question. Annie rolled her eyes. Of course Chrissie would know. Annie had been big news – *massive* news – when she'd survived a murder attempt up in the hills beyond her house, among the ruins of a lost settlement.

She could feel his hands around her throat even now – Chris Jenkins, the pastor at a church in Glasgow. It was only later that Annie was able to see that he had sought her out and wooed her because he wanted to know just how much her psychic ability had revealed to her about him. When she'd arrived within the confines of one of the ruined houses she'd not only seen a beautifully arranged picnic, but she'd somehow seen, under and within the roots of a tree, the bones of two women.

Her shocked reaction at this discovery had pushed him to try and kill her. She gasped at the memory, as she always did – surprised, and yet not, that it still had the power to frighten.

Following the events of that day it seemed that she had been on the news cycle for months, and it was only now, almost a year later, that she was being left on her own. Movie and TV producers had thrown various sums of money at her, pleading for her to tell her story, but she'd refused them all, determined that she would use this gift, this curse, as little as possible.

Despite all of that attention, she'd managed to keep this little house in this far glen a secret from the media. The hillside higher up the glen had been crawling with forensic scientists, newspaper reporters, and curious members of the public, but none of them had turned their eyes towards her home down by the loch. She occasionally wondered if the spirits who lived in the glen had somehow made this possible.

'When does your shift end?' Mandy asked, pulling Annie from her thoughts.

'I ... eh, I'm off today.'

'Right. We'll be there around four or five pm.'

'What? We? Who's we? You're not coming up here, are you?'

'We've booked a B&B in Mossgow.' Mossgow was the village twenty minutes away where Annie had spent a chunk of her childhood.

Annie shivered. Cold fingers of dread gripped her heart. Her curse was hard enough to bear without actively seeking it out.

'Hear Chrissie out, Annie,' Mandy pleaded. 'I've never seen my sister so worried.'

Annie closed her eyes. Tight. Clenched her fist.

Clever, clever, Mrs Mac. Saying that she was going to drive all the way up from Glasgow. Many knew, no matter how difficult it might be for Annie, that she was never able to refuse her anything, especially when she was standing in front of her.

'Will you please help my sister?' Mandy said. 'Help her find her son?'

Chapter 5

Annie

At five minutes to five that afternoon Mandy breezed into Annie's little house, carrying a large casserole dish. 'Didn't think you'd have time to cook, Annie, so I brought us some of your favourite fish pie. Hope you don't mind. I'll just put it in the fridge.' By this time she was in the kitchen so she shouted over her shoulder: 'Unless you're hungry, in which case I'll put it in the oven now.' Then. 'It's been a while since you last saw Chrissie. Don't just stand gawping at the door, Chrissie. Come on in.' Then to Annie. 'We're staying at The Lodge, by the way, but we thought it would be nice to have a wee girlie evening with some food and wine, and I'm driving, so Chrissie and you can get stuck into the prosecco.'

Annie felt like holding a hand up, making a stop sign with it, just to get a word in. Mandy was a talkative lady, but even for her this was a bit extra. It was a sign that she was uncomfortable with the whole situation. Her love for Annie and her need to protect her had clearly been overridden on this occasion by her concern for Chrissie.

Annie took a step closer to Mandy's sister, unsure of the protocol. It had indeed been a number of years since she'd seen Chrissie. She and her family hadn't been that regular in their visits to see Mandy, and while Annie had got to know Damien as a child, she'd never really developed any kind of relationship with his mum. Not that the blame was all Chrissie's. Annie freely admitted that she was hard work as a teenager, stomping about the house, slamming doors, avoiding any kind of contact. But seeing Chrissie standing in her doorway, her face a mixture of trepidation and desperation, her heart went out to her.

Chrissie was so unlike her sister it was hard for Annie to accept that they were siblings. Where Mandy was short and slight, Chrissie was a good four inches taller and four stone heavier. Mandy's dark hair was slowly giving way to the silver, but Chrissie's was dyed resolutely blonde. There was something about the eyes, though, that hinted at a family connection. Those eyes were carefully scrutinising Annie and her little house.

'Hey,' Chrissie said, still in the doorway, as if afraid the strange phenomenon that affected Annie was contagious in some way. But instead of being insulted, Annie found she was resigned. She'd suffered a much stronger reaction very recently. If the woman turned nasty on her she'd deal with it. In the meantime she'd try and be a friend and see where that led.

Should she shake her hand? Give her a hug? She settled for a raised hand and, 'Hi. Come on in. Have a seat.'

'Your wee house is lovely,' Chrissie said as she moved to the folded-up futon under the window. 'It's a bit out of the way, right enough.'

'Aye,' Mandy said as she re-entered the living room. 'I forget each time I drive up here how far it is from the big city.'

Mandy and Annie hugged, and before Mandy let her go she sent a silent query with her eyes: *You okay*? Annie should have known Mandy would notice something wasn't quite right.

Annie smiled in reply, realising that a smile that didn't go anywhere near her eyes wasn't going to convince Mandy of anything.

'We can talk about it later,' Mandy whispered. Then she sat, looking around as she did every time she came to visit. 'It is lovely and peaceful, Annie,' she said. 'I can see why you'd never want to leave the place.'

'Yes,' said Chrissie as she released her handbag from her lap, where she had been clutching it as if it might offer some sort of protection. 'There's a nice atmosphere in here, eh?'

Annie sat on the chair nearest Chrissie, thinking it best they got on to the subject at hand. 'Damien,' she said. 'What happened?'

'Right,' Mandy said. 'I'll go and see to the food. Let you two talk.' With that she disappeared into the kitchen.

Chrissie watched her go, and Annie read that she'd rather Mandy had stayed. 'It's ... well ... I don't *really* believe in all this voodoo stuff. I mean it doesn't make sense, does it? How can you know these things? And I'm a good Christian.' Her eyes filled with tears. 'But this is so unlike Damien. He's a changed boy, so he is. Dotes on that kid of his, so he does. There's no way he would just up and vanish unless something bad had happened to him.'

She leaned forward, crossing her arms as she did so. 'So, how do you do this thing? Do I give you something of his and you get some kind of signal?'

Chapter 6

Annie

Annie felt hopeless. She could see the distress that Chrissie was in, felt it deeply, but had no idea how she could help.

Playing for time, she said, 'Let's just talk for a little while.' She paused. 'This thing has no real pattern to it. Comes and goes, and it's mostly when the person is in front of me that I sense things.' She hoped her expression of sympathy would be appreciated.

'Oh.' Fresh tears sparked in Chrissie's eyes. 'But you helped that man find his girlfriend, didn't you?' She looked around, out of the window behind her, and at the hills beyond.

Annie felt herself heat with anxiety at the thought she might not be able to help Chrissie and her son.

'You mentioned Damien's wee boy. Tell me about him?'

'Oh,' Chrissie brightened a little. 'Bodie. I thought that was such a stupid name at first, but it's growing on me. He's a love. The cutest wee boy you could ever imagine. Bright as a button, with this mop of blond hair.'

'Do you get to see plenty of him?'

'Not as much as I'd like.' Chrissie's expression fell back to a slump. 'People forget about the grandparents, you know? The courts. When they work out visiting rights and all that, they don't give a moment's thought to how the grandparents might feel, hardly ever getting to see the wee one...'

Mandy reappeared in the room, telling them she'd put the food in the oven, and before long they'd be able to sit down to eat. When it was warmed through they all took their places around the small table in the kitchen and were soon eating the fish pie, and to Annie's relief, the conversation maintained the same general tone as before.

As Annie was finishing off her meal, she heard a noise from the front of the house. She turned towards the window, trying to work out what it might be.

'Are you expecting anyone, Annie?' Mandy asked. 'Lewis hasn't decided to pop up, has he?'

'Not that I know of.'

There was a loud crashing noise. Breaking glass, and the squeal of tyres. Then shouts:

'Fucking witch!'

An engine revved – a whine as it moved too fast in reverse, wheels spun, and a car tore away.

'What the...?' Annie rushed through to her living room. Saw a rock that had landed in the middle of the floor and the glass of the window scattered all over her couch. Anger heated her limbs and she ran to the door, pulled it open and saw the brake lights of a car as it crested the hill.

'The utter, utter shits,' she cried.

Then she heard a gasp from Mandy, and turned. Her door had been splattered with red paint, and the matted fur and headless corpse of a rabbit lay on her front step.

Chapter 7

Ben
1958

It was hate at first sight.

But that wasn't unusual; Ben hated everyone when he first met them, and it was only when he was older he realised that this was simply so he could save time.

It was 1958, his first day of school at Clevelland Academy in the Scottish Borders, and a girl with blonde hair was told to sit beside him. She did so without even looking at him, and while other children around them cried for their parents, the two of them sat in confused and judgemental silence. Why would anyone cry when left behind by their fathers and mothers? Parents did that all of the time. Benjamin's parents left him to go on holiday, to go to work, to go to friends for the weekend, to go into town, to take the dog for a walk.

There were any number of reasons that they avoided spending time with their only son, leaving him with a string of au pairs and nannies – few of whom lasted more than two weeks. He didn't have to say much to scare them off. Simply standing at the door, silently, for however long it took them to have what his mother described as a 'conniption'.

His mother said they were sending him to this school because he was special, that only an establishment such as this could cope with his particular abilities. Which he knew was a lie the moment the words spilled from her mouth.

She was a thin woman, with severe cheekbones and lips so pale they were almost blue. Ben couldn't remember a soft, or a kind, word ever coming out of her mouth; she only ever spoke in commands or judgements.

'You're a little man. Behave like one.'

'Boys should be seen and not heard. Silence.'

'Shake Mother's hand. Silly boy.'

At least she spoke. Father was as quiet as the grave. He would simply give his mother or the nanny a look, and whatever he intended they said. Except when Ben did something wrong, and then Father would strip the belt from his trousers, and words full of hate and spite would flow from him like a purge as he beat Ben. 'Bruised but never bloody,' Father said to Mother each time. 'That is how man differs from the beasts. And I fought the Germans across Europe, so I know beasts.'

Ben knew he deserved it, that he should be a good boy, but the sins of children were too numerous and confusing, and what was a cause for remonstration one day would produce a half-grin perched over a full whisky glass the next.

At the huge front door to the school his father put a hand on Ben's shoulder. Ben flinched at his touch. It was rare that his father touched him with anything other than anger. His father stepped back, craned his neck to take in the scale of the establishment, a look of pleasure on his face, as if he'd built it himself. 'Didn't do me any harm, dear,' he said to his wife. Then he looked at Ben and offered him a rare piece of advice. 'It's all about power, my boy. Grab it. Use it.' And without another word he turned and walked away.

And there, sitting on that chair, next to the girl with the chin-length blonde hair, taking in the crying, upset children around him, noting her lack of emotion, he decided he would try to make her cry as well. That was power of a sort, wasn't it?

Chapter 8

Annie

Mandy sprang into action. She ushered Annie to a seat then rushed to the kitchen to grab a scrubbing brush, a mop and a pail. Seeing what she was doing, Chrissie found a plastic bag, ran to the door and scooped up the poor little rabbit.

'Unless you want it for tomorrow night's dinner?' Chrissie said with a wan smile.

'Not funny, Chrissie,' Mandy replied.

'Kinda is,' Annie said, and laughed. And laughed. Her laughter turning into tears of anger. This was her home, her safe space, her sanctuary, and these idiots had ruined it.

No: they'd tried to ruin it. She would not be cowed by their tactics.

People fear what they don't understand.

The thing was, she understood that impulse to action, driven by fear. Who knew better than her how terrifying her curse could be?

After they'd cleaned the door and step as best they could Mandy gathered her into a hug. 'You okay, pet?' she asked.

The display of caring caused a surge of emotion. Until that moment Annie had thought she was okay. Angry, but not really that upset. Now, though, she felt the tears build.

'Hey.' Mandy rubbed Annie's back. 'Thinking is difficult,' she said. 'That's why lots of people judge instead.'

'That, and the fact that they're arseholes,' Chrissie added.

Annie snorted, laughed again, and soon all three women were giggling.

'Best medicine,' Mandy said, as she wiped tears from her cheeks. 'We'll get the rest of the paint in the morning. And, by the way, you're not staying here on your own, young lady. You're coming with us to the hotel.'

'No, I'm not,' Annie replied.

'You can't stay here after that,' Chrissie said, her eyes straying towards the hill the car had disappeared over.

'Yeah, what if they came back?' Mandy asked.

Since her ability to see how people would die had become common knowledge, she had been aware of how many people reacted to her: the stares, the suspicion and the whispers. Thankfully there had been little of that kind of behaviour in this small community, and she had originally thought that was because no one here realised who she was.

Now she had been proven wrong. They'd known who she was all along. A thought that made her neck heat with embarrassment. Idiot.

She thought of the paint on her door. The broken window. That poor little rabbit. And she crossed her arms. Felt herself shrink. This was her sanctuary, and those arseholes, as Chrissie called them, had ruined it.

No. She refused to give credence to the thought. They hadn't ruined anything. She wouldn't allow herself to be pushed out by narrow-minded, knuckle-dragging *children*. In any case, how would she manage to live around other people in busier places – the knowledge of whose deaths would be broadcast into her mind on a much more regular basis. She simply couldn't, wouldn't, move away from this little cottage, the one place where the murmurs didn't constantly tear into her mind.

Annie became aware that Mandy and Chrissie were staring at her, waiting for her decision.

She set her jaw. 'I'm going nowhere.' She moved to the other side of the fireplace, and looked over at the sharp edges of the broken window, at the glass shards scattered all over the sill, futon and floor – an opaque, razored jigsaw.

'We'll help you clean the glass up,' Mandy said. 'Do you have any board you could cover the window with?'

Annie snorted. 'There was none left in the local supermarket last I looked.'

Mandy ignored her sarcasm and offered a smile. 'We clean this up and then we're taking you to the hotel. They're quiet so they'll have plenty of rooms. And besides, Mr Burns is extremely grateful to you so he'll be happy to help.' Then she added with false brightness: 'He might even have a handyman he uses for hotel stuff who he can send out to fix your window.'

Mr Burns, the hotel manager at The Lodge on the Loch was indeed appreciative towards Annie. His daughter, Jenny, had been one of the women murdered and buried up in the lost settlement. She'd disappeared without a trace years ago, and he and his wife had spent most of the time since suspended in the agony of not knowing where their daughter was. Anytime Annie had been in the hotel since the truth was uncovered he was so happy to see her and so desperate to do what he could for her, that she felt deeply uncomfortable. It was the last thing she needed tonight.

Mandy and Chrissie had already started working quietly and

efficiently to clear away the broken glass. Then Mandy found a towel and a stapler and fixed the towel over the window frame. 'It's not great, but at least it will keep the rain out,' she said. Then she looked at Annie. 'Pack your bag, and we'll go, eh?'

Annie knew it was pointless protesting, so she nodded silently, then went into the bedroom, took a small rucksack from the back of the door and mechanically filled it with a change of clothes and some toiletries, all the while knowing that she couldn't leave, couldn't risk the murmurs kicking off the moment she left her home.

Back in the living room, Mandy and Chrissie were standing by the door, waiting for her, jackets on and holding their handbags.

'Ready to go?' Mandy said, jiggling her car keys.

'Oh.' Annie faked surprise. 'Better get the charger for my phone. You two go on to the car, I'll just be a sec...' She turned, pretending she was going back to her bedroom, but when she heard their footfall on the gravel path outside, she dashed to the front door, slammed it shut and turned the lock.

'Annie,' she heard Chrissie protest.

'You can't stay here, honey,' Mandy shouted through the wood of the door.

'I can't spend the night away from here either,' Annie shouted back.

She had slept every night in the cottage ever since she'd first moved in, and had slept soundly and without nightmares. She just couldn't countenance a night somewhere else. She was terrified the dreams that had populated her nights previously would return with a vengeance.

'I'll be better here than in the hotel,' Annie shouted through the letter box. 'Come back in the morning with a number for the local handyman and we'll laugh at those idiots.'

Annie could hear the two women holding a mumbled conversation.

'And I won't be too annoyed if you bring some bacon rolls with you for breakfast.' Annie was aiming for a jocular tone, sending the message that she was okay.

'Brown sauce or tomato sauce?' Mandy asked after a moment, and Annie sighed with relief. Her adoptive mother was sending a message back: she understood.

'Brown, please. Bye,' Annie shouted, and Mandy and Chrissie called their goodbyes back.

Annie waited, listening to the women walk to their car. Then the car started, and they drove off. Annie made her way to her kitchen, threw the remnants of the spoiled meal into the bin, washed the dishes and then went to bed.

Head on her pillow, staring sightless at the ceiling, her mind was bright with the image of young Lachlan at the café. The shine of youth in his skin and eyes. And the terror in them the moment before his car hit the tree.

A waste of a life. He might have saved other lives as a crew member on the lifeboat. He might have had a wife and children. Now, none of that would happen.

She could have saved him.

She could have spoken up.

Shame washed over her, then set and solidified over her skin, muscle and bone until she was nothing but an unmoving length of granite, within which pulsed an overactive, punishing mind.

Chapter 9

Annie

At first light, feeling more tired than when she went to sleep, Annie slipped from her bed, dressed and made her way out to the little beach behind her home; a curve of sand that edged the loch. She sat on a rock there, a red tartan blanket over her shoulders, the breeze like velvet on her cheeks, and sipped from a flask of coffee, watching a pair of ducks as they dived for food just yards from where she perched.

She had fallen asleep the night before, eventually, but tiredness was like grit in her eyes, and guilt at not intervening before Lachlan died was still a weight on her limbs. Movement in the far right of her vision had her lift her face to the sky, and she watched a bird of prey as it flew in her direction.

The ducks were aware of the danger, it seemed, and they swam for the shelter of the long grass edging the banks further down the shore.

She loved this spot, and would often sit here for hours, savouring nature and its healing arts, and she was tempted to just stay here and allow that soothing, but the thought of the blood-red paint splattered on her door nagged at her. She wouldn't be able to settle until that was cleaned off completely.

With a sigh, she aimed herself back indoors, to the sink and a pail and a scrubbing brush, and then she stood before her front door to assess the damage and to work out what needed to be done.

The paint was mostly on the bottom half of the door – a rich red against the stained oak – and some had made it onto the walls and the doorstep. Annie noted there were no footprints anywhere, meaning Chrissie and Mandy had managed to avoid stepping on it as they made their way over to their car.

As she studied the mess she realised she actually liked the colour. Against the white of the walls it was quite striking. Rather than clean it all up she could simply buy a tin of the stuff and paint the rest of the door. And it would be the work of moments to touch up the splashes on the walls with white masonry paint. Then, once the colour was cleaned off the doorstep it would all look quite smart.

This cheered her, and in her mind she gave a two-finger salute to the men who'd done this.

And then she thought of Lachlan again. Why hadn't she been clearer?

A crush of guilt landed on her, and she exhaled, long and slow.

Enough. She had work to do to clean the doorstep and make the door ready for its new look.

Sometime later, over the noise of the brush against the stone, she heard an incoming car. She jumped to her feet in alarm, holding the brush in her hand like a weapon. If those guys, or any other idiots, were on their way to try and intimidate her, they'd find she was ready for them.

A car crested the hill, and she relaxed with relief as she recognised Lewis's black Honda. But then she became annoyed. It was only nine am. He must have left Glasgow at the crack of dawn to be here at this time. Mrs Mac must have phoned him and told him about the attack on her home.

Lewis parked. Climbed out of the car and walked towards her, holding a little brown bag in the air. 'Did you order bacon rolls?' he asked. A smile hovered across his face, but his eyes betrayed his concern. He looked past Annie at the paint on the door. 'You okay?'

'You didn't need to come driving up here like a white knight,' Annie said, aware that she was bristling, but also pleased to see her brother. 'When did Mrs Mac phone you?'

'Last night. And if I was interested in doing the white-knight thing I would have left straight away. But fuck that, I need my beauty sleep.' He grinned. 'I did leave pretty early, right enough.' He looked into her eyes. 'But you're okay, yeah?'

Annie studied her twin.

'What?' he asked. 'You're doing that thing.'

'What thing?'

'The looking me up and down, assessing thing.'

'Just trying to work out how my brother is.'

'And?' Lewis stood still and held his hands out wide.

'New expensive jeans. New girlfriend? Flatter stomach. Been working out?'

'No, and yes,' Lewis replied with a chuckle.

He reached out to her and they hugged.

'You don't need to worry, you know,' Annie said after she'd stepped back. 'I can look after myself.' After her near-death experience the previous year, Lewis had taken up Krav Maga and running, apparently to fulfil his role as her protector. When she'd challenged him on it, he'd reminded her that their father's instruction to him on the day before he committed suicide, when Lewis was just turned thirteen, was to look after her. 'And that shit is difficult to deprogramme,' he'd added.

'Nice repaint,' he said now, looking over her shoulder at the door. 'Half and half. Kinda works.'

'I'm thinking of keeping the red,' Annie said.

'Making lemonade?'

Annie laughed.

'Is it coming off okay though?' Lewis asked.

Annie wiped at her mouth with the back of her hand. 'They used emulsion paint.' She offered Lewis a half-cocked smile.

'Amateurs,' Lewis said.

Annie dropped her scrubbing brush into the bucket of soapy water. 'C'mon in and I'll put the kettle on.'

As they passed through the living room, Lewis gave a low whistle at the window, and the towel covering it. 'Quite dark in here without that window, eh?'

'Let's hope the weather doesn't grow cold for a wee while yet,' Annie replied. 'Can you imagine the draughts coming in when the wind's up?'

'You can't really stay here with a hole in the wall like that, Annie.'

'Don't you start,' Annie replied. 'Where would I go? I can't face leaving. It's been so nice to have this long break from all that madness.'

Lewis gave her a shoulder a squeeze. 'We'll think of something.'

In the kitchen, each with a coffee and a half-eaten bacon roll in front of them, Lewis asked, 'How are you, really?' He was the one person in the world who understood her – better, almost, than she knew herself, so she didn't even bother to disguise how she was feeling.

'I'm furious,' she said. 'At those arses. How dare they try to ruin my wee home.' She looked at her brother, just for a moment, his eyes suggested a hint of anger. Annie guessed that it was on her behalf, and that it was fresh. 'What happened?' she asked.

Just like Annie, Lewis knew there was no point in obfuscating. 'When I was in the café, waiting for the coffee and rolls, a couple of old biddies were talking about you.'

'Pay no attention, Lewis.'

'It wasn't nice, Annie. They'd heard that some kids had thrown paint at your door, and they weren't criticising it. It had the tone of "serves her right".'

Annie sat with that for a moment. 'I get it,' she then replied. 'I could have saved that young guy.'

There was the sound of a car horn.

Lewis stood up. 'That'll be Mandy and Chrissie.'

'I locked them out last night,' Annie said with a grimace.

'I know.' Lewis smiled. 'Mandy told me.'

Annie got to her feet too. 'Better face the music.'

Annie opened the door just as the two sisters reached the front step. There were cries of hello as they entered the house and everyone hugged. When it was Mandy's turn to hug Annie, she held it for a long moment, stepped back and looked into Annie's eyes.

'Okay?'

Annie looked at the floor, tugged a strand of hair behind her ear, and nodded.

They were soon gathered around the kitchen table with tea and coffee.

'I spoke to Jenny Burns' dad,' Mandy said with a quick glance over her shoulder at the broken window. 'He's going to get his guy to come out and fix your window. But he's on holiday for a few days.'

'Great, thanks for arranging that,' Annie said.

'He was delighted to help. And scandalised that you'd been treated so badly,' Mandy added.

They all sipped in silence for a moment, and Lewis pulled his phone out. Annie noticed Chrissie widening her eyes at Mandy, who gave her sister a tiny shake of the head in reply. It was clear to Annie what the exchange between them meant.

'It's okay,' Annie said, putting her cup down on the table. 'You came here yesterday to talk about Damien. So ... let's talk about him.' She turned to Chrissie. 'What can you tell us about that boy of yours?'

Chrissie swallowed, and her eyes instantly welled up. She tugged at the little silver St Christopher at her throat, running the medal back and forth along its silver chain.

'He was back,' she said. She looked each person in the room in the eye. 'He was,' she protested, as if they'd refused to believe it. 'I had my boy – my real boy – back, but then he goes and vanishes. The police won't listen. My friends all think I'm deluded, that he's a bad sort and he's got what he's due.' She paused. Prodded her sternum with a stiff index finger. 'A mother knows. His days going gadabout and getting up to God knows what are over. He's turned his life around for wee Bodie. He's desperate to get more time with the wee fella. So this time, his leaving is out of character. Something's happened to him, I'm sure of it.' Again Chrissie looked at each of them in turn, as if desperate that they should all believe her. 'Something bad.'

Chapter 10

Lewis

Lewis watched as Chrissie talked and could see how earnest she was, that she truly believed in her son; that he had turned his life around, only to vanish.

'And grown men don't just go missing,' Chrissie asserted.

Well, yes, they do, Lewis wanted to say, but he didn't want to upset Chrissie any further.

'When did you last see him?' Lewis asked.

Chrissie's eyes bored into his, seemingly grateful that he was taking her seriously. 'A couple of Sundays ago.' Her bottom lip trembled. 'He came by after he'd been down to see Bodie. He always pops in to get me up to speed with the wee fella's antics.'

'What was his state of mind?' Annie asked.

'Agitated.' Chrissie's head jigged from side to side. 'Aye. That describes it pretty well. He was fed up that he only got to see Bodie on Sunday afternoons.' She huffed. 'Said, how are you supposed to build a relationship with your kid if you only see them for two hours a week?'

'Fair comment,' Lewis replied. 'Why only two hours?'

'That's all the courts will allow. For the moment.' Chrissie leaned forward. 'That's why I know he's not off on some drug-and-drink bender somewhere. He's determined to prove he's an upstanding member of society, and then he's going to apply for more time with the wee fella.'

Lewis stole a look at his sister. Annie was sitting hunched in her seat, arms tight across her midriff, as if making herself as small as possible. He knew she was uncomfortable with being asked to use her curse and that she was deeply reluctant to leave the house. He also knew she wouldn't be able to refuse Mandy any favour, no matter how difficult. His heart went out to her as he watched her in a torture of indecision.

'I want to help, Chrissie,' Annie said, reaching out to grip Chrissie's forearm. 'I really do. I just don't know how.'

'Do you have anything belonging to Damien?' Mandy asked her sister. 'That's how you see psychic people do stuff in the movies and all that, isn't it?' She turned to Annie, her expression one of apology.

Chrissie rummaged in her handbag, pulled something out and

placed it in the middle of the table. It was a small gold cross. There was something about the briskness with which she did it that made Lewis think this had already been discussed between the sisters.

Everyone looked at the piece of jewellery.

'Is Damien religious?' Lewis asked. 'I don't remember him that way.'

'Not really,' Chrissie replied. 'Not at all, to be honest. His grandfather bought him this for his thirteenth birthday. Don't know what he was thinking. Damien did wear it for a time, then I found it...' She paused, and the weight in her eyes betrayed her shame. 'I found it when I was clearing out his stuff from the loft after he was sent to prison.'

'Hey.' Mandy leaned closer to her sister and gave her hand a little squeeze. 'No one here blames you for that.'

'I'm his mother,' Chrissie shrugged, then dabbed at her leaking eyes with the pad of her palm. 'You might not blame me, but plenty of people judge me for it.'

Lewis saw a movement out of the corner of his eye. Annie was silently holding out her hand. Chrissie and Mandy froze for a second. Then Chrissie reached out, picked up the cross and dropped it into Annie's palm.

Annie closed her fingers, and her eyes, and they all waited.

Chapter 11

Ben
1965

Ben never ever managed to make that girl cry. She was made of sterner stuff – even than most of the boys. But he did develop a bit of a fancy for her when he was a little older, and instead of trying to make her cry, he would try to make her smile – and got even less reaction for his efforts.

He hated school. After seven years he'd never got used to the masters with their hard lessons, hard eyes, and even harder fists. The draughty dormitory full of snoring, farting, crying lonely boys. Food that was either mush, or leather, and could only be made palatable with a liberal coating of salt. Physical education that consisted of moving more speedily than his body was designed to, getting dirty and covered in bruises. And other children who, in his opinion, were either too stupid, too cruel, or too ill-bred to be allowed to even live.

One such boy, Thomas Quick – Ben would remember that name for the rest of his life – was taller and heavier than any of the other boys in the dorm and worked like it was his mission to make everyone else's life more miserable than it needed to be. Two boys in particular grabbed Quick's attention: Ben and a small boy called Rupert Hervey. He would spit on their food, when he wasn't stealing it off their plates, stab them on the hand with a compass needle when the master was distracted, and then adopt the expression of a saint when their inevitable cry brought a glare. And his special treat, whenever he passed either of them in the corridors or hallways, would be to flick them on the balls.

Quick had a name for Ben – Boney Ben – which he decided was apt because Ben was so skinny and because of the alliterative effect. He regularly chanted it until all of the other boys felt they had to join in.

'I hate that boy,' Rupert told Ben one afternoon. 'I wish he was dead.' They'd both been late for first class after lunch, held back because Thomas Quick had thrown their lunches on the floor. None of the masters saw it happen and therefore both had to stay back and clean up the mess. Phineas Dance was the youngest master in the school and was often left with lunch-monitor duties. As well as being the youngest, he was the one with the cruellest bent of mind. The task was to be done without tools, he ordered, his eyes full of loathing for his small charges. They had to clean the floor with their tongues.

This meant they were late for class. And they were punished again. This time they were given detention and told to fill one half of the blackboard each, with the line: *I shall not be late ever again.*

'You wish he was dead?' Ben replied. 'Let's make that happen.' Where the words came from he had no idea, but when he saw the look of delight, and horror, on Rupert's face he wondered how he could indeed make it happen.

That very night he had his chance to see the Quick boy fall to some harm.

After lights out, a whispered chant ran the length of the room: *'Tuckshop run, tuckshop run, tuckshop run...'*

Only the bravest boys would ever take this on, and whenever the chant started Ben buried himself under his blanket, pretending he was asleep, but on this occasion, he sat up, said he would do it, but only if Rupert Hervey and Thomas Quick joined him.

'What the bloody hell are you up to?' Quick hissed.

Rupert said nothing, but in the dim light Ben could see him sit up in bed, the whites of his eyes shining with fear.

The tuck shop was situated above the dinner hall on the first floor. Being successful on the run entailed making your way from one end of the school to the other, along dark and draughty corridors, and taking the fire-exit stairs down to the bowling green. On the far side of this, the bravest boy would scale the drainpipe to the roof, help the others up then prise open a skylight that famously had a wonky lock, and the smallest boy would drop through it. Once he did, his job was to fill his pockets and his pillow case with as much booty as he could find.

Ben calculated that Quick couldn't be seen to back down and Rupert would be too scared to – and he was right. They each put their jumpers and trousers over their pyjamas, and made their way to the dorm door, but not before Ben pulled the linen cover from his pillow.

'I'll bloody kill you, Boney,' Quick hissed.

'Bloody b-b-bastard,' Hervey stammered.

'C'mon, scaredy-cat,' Ben said, emboldened by the enormity of what he was about to attempt.

They quickly made their way along the corridor, down the stairs, up another set of stairs, along another corridor, which held the year four girls' dormitory, and to the fire exit and stairs at the far end. Only once did they need to scold Rupert for lagging behind.

At the bottom of the stairs, they skirted the walled garden and approached the bowling green. This was the place they were most likely to be caught. They were out in the open, and the masters were known to loiter in this area of an evening for a quiet beer and a smoke. The masters were also hideously protective of the bowling-green surface – may the angels protect any boy who was seen to cause damage to a single blade of the carefully manicured grass.

The angels were on their side for now, and they hustled their way across the soft surface without any shouts of alarm. From there they made their way to the drainpipe. At the wall of the dining hall they all stopped.

There was a noise. Shoe on pebbles. They held a collective breath. Over in the far corner Ben could make out a little red dot as someone pulled on a cigarette. He stuck his head out to see who it was.

'What are you doing?' Hervey whispered. 'You'll get us caught.'

Ben thought he recognised the shape of the person across the quadrant, his hand in his pocket, that familiar wide stance. He ducked back in.

'Bloody Dance.'

Even in the weak light Ben could see Quick grow pale.

'If he sees us,' Quick said, squeezing his eyes shut, 'we're dead.'

Ben sensed fear from the bigger boy. He tucked that away to exploit later.

Finally, they heard Dance move. A scrape of leather against stone as he stubbed out his cigarette. And then his footsteps retreating into the distance.

'Right,' Quick whispered to Ben. 'You first.' Again Ben could see the bigger boy was afraid. He'd always thought that Quick was one of the most courageous boys in their year, but with a flash of insight he realised this was an act – a tactic to allow him to do the nasty thing before it was done to him.

Emboldened by this realisation, Ben made his way up the pipe. He'd never been much of a climber, but somehow he found the necessary ability, and clambered over a knee-high parapet and onto the roof. He stopped to catch his breath. Then knocked on the pipe as a signal for Quick to make his way up.

Quick had a moment halfway when his shoe slid off the wall, but he managed to hold on, correct himself and make it to the top.

Hervey whispered up at them, 'Can I not just act look-out from here, chaps?'

'Can you, billy-o,' Quick hissed down. 'If we're doing it from here, so are you.'

Two minutes later Hervey's head appeared through the gloom and the other two pulled him up. Once there he lay back on the steep pitch of the roof and took a breath.

'Right,' Ben said. 'The skylight is just over there. Quick, you lift it up and I'll let myself into the room.' He was keen that he be the one to hand out the bounty back in the dorm.

'Who made you king for the day?' Quick protested.

'You want to jump down into the tuck shop, be my guest.'

'You're lighter than me,' Quick shrugged. 'It will be easier if you do it.' Then he turned to Hervey. 'See anyone?'

'It's bloody dark,' Hervey replied. 'I can't see buggery.'

'Keep an ear out then.'

Ben and Quick carefully edged along the rooftop towards the skylight. Quick tugged it open, propped it up with a straight arm, and Ben slipped inside. He dropped onto the floor. Heard the noise of his impact and froze.

Nothing.

A light shone from above.

'At least someone thought to bring their torch,' Quick said from overhead. The weak light roved around the room. 'Get me some of those dib-dabs. Hurry,' he urged.

Ben whipped his pillow case from under his jumper and set about collecting as much booty as he could, then turned to assess his way out. A chair was conveniently positioned at the side of a pipe that ran from a radiator up to the ceiling. He got there, and with one jump caught the lip of the skylight edge and pulled himself up.

'Give me that,' Quick hissed, grabbing at the pillow case as soon as Ben was back on the roof.

But Ben snatched it away. 'Here,' he said, and handed Quick a yellow packet.

'Dib-dabs,' Quick sang, apparently satisfied. 'Right. Let's go.'

They joined Hervey at the roof edge, each of them leaning against the pitch of the roof. Ben was now rather fearful of their return trip. *Down* looked a good distance away from this vantage point.

A voice rang out into the quiet. 'You, boy. You!'

Dance.

'You were supposed to be on look-out, Hervey,' Quick whispered. And punched him on the arm.

'I did. I was,' Hervey replied, rubbing the spot.

'There's no point in us all getting caught,' Ben murmured. 'One of us has to play decoy to let the others escape back to the dorm with the booty.'

'Not bloody likely,' Quick said, and Ben saw something in the glint of his eyes. More than the fear of being caught. It was a fear of being caught by Phineas Dance. Ben had heard the rumours – they all had. Dance was said to be a bit 'handsy', and Ben wondered if Quick had been subject to this.

Ben looked back down at the bowling green. It wouldn't be fatal, he thought. The grass would cushion any fall. Broken bones at the most.

With a glance at Quick – a look that said, *See what I'm capable of? It could have been you. You will owe me forever* – Ben put both hands on Rupert Hervey's back and pushed.

As he listened to the small boy's cry and the thump as his body hit the ground, he saw Quick's expression turn to horror and remembered his father's words of advice on the first day he arrived at Clevelland:

'It's all about power, my boy. Grab it. Use it.'

With a rush that made him feel twenty feet tall, he realised he'd finally learned what that meant.

Chapter 12

Annie

Aware that Chrissie was watching her closely, Annie closed her eyes and concentrated on the slight object resting in her hand. She curled her fingers over it.

Nothing.

All she could sense was the expectant breathing of those around her, every eye focused on her.

She shut that thought off. Concentrate, she told herself. Think only of the little cross. An image of Damien appeared in her mind. It was probably the last time she'd seen him. The occasion was the wedding of a distant family member of the McEvoys. Annie guessed she would have been about fifteen. Damien was about two years older. He'd just signed a contract with one of the big Glasgow football teams, and all the other boys were hanging around him as if some of his good fortune might rub off on them. Annie knew nothing about football, but Lewis assured her this was a big deal; that Damien was a talent who had the potential to go to the top of the game.

Annie recalled she had caught Damien in an unguarded moment. For a split second, when all eyes had moved somewhere else, Damien looked like a lost little boy, like he didn't feel he deserved the success or the attention; but then, when an older, male relative approached to shake Damien's hand, the boy moved back into cocky mode. He transformed so swiftly and smoothly that Annie wondered if she'd imagined what she'd seen.

As this memory unspooled in her mind, Annie knew she was seeing it from her present-day perspective. She had thought none of that at the time; only now did she understand that what had been a shining moment for Damien actually had many more levels.

His eyes in that moment had looked haunted. He saw himself as unworthy.

Shameful.

'What happened to Damien back then?' Annie asked.

Hand over her heart, Chrissie asked. 'What do you mean? What did you see?'

'He signed a professional contract...'

'Yeah, at Celtic.' Chrissie replied, a quizzical light in her eyes. 'But he got a bad injury and his career was cut short. That was when he went off the rails.'

'No. Before that,' Annie said. 'Even before the football thing. Something happened to him.' And as she spoke she was aware she was echoing Chrissie's words from earlier. 'Something bad.'

Chapter 13

Annie

After Chrissie and Mandy left, the twins walked out of the house and over to the little beach. While Annie sat on a fallen log, Lewis searched the rough sand along the water's edge for some smooth, flat stones he could skim across the loch's surface.

'How disappointed was Chrissie...' Annie said. 'But I get it,' she added. A sudden wind whipped her hair in front of her face. She tossed her head, and pulled it back behind an ear. 'It was just...' She took a moment to work out how best to express what happened earlier. 'I saw a *memory* of Damien. I saw nothing of where he might be now. I don't think this curse works in that way.'

'You haven't really tried though,' Lewis replied. 'To work with it, I mean. You've mostly been fighting it off.'

Annie stared at her brother. 'So would you, Lewis. It's bloody terrifying.'

He held his hands out. 'I'm not judging you, Annie. I'm just saying it might be like...' He paused. 'I was reading up on fear, you see, and how we react to it.'

'Right.' Annie could feel herself tighten, about to spring to her own defence, but she held herself still.

'It's like when you're driving and you skid, and you're told to drive into the skid because you then get some traction and can straighten up, whereas when you try to correct, to fight the skid, you end up worse off.'

'Lewis, what the hell are you on about?'

'Anxiety, fear, phobias are all like that. You tighten up, fight the bad feeling, and that tells your brain this is something awful, and that tension makes it feel so much worse and that, apparently, is how we perpetuate our fears and phobias. Whereas if you go with the feeling, relax into the skid, kinda thing, it tells your brain: "This is fine, you can cope. You're safe."'

'Oh piss off, Lewis, you have no idea.'

'Okay. Sorry.'

He looked so crestfallen Annie felt she had to try and appease him. 'No. You're ... you have a point. I can see how relaxing into a bad feeling might help when there's nothing behind that bad feeling but an old or imagined fear.' She chewed on her lip, thinking that through. 'And I can see how that might help reprogramme the impulse, and the build-up of adrenaline and all that stuff. But this is very fucking real. This is here, in my head, and it's almost ever-present. There's no relaxing into that shit, Lewis.'

They were silent for a time as Lewis returned to skimming stones. One bounced four times across the surface of the loch.

'Nice one,' she said.

He accepted her peace offering. 'Before they left, Mrs Mac said something to me – in the kitchen, away from Chrissie.'

'What?'

'About us looking into this.' He looked into Annie's eyes. 'We did a proper good job investigating Bridget's whereabouts.'

'Right,' Annie replied, and felt a surge of sadness, as she always did when Bridget's name came up. They began looking into Bridget's whereabouts as a way of helping her cope with the rise of her murmurs. At the start they believed Bridget was their aunt – their mother, Eleanor's sister – but they were to discover she was in fact their biological mother.

'And you didn't need to rely on the curse then,' Lewis continued.

'No, but I triggered a man into trying to kill me.'

'That's one interpretation of what happened, Annie. He'd been on your case since the moment he read about you in the newspaper.'

One of Scotland's top rags had run a piece about her premonitions and her wish to help convicted killer, Edward Trainer – who was protesting his innocence after a twenty-year jail term – to find out what had really happened to his fiancée, Tracy Dobell.

'The point is we kicked ass,' Lewis went on. 'We tracked down Bridget and Aunt Sheila. We uncovered the truth. Maybe we could so some super-sleuthing and find out what happened to Damien?'

He looked so keen she didn't have the heart to tell him the idea was nonsense. 'What, like, I'll be Nancy and you'll be Drew?' she said instead.

Lewis laughed.

'Dunno,' she finally admitted. 'I can't leave this place, Lewis. You know that.'

'And you can't stay,' Lewis argued. 'You have no front window, and the natives are a lit pitchfork away from storming the place.'

'They don't light pitchforks, Lewis. They're for stabbing the monster with.' Annie looked away, up to the hills in the distance. 'And in this case, I'm the monster.'

Chapter 14

Sylvia
1965

When you were familiar with death, and with talking to the dead, at such a young age, the power games of other children were difficult to engage in. Even so, there were occasions when they became too much and action had to be taken.

Sylvia had no need of anyone, for she had Sarah – the name she'd given her constant companion, her shadow. And because of this she had gained a reputation for being remote and a little strange. As a result, during her early years at Clevelland the bullies were merciless. They pulled her hair, called her names, and she was regularly shunned. Rumours of her promiscuity adorned the toilet walls in terminology that had Sylvia scratching her head. Even the teachers dialled up the sarcasm and the punishments when dealing with her. Sylvia suffered it all quietly. But when a new girl, Emily Montague of the Halifax Montagues, arrived in her first senior year and decided that Sylvia would be her lackey, she was forced to take a stand.

When she returned home during the Christmas break her

grandmother could tell instantly that Sylvia had something on her mind.

'Come, Sylvia,' the old lady said over an afternoon tea of scones and ginger preserve. 'Stop snivelling. Out with it.'

'I've had enough, Grandmama,' she said. 'I've tried to ignore it, hoped it would go away, but it's only got worse. And now this new girl...' Sylvia explained who the new source of her problem was, and to her surprise found herself crying when she detailed some of the excesses of the young Montague.

Maude looked distant for a moment. 'Emily is the grand-niece of my cousin, Gwendaline, who was a monster as a girl herself. *What* goes on in that family...?'

'Emily hits me, calls me names – now *everyone* calls me Slack Sylvia. She trips me up during netball. She even claimed to have lost a locket, a family heirloom, and then managed to find it under my pillow. I'm no thief, Grandmama.' Sylvia cried a little more. 'I don't know what I've done to upset her, and why she hates me so.'

Her grandmother thrust a cotton handkerchief into Sylvia's hand, and gave a little sniff – she had always been troubled by displays of emotion. 'There, there,' she said coldly. 'Other girls can be so cruel. I daresay a punch on the arm would be easier to take than Montague persuading the other girls to call you names and ostracise you.'

A further release of emotion from Sylvia had the old woman give her head a little shake that made the wattle under her chin wiggle. 'Sylvia,' she said sternly. 'What do we Villiers do when faced with bullies? We take them on and teach them a lesson they will never forget.' She sipped at her tea. 'Now eat your scone.'

After tea, they retired to her grandmother's special place – an anteroom the size of a large cupboard, tucked in behind her dressing room. It was accessed via a hidden door disguised by oak panelling and a reputedly priceless Vermeer, and held nothing more than a table with four chairs, a bookcase full of leather-bound volumes, and a window with dark-purple curtains so heavy Sylvia had been unable to pull them shut when she was smaller.

Maude lit a couple of candles, closed her eyes, and stretched across the table to grab Sylvia's hands. Sylvia was always surprised by the strength with which she did this – that someone so old would have such vigour.

'Now, let's have a word with your mother,' Maude said. She threw herself back in her seat, looked to the ceiling with milky eyes and began to speak in a language that to Sylvia's ears had no rhythm, meaning nor rhyme.

Maude stopped speaking, her head down, face now inches from the table's surface. When she next spoke her voice was at a slightly higher pitch.

'Darling, Sylvia,' she said. 'It's advice you seek.' A statement, not a question.

'Emily Montague hates me. She's does everything she can to hurt me. Setting me out as a thief is the last straw,' Sylvia answered without pausing. Speaking to her dead mother was perfectly normal to her.

'What would you do to get your revenge on her?'

'Anything.'

'What would you give to get your revenge on her?'

'Everything.'

'Be careful what you wish for, my little one. The price you pay is never the one you agree to.'

Wind sang hollow in Sylvia's ear and somewhere in the house a door slammed shut. Sylvia felt a moment of fear at the warning, but gathered her strength.

'Nonetheless...' she said. She thrust out her chin. 'Enough is enough.'

'Very well, my precious daughter. Here is what you do...'

The little doll was easy to make. Emily Montague was very proud of her hair and acted as if the advised hundred brushstrokes before bed was a bare minimum. Therefore securing a few strands of her hair was easy. The doll also required a small token that held emotional value for Emily. It wasn't lost on Sylvia that securing this would turn her into the thief Emily accused her of being.

Emily was rarely without a locket her grandmother willed to her. She only ever removed it for Thursday-morning swimming lessons.

Sylvia convinced the nurse that she had an extremely painful period that morning, thereby absenting herself from the pool. She bribed one of the boys – Boney Ben – to create a diversion. He pretended he was drowning. While the teacher and most of the girls flapped in near panic at the side of the pool, Sylvia slipped into the changing room and found it in Emily's blazer pocket.

The tantrum Emily threw when she discovered the precious locket was missing was so satisfying Sylvia was almost tempted to rein in her use of the doll and the intended curse, but she had put herself on this path and would not budge. If only to see if it would work.

And did it.

Sylvia overheard two of the teachers discussing Emily's death only a few short weeks later. 'Acute myeloid leukaemia...' 'It's rare for children to survive...' 'Cerebral haemorrhage...' The teachers continued their discussion in more hushed tones.

She cried that night. Her pillow stuffed into her mouth, she was swamped by emotion. Surely a cloth doll, some hair, an earring and a long pin were not enough to cause such an illness and such an accelerated death...

Had she really done this?

Had Emily Montague deserved to die?

Might she have died anyway?

Out of the corner of her eye she caught movement; Sarah her shadow – and it seemed that just for a moment she glowed. Then there was nothing.

Sarah approved of her actions, and when the tears subsided

and the heat of her face became cool, Sylvia was able to distance herself from events. This was not her fault. Maybe it was her doing, but it was not her *fault*. Emily Montague had brought this upon herself.

Chapter 15

Lewis

Since he'd been visiting Annie in the cottage, Lewis had wondered why being in this little house calmed her murmurs. Was it the area – did being close to the original homes somehow offer some form of protection? Or was there something in the fabric of the building that helped?

'Haven't you wondered why your murmurs are less of a problem for you while you're here?'

'They're quiet. That's all I need to know,' she replied.

'Maybe there's something about the building? Or where the house sits here in the valley?' He looked around, at the hills, the loch, and back at the cottage as the sunlight blinked off a window.

He dropped the stones he'd been skimming, headed over to the little house and began to walk round its periphery, studying the walls, the roof and the garden. As Annie followed him he asked, 'You feeling anything? An energy or something?'

Annie paused as if listening. Shook her head. 'Nope.'

'What if we could work out why, or what helped you, and you took something that represented that with you everywhere you went? Might that mean you'd be able to leave and get some peace?'

'That would be brilliant,' she replied, but she looked doubtful.

'Bear with me.' He held a hand up. 'Let's investigate, eh?' He looked up the hill towards the abandoned settlement. 'Our ancestors lived up there, aye?'

Annie nodded.

'But, you're fine down here?'

Another nod.

'So, what is it about this house that works?'

They stared at each other for a moment, then Lewis headed indoors. He walked to the hearth, and as he looked up at the stones of the chimney breast he realised it was different there than the rest of the little home. He looked around the room and assessed the stonework. Here by the hearth the stones were larger, more irregular and looked older. He stepped closer and held a hand up to it, running his fingers over the ancient stones.

'What are you doing?' Annie asked.

Lewis looked from the wall he was touching to the other four walls of the room. 'This stone. It looks older than the stone everywhere else in the house. Here, on this gable end. Doesn't it?'

'What, you're a stone mason now?'

He cocked his head. 'C'mere. Put your hand on the stone. See how the murmurs react.'

Annie got to her feet, stepped up onto the hearth and put her hand on the wall. 'Okay. It's rough, but smooth at the same time. Warm, and cool. What's your point? ... Oh.'

'What?' Lewis studied her reaction

'There's a sound in my mind. A low hum. A low *satisfied* hum.'

'Okay,' Lewis nodded, reading her reaction. 'That was a guess. I wasn't sure it would work.'

'The murmurs mostly reduce in level and in pitch whenever I come in the house but they're rarely this peaceful.' A tentative smile shaped her face. 'What are you thinking, Lew?'

'The memoir we found, by Moira McLean?' On one of their first visits to the house, they'd noticed a loose stone on the hearth, lifted it up and found a little hand-written journal wrapped in hessian sacking. It detailed the origins of the curse – the poor people who'd been executed as witches in the early 1700s – and how the small girl who'd grown up to make the curse had found her home in this valley, only to be thrown off the land nearly a century later, as part of the local Clearances. 'When you compare the ruined houses up the valley with this one – this is a very different, more modern construction, yeah? Probably built a while after the McLeans were turfed out.'

'Yeah,' Annie agreed.

'But this stone here.' He looked up and down the wall. 'It's the same as the stone used in the homes up in the old settlement. I bet you these stones here are from old Moira's actual home, and that's why the curse is quieter when you're here. She's back home,' he added with a note of triumph.

Annie sat with that. Nodded. 'I think you could be right. But how is that going to help?'

'It's a theory. Just a theory. But if this stone calms the murmurs down, what would happen if you were to carry a little piece of it with you whenever you left? Might that keep it a little quieter when you were out and about in the wider world?'

'I dunno, Lewis. It might piss them off even more if you go knocking great big chunks off the wall.'

Lewis stepped back so that he could survey the full height and width of the wall.

'What are you doing?'

He got to his knees and wiggled the stone on the hearth under which they'd found the memoir. 'There's a bit here that's come loose without me having to hack at it.' He held up a chunk of stone about the size of his thumb. 'Here.' He handed it to Annie.

Palm up, she moved her hand up and down slightly as if measuring the weight of it in her hand. 'What now?'

'Now, we go for a run in the car – somewhere not too far, but a place where people might not know you. And we'll test my theory.'

Chapter 16

Gaia
NOW

First, she took a long, hot bath, making sure every inch of her was clean, then she padded up to her altar room at the top of the house, naked, and stood in front of a full-length mirror, arms wide until she dried.

As she stood there, eyes closed, she hummed the words to her spell over and over again, and as she chanted she checked them for meaning and rhythm and rhyme. She had a particular fondness for a spell that had rhyme.

Once dry she moved to her altar, a large, wide slab of elder wood covered in pristine lace. She reached for a little bottle of oil – essential oil she had distilled herself – and dabbed her third eye, both pulse points of her wrists, her throat, her heart, and lastly, her umbilicus.

On top of the lace was a large wooden slab made of hawthorn. On top of that lay three images – the house in which she presently stood, a drawing of the Baobhan Sith, and a photograph she'd taken herself of the target of her spell.

Making sure a corner of each image was overlapping the others but the main parts were not obscured, she placed a small, fat candle on top and lit it with a taper.

She knelt before the altar for as long as it took for the wick to burn slowly through the wax. Beneath her bare knees were grains of uncooked rice. She bore the discomfort with determination – the pain caused stress hormones to flood her system, raise her body temperature and increase the beating of her heart. The pain made for a more efficacious spell, she believed, so she twisted each knee a little to boost the effect. And all the while, she continued to chant her intention, her pulse a thick thud in her neck.

Time lost meaning. The wick burned low and she placed the

images one by one on to the candle so that the centre of each blistered and burned. Last to catch was the unsmiling face of her intended.

'This house will loom large in your mind, as will the Baobhan Sith, young lady.' She held her hands out over the flame, feeling the heat dry the oil she had just placed there. 'I'll expect you soon. Very soon indeed.'

Chapter 17

Annie

As she sat in Lewis's car Annie felt a surge of worry twist in her gut and her heart was a heavy clamour in her chest. She stopped to listen.

The murmurs were silent. Completely silent, and part of her wondered if yet again they were toying with her. Waiting for the moment to rush in with all the virulence they could manage.

'What are you thinking?' Lewis asked.

'The minute...' Annie pulled her eyes up from the stone to look at her brother. 'The *second* I say I want to go back home, you turn the car round.'

'Okay.'

'I mean it, Lewis. Not a moment's hesitation. No trying to cajole me into staying for one more second. If I'm going to end up frozen in terror I don't want to do it where other people can see me. They have a bad enough opinion of me as it is.'

Forty-five minutes later, including single-track roads and vistas of heather and hills and gleaming lochs, they approached the Corran ferry and the little white hotel just beyond.

Lewis parked then looked across to Annie. 'So far, so good?'

Annie nodded. Listened for a moment. 'I can hear the odd

cackle, the odd kind of hum.' She screwed up her face, reluctant to admit it out loud in case that set the voices off. 'It's not just as quiet as it is back home, but it's not as bad as I expected.' She looked around and noted the long trail of cars waiting for the next ferry. It rocked in the swell, just off shore, almost ready to dock.

'What now?' she said. 'Are we going back home?'

'Depends on how far you want to test this. We could go on the ferry and drive up to Fort William. Do a little retail therapy there? Or' – he nodded in the direction of the hotel – 'it's almost noon. We could go for a bar lunch?'

Annie looked at the long, white building lining the road. It had an inviting, friendly air; as she watched, a couple in hiking gear with a small black dog walked towards the door. But, they were pretty close to home here, so there was a chance of meeting someone from Mossgow, and all that might entail.

She listened in to her murmurs. Silence.

She looked back to the ferry. If they went across to Fort William, there was more to do, more shops and cafés, but, importantly, more people. And one of those people might be facing imminent death.

Her stomach grumbled.

'That's your body deciding for you,' Lewis laughed, and released his seatbelt.

The restaurant at The Inn at Ardgour was a modest affair. White walls adorned with framed photographs of the local views, tables with chequered cloths, straight-backed wooden chairs.

'Busy place,' Lewis said as they were directed further into the room.

As they moved through the tables, a group of people got up to leave. They stepped aside, and Annie realised she was face to face with the woman who'd tried to talk to her at the café the day that Lachlan died.

Annie blinked and looked away, but this time the woman didn't even give her the time of day. She simply walked past her.

And as she did, Annie felt something lightly flicking the back of her hand. Something damp, like a smear of light oil. She paused. Rubbed her hand. But it was dry. She shrugged and followed Lewis to their table by a window.

As Lewis hungrily perused the menu, Annie studied the other customers from underneath her fringe. Her grip was tight on the stone in her pocket, and there was nothing – no reaction, no noise from her curse. But she did feel unaccountably dizzy. Just for a moment.

'The menu is pretty standard,' Lewis said. 'I fancy me some smoked salmon to start.'

'Right,' Annie replied absently. A surge of nausea hit her suddenly, then passed. She shook her head. She was fine now. Strange, she thought.

A movement at the far end of the room caught Annie's attention. A woman of indeterminate age, sitting alone at a table, her face an unearthly pale framed by long black hair. She was wearing a long dress the colour of moss. It had the look of a style from another age ... What was that? A foot emerged from the folds of fabric. But it wasn't ... No, she thought, that was more like a hoof...

Annie blinked. Rubbed her eyes. What on earth was she looking at?

The room began to spin. It shrank. There was just Annie and this strange woman.

What on earth was going on? She felt sick again. Fear bloomed in her mind. A cold hand gripped her heart. Squeezed. Voices wove themselves through the noise of flames. A susurration of disjointed syllables, notes from an instrument long since off-key. The woman's mouth peeled back in a smile, displaying black teeth filed to points.

Annie then became aware of Lewis getting to his feet. A woman, a different one, approaching from the right. Mouth moving.

Now standing over Annie.

Her words became clear: 'At least look at me when I'm talking to you,' she demanded.

'We're just here for a quiet lunch,' Lewis was saying. 'We're sorry for your loss. It was truly a terrible thing to have happened.'

'You witch,' the woman said, her finger in Annie's face. 'You could have saved our Lachie. Instead you come up with some nonsense about checking his tyres. How can you live with yourself?'

All eyes in the place were on them now. Everyone staring. Annie shrank into her seat and looked up at the woman. There was a family resemblance to Lachlan. This woman looked to be in her mid-fifties, so his aunt, maybe?

'I'm sorry,' Annie managed.

'Hey. Enough.' Lewis moved in front of Annie now. 'We're just here for a wee spot of lunch, like everyone else.'

Upset as she was at the woman's outburst, Annie's mind was still fixed on the woman draped in green in the far corner. She bit her lip, almost too scared to look over, but she felt like she had no option. She stole a glance.

The woman was gone.

In that corner of the room was a table with two chairs, and they were occupied by the couple she'd watched walk in earlier with the little dog. She looked around the room. Where was the woman?

Skin prickling with fear, Annie jumped to her feet. 'We'll go,' she said, desperate now to get away.

'You can't let people scare you off, Annie,' Lewis protested.

Annie approached the angry woman. 'What's your name?' she asked.

'Doris,' she replied. 'I'm his Auntie Doris.' Tears welled in her eyes.

Annie manage to push her fear to the side and reached out to Doris. 'I'm so sorry,' she said.

Doris lifted her arm out of Annie's reach. 'Don't touch me, you witch,' she spat. 'Don't you fucking touch me.'

In the car, it all became too much for Annie.

The tears flowed. 'That was horrible,' she said. 'That poor

woman. She was distraught. And who can blame her? Lachlan was a lovely wee guy.'

'That's not fair, Annie,' Lewis said. 'You're being too hard on yourself.'

Annie cried some more, unable to articulate the depth and complexity of her thoughts. Even though Lewis was by her side, hand on her shoulder, she had never felt so alone, so adrift from other people. Since this curse had reappeared in her adult life she'd experienced some real trials, but to have witnessed that young man's death, to have done little about it, and then to experience the grief of his relations was too much.

She'd moved to this area to get away from people, to reduce the possibility of just this thing happening. What was she to do now? Where could she go?

'Let's get you back to the cottage,' Lewis said, and started up the engine.

Annie was silent the entire way back, and once home she ran through to her bedroom, burrowed under the covers and gave into her emotions.

After a time the wave had passed and she found she could think more clearly. She got up and returned to the living room.

'You okay?' Lewis asked, studying her.

She nodded. 'I should eat something.'

Lewis appraised her. 'Want me to rummage up a sandwich or something?'

She sat down on the armchair, arms wrapped around herself. 'You know, everybody I see who's going to die – every single one of them – I carry a little bit of guilt for them.' She felt she was admitting this for the first time. She'd had the thought, but had never allowed herself to express it out loud.

'Annie, that's not fair.'

She held a hand up. 'And that's fine ... I'll have to learn to accept that's just the way it is. Accept what you can't control? All that seren-ity-prayer stuff makes sense. Whatever I choose to do, this curse is going to be there.' She paused. Shuddered. She was back in the restaurant, skin prickling, frozen to the spot. 'But ... the other woman...'

'What other woman?'

Annie explained what she saw in the inn.

'She was in the corner of the room? And then she wasn't? You don't think she was, like a ... ghost or something,' Lewis replied.

'You believe in ghosts?'

'After all the shit I've watched you go through, I really don't know anymore ... Do you think it's a new development in your abilities?'

Annie shook her head. 'Who knows.' Her breath caught in her throat as she thought through the implications of the vision. 'This woman in green, whoever she was – *whatever* she was...' She didn't mention the hooves. Couldn't mention the hooves, or Lewis might think she had really lost it. '...I know that she was waiting. For me.'

Chapter 18

Lewis

Lewis offered to go into the village and buy them some food, and he was pleased when Annie accepted his suggestion. Fear and anxiety always robbed her of appetite, so it was a good sign when she wanted to eat.

He also wanted to give Annie space to think, to consider what came next. And he fully expected that she'd face whatever that was with her shoulders back and chin up. He didn't know anyone with the courage of his twin sister. All the stuff she'd dealt with in life, and she just got back on her feet, dusted herself down, and took one more step forward.

Lewis returned with a bag of food that could be easily thrown together in a pot. He cooked. They ate. Then Lewis cleared the table and did the dishes.

Watching, Annie said with a half-smile, 'I should have a crisis more often.'

'Please don't,' Lewis replied.

'You know,' Annie began. 'When I leave the cottage bad stuff happens, and when I stay bad stuff happens.' She shook her head slowly, her eyes heavy. 'Wherever I am, wherever I go, the consequences of this curse kick me in the arse.' She bit her lip for a moment. Crossed her arms. 'Jesus.' She sighed. 'I can't win. Whatever I do.' She squared her jaw, and looked Lewis in the eyes. 'So, I've decided...'

'Yeah?'

'As much as I love this place, I can't hide away here for the rest of my life. I'm going to come into contact with people wherever I go – there's just no getting past that. And I'm not into avoidance. I faced up to Chris Jenkins, Pastor Mosely and this curse, didn't I?'

'You did.'

'And the stone does work. A little.'

'Good. So where does that leave us?'

'I make myself useful.'

'Meaning?'

Annie looked pointedly towards the front door. Lewis turned his head and noted a small bulging suitcase standing beside it.

'Meaning I get away from here for a while and let the natives cool down. I kip on your sofa, and we look into Damien's disappearance.'

Lewis rubbed his hands together with a grin. 'When do we get started?'

Chapter 19

Annie

It took a couple of days before the handyman at The Lodge could come out and replace Annie's broken glass. But once that was done, knowing her home was wind- and water-tight, she got herself down to Glasgow and Lewis's flat.

From the moment she walked into his building, with what she'd come to think of as the lodestone firmly in her grasp, she was hyper-vigilant to any noises going off in her mind.

'You getting anything?' Lewis asked as she entered his living room, instinctively knowing her thoughts.

Annie held a hand out and made a so-so motion. 'They're definitely less intrusive. I can hear whispers, and the odd bout of mocking laughter.' Her smile was tentative. 'Not as bad as it was last time I was down here.'

'I'll take that as a win,' Lewis replied.

After she'd settled in, they sat down in the living room and got down to the business of how they should go about finding Damien. They decided to retrace what they knew of his last journey. Chrissie had been able to tell them that the day he disappeared he'd been to visit his son, Bodie, who lived with his mother in the small Ayrshire coastal town of Girvan.

They talked late into the night – Lewis brought his own quilt and pillow through from his bedroom and camped out on the floor beside the sofa. Annie smiled, remembering times when they did this as kids. It was the two of them against the commanding nature of their mother – their adoptive mother – and they would team up like this while the grown-ups were sleeping. It was a small act of defiance – because Mother wouldn't want either one of them out of their bed in the middle of the night.

Finally, Annie slept.

There was a woman there, in her dreams. Long black hair, eyes gleaming and teeth shining.

Annie felt a pang of loneliness, and *knew* this feeling belonged to the other woman. The woman came closer. Floated above Annie in her dream bed, her hair like black silk curtains extending down either side of Annie's face, her breath on Annie's skin. Warm and moist. *Lonely*.

She floated closer. Noses almost touching.

Trust, the woman sang.

Annie's murmurs laughed. Mocked.

Love, the woman sighed, and kissed Annie on the corner of her mouth. It was so light, Annie barely felt it, but then, she was aware of its lingering weight. It made her feel looked after. Cared for. That someone was on her side.

The murmurs cackled.

Be gone, the woman said. And silence echoed in her mind. And Annie knew nothing but quiet for the remainder of the night.

Chapter 20

Ben and Sylvia
1966

It was the start of a new term and while the world outside their doors talked of the Vietnam War, a sniper killing fourteen people from a tower in a university in Texas and England winning the football World Cup, against West Germany of all nations, Phineas Dance called Ben and Sylvia to his chambers to change their lives forever.

When he opened his door and saw them both standing there, confusion clear in the semaphore of their stance, his mouth formed a smile that was thin but heavy with satisfaction. He ushered them inside, closed the door behind them and walked over to the window.

'A little voice told me, Boney Ben,' he began, 'that it was you who pushed Hervey off that roof.'

Ben opened his mouth to protest, but Dance carried on. 'A little voice belonging to one with a less than Quick mind.' An actual smile now. 'Good job that his fall wasn't that injurious. A boy with his lack of ambition doesn't need the use of both legs.'

Hervey's parents had moved him to another school once he got out of hospital. According to rumour he would walk with a permanent limp.

'And you, Slack Sylvia: that doll you made of Emily Montague had stunning results.' He turned away from them. 'What to make of you both...' He looked into the distance, his hands behind his back, the hook of his nose pushing at the space before the glass. 'Hmmm, what to make of you...' he repeated in a tone that suggested he knew exactly what to make of them.

'Sit,' he commanded. And his tone told them that he expected no reaction from them, just silent obedience.

They sat.

He turned and faced them, his gaze fixing on a point about an inch above their heads.

'Superior establishments such as this have sent young men and women to all corners of the globe, where they have done much to secure success for our great nation over the centuries.' He sat down. Crossed his legs. Chin up. One eyebrow higher than the other. Long, thin fingers clasped on his lap. He appeared to be in command of every aspect of his being.

'However, the work you do with me will never be spoken of openly. You will always be behind the scenes. And your teachers will be Comte De Saint Germain, Madame De Montespan and Aleister Crowley. Among celebrated others.'

He paused, looking again just above their heads.

'You will appear as a couple, even though relationships are frowned upon here at Clevelland. And you must *never*' – he invested the word with the power of a command – 'actually couple. Unless I say so. If you do I will scourge the tender skin from your backs.' He wrinkled his nose and said, softly and with relish, 'I might just do that anyway.'

Sylvia opened her mouth to protest, but Dance shut her down before she could make a sound.

'I will break you. Both. And remake you. And it will be the

crowning achievement of my life. Don't think for a moment that either of you can escape me. I know things. I have the ear of everyone. You think your time here has been difficult? Refuse to do as I ask and your life will be hell. Make no mistake, I have the power of life and death.' He held his arms out, and paused in his speech long enough for Ben and Sylvia to dare a glance at each other.

'Welcome ...' he said eventually '...to the Order.' Dance stared into their eyes – Sylvia, then Ben. 'Tell anyone of the Order and what we are about and the punishment will be severe. Not only for you, but for your loved ones too.' He sneered at Ben. 'Not that that is an issue for you. You care about no one but yourself. Power and the idea you might belong to a group worthy of your ambitions will be enough for you, I believe. But you...' He turned to Sylvia. 'How's your dear grandmama?'

Sylvia said nothing.

Dance supplied the answer. 'She's in her dotage. Money is running out and if she doesn't have access to your trust fund soon she will lose her home.'

'But...' Sylvia jumped to her feet, panic bright in her head.

'But we can fix this issue for her, provided you promise to do as we say.'

'I promise...' Sylvia sat back down. 'I promise.'

'Be careful, young Sylvia.' Phineas Dance leaned forward, his eyes gleaming with threat. 'The price you pay is never the one you agree to.'

A warning she instantly recognised. And for a moment she wondered if Dance and her grandmother were somehow connected. Sylvia was distraught to discover her beloved grandmother was in danger of being made homeless. And she was also aware her trust fund was inaccessible until she was twenty-five – and here she was, only thirteen. But more than either of these things, she burned with interest. There was something in what Dance was saying that drew her. There was an avaricious shine to his eyes that promised much in the way of learning and riches. Of the people he'd mentioned, one stuck out: Aleister Crowley. She was sure this name was gilded onto the leather spine of one of the books in her grandmother's bookcase.

'First, you must know the truth about your parents.' His gaze suddenly pinned her to her seat. 'The African plane crash is a fantasy, cooked up by your grandmother to mislead you into thinking your progenitors were normal people. We have secured information that proves your parents entered into a murder-suicide pact. Your mother was unhinged, Sylvia. Convinced there were voices in her head tormenting her, telling her you were all going to die a horrible death. So rather than wait for fate to deal you that cruel and painful blow, she decided that you should all die at a time of her choosing.

'She wore your father down – convinced him. And they made a poisoned brew, drank their fill, and gave you some before they passed out. You were found hours later, crying in your cot, covered in vomit. A reflex that surely saved your life.'

Sylvia gasped.

No.

Could this be true?

She felt a light breeze on the back of her neck. Comfort from Sarah, she believed. And confirmation.

Dance handed Sylvia two documents. They were yellow with age, their boxes filled with a neat cursive script. They both bore the title *Death Certificate*. One of them was her father's – the other, her mother's. And there under 'Cause of Death' it read – 'anaphylaxis – catastrophic heart failure – poison'.

Chapter 21

Lewis

Bodie's mother's name was Alison Oldfield and she lived in a sandstone villa facing the sea on one of the main roads in Girvan. The drive down from the city was mostly a long, black-tarred line of dual carriageway streaking through moor and farmland until they got past Ayr. Then it became one lane either way, greenery on either side, punctuated by the occasional dwelling.

When they parked outside Alison's house, Lewis gave out a low whistle. 'Nice. If this was in Glasgow it would probably be worth close to half a million.'

There was a small front garden, mostly lawn with a border of flowers. It was well cared for and looked like it was intended to outshine its neighbours. Lewis noted the absence of weeds from the path, and that the window sills and door seemed to have just been given a fresh coat of paint. Even the pointing around the large sandstone blocks looked like it had been recently renewed.

'If Damien had a girlfriend who could afford somewhere like this, he must have been kicking himself when she dumped him.'

Annie raised an eyebrow. 'There's also the fact that he lost daily access to his son.'

'There is that.' Lewis shrugged. 'Once an accountant...' he grinned.

'Are the bosses happy with you taking so much time off, by the way?'

Lewis had made a point of not discussing his work with Annie recently. She wouldn't be happy to know that following the Jenkins scandal, Lewis went from being close to becoming a partner, to being accountant *non grata* – 'let's pretend he doesn't exist and hope he goes away'. Which he was seriously considering. After the way he'd been treated, accountancy had lost its shine for him. It was hardly his fault that a client of the firm went so bad. But if he told Annie all this it would just add to her guilt.

'I'm not happy at Taylor and Gilfinnan's,' he said, trying to keep things vague. 'I'm going to take the next wee while to think about my options.'

'But you still have a job, right?'

Lewis nodded. 'Got your stone to hand?' he asked, to change the subject.

Annie opened her right hand, closed it tight again. 'So far, so good,' she said. Then realised that if she kept it there it might be obvious to other people, or worse she might lose it. Her jeans only had back pockets so that wouldn't do. With a small smile she thought of the perfect place and opened the top button of her shirt and tucked it into the left cup of her bra.

'Really?' Lewis asked.

'Works for me,' Annie shrugged. She listened for her murmurs. Nothing. And with a smile she patted it in its little pocket.

Lewis had a hand raised to knock on the door when it opened. A man in a black T-shirt bearing an album cover by The Eagles and faded-blue jeans stood there. He was tall and broad-shouldered, with dark cropped hair and a bowling-ball belly. His look as he assessed them was cold and uninterested.

'Alison,' he shouted over his shoulder, 'tell Mum I'll talk to her later.' Then he brushed past them without another word.

A woman appeared, almost as tall as the man, with sleek chestnut hair. The family resemblance was clear. She was wearing leopard-print leggings and a white off-the-shoulder T-shirt with a diamante heart in the middle. She nodded in the direction of the man as he walked up the path to the gate, shook her head and said, 'Apologies. My brother is a dick sometimes.' Alison continued looking over their shoulders, and Lewis turned. She was watching her brother get into a large black car. It was only when he'd driven out of sight that she finally spoke. She studied them both. 'Sorry about that. Now ... how can I help you?'

Lewis smiled. 'No worries. Don't know if you remember us? I'm Lewis. This is Annie.'

Annie offered a little wave.

'We're Chrissie's nephew and niece – sort of.' Lewis smiled. 'I think we must have met you at a family wedding, or a christening, or something. Would have been ages ago, right enough.'

Alison looked at him and then Annie, and sudden recognition

flashed in her eyes. 'Gosh, Annie. It's you. Wow. You look so well. After everything.' She stepped forward. Paused, holding her arms out wide. 'Can I? I mean is it okay if I hug you?'

Annie shot Lewis a look; as if she was slightly embarrassed at eliciting such a reaction, but Lewis could tell she was pleased. This would mean they would get a hearing, and maybe even some help.

The women hugged.

'God, you were so brave,' Alison said as she stepped back. 'I'm a true-crime junkie. I watched it every day on the news. As they found the bodies and everything. Oh my God. It was awful.' She looked back into the house. 'And Mum will be so chuffed to meet you. She was even more caught up in the story than I was. But...' She made a little face of disappointment. 'But she's seeing to Bodie right now. His midday nap. Please say you won't leave without saying hello to her?'

'Sure. Of course,' Annie replied.

'Where are my manners?' Alison said. 'Please come in. Come in. I'm in the middle of some work so ignore the mess.'

The hallway was filled with natural light, wood panelling on the lower half of the wall painted the same dark grey as the stair banister, the stairs themselves carpeted in a plush, light-grey carpet.

A glass-topped occasional table sat to the side, with a large fern inside a brass plant pot sitting in the middle. A little brass plate held a set of keys, and under the table there were three pairs of small shoes, each of them with the toe tops badly scuffed.

Alison led them through a doorway to the right and into a large living room with bay windows. It held two cream-coloured sofas, a floor-to-ceiling bookcase in one corner, and a large oak fireplace, which stood in the centre of the far wall. The floor was covered in a child's toys.

Alison wove her way through them. 'Sorry, again. If I'd known I had a celeb coming to visit...'

She took a seat on the corner of one of the sofas and indicated that they should sit on the other. On a low, glass coffee table between them sat an open MacBook as well as piles of wedding paraphernalia: images, fabric samples, little blue-and-pink boxes, and cheesy artwork about love and togetherness.

'I'm a wedding organiser,' Alison said, flicking her hair. 'I have a big commission coming up, and oh my God, the family is a nightmare.' She grinned, and Lewis couldn't help but think she thrived on this pressure, and that the size of the house and the classy furnishings suggested she was very successful. Alison reached forward and closed the lid of the laptop. 'Bodie is having a wee nap, so we should get some time to talk without him interrupting ... So, to what do I owe this honour?'

Lewis glanced at Annie. 'We wanted to ask you about Damien.'

Alison heaved a sigh, her demeanour instantly changing. Then she looked from Annie to Lewis. And back again, her eyes narrowing in thought. Lewis could see that she was already working out why they were here.

'You helped that Trainer guy clear his name,' she said. '...And Chrissie has asked you to try and find Damien, am I right?'

'Correct.'

'The police aren't interested because—' Lewis began.

'Because he's an arsehole,' Alison interrupted.

Annie sat forward and quickly picked things up. 'We're hoping to retrace his steps on the day he disappeared. See what comes up.'

'Right.' Alison nodded a couple of times. 'A bit weird, to be honest, having his relatives act like private detectives.' She sat back, crossing her arms and legs as she did so. 'Chrissie's that worried?'

Annie nodded. 'She's frantic.'

'Really?' Concern momentarily wove its way through Alison's expression. She bit her lip as if warding it off, and then exhaled. 'To be honest, I don't know that I'll be able to tell you much. Damien took Bodie out for a couple of hours. Brought him back. Spat out some angry shit at me – the usual – and then left. And I haven't heard from him since.'

'If you don't mind me saying,' Annie said, 'you don't seem all that worried.'

'It's resignation, Annie.' Alison uncrossed her legs. 'I've been with Damien long enough to know he's reliably unreliable.'

'Prior to now has he missed any of his arranged visits with Bodie?' Lewis asked.

'To be fair,' Alison replied, 'since Bodie was born, he's the one area where Damien has been true to his word. If he says he's going to be somewhere for the wee man, he is.'

'Which could suggest,' Annie said, 'that rather than being off on some jaunt somewhere, something is very wrong indeed...'

Chapter 22

Annie

Alison pursed her lips and crossed her arms. She looked past them out of the window, in the direction her brother's car had left in minutes earlier.

'We've kinda lost track of Damien over the years, to be honest,' Annie said. 'What kind of man he turned into and all that. So don't be concerned about any loyalty we might have to him. Please speak your mind. If it wasn't for his mother coming to see me we wouldn't be looking into this.'

'How does it work then?' Alison gazed intently at Annie. 'This psychic thing? Do you hold something belonging to him? And then what?'

'I'm not really sure how it works.' Annie crossed her own arms now, aware of the pressure of the little stone. She listened for her murmurs. Nothing.

'Right,' Alison nodded. 'And what about the memory thing? That must have been so weird. Losing your memory as a teenager and then getting it back, *while someone was trying to kill you*.' Her mouth was hanging open. 'Sorry. Listen to me getting all star-struck. I love all those true-crime podcasts, and here's this terrible thing that happened, and I actually know one of the key people...'

'Wow, when you say you followed the story, you really did,' Annie replied, and hoped that her tone was neutral. She wanted Alison's help, but she was uncomfortable with this level of interest.

'It must have been awful,' Alison said, leaning forward. 'I don't know how you're not a wreck. That guy trying to kill you? Were you and this Jenkins fella ... were you...?' Her face flushed. 'Sorry. I've ... It's just when it was on the news and stuff I couldn't keep my eyes off it. You were so brave.'

Alison bit her lip, and Annie could see she was building herself up to ask her next question.

'The newspapers said you know when people are going to die. Do you have a feeling – a sense – that Damien's okay, or...?' She asked this quietly. She *was* concerned.

'I only get a sense if something bad is going to happen when the person is in front of me,' Annie replied. 'And only, I think, when it's imminent. I really can't say if that's the case here. I'm sorry.'

'No need to apologise.' Alison tossed her hair over a shoulder, as if that switched her back into don't-care mode. 'He is a colossal dick. But he is the father of my son, so I don't wish him dead or anything.' Again she looked out of the window towards where her brother had driven off.

'How was he that day, when you two last spoke?'

Alison shrugged. 'The usual. He's all sweetness and light when he picks Bodie up, then all attitude when it's over and he's got to leave.' She picked at a thumbnail. 'And I get it. If I don't see Bodie for a while, it's a welcome break.' She made a face. 'I love him to bits, but jeez he's hard work. From Damien's point of view, though, when he doesn't see him, he's being deprived of his son. I can't imagine only getting to see Bodie for a couple of hours a week. But, you know,' she shrugged, 'Damien's the source of his own problems and until he deals with them and...' She paused. 'Sorry, I don't want to be disrespectful. He's your family...'

'That's okay,' Annie assured her. 'We want to hear what you have to say. Warts and all.' She smiled. 'How long have you guys known each other?'

'God, it's been like, forever. I can barely remember a time he wasn't in my life.' She slumped back in the sofa. 'We met at school. Teenage sweethearts and all that. We were around thirteen? He was this cocky, handsome footballer type – so not what I was into at the time, but I fell for his charm. He was sweet as a young man, so much fun, and he would *listen*, you know, like he was actually interested in what I had to say.' She raised an eyebrow in Lewis's direction. 'Men should learn how sexy that is.' Then her face clouded. 'Then he got a bit weird. Had all this anger. He never hit me though.' She held a hand up. 'I wouldn't have stood for that. And then he got injured within the first year of his big contract at Celtic, and totally went off the rails. It felt like self-sabotage at the time, to be honest. As if he didn't think he was worthy? Drugs, drink, gambling, other girls, you name it. We'd fall out. Get back together, fall out again. This is all over a, what, fourteen or fifteen-year period? I should get a bloody medal for putting up with his nonsense.'

'Was vanishing like this ever part of that nonsense?' asked Annie.

Alison pursed her lips and blew. 'Yes. All the time. He'd go off on these benders then turn up days later, all sorry and knackered-looking, begging me to take him back.'

'Does this disappearance feel any different to you?' Annie asked.

Alison sat up. Looked off into the distance. Crossed her legs. Then her arms. 'When Chrissie called to ask if I'd heard from him, I was like, here we go again. Damien's up to his old tricks. But, as I said earlier, he's been on the ball since he was awarded visiting rights with Bodie. He's at the door on the dot, as arranged, every week. So yeah, this isn't good.' She looked at Annie, eyes wide. 'Should I be worried?'

Before Annie could reply, they heard rapid footsteps, and a yell. 'Mummy?' More rapid steps along the hallway and then a little boy with sleep-fussed hair and bright eyes appeared at the door. 'Mummy,' he repeated, and then paused at the door at the sight of the two strangers in the room.

A woman appeared over Bodie's shoulder. 'Sorry, honey,' she said. 'He heard your voices...' She looked over at Annie. 'And couldn't wait to come and say hello.' At that she offered Annie a large smile. 'Hi,' she said. 'I'm Evelyn.'

'My mother,' Alison added. 'Your biggest fan.'

Annie ducked her head, uncomfortable now.

Evelyn was a tall woman, with short white hair. And thin. So thin Annie wondered if that was why her eyes appeared so large – eyes that were staring at her, lingering over her so greedily that Annie shifted uncomfortably in her seat.

'Mummy,' a little voice pipped in.

'Guys,' Alison said, 'meet Bodie.' She smiled. Doting. 'This is Annie and her brother, Lewis.'

Lewis looked over at the boy and waved. 'Hi Bodie. Did you have a nice nap?'

'I'm so sorry, everyone,' Evelyn said, creeping into the room as if she didn't quite belong. 'If I'd known you were having guests I wouldn't have let him out of his bed.'

Annie sent the older woman a smile to signal she was happy enough for the interruption, and thinking this was a strange thing for Evelyn to say. She must have heard their voices and was curious herself, judging by the way her eyes never left Annie's face.

The little boy ran to stand by his mother's side, leaning his belly against her knee. He sucked at his thumb, and lifting a leg over one of his mother's, placed a hand behind her neck and pulled himself up onto her.

'Oww, Bodie,' Alison said as she freed a clump of hair from his grip. 'That was sore.' Bodie's eyes were large and blue, and they were now focused on Annie's face. His gaze was so unaffected and direct that Annie felt a little discomfited. It was as if he could see right into her heart.

'I had a dream, Mummy,' he said as he put both arms around her neck. He was now fully in her lap, all the while staring at Annie. Then he glanced towards the door, and his grandmother. 'The green woman,' he said to Annie, eyes back on her as if she was the only other person in the room. 'She said you've not to be afraid anymore.'

Chapter 23

Annie

All the adults looked at Bodie in surprise.

'What did you say, Bodie?' Alison twisted to the side, turning him round and looking at him face on. 'What did you say, honey?'

Annie held a hand over her heart, aware of its heavy thump. She shot a look at Lewis.

Bodie closed his eyes and allowed his head to fall against his mother's chest. 'I didn't say something,' Bodie replied. 'I'm a sleepyhead.'

'Want to go back to bed?' Alison asked as she exchanged glances with Annie. Her look seemed to ask: do you understand what just happened?

Bodie lifted his head with a jerk, and placing a hand on his mother's cheek, turned her face to his. 'Now I'm awake,' he replied.

'Now you're awake,' Alison laughed. 'Can you tell us about your dream?'

'You said I could watch the *Lion King*?' Bodie asked, his face a blank, as if any notions of a dream were completely gone from his mind. 'Can I, Mummy?'

'A deal's a deal,' Alison said, replacing her worried expression with fake brightness. She reached for a remote, pressed a few buttons and soon the TV screen was filled with bright colours and movement, and a familiar tune filled their ears.

With Bodie on her lap, entranced, all thoughts of his dream gone, Alison looked over his head at Annie. 'I don't know what that was all about,' she said. 'He's never said anything like it before.'

'Kids have such vivid imaginations,' Annie said, waving off Alison's concerns, happy to avoid any further chat about psychic abilities. 'Mind if I ask you something more about Damien?'

Alison nodded. 'Sure.'

'It's just, I ... I remembered a family event we were at years ago. Damien would have been around sixteen at the time. He'd just signed his first professional contract to play football. Is there anything that might have happened to him around that time? Something significant?'

'What do you mean?' Alison frowned.

'It's just ... I know this is going to sound weird, but I caught a vibe off him. He wasn't happy. We were at a family wedding. He'd just signed up for what must be every boy's dream, but I saw him when he thought no one's eyes were on him. He looked like he wanted the earth to swallow him up. Like he deserved none of it, you know?'

'When he was around sixteen you say?'

Annie nodded. 'At a guess.'

Alison sucked in her top lip. Then: 'That would have been around the first time we fell out, I suppose. He'd been really horrible to me. Completely out of the blue, you know? Until then he'd been this sweet kid.' She put a hand on her chest. 'Gosh. Do you think something happened around then that sent him off the rails?' She paused, staring into Annie's eyes. 'Are you *getting* something?'

Annie felt her face heat a little. She didn't want this to be about her and her 'gift'.

'There is one thing that happened around that time,' Evelyn

interjected, shaking her head slowly, 'although I'm not sure how much it affected Damien. A boy called Rab Daniels died.'

'Who?'

'Rab Daniels,' Evelyn answered. She had moved to sit on the arm of the sofa by her daughter's side now. 'Used to hang around our Craig. *Not* my favourite of his friends.'

'How did he die?' Lewis asked.

'The details are a bit foggy,' Evelyn replied. 'If memory serves, it was a hit and run. But they never found the driver of the car that hit him.'

'And Damien and this Rab guy were pals?' Lewis asked.

Alison rocked her head from side to side. 'Wouldn't say they were exactly pals. Rab kinda hung about, hoping for some of Damien's shine to rub off on him. Every now and again he'd turn up at ours, asking my brother Craig to go out and play, but Craig couldn't stand him. Don't know why he kept coming around.' She shrugged.

'And to make it more awkward,' Evelyn added, 'his mother worked in the lawyers' office for Dad.'

Alison sat back in the sofa. 'Yeah, that was tricky. I don't know how his mother coped with the loss, though. The whole family was devastated.' Her eyes softened, and she slowly, deliberately fixed a strand of Bodie's hair back into place. 'I can't imagine how it would be for a mother to lose their son.'

Chapter 24

Lewis

Back in the car, after they'd said their goodbyes, Lewis clicked his seatbelt into place and said, 'What did we learn then?'

'It's interesting that Damien's behaviour changed after Rab Daniels' death.'

'Think it's significant?'

'It's certainly worth looking into,' Annie replied. 'Wonder if Chrissie can tell us anything more about what was going on at that time.'

'What about Bodie's "dream" woman?'

Annie exhaled, and they both looked out of the windscreen at a grey panel of sea and sky. 'I thought it better not to get into it,' she said. 'If this dream woman wants to send me information through other people, that's kind of worrying. And scary if it's coming through a child.'

'What are you not saying, Annie?'

'Godsake,' she swiped at him. 'Do you have to be so good at reading me?' She shook her head. 'Last night I had a dream where a woman, a very strange woman, was comforting me. I'm not sure if "comforting" is even the right word, to be honest. But when I woke up I realised I'd seen her before.'

'Aye?'

'It was the woman in green I saw at The Inn at Ardgour.'

'Whoa. Really?' He swivelled in his chair to look at Annie.

'And Bodie? If the woman's sending you messages through the kid...' He took a moment to consider how weird those words might sound. 'Do you think he's got some kind of gift as well?'

Annie exhaled. Threw her hands in the air. 'God. I don't know.' She looked back at the sea. 'What about Evelyn? What did you make of her?'

'She couldn't keep her eyes off you,' Lewis replied.

'You noticed that as well?'

'Couldn't not. She was a bit intense, eh?'

'You can see they're mother and daughter. I liked Alison on the spot, but her mother...?' She shivered. 'There's something off about her.'

'Nah, she was just caught up in meeting a celeb.'

Annie pursed her lips and blew some air out dismissively. 'Hardly.'

Lewis fired up the engine, judged the traffic in the mirror, and slipped onto the road, and as he did so, something snagged his attention. Someone, rather. The driver of a parked car, looking right at him, scowling.

'What's his problem?' Lewis said. Then realised he recognised the man. It was Alison's brother, Craig.

As he drove on, he looked in his rear-view mirror and noted that the car had joined the traffic just behind them.

'That black car,' he said to Annie. 'Just two cars behind?'

Annie swivelled in her seat. 'What about it?'

'That's Alison's brother.'

'Why would he ...? Do you think he came back and was waiting for us to leave?' Annie asked. 'I noticed that she looked out of the window a couple of times. Maybe she was expecting to see his car come back.'

'Watch this,' Lewis said, indicated, and took a right. The black car followed. At the next junction Lewis took another right. The black car followed again.

'What's going on, Lewis?'

Lewis sped up.

The black car kept pace with them.

Lewis drove to the end of the long road they were on. Most of the shops on it were shut, and weeds sprouted up from many of the gutters. It was a listless place and had the air of a high street where the rents were too high and most of the residents had abandoned it, lured by the cheaper goods in the supermarkets.

They came to a roundabout. Lewis knew the left turn would take them onto a small country road that bypassed the town, eventually coming out near a bigger roundabout that would lead them back north to Ayr. He took the country road, and sighed with relief when he noted Alison's brother didn't follow them this time.

'I'm thinking we need to look into Craig,' he said. 'I have the feeling we've just been escorted out of town. That guy doesn't want us here, and we need to know why.'

Chapter 25

Annie

On the drive back up to Glasgow, the motion of the car pulled Annie into a dream-like state. Her mind was full of the little boy's message, the brisk attitude of Craig Oldfield as he brushed past them at the door, and Evelyn's near-constant stare. It was almost as if she was committing Annie's face to memory in order to render it into a piece of art once she left.

Fifteen minutes into the journey and something snagged her attention, tugging her from her thoughts. The car had slowed at a bend, and off on the other side of the road she spotted what might be the entrance to a dwelling – two stone pillars about six feet tall. Metal gates hung off each pillar but they were open. Her eyes were drawn upward, beyond some fir and oak trees, a rhododendron hedge, and to the top of a small hill, where a large house stood. Annie felt a shot of the familiar. She knew this place. Had seen this house before, and although they were a good five hundred metres away, Annie somehow could make out a figure at one of the windows. And she had the strong feeling that this person could see – and read – her.

'That's...'

She couldn't articulate what she was feeling. And Lewis wouldn't understand even if she could. And then she had the strong sense that she mustn't tell him. All she knew was that she had to come back here, on her own.

'Annie?' Lewis asked.

'Eh?'

'You're looking weird.' He moved his eyes from the road, to search hers. 'What's going on?' He followed her line of vision and looked up at the house retreating into the distance.

'What? Nothing.' She shot him a smile.

Her hand strayed to her chest, the pad of her thumb rubbing

at her lodestone, and she recalled her dream of the night before – the woman, her voice. Annie felt an ache, a loss, a longing she'd never experienced before.

Come to me, she heard, the words woven into the wind, knitted through the swish and hiss of the car tyres on the road, and laced through the off-key hum of her murmurs. It was the sweetest voice and it was for Annie's ear, and Annie's ear alone.

Come to me.

Soon.

Chapter 26

Ben
1967

After that first meeting with Dance, Ben and Sylvia were in his chambers at least twice a week. For the first year the things they learned were so terrifying that the men, women and creatures Ben learned about inhabited his dreams, and he developed the habit of wetting the bed.

Each time he woke up and felt that faint, urine burn on his skin from groin to knee, he burst into tears. With the result that, each night, after his sessions with Dance, he would return to his dormitory, slip under his covers and pray that his dreams would not be nightmares and he would not wake up with his sheets plastered to his legs.

Of course, the other boys teased him horribly about this, all of them apart from Thomas Quick. His eyes would slide from Ben's face as if even looking at him would hurt.

Dance was a brilliant orator and he brought his lessons vividly to life, and while in that room, listening to tales of horrible and fantastic happenings, Ben's fear and excitement had his pulse high and his cheeks so red he looked like he'd been slapped.

The lesson that affected him most during this time was that of Urbain Grandier. In France, in 1633, he was suspected of being a witch in league with the devil and of causing a group of nuns to be possessed. He was tortured, his legs smashed and his broken body dragged through the streets before he was burned alive. Within five years, two of the nuns died insane, and the third was said to be possessed by an evil spirit for a further twenty years.

Despite the warning the tale contained, Dance told the story with such brio that Ben imagined himself in the roles of both Grandier and the long-lived nun. He didn't know which might be worse – the hours of torture, or the years of being driven mad by an evil spirit.

Eventually, news about Ben's bed-wetting reached Dance's ears. He was furious. 'Not only do you wet the bed, you cry when your soaking sheets are discovered!'

Ben's face burned. He felt more shame than he'd ever felt in his life. What manner of man would he become if he pissed his sheets every night?

Dance was standing in front of his desk. 'Come here,' he ordered.

Ben shifted, slowly, until he was about two feet away. Just out of reach.

'Closer,' Dance said.

Ben shuffled a little.

Dance's hand shot out and he slapped Ben. Hard.

'Weakness is not to be tolerated,' Dance shouted. 'These nightmares have lasted over a month. I've never known a student to be so affected by his lessons. You must be possessed yourself.'

'What?' A current of fear ran through Ben. It was so strong he barely noticed the heat and pain on the side of his face.

'It is of no matter,' Dance said, now with an appearance of preternatural calm. He seemed to have the ability to switch from a towering rage to the serenity of a monk with the tick of a clock. 'We shall perform a banishing ritual. Sylvia has been taking extra lessons for just such an occasion.'

Ben felt a pang of jealousy and shot Sylvia a look. Her gaze was distant, as if concentrating, frightened to forget anything.

'And you will be renewed,' Dance said.

The master then whipped back the rug that was in front of his desk, revealing a magic circle carved into the floorboards. This was something they'd never seen before. Or Ben hadn't. He shot another look at Sylvia and with another pang of jealousy judged that she evinced no surprise at all. He looked down at the circle and thought it looked permanent. The artwork was intricate and detailed, and, caught up in wonder and not a little fear about what he was going to experience next, Ben forgot his envy.

When Sylvia asked him later what the experience was like, he couldn't answer her. It had been thrust upon him and was magical and terrifying at the same time. All he knew was that he was ordered to stand in the middle, lit candles were placed at the points of the compass. Voices chanted around him – two of them, then multiples of two. There were others here? He looked around and saw no one. A great burning sensation worked its way up from his feet to his thighs. He felt sure he would vomit.

His parents loomed over him, their faces contorted with hate, their mouths moving in a concert of derision.

'A towering disappointment.'

'A disgrace to the family.'

'Should have strangled you at birth.'

He shook before them, his mind and body unable to do more than tremble in reaction. Words queued in his mind. Replies that would put them in their place, but such was his terror, sound was beyond him.

His mother handed his father a leather strap and pulled down Ben's trousers and underwear. 'Spare the rod, dear, and you spoil the child,' she said, the only emotion on display from her was a cold gleam in her eyes.

Blinding pain on the back of his thighs, his buttocks, his calves. He fell to his knees.

They laughed.

Then. From somewhere, a shimmer of defiance. He stoked it with his resentment and spite. Every slight, every petty and large cruelty, every moment of hurt they'd ever placed on him built in his mind until he was alight with hate for them.

A knife appeared in his hand and he was so strong with this dark energy that the tip shone with heat. He struck out. Again, and again, and again. He lashed at them so many times with that knife that his arms and lungs burned with effort, until, exhausted he stepped back to see them as a tumble of bones and rent flesh, and his clothes crimson with their blood.

When he came to he felt better, lighter, stronger than he ever had.

So much so that he started crying with relief.

Dance slapped him so hard he flew out of the circle and landed in a heap at the master's desk.

'If you ever show such weakness again,' Dance thundered, his face puce with rage, 'I will cut off one of your fingers, use it in a golem and you will never know a moment's peace ever again.'

Ben hiccupped a sob. He didn't know what a golem was or how this lack of peace might articulate itself, but he vowed there and then to close off his emotions. He would never risk such a punishment ever again.

Chapter 27

Sylvia
1968

Sylvia felt a thrill like none she'd ever had when she and Dance performed the banishing ritual on Ben. To have that power was intoxicating.

The relief Ben expressed was palpable. And made him a little more bearable for a while, until his usual detached persona took over.

Their act – that they appear like a couple to explain how often they were together – had produced many awkward moments for Sylvia over the years. But it helped that relationships were frowned upon at Clevelland – it meant that she could be in Ben's company without having to hold hands, or worse, cuddle.

'He never slaps you,' Ben said to her out of the side of his mouth as they made their way back to their respective dorms after a lesson with Dance.

'Words,' Sylvia said simply. 'That's his choice of weapon for me.'

'He's only ever polite to you,' Ben protested.

She looked at him from the corner of her eye. 'For someone so smart you can be pretty dim, Benjamin.'

'What do you mean?' he asked.

They'd reached the end of the corridor where they would part ways. She stopped walking, and aware that there were eyes on them, she reached out and touched his right forearm, aiming for a supportive, friendly gesture.

'Pay attention,' she said. 'Read between the lines. That's where the punch sits.' With that, she turned and walked away.

Later, after lights out, Sylvia lay on her back, staring at the ceiling, thinking once again about the ritual. Ben had been terrified, but when he was in that circle he had changed, staring at something in the far distance that only he could see. Then he began to shake – so hard Sylvia wondered at how he managed to stay upright. It passed almost as quickly as it came, and his face then was a picture of relief, his features softening to an expression that almost made Sylvia like the boy.

Over to her right, in a bed at the end of the row, someone sobbed.

Lucinda Armitage. Stupid girl. It was probably over some imagined slight – reading too much between the lines of a comment by one of the other girls.

That's where the punch sits, she'd told Ben. You just had to know where and when to look for it. Dance was a master at saying little while meaning much. His tactic with her, after telling her the truth about her parents' deaths, was to make continual little jabs about them.

Over the years she'd learned not to ask her grandmother about her parents, because when she did, the old woman would clutch her pearls and fan her face. 'Am I not enough?' she'd demand.

'I just want to know about them.'

'They're dead,' Maude replied each time. 'A terrible, tragic accident. They died in each other's arms. Like something from the classics. Shakespeare couldn't have written better. What more do you need to know?' And then she'd distract herself and Sylvia with some form of frippery. And in those moments Sylvia would feel a hate so pure for her grandmother that it stole her breath. She couldn't help but feel betrayed. Her parents would rather kill themselves than be with her, care for her, love her? And whenever she was assailed by those torments, her shadow, Sarah, would disappear, leaving her alone with the tumult in her mind.

Why couldn't Maude just tell her the truth? At least if she'd known it from the start, she would have got used to it by now, and would be better able to put up with Dance's digs: 'Just like your mother.' 'A little unhinged there, were we?' 'If only your father had loved you more.' A drip, drip of words that had her feeling worthless. Until. The moment when Ben was in the circle. The rush as the words Dance taught her caused such a change in Ben.

This was what it was all about.

Dance had held Sylvia back for a moment after Ben left his chambers. He bent down, peered into her eyes.

'There,' he said. 'Right there. That's what you are capable of, Sylvia Lowry-Law.' He touched her cheek with an unexpected lightness, and she felt this man knew her, cared for her, wanted only the best for her. And her spirit soared.

Chapter 28

Lewis

When they arrived home Lewis offered to make them both dinner, and after a simple meal of steak and chips they sat and watched TV. As they did, Lewis couldn't help occasionally turning to check on Annie.

'Lewis,' she said slowly. 'You're doing that thing.'

'Excuse me?'

'Stop it.'

'Stop what?'

'You're worrying about me. I'm fine.'

'Okay. Whatever you say.' He crossed his arms.

The programme ended. He hadn't really been watching it anyway. Adverts. And then another programme started. A soap. His mind trailed off into thoughts of the day. The little boy. His mother.

Craig trailing them as they drove out of the town.

He stretched to the side of the sofa and picked up his laptop. He opened it, and brought up a search engine. 'I'm going to look up Alison's brother online,' he told Annie. 'See what I can dig up.' Lewis thought about the size of the house Alison lived in, her brother's large BMW. 'Do you know if they come from money?' he asked.

'Evelyn did say something about Rab Daniels' mother working in their dad's lawyer's office. So I'm guessing daddy's the one with the cash. In any case,' she added, 'there's someone we both know who could add a little detail about Alison and Craig's parents.' She picked her phone up as she said this and Lewis saw her dial Mandy McEvoy, putting it on speaker phone as it rang.

'Hi, honey,' Mandy answered almost immediately. 'How was your trip down the coast?'

'Interesting,' Annie answered. 'Not sure we learned that much, to be honest.' She looked to Lewis for confirmation of this assessment. He nodded. 'The little boy, Bodie, is so cute.'

Lewis wondered if Annie would tell Mandy about the strange moment when Bodie had told her she shouldn't be afraid. But Annie moved straight to the point of the call.

'Are they from money?' Mandy repeated the question. 'Oh yeah,' she replied. 'That was one of the reasons why her family weren't too happy about Damien. Thought he was a crook and a junkie, and only interested in Alison for her cash.'

'We met her brother Craig today,' Lewis said towards the phone.

'Oh yeah? And what did you make of him?'

'Bit of an arsehole,' Lewis said.

Mandy's laughter sounded out.

'What do you know about him?' Lewis asked, as he thought of the black car behind them, the driver not visible when light bounced off the windscreen.

'Not much, to be honest,' Mandy replied. 'Chrissie wasn't too impressed by the family. She liked Alison well enough, and to my mind that makes the woman almost saint-like; if she was good enough in Chrissie's eyes for her precious boy she must be some sort of female paragon.'

'What was it about the rest of them she didn't like?' Lewis asked.

'According to her, they thought they were too good for her family. Too big for their boots, she reckoned. Thought the mother, and I quote, was a "stuck-up cow", and Damien's father was a dick. He's a lawyer, apparently, and Chrissie said the first time she met him she'd never been made to feel so insignificant. It was as if she wasn't even in the room, he paid so little attention to her.'

Lewis thought about the way Craig barged past them as they stood on Alison's doorstep. 'That attitude was obviously passed on to the son. Do you know if he went into the family trade, became a lawyer?' Lewis asked.

'The way Chrissie tells it, Craig is a huge disappointment to the father. Nothing outright was ever said – they want to be seen in a certain way: well-heeled pillars of the community and all that – but Chrissie could see it in the way the father dismissed Craig. Every time he spoke, his father either talked over him or sneered. It made her feel very uncomfortable at any family gatherings she was invited to. Not that there were many of them.' She paused. 'But as far as what Craig does for a living, Chrissie has never said.'

Annie told her about Craig following them as they made their way out of the town. 'Was it for his own benefit,' Annie wondered. 'Or is he reporting back to someone?'

'Not the behaviour of a well-balanced young man,' said Mandy. Then before she rang off she gave them a warning: 'Look after yourselves, kids. I mean it.'

With the computer still on his lap, Lewis budged round in his seat so that Annie could follow what he was doing. He entered a social-media site and looked up the name Craig Oldfield. 'Let's see what kind of clues we can get on here.'

More than fifty profiles popped up. They were able to discount many of them, because they displayed the wrong location. Some of them showed no location at all so they required further investigation. There were some others that showed pictures of men who weren't Craig. They were finally left with three possibilities.

Annie pointed at the screen. 'That one has no image. The guy we met doesn't strike me as being that private.'

Lewis laughed. 'Good point.' He clicked on the name below and a profile appeared that displayed nothing but photographs of tractors.

'Ehm,' Annie laughed. 'Don't think so.'

'That one' – Lewis's turn to point – 'has a snarling bulldog as an avatar. Bet that's him.'

He clicked and they watched as a page loaded. This man lived in Girvan. He was a businessman. 'Whatever that means,' Lewis said as he read it. He had 306 friends and his last post – from six months earlier – was of a shiny little face blowing at a birthday cake with three candles on it. They recognised the child instantly.

'Aww, Bodie. That's so cute,' Annie said. 'So, we've found him.'

Lewis scrolled down Craig's page. It was mostly memes of bad, sexist jokes and birthday wishes he hadn't responded to. There was one picture of him, a leaner, more muscular and slightly younger version of the man they'd seen that day. He was wearing a football strip with muddied shorts and a smear of dirt across his forehead, as if he'd slid across a mud patch using his head as a brake. There was an arm across his shoulder but the owner had been cropped out of the image. Craig was cheering as if he had just won something.

'Not much going on with this guy, is there?' Annie said.

'At least, not in social-media land.'

'Which kinda makes me want to like him.'

'Damien and Craig were buddies as boys...' Annie reached over and scrolled up and down the page. 'I can't see any interaction on here between them though. But here, look – they're "friends". But there's nothing going on between them, at least publicly. No likes or shares. Wonder what happened?'

Chapter 29

Lewis

With his laptop tucked under his arm Lewis made his way to his bedroom. There, he arranged his pillows so he could sit up against them, and got himself into position for another session of internet searching.

Damien's social-media presence was even worse than Craig's. The last page that Damien had posted was from ten years earlier. Before his stint in prison.

Lewis wondered what kind of impact that experience had on Damien. How had the man been changed by his time inside? According to his mother and his ex-girlfriend, he had matured and taken his responsibilities as a father seriously. But as far as social media went, there'd be no new contact between him and Craig. He wondered if Chrissie might be able to cast any light on their relationship.

He gave her a call and she picked up after only a couple of rings, as if she'd been waiting.

'What's going on? You found out something?' she said without preamble.

'We met Alison and Bodie today. Nothing new to report. Met Craig, the brother. Strange man. Do you know how him and Damien got on? Annie and I thought he might be worth talking to.'

'I never quite took to that boy. Him and Damien were pals when they were younger. Then they played for an amateur team together when D's injury meant he couldn't make it in the big leagues. But they were never as close as before, as I remember. I thought Craig was jealous of Damien. I mean, for a while he was the star among the boys, you know? Being with a big club and all that. I thought there was more to it though, but D wasn't telling.'

'There was nothing recent between them, once Damien had a kid with his sister? They would have seen more of each other, wouldn't they?'

'D did mention that Craig wanted him to go into a business deal with him. But he didn't have the cash. Why do you ask all this? Do you think Craig's had something to do with D vanishing?'

'Just fishing, really,' Lewis said. 'We don't have enough to go on yet to pin anything on him.' He decided not to tell Chrissie about Craig following them out of town.

After they said their goodbyes, Lewis went back to Craig's page and trawled it for any connections he had with Damien, looking to see if there was someone who might be willing to shed some light on anything that might have happened between them.

A good while later, eyes sparking with tiredness, Lewis had found a couple of possibilities. Two men: Ryan Henderson and Steve Murphy. From what he could gather they'd played in the same amateur football team as Craig and Damien. By the looks of it they'd kept in touch with Craig, and there were some regular birthday wishes from them both on Damien's page, although he hadn't bothered to reply.

Lewis read that Murphy was a personal trainer, so he sent him a message asking for a note of his fees. To Henderson he simply sent a friend request.

Murphy replied almost instantly.

What are you looking for, Lewis?

Need to get fit in a hurry, dude, he wrote, trying to sound keen. *Build up some positive habits, you know? When is your next free appointment? Want to start ASAP.*

Not much until a week on Thursday. Unless you want to meet first thing tomorrow. I can fit you in before my other clients – if you're up for it?

The time Murphy suggested was seriously early. But a private investigator had to grab his chances when they fell in his lap like this, Lewis thought. He replied with a yes, noted down the time and place Murphy gave him, then turned out the light.

Steve Murphy was short, with thighs like a sprint cyclist, the waist of a teenager, and the shoulders of an Olympic swimmer. His eyes were bright and his teeth looked so shiny Lewis thought he might have to wear a pair of sunglasses every time the guy smiled.

They shook hands. Steve's grip was firm but measured – demonstrating strength and the ability to channel it. They chatted briefly; about the weather, the traffic, how easy it was to get to the park where they'd met, and the open-air calisthenics Steve specialised in.

'Let's warm up with a gentle jog round the park,' Steve said, and without waiting for a response from Lewis, he began running. Relieved that he had at least done some jogging in the last few months, Lewis matched Steve's stride. 'You look as if you've been taking care yourself,' Steve said, running his eyes up and down Lewis's body. 'What kind of exercise have you been doing?'

'A little bit of jogging,' Lewis replied. 'Two or three times a week. I started a Krav Maga class last year. Go there twice a week.'

'Cool.' Steve nodded. 'Mind if I ask how you heard about me?' he added. 'I'm trying to work out whether social-media posts or adverts, or word of mouth is how I get my clients.'

Here's my 'in', Lewis thought. 'Through my cousin, actually. Damien Fox?'

'Foxy?' Steve's stride was momentarily shortened with surprise. 'Haven't spoken to him in ages.'

'Yeah, we caught up at a family wedding a few months back. I mentioned I wanted to get fit and he told me about you. Took me ages to work up the courage to book you, to be honest. Didn't want to look like an idiot.'

'And see,' Steve grinned, 'you're doing fine.'

They stopped at a wide patch of grass at the bottom of a hill, edged with fir trees and rhododendron bushes, where Steve put Lewis through a thirty-minute workout of press-ups, burpees, sit-ups and squats, which Lewis took on as best he could, while trying not to feel self-conscious as other Glaswegians walked past. They finished the main session with a dozen sprints up the hill.

When Steve finally said they were done, a tired and panting, but strangely happy Lewis lay back on the grass, staring at the sky. 'Jeez,' he managed to say. 'Those last two times up that hill. Thought I was going to throw up.'

'You did well, man,' Steve said. 'Right,' he clapped his hands. 'Before you cool down let's finish with some stretching and mobility work.'

As they worked and stretched, Steve asked, 'How is Damien these days?'

'When was the last time you spoke to him?' Lewis asked.

Steve shook his head slowly. 'Can't remember, to be honest. Was a time we were thick as thieves.' He grinned. 'The shit we got up to? Should have come with a health warning. But...' He got down to a crouch so that he was eye to eye with Lewis sitting up on the grass. 'Older and wiser now.' He'd crouched so low that his buttocks were almost hitting the ground. He placed his elbows inside each knee and pressed outwards. 'This is a yoga pose called the garland. Great for thighs, groin, legs and ankles.' He watched as Lewis copied him. 'Not bad, dude. Sit back on your heels a little more – try to get lower. Cool. We try to work up to two minutes on this. Do it every day, yeah?'

Lewis nodded. 'I take it you haven't heard, then? About Damien?'

Steve shook his head, forehead furrowed.

'He disappeared about two weeks ago.'

'Really?' Steve gave that some thought. 'I'm not that surprised, to be honest. I'd heard he'd calmed down since the wee fella was born, but he was always one for going on benders. Would disappear for days, then turn up looking like he'd been living in a hedge, ingesting nothing but alcohol and cocaine.'

'Did a bloke called Craig join him on these benders?'

Steve cocked his head. 'Craig Oldfield? That prick. Sorry, I try not to use language with a client I barely know, but I wouldn't piss on that guy if he was on fire.' Steve got to his feet. Gave a little kick out with each leg. Lewis copied him, aware of the ache behind each knee. 'Like father like son,' Steve went on. 'A right pair of dicks: no wonder Craig turned out like he did. And to answer your question: yeah, it felt like Craig was the ringleader in their wee bouts of debauchery.'

'I met Craig for the first time the other day,' Lewis said. 'It's hard to imagine them as friends, to be honest. Until he vanished Damien seemed like a good guy. Got his life back together after being inside, you know? But there's something about that Craig fella that leaves me a bit cold...'

'You're right there. Craig was jealous as fuck of Damien's success. I'd put money on him being part of the reason Damien lost it back then. I reckon Craig was egging him on to get wasted all the time.'

'You ever meet Damien's mum, Chrissie?'

'Aye,' Steve replied. 'Nice wee wummin. Used to bring treats for full time for all the players. None of your half-oranges.' He grinned at the memory. 'Mars Bars and the like.'

'She's my mum's sister. She was at ours not long after Damien disappeared.' Now Lewis decided to fabricate a little. 'She suggested that something might have happened back then – before Damien's injury, I mean. That he'd started to self-sabotage before that, and there was a reason he did. You got any idea what that might have been?'

'Here...' Steve paused. Looked at Lewis hard. Really looked. 'What's going on? Why all the questions?'

'I'm just asking because we both know Damien...'

'No, no, no. There's more to this than you wanting to get some PT. You're here specifically because of Damien, aren't you?'

'Sorry,' Lewis held a hand up. Time for some honesty. Since meeting Steve he'd warmed to the man and throughout the session he'd definitely considered rebooking. 'I did want the PT, and I'd like to book you again, actually. But, you're right, there is more. Chrissie's asked me and my sister, Annie, to look into Damien going missing.'

'What? Are you like some kind of private investigator?' Steve seemed amused now. 'You didn't need to go through that elaborate charade, man, just to ask me some questions.'

'Well, we're not PIs exactly. Not really. We just think we can help.' Lewis looked around them and spotted a bench. 'Got a minute or two before your next client?'

Steve looked at his watch. 'Not much more than that, to be honest. But crack on. What do you want to know?'

'Craig Oldfield,' Lewis said. 'We saw him the other day.' He told Steve about Craig bumping into them on Alison's doorstep and then escorting them out of town. 'What's his deal? I can't help but think he might have something to do with Damien going missing.'

'What, like he's murdered him and hid his body somewhere?'

Steve's tone was jocular, but when Lewis glanced into his eyes, they told a different story. There was no surprise, only the look of someone who'd long suspected something. He looked away for a moment. Crossed his arms, biceps bulging, then turned back to Lewis.

'Damien told me something long ago. Something bad. But he swore me to secrecy. To be honest I didn't really believe him at the time – it seemed too ridiculous. And he was wasted, too, I mean completely and utterly out of his mind. But this...' He narrowed his eyes. 'Damien going missing ... And I've heard other shit about Craig Oldfield that makes me wonder...'

'Makes you wonder what?'

Steve's eyes clouded over. 'I've said too much.' He held both hands out. 'I can't, man. He made me swear on my mother's grave.' He chewed on the inside of his cheek.

'Whatever you know, please tell me, Steve. His mother is going out of her mind with worry. It sounds like Damien really did turn a corner, got his life back together. Even his ex, Alison, will tell you that. This disappearance is out of character. If you know something from back then that could help explain what's going on now...'

'OK ... If I tell you this, you can't take it as gospel. You need to verify it from other sources if you can. As I said, Damien was well out of it when he told me. And you sure as fuck can't tell his mother. It would destroy her.'

Chapter 30

Annie

After Lewis left for his PT session, Annie jumped into her clothes and made her way downstairs to her car.

She hadn't slept much, and when she had, her dreams had been full of the strange woman in the green dress. What the woman was doing and saying during her dreams was lost in the light of day, and Annie was left with a feeling of loneliness; a pang of missing. And one image: the woman at the window of the large house up on a hill – her long, black hair and green dress merging with the shadows. The very house she and Lewis had passed the day before.

Annie sat in a lay-by just beyond the house. As she'd approached, she'd almost indicated to take the car up the drive. But how on earth would that have looked to whoever lived there, if she'd just knocked on the door, and said, 'hi, I've been dreaming about your house'?

From where she was parked, she could make out the roof above the treeline, and nothing else. She got out and walked along the grass verge a few yards, until there was a break in the trees and she could see a little more – the roof and the top row of windows. The house looked in good repair.

As with the dream woman, there were good and bad emotions pushing at her mind as she looked up at the building. A sense of foreboding, as well as a sense, unbelievably, of somehow belonging. She could see herself in that house, making a cup of tea, or in the garden doing some weeding. But more than anything she wanted to be close to it.

What on earth was going on? Why was she so driven to visit this house?

She wondered if she could just knock at the door and come up with some bullshit story why she was there and see what happened. But then she recalled the day before when she and Lewis had driven past on the way down to Girvan. There had been a village just a few minutes away with a little shop on the main street. Perhaps she could engineer a conversation with someone there who would be able to give her some sort of clue about the house.

Minutes later, she had parked again, this time in a bay just off the main street in front of the little cabin-style shop. It was fronted with freshly stained planks of wood, hanging baskets either side of the door, with large display windows and a sign reading *Kirkronald Stores*.

A little bell tinkled above the door as she opened it. A wide counter faced her, a smiling woman behind it. On the counter were a number of glass, bell-shaped covers over plates of cakes and scones. To the far side, a display of lottery tickets.

'Morning,' the woman sang. 'Anything I can help you with?' Curiosity was large in her eyes, instantly pegging Annie as someone who was not local.

'Those scones look amazing,' Annie said.

The woman preened. 'Fresh out of my oven this morning.' Her smile grew. 'They might still have a little heat in them.'

'You don't sell coffee, do you?'

'We sure do,' the woman said. Annie guessed that she was in her mid-fifties. She was slim and tall with blonde-grey hair in a sharp bob to her chin. 'And none of your instant muck. We have a lovely wee bean-to-cup machine back here that's the main joy in my life,' she chuckled.

'If you can butter me up a scone,' Annie replied, 'and fashion a cappuccino from that machine of yours, you have yourself a happy customer.'

'Coming right up, dear.' If her scones were as warm as her smile, Annie thought she was in for a treat. 'You can take it away, or there's a wee stool here at the side of the counter where you're welcome to sit,' she said over her shoulder.

'I'll sit in please,' Annie said and took her perch. This was exactly what she'd hoped for. If anyone possessed any intelligence about the house back there she was sure it would be this woman.

'I'm Jo,' the woman said, turning with her hand on her chest.

Annie introduced herself in return.

'Passing through, Annie?'

Annie nodded.

Jo pressed a button on her coffee machine and it whirred into life. Moments later she handed Annie a white, china mug. Then the scone appeared, with a pat of butter, and as Annie cut it, she asked, 'There's a house just back there, on the bend before the village—'

The bell above the door tinkled.

'Good morning, Ina,' Jo said to the woman who entered.

'Aye,' Ina replied. 'It'll be better when I'm back home and I've got the kettle on.' She was a tiny woman, as slight as a clothes pole, her hair covered by a blue and heather-coloured scarf that was tied under her chin.

'How's Bob today?' Jo asked.

'Slower by the minute, the wee soul. I'm trying him wi' a new feed. It's got multi-vitamins in it, so I'm hoping that'll put a pep in his step.'

Annie had initially thought Bob would be her husband, but perhaps it was her dog...

'The usual?' Jo asked.

'The *Herald*, and two well-fired rolls. And make sure they're almost burned. Yesterday's were much too pale.'

'Sorry about that,' Jo said as she selected two very dark-brown rolls and put them into a paper bag.

Ina brought over the newspaper from the shelving by the door, then fished out her purse and counted out the exact number of coins. Then stood aside and opened the paper.

Jo resumed her conversation with Annie. 'You were asking about the house – the big sandstone one, you mean?'

'Yes. It's lovely. It sits so well in the landscape. Looks like someone's spent time and love on it.'

'Summerhill Hall, it's called. Do you work in property, Annie?' Jo asked. Annie grabbed at the cover story. 'Yes. My brother and I have a portfolio.' The lie slipped easily from her mouth. 'We're always looking for new properties. That one would make a lovely wee boutique hotel ... Do you know the owners? Might they be open to an offer?'

Jo nodded. 'A woman called Gaia lives there.' She made a face. 'Pretentious or what?'

Ina looked at them over the top of her paper.

'She lives there on her own, I believe,' Jo went on. 'Occasionally takes in guests – offers refuge to women having a hard time. Drugs, domestic violence and such like.' She nodded in the direction of her shelves. 'She supplies us with honey. And beeswax soap.' Her smile wore a hint of commiseration. 'She's been there for about five or six years. And whenever I've spoken with Gaia she's sounded like she's very happy there.'

'Seven years,' piped up Ina as she made her way to the door.

'There you go,' Jo smiled as the door closed behind Ina. 'Seven years. If anyone knows anything about anyone in this village it's our Ina. She's eighty-four, which she'll happily tell you if you spend more than five minutes in her company.' Jo leaned closer. 'Word is that our Ina is a bit fey.'

'Fey?' Something buzzed in Annie's heart.

'Yeah, sees things that no one else—'

The bell above the door sang out for another new shopper. And another. Both were hailed by Jo, and whatever she'd been going to say was lost to the moment. Jo chatted on at length to her latest customers, and as Annie ate up the last of her scone, she spotted someone standing by her car outside, apparently studying her newspaper, but glancing back at the shop regularly. Annie knocked back the last of her coffee, left a ten-pound note on the counter and rose from the stool.

'Not wanting your change, Annie?' Jo called as she neared the door.

'Put it in your charity box,' Annie replied. 'And thanks for your time.' And with a wave she left the shop.

Outside, Ina was still standing by Annie's car, a yellow Lab on a leash sitting by her side. The dog's tongue was hanging out and he looked as if he'd be happy if he could stay in that one position for a time.

'You were asking about Gallows Hill?' Ina asked briskly as Annie approached.

Annie felt an odd shudder at the name, and frowned. 'Do you mean the house just outside the village? But isn't it called Summerhill Hall?'

Ina raised her eyebrows. 'The owner of the first house built there quite liked the macabre-sounding name of the place.' She nodded, as if agreeing with herself. 'It's where a gallows stood centuries ago. A man murdered his family: a wife and two girls. A terrible, terrible thing,' she huffed. 'Most executions were handled in Ayr back in those days, but the locals were so upset they took matters into their own hands...' She grimaced. 'The new folk changed the name, and nae wonder. As Jo said, it's called Summerhill Hall now.' Ina humphed. 'They have beehives,' she added, as if that was a strange thing to do.

She stared at Annie for a long moment from under her heavy eyebrows.

'You're not really in property, are you, hen?'

Annie shook her head slightly. Caught out already.

'What's your interest in the place?'

'Just curious,' Annie replied. 'It draws your eye, doesn't it? I've driven past a couple of times now. Looks a lovely place to stay.' Fey or not, Annie thought it would be too much to tell the old woman that she felt compelled to go there and knock on the door.

'They did some work on it when they moved in. My neighbour's boy was contracted to do the joinery. Said the place gave him the creeps.'

'Oh? Did he say why?'

'He worked there for about five months. Said all these women came and went. Not that that was a problem for Dan. Has an eye for the lassies so he does, but' – she lowered her voice – 'there was a basement room he was asked to fit out. Like a bedroom he said, with space for a toilet and shower.' She tutted. 'Who wants a bedroom in a basement without any windows? And,' she continued pointedly, 'he said there was something very strange about the owner, thon Gaia woman.'

'Yeah?'

'Aye, snooty cow. Dan said that whenever he turned round, she was standing there, watching him.'

'I thought you said he liked the ladies.'

'He does that, hen, but as he tells it, her look was cold – assessing, you'd call it. He couldn't make up his mind if she was sizing him up for her own bedroom, if you get my meaning.' She winked. 'Or measuring him up for a coffin.'

Measuring him up for a coffin: those words were familiar, too familiar – and brought up a painful memory. They were the very words an old man had said to Annie on her first day working at a care home. Which was the first time, as an adult, that she received a premonition that someone was about to die. Sadly, that old man had passed away just as she'd seen he would.

Lost in thought, Annie hadn't noticed that Ina had moved closer to her. Almost too close. She was right in front of her, and stretched a hand up and placed it under Annie's chin. She pushed it up a little, her touch intimate, and slightly uncomfortable.

'Chin up, dear,' Ina said, and there was a kindness in her voice. 'You've the eyes of someone who's seen a lot for one so young.' Her own eyes narrowed. 'But there's as much in front of you as there is behind you,' she warned.

'What…?'

Ina waved a hand in the air. 'Och, dinnae mind the blethers of an old woman, m'dear, but if I can offer one piece of advice?'

'Yeah?'

She met Annie's eyes, and held them in her gaze. 'There's nothing here for you. Nothing good anyway. Go home.'

Ina gave Annie one last hard stare, then turned and slowly walked away.

Chapter 31

Sylvia
1975

A few weeks before the end of their last term at Clevelland, Ben and Sylvia were given their instructions: Ben was to study law and Sylvia medicine – both in Edinburgh so they could maintain contact. Dance had secured employment in an Edinburgh private school of some renown so he could be nearby to continue their education.

During her holiday at home with her grandmother, before she moved north to Edinburgh, Sylvia went off her food. Regardless of what Maude had the cook prepare, Sylvia's stomach turned, and fearful that her charge might lose too much weight, Maude had her doctor come to visit.

He was an old man – far too old to be still working, judged Sylvia. His hands shook, and his eyebrows jutted at least two inches from his forehead, where the lines were so deep Sylvia wondered if he had a special implement to keep them clean. But he was a kindly man and his care for her was clear in his soft touch and tender tones. That he examined every part of her was deeply embarrassing, but he was her doctor.

'I was present at the birth of your grandmother, and both your parents,' he said after she had put her clothes back on. 'But, look at you now. Soon to be a mother yourself.'

Sylvia sat up. 'A what?' She'd been about to ask him for the details of her parents' death but that thought was now driven from her mind.

'Children marry so young these days.' He turned away from her to put his instruments back in their little leather case. 'Nonetheless, love must have its day, I'm sure. Where's the father; he'll be tickled pink at the news.'

Her grandmother chose that moment to enter the room, and

Sylvia was sure she'd been standing with her ear to the door the entire time the doctor had been examining her. As she ushered him down the stairs and to the door, Sylvia could hear that her grandmother was very keen to remind him of his duty to keep information about his patient confidential.

Sylvia lay back on her bed, stunned. Pregnant. Her life was over. She was only just turned seventeen ... Her thoughts turned to a particular night some weeks ago.

Dance had taken Ben and her to a small clearing in the middle of the woods to the north of the school. It was midsummer, he explained, and there were many customs around the world – pagan, Christian and occult – to mark the occasion.

'While it is the time of greatest strength of the solar current,' she remembered him saying, 'it is also a point of change, because the sun begins to decline as the wheel of the year turns.' He then went on to talk about some customs: fires being lit, people adorned with flowers, dancing. While he spoke, they'd sat cross-legged facing a fire, passing a flask of tea back and forth. A strange tea. Sylvia had been able to taste honey, cloves, and something earthy. Her head spun, and she recalled having to lie down, and noticing in the corner of her vision that Ben and Phineas Dance were doing likewise. Of her shadow there was no sign.

And then she recalled what happened next. How could she have been so wanton?

First, there had been a wonderful feeling – a sense of connection. Then they were all hugging and sobbing, and she had a memory of being on top of Phineas Dance and they were all naked. And unrestrained.

Such freedom of thought and movement and lust. Feelings of being intoxicated, and of being intoxicating. Both men kissing her, worshipping her.

She wasn't a virgin, of course she wasn't. There had been some experimentation at school, with girls as well as boys. The 'slack' moniker had stuck, leading to many proposals – most of which she turned down. But from time to time curiosity got the better of her and she'd decided she might as well have some fun.

Ben.

A flash of him over her, his expression one of bliss. Dance over his shoulder, hand on his head, finally allowing them to couple.

She couldn't believe she'd had sex with Ben. She must really have been lost in the moment. He was such a bore. She hoped Dance was the father instead. Not that it mattered, of course, if she wasn't going to keep it anyway.

At that thought she felt a pang of something. She refused to name it, and tucked it away in the back of her head. Grandmother was going to arrange everything, likely with the help of her cousin, Gwendaline Montague, who seemed to have her fingers – and toes – in everything. Phineas wouldn't want her to have a child – it would get in the way of her studies and whatever purpose he had in mind for her within the Order.

A year out, was the convenient lie broadcast to the world, and Sylvia was carted off to Switzerland before her condition became apparent. There followed months of what felt like terminal boredom, and after a twenty-hour delivery the child was whisked away before Sylvia could even touch it.

'It's a lovely, healthy boy,' one nurse exclaimed before a hard stare from a colleague reminded her of the situation.

Sylvia returned to London and for a few weeks after the birth, she couldn't get out of bed. Her mind was as leaden as her limbs. But finally, one morning, her grandmother entered her bedroom, pulled the drapes open, and said, 'Time you were up and about. You're a young woman with your whole life ahead of you. No need to waste it under those covers.'

Sylvia understood that she was being told not to feel sorry for herself, that she'd have plenty more chances to have children.

For a time she regretted not saying something, doing something, and simply going along with everyone else's plans for her.

Choosing the path of least resistance, like she had all of her life so far, as if she was nothing more than a puppet. Whenever she cast her eyes to the side, looking for Sarah, for reassurance – she caught something, but it appeared to be less somehow, as if even she was diminished by recent events.

Buck up, Sylvia, she told herself. Enough. You'll be fine. Utterly fine. Life had other things in store for her than bringing up a child.

But if that was the case, why were her fingers so cold over her heart? Why did she sense a dull ache and a chill weight there, layered through the thin seams of skin, bone and muscle? As if something within her had died. Forever.

Chapter 32

Lewis

'They killed a guy,' Steve said, eyebrows high, the shock still felt. 'He said it happened when they were around the age of sixteen or seventeen. Dumped the body out on the hills and set the car on fire somewhere else to try and cover their tracks. He made out like it was a hit and run – but when he told me that part it sounded made up, rehearsed, you know?'

'If they didn't kill the guy in a hit and run, how did they?' Lewis asked.

'No idea, mate.'

'They really killed someone? This wasn't Damien on a bad trip?'

Steve looked into the distance for a moment. 'Damien was a fuck-up at the time he told me all of this. Totally wasted, you know? But he seemed to be feeling real guilt and shame about the dead guy, so...' He shook his head. 'Look, I bought the part about them disposing of the body, but the hit and run – I didn't buy that.'

'Why not?'

'Craig was scared of his old man. Really scared. One time a bunch of us stole a car and went for a joyride – young and daft, what can I say? Craig had to be talked into coming along. Anyway, he did, and we got caught. Craig's dad – who's a lawyer – sorted for us all to get off with just a warning. But a few days later at training, Craig took his top off and his back was covered in cuts and bruises. He quickly covered it up, like, when someone asked what the hell had happened to him. I think his dad hammered him with a belt or something. But put it like this – after that, I thought he'd be too scared of the consequences to do a hit and run.'

'Who was the guy they killed?' And as Lewis asked, he remembered what Alison had said about Damien's personality changing after Rab Daniels died. She'd said that was a hit and run.

Steve didn't answer him, but instead said, 'They left the poor lad on the side of the road, and his death was still unsolved, according to Damien. 'Man, it fucked him up. Makes sense, right enough. Guilty conscience. This kid's dead because of him, and Damien goes into self-destruct mode cos he can't handle it.'

'Who was the boy they killed?' Lewis repeated.

'Rab Daniels. He was a wee shit as well. A wannabe – and never gonna-be. Harsh but true.' Steve crossed his arms.

'Jesus,' Lewis said. 'So … I wonder if all that could have anything to do with Damien's disappearance now. If Craig Oldfield is involved, could it be something to do with what happened back then? But why wait all these years?'

'Mate,' Steve said, arms wide, 'your guess is as good as mine.'

Lewis chewed on that for a moment. 'So what's Craig's deal? He was clearly fucked up as a kid…'

Steve nodded. 'I don't for a second think that hammering he got from his dad was a one-off. The guy was brutalised as a kid, and that shit leaves its mark.' He scratched the side of his face. 'You know, I think it's too easy to say someone is evil, or just wrong in some way. That's a cop-out. Means we don't have to look too closely at how poorly our society works. We just write the fuckers off.' He made a face of apology. 'Sorry, man. This is my soapbox material. I work with some disadvantaged kids, and it really pisses me off how they get talked about.'

Lewis nodded. Tried another tack. 'Craig's dad was a lawyer, then...'

Steve was silent for a moment. 'My old man was in business with him for a while.'

'Your dad was a lawyer too?'

He nodded. 'And he said Oldfield Senior was the single most self-serving man he ever met. Ambition way beyond his capability.'

'Right? From what I've heard, Oldfield was successful though.'

'Ever heard of Joe Beltrami?'

Lewis nodded. He was a sharp-suited lawyer, rarely out of the Scottish broadsheets, who defended a number of high-profile cases, leading to the catchphrase 'get me Beltrami' anytime a miscreant was caught by the police.

'Well, Craig's dad became a south of Scotland equivalent. Which totally threw my old man. Every time he was mentioned in the news or the papers my dad would just shake his head and wonder if he'd made a deal with the devil.'

'Meaning what, exactly?'

'Basically, Dad thought Oldfield was crap at his job. After a while working with him, Dad wrapped up the partnership and moved to Glasgow, to avoid Oldfield dragging him down with him, Dad thought he was that bad. But then Oldfield changed – like, overnight, Dad said. Became successful. The old man just couldn't understand how he achieved what he did.'

'Was the mother around?'

Steve nodded. 'I met Mrs Oldfield a couple of times. Didn't have much to say for herself. I couldn't get a read on her, to be honest.' He paused. 'You say you met Craig's sister, Alison?'

Lewis nodded.

'A proper gem, she is. Doesn't fit with that family at all. And she's gorgeous too. Wouldn't have minded getting together with her, but she only had eyes for Damien.' He thought for a moment. 'And you know, my dad wasn't the only relative among our crowd that worked for Oldfield Senior. Wee Rab's mother also worked in the office. Some kind of secretary.' He leaned closer. 'And you know what they did to her? A few months after Rab died they sacked her. They fucking sacked her. Imagine doing that to a grieving mother.'

'Did you hear why?' Lewis asked.

'Dad said it was something to do with missing money from a client's account, but he didn't believe it. He thought Mrs Daniels was as honest as the day was long. Tells you everything you need to know about the Oldfields,' Steve added. 'Arseholes. Oldfield Senior probably got fed up with the poor woman being so upset about her son's death that he concocted a bullshit story to get rid of her. Who treats people like that?' he asked with disgust.

Back in his car Lewis gave Annie a quick call to fill her in on his discoveries, but there was no answer.

And when he got home the flat was empty, so he tried her number again. Again, no answer. He showered, and as he had something to eat he reviewed what Steve Murphy told him.

The details he'd given Lewis were chilling, and had the ring of truth, but Lewis wanted to get this right, and to act only on fact. He was just a burgeoning investigator, after all – even calling himself that made him cringe a little – so if he was to take this seriously, if he was to consider it a career option, he had to get it right.

Forty minutes later he was back in an old haunt, the Mitchell Library in Glasgow city centre, looking up some old newspapers on their microfiche. He laughed to himself; Annie had always said he was one-hundred-percent geek.

Eyes on the screen, Lewis thought about the murdered boy and discounted the national newspapers as good source material. He doubted that would be something that would reach their radar. Perhaps if the victim was young, blonde, pretty, white and female it would, but a wee ned from the provinces would be ignored. That meant a local rag. He searched online for the newspapers that covered that part of the country, and found one called the *Carrick Gazette*. It was out of publication now, but it ran from 1973 and would have been in circulation at the time of Rab Daniels' death.

Steve had told him that Damien said the death had happened when he was sixteen or seventeen, during the summer holidays. So that meant July or August of 2009 or 2010. Lewis located the correct fiche, loaded it onto the reader and began to wade through the images of newspapers.

He'd been searching for an hour or so, and felt the screen was becoming a bit of a blur, when a face and headline came into focus.

'Boy, Fifteen, Killed in a Hit and Run'. According to the report, the police were scratching their heads as to who could have done it, and they were appealing to locals for any information they could provide. The image of Rab Daniels was in black and white. He had a thin face with cropped, light-coloured hair, and he was sending out narrow-eyed, buck-toothed defiance to the world.

Further down the report it said that Robert Daniels was survived by his parents, Paul and Kate, and his twin sister, Rose.

Lewis sat back in his chair. A twin? If Rab and Rose were anything like him and Annie – telling each other pretty much everything – might Rose Daniels, wherever she was, have a story to tell?

Chapter 33

Annie

Annie parked at the entrance to Gallows Hill House. She caught herself. It had been renamed Summerhill Hall, so why was she automatically thinking of it with its previous name?

Gaia, the new owner, had changed it – the woman Ina said had so disturbed her neighbour, Dan. Annie wondered about the cold, assessing looks Dan had apparently described. Might Gaia have a gift similar to her own? Was that why she was so drawn to the place? She should have asked Ina more about Dan's time working at the hall.

Looking up the drive towards the house she considered phoning Lewis to tell him where she was. In a minute, she decided, once she'd actually gone up there and faced whatever it was that was pulling her towards this place. If she spoke to Lewis now he'd only persuade her to wait until he was with her.

Something told her she had to do this on her own.

Ever since they'd driven past the house yesterday, she'd imagined herself walking up to that door. She'd approached it in her imagination a number of times – heard the pop of gravel under her feet, the scuff of her heel as she walked up the steps, the creak of a weathered and rusted brass doorknob as she lifted it. The images were so vivid it was as if she'd been spellbound in some way.

She shook herself. Right. Okay. She started the car. And as she did, something moved in the periphery of her vision.

Startled, she turned. There was nothing there but a tall tree, its branches wide, like arms waving in the stiff breeze. Idiot. She held a hand over her racing heart and forced a long, slow breath.

She released the clutch, aimed the car up the long drive and headed for the large circular lawn in front of the house. Pulling up on the nearest side of the building, she sat for a long minute.

Then another. Get out, she told herself. If there was anyone watching they'd think she was crazy. She opened her door.

The house was tall and narrow – three storeys, with four windows on each. The steep steps that led to the large central doorway were edged with plant pots of various sizes, all of them bursting with colour.

Annie stood at the bottom of the steps and looked up at the house. All was still. There was no movement around her, and no sound reached her from the road only five hundred metres away. She couldn't even hear any birdsong.

She swallowed. What was she doing? Reaching through her thin top she pulled her stone away from her skin to see how her murmurs would react. They were silent. At first. Then a susurration sounded, faint and thin, like an echo of past mockery. Her murmurs were always as unhelpful to her as possible, so she'd hoped for a strong signal, something she could react against – to behave in a way opposite to what they intended. But there wasn't enough there to guide her. She released the stone back into its little pocket and began to climb the steps.

The wind lifted and sighed through the leaves of the nearby oak and sycamore trees.

Welcome, she imagined she heard. *Welcome, sister. Just one more step.*

This voice was friendly. Its intent warm, and it was much stronger in her mind than it had been on the previous times it had spoken to her. It was the woman from the inn, she was sure.

Annie took the last step, and lifted her hand to grab the brass door knocker, but the door opened before she could.

A woman stood before her. A woman who looked vaguely familiar.

'Have we...?' Annie began.

She could have been anywhere between forty and seventy. She wore her thick, grey-white hair in a chin-length bob, and her face was unlined and seemed clear of any make-up.

She tilted her head to the side and smiled. 'Come in,' she said, her hand extended in invitation. 'We've been expecting you.'

Chapter 34

Ben
1985

It was not quite eight o'clock in the morning. Ben was in his new office looking out onto a row of Georgian buildings in Edinburgh's New Town. Certain that the police would arrive at any moment, he was jumping at every noise, sure that guilt was etched into every muscle in his body.

When he'd called Dance the night before to clean up his mess, the older man had reassured him that they would pay off the authorities and his father's death would be treated as a terrible accident – he'd simply been out walking on his estate, tripped and hit his head on a log. The branch Ben had actually used to hit his father would soon be nothing but a pile of embers in a fire.

Ben had been summoned to the family home for the weekend – his first visit since his mother had died the year before, from lung cancer. His father had never been an easy man to please, and from the occasional, dutiful phone calls he made every month, it was clear to Ben that he'd become a withdrawn and bitter old man. Nonetheless, when he secured employment at a prestigious law firm in the capital, he was keen to show his father he would be his own man.

Every time he walked through the doors of Lindean Hall, he did so with mixed feelings. This had been the scene of many unhappy moments in his life, and he could barely enter the grand entrance hall without shrinking into a little boy and hearing his mother say something cruel and disparaging to him. Or feeling the spray of his father's spit on his face as he worked himself into a fury while he pulled his belt from his trousers. At least, he thought, as his fingers lingered on the brass handle of the door, this would be his – just as soon as his father had the good grace to breathe his last.

Ben was met at the door by Betty, the long-suffering and last remaining member of a staff that had numbered around a dozen when Ben was a boy. She was a tiny woman, thin as a broom handle, always wore a navy cardigan, and hadn't aged, at least to Ben's mind, since she'd tried to help him negotiate the moods of his parents as a small boy.

'Look at you,' she said. 'All grown up.' She coughed. 'Your father is in the study.' Then under her breath: 'He's been at the whisky.'

Ben's father, Maxwell, was sitting behind a large desk at the window, a dark figure against the daylight. And not for the first time Ben thought that he chose that position so that people would find it difficult to read him. 'Good of you to come,' he said, his tone suggesting completely the opposite.

'Nice to be here,' Ben replied, deliberately choosing to sit on the dark-red chesterfield by the fire.

'I'd rather not shout,' Maxwell said.

'Nonetheless...' Ben replied. He placed his right foot on his left knee and spread his arms along the top of the sofa. From his new vantage point, his father no longer had the benefit of the light at his back, so Ben could see that his father had aged, even in the months since he last saw him. Such was the timbre of their relationship since Ben became an adult: barbs and small victories.

'I might as well get to it,' Maxwell said. 'We've sold the house to the National Trust...'

Ben sat up.

'...to cover the family debt.'

Maxwell picked up his half-full crystal glass, moved it back and forward so that the ice sang against the sides. Then he put the glass on the desktop and pushed something across the desk towards Ben.

'You disgust me,' he said, and turned to look out of the window. 'I can't bear to look at you.'

Ben moved to the desk and saw a large brown envelope. 'What is this?'

'I believe it's the only copy. Take it with you,' Maxwell said. He turned in his chair, his head low, staring up with a look of contempt. 'And never come back.'

Heart a hammer in his chest, Ben opened the envelope and pulled out its contents. Photographs. Black and white, and colour. Ben was front and centre in all of them. In some he was wearing a black cloak. In others he was naked. In one he was holding a goat's head, blood a dark smear down his chest and abdomen.

'How did you get these?' Ben demanded.

'That's your response?' his father was struggling to his feet. Shouting. 'Can you imagine my horror when I opened that envelope and saw that? I knew you were some kind of deviant, but this? This?' Maxwell picked up his glass and hurled it at Ben's head. He ducked and it crashed against the wall behind him. 'One bright point in all of this is that your mother is not alive to see what became of her only son.' Maxwell sneered. 'The other bright point is that you get nothing. This...' he waved a hand at the images '...is the final straw for the estate. We've been struggling to hold it together for decades. I was actually happy to pay, because it means you get nothing.'

'What do you mean? Has someone ... How did you get these?' Ben repeated. His mind raced. The numbers of people at the ceremonies he'd attended over the years had always been low, and all of them were heavily vetted. This could only have been an inside job. But who in the fellowship would do something like this?

'They arrived by courier last week. Along with a letter. Pay three hundred thousand by close of business that day or the negatives would be sent to every tabloid newspaper in the country.' Maxwell leaned towards Ben, his knuckles on the desk. 'Know this: I care deeply about the family name. I care *nothing* for you.' He collapsed back on to his chair as if exhausted. 'I never want to see you again.'

Ben had run from the house, jumped into his car and raced down the drive to the gate. There he had braked, sat, engine running, mind racing and fury a simmer in his gut. He couldn't lose the house. That couldn't be allowed to happen. That was the only reason he'd put up with his father these last few years, so the old man wouldn't write him out of his will.

All of that for nothing? There must be something that could be done. A condition on the gift to the National Trust? They could allow him to have life rent in one of the apartments?

And who would blackmail his family? The only people who would have had access to take such photographs would be other people in the Order. And they would want this exposed to the press no more than he did. Which meant it had to be someone who was pretty confident his father would pay out.

Dance?

Was this part of his plan to break and then make him? He wouldn't put it past Dance to come up with something like this.

He sat there, lost in his anger, hurt and disappointment, until he could bear it no longer. He had to do something. The clock on the dashboard read that it was one-thirty in the afternoon. Father would have had his lunch and would have gone on his walk through the woods and along the river, before returning home for the nap he always took before pre-dinner drinks.

Ben knew the route well, had endured it with his father on many occasions. He calculated where he might be and jumped out of his car.

As he walked he imagined himself talking to his father, persuading him, giving him all the reasons why he, the only son, should not be punished in this way. The photographs were nothing more than a young man trying to find his way in the world. They were harmless ceremonies. Just a bit of fun, and what decent newspaper would want to print them?

The breeze was cool on his face, the river low, providing a calming gurgle. So Ben surprised even himself when he picked up the large branch on the path, just before he met his father, and with everything he had hammered him on the side of the head.

Chapter 35

Lewis

Lewis moved from the microfiche reader to a computer and entered a simple search for the name Rose Daniels. The screen filled and he scrolled down. Rose would be in her mid-thirties by now. None of the entries seemed helpful. One woman was a CEO in the US. Another was a triathlete from Oz. Yet another was leading a charity drive in London for a brain-tumour organisation. And if Rose had married and changed her name he was never going to find her.

Maybe a change of tactic was in order here. He made his way down to the café, ordered a coffee, then took a seat, pulled out his phone and made a call.

'Hi Chrissie,' Lewis said when she answered.

'Any news?' she asked breathlessly.

'Sorry. Still nothing to report.' He heard a sigh. 'I'm trying to get a handle on who Damien knew back in the day. I'm sort of working through a theory just now...'

'Oh?'

'I'm thinking that something may have happened years back that he kept from you? And maybe it's come back to bite him on the backside.' Lewis didn't want to put all his cards on the table at once.

'Right.' Chrissie sounded disappointed. 'What about Annie? Did she find anything when you drove down to Girvan?' Now she seemed a little bit desperate. 'I thought she'd be like some human divining rod and she'd pick up on...' She trailed off. 'Sorry. That is such a stupid thing to say.'

'We don't know how Annie's thing works, Chrissie,' he said, trying to inject his voice with calm and care. 'Or even if it will for this sort of thing, so we're approaching it from both sides – the otherworldly and, I suppose you'd say a real-world angle. So I'm chasing down events from the past, as I said.'

He paused a moment before asking his next question.

'Do you recall a hit and run? A boy called Rab Daniels was killed. Were you living down in Girvan in those days?'

'Oh, aye, that was a terrible, terrible time. His poor parents.' She sighed. 'I'm getting a real sense now of what they must have gone through.' Her voice cracked. Then grew sharp. 'You don't think our Damien had something to do with that, do you?'

'Could be a coincidence, but it was just after that when Damien started to act up. Before that he was just a normal young guy, kicking a ball, chasing his dream.'

'I don't like where you're going with this, Lewis.'

'It may be nothing – quite likely is.' He screwed his eyes tight. Maybe it was a bad idea to bring this to Chrissie before he had the full facts. 'Look, I heard that Rab had a twin sister, Rose. And I thought it might be worthwhile to chat to her, see what she remembers from that time.'

'Okay, well, I can tell you a bit about her.' Chrissie sounded a little more amenable now.

'Yes, please.'

'I did hear she's been married, divorced, and then she got remarried. Her and her hubby have got one of them blended families, or whatever they call it. She's got three kids of her own and the new guy has two. Must be bedlam in that house.' Her voice cracked with emotion again. 'Och, thinking of that makes me miss my wee Bodie.' She paused. Came back more business-like: 'Give me ten minutes. I've got a cousin who still lives in the town. I'll give her a ring and see if she knows any more.' She hung up.

Lewis took his time over his coffee, and then made his way out to his car. He'd just sat down when a text arrived, then Chrissie phoned straight after.

'I've just sent you a text with where to find Rose.' She sounded excited but a little wary at the same time. 'Turns out my cousin is actually a good pal of hers. So she phoned her and told her what you'd said, and then she phoned me back with what Rose said.' She laughed nervously. 'I don't know if that makes sense. The gist of it is, Rose hates Craig Oldfield, and is keen to talk to you. Very keen.'

Chapter 36

Annie

Annie stepped inside Summerhill Hall like a small creature brought into a new home, warily putting one foot in front of the other.

Ahead of her was a wide stairway that reached up to a landing with a large window that flooded the hall with light. The floor was covered in polished oak, and the walls were bare. Looking down, beyond the stairway, the hall narrowed, and the area beyond was draped in shadows.

A noise echoed from somewhere overhead, as if a chair had been dragged across a wooden floor. But it stopped so suddenly and the silence after was so complete, Annie wondered if she'd imagined it. Then: *Welcome*. It was as if the sound had been issued high above her and grown in volume and clarity as it swooped to reach her ears.

Welcome home.

'My name is Gaia.' The woman offered her a reassuring smile.

'I really don't know why I'm here,' Annie admitted. 'This is … it's all a bit much.' She turned back to the door. 'I should go.'

But her feet wouldn't let her.

What was going on? She was both discomfited, needing to get out of this place, and desperate to stay at the same time. How could her brain contain such disparate emotions?

'You felt a calling, yes?' Gaia's hands were clasped in front of her as she laughed, the music of her joy echoing in the large space. 'And you heard Her just now, didn't you? You wouldn't believe how many times I've had this conversation.' She stretched forward and lightly touched Annie's forearm. 'There's a magic to this place that calls out to a certain kind of woman.' She took Annie by the wrist and pulled her a little so that they were standing side to side. 'Come on through to the kitchen. At least let me give you a cup of something before you leave.'

Her welcome seemed so warm Annie simply couldn't reject it.

'A cup of something would be lovely.' She returned the woman's smile.

'See,' Gaia said, lightly bumping shoulders with Annie. 'I can already tell we are going to be friends.'

Gaia led her into the gloom at the back of the house. Closed doors led off either side of the hallway, and a small, low door faced them. She pulled it open and walked through, Annie left with no choice but to follow.

'Wow,' she said as she entered the room. 'I did not expect this.'

It was as if the back of the house had been demolished and given over to a barn-like kitchen with floor-to-ceiling windows displaying a panoramic view of the wood-edged fields of South Ayrshire. Hills pushed in at either side, and in the distance the land eventually led to a small skirt of sea.

'I know,' Gaia said. 'I love the surprise I get almost every time I walk in here. It's like a portal into a different world.'

She invited Annie to sit at the large table, but Annie felt strangely reluctant, remaining comfortable. 'I'll just...' she replied, gesturing at the view.

'Coffee? Tea?' Gaia asked. 'Or something herbal?'

Annie's murmurs burst into her ears – a mix of a shriek and a howl – and icy fingers of dread pulled at the muscles of her jaw. She held a hand over her protective stone, wondering why it wasn't working, and felt a tremor of fear in her thighs.

Gaia offered her the cup. It was hot to touch, but Annie managed to put it to her mouth and sip.

'That's nice,' she said, and took another sip. It was sweet with an undernote of something earthy – mushrooms maybe...

Her murmurs surged once more and the urge to turn and leave suddenly overcame her.

'Sorry,' she said. 'Got to...'

Just about managing to stop herself running, she made her way to the front door, and outside to the safety of her car.

Chapter 37

Sylvia
1990

Maude died while Sylvia was away at her studies in Edinburgh. Everything that could be sold was, and the rest of her grandmother's possessions were boxed and stored at her cousin Gwendaline Montague's manor house in the Cotswolds, and an invitation was extended to Sylvia that she was welcome to look through it all at any time, and keep something as a personal reminder.

'Why have you chosen Gwendaline to help you manage your affairs, Grandma? She's been horrid to you in the past,' Sylvia had asked Maude on her last visit before the old woman died. Maude had told Sylvia many stories over the years about her relationship with her cousin – which seemed to be a strange mix of tit-for-tat cruelties and kind favours. Sylvia couldn't understand it at all.

'If you can't be conciliatory on your death bed, when can you be?' Maude finally answered. 'She's my only surviving relative. She'll invite you down to her place in the Cotswolds after I die, and you must go. But you mustn't listen to a word she says. Especially if she is drinking. She's a damn nasty drunk.'

Now, here she was, seven years after Maude's death, on the train on the way to Bourten Hall, wondering what kind of reception she would receive. As the train wound its way through the English countryside, Sylvia acknowledged she hadn't accepted the invitation for so long because she felt a deep sense of disappointment with her grandmother, both for refusing to tell her the truth about her parents' death, and for pushing her into giving her child up for adoption. She felt that particular ache and lack every day of her life, and was grateful that she still had her studies, her connection to the Order and Phineas Dance, and that sense that she had a greater purpose.

She'd met with Dance, not long after she took up student digs in the city.

'But what is it all for – the Order, the ceremonies?' she'd asked.

'We belong. We serve the Master, that is enough.' There was a stern, and final note to Dance's reply, so she set the thought aside for consideration another time. As much as she appreciated how the Order made her feel apart from, and above, the vast flock of human sheep, she felt there had to be more to it all. She determined that she would find out what that was.

In the meantime, she had become a perpetual student, and would soon be on her way to a series of lectures in California. Having started in general medicine, she had then specialised in herbs and a study of 'white magic' – the notion of which seemed laughable to her. In her opinion, all magic was knowledge and power – the *intention* behind it was what made it black or white.

She only studied 'white magic' because it was more palatable to those around her.

Ben was still a presence in her life. It was as if, she remarked to Dance, Ben was an annoying little brother. After thirty minutes in his company she had to leave, and yet, from time to time, she sought him out. She had always seen him as an ambiguous character, holding himself remote from everyone while seeking approval and validation at the same time. It was fair to say that he'd been brutalised – by his parents, his teachers, and his peers. Perhaps all he'd needed to develop a kinder mindset was a hand on his shoulder, a kind word or two and a positive example. Instead, the greatest influences in his life would prove to be Dance. And her.

She was aware of the truth of his father's death, and the blackmail that had prompted it – orchestrated by Dance, naturally. Dance had judged the blackmail amount perfectly so that it would both be payable and enough to force the sale of the estate to the National Trust. Dance had inserted himself into her family's affairs in a similar way. Meaning Sylvia didn't inherit huge wealth either. Was this all part of Dance's aim to break and make them? Ensuring she and Ben wouldn't be independently wealthy, but reliant on the Order?

Aside from all of that, Sylvia knew Ben was a little bit in love with her – always had been. And she knew she could make use of that fact.

When she arrived at Bourten Hall she was shown to her quarters, and then spent an agonisingly long afternoon and evening with Gwendaline, who spent the entire time drinking gin and bragging about the royals she had met, the countries she had visited, expressing her concern about Sylvia's singleton status, and detailing her medical conditions. 'And then when you think it can't get any worse, God adds diabetes onto the pile,' she complained.

Next morning, Sylvia was shown to the room where her grandmother's last effects had been stored. It was a little space just beyond the kitchen that might have been a larder at some point.

Sylvia could see the room was full of boxes, many of them, she guessed, filled with books. One day they would take pride of place in her own home, when she finally settled down.

A wide window took up the top quarter of the far wall. Dust motes danced in the morning sunlight. The walls were lined with cardboard boxes, regimented, each tan surface bearing the detail of what was inside in large black letters. She surveyed the room. That grand apartment, in one of the most sought after areas of London, reduced to this. She felt bitter that her grandmother was such a willing participant in Dance's plans to waste the bulk of her inheritance, but she was more concerned with the lies. Why couldn't she be trusted with the truth about her parents' death? Perhaps the answer lay in one of these boxes.

The ones off to her left, labelled *Personal Effects* were the first to attract her. She pulled the top one from the tower of boxes it rested on and carried it to the table. The shiny tape pulled off easily and the first thing she pulled out was a Ouija board. She couldn't remember Maude ever using one of these.

Sylvia turned the Ouija board over, and saw a name inscribed on the back. *Georgia Lowry-Law.* This had been her mother's? In all the time Maude had performed seances, she hadn't mentioned that her daughter had also been interested in the occult. Had it been a passing phase, or something more meaningful? Sylvia slid the board back into the box – she'd never know.

In another box she found some of her grandmother's costume jewellery. She had copies made, she'd explained, and the real stuff was kept in a vault. It had probably all been hawked off to pay creditors. Sylvia wondered what had happened to the Vermeer painting that had disguised the door to Maude's special room. Had that been sold as well? It was reputed to be priceless. How much had the old woman lost?

More questions without answers.

The next box she lifted was labelled *Bedroom Personal Effects*, and Sylvia recalled a bedside cabinet in her grandmother's bedroom in which she housed her more precious items.

She tore off the tape and looked inside. A bottle of Chanel No 5. She held it. Felt her hand warm the glass, and that familiar fragrance suggest itself to her nose. Oh, Grandmama, she thought, feeling the usual complex round of emotions – including fondness and spite – and put it back. There was a little bottle of what Sylvia knew to be sleeping pills. A pair of gold-and-brass hairbrushes with an embroidered back. Another bottle, dark purple, half full, in its own little green velvet purse. After a little sniff that told her it smelled of almonds, she put it back in its place.

And there? Something filled the bottom of the box.

She pushed her fingers down the side and pulled. And lifted out a pair of leather-bound journals. Interesting. Sylvia hadn't known her grandmother to write. She lifted them out and took a seat.

Clever girl, she read, in her grandmother's neat script, *I knew you'd find these eventually. It's time you learned some answers...*

Chapter 38

Lewis

When he got back to the flat, Lewis was relieved to see that Annie's car was back in her usual space, and he rushed inside to tell her everything he'd learned so far.

'Well done,' Annie said. She was curled up on the sofa, wrapped in her quilt. She didn't seem as pleased with what he'd come up with as he thought she'd be.

'What did you get up to?' he asked. 'Where have you been all day?'

'Och, just went for a wee drive in the car,' she said, her gaze slipping from his face as she spoke. 'Had to get out of these four walls. Know what I mean?'

Lewis nodded, and refrained from asking exactly where she'd gone. He could sense she was hiding something from him, but she would tell him, eventually. Annie always preferred her own counsel in the first instance and would share with him whatever was going on in her own good time. He knew that if he tried to dig she would just become more entrenched in her silence.

'As long as it helped,' he said. 'By the way, I'm heading back down Girvan way tomorrow morning to meet Rab's sister, Rose. Up for another drive down the coast?'

'Sure,' she replied. And the way her eyes shifted made Lewis feel that she really was hiding something from him.

Rab's sister, Rose Russell, as she was now known, worked in a farm shop located between Maybole and Girvan. It was a long, low building facing the sea, with large windows giving a panoramic view of the coastline.

As they pulled in, a woman in black trousers and a white shirt walked out of the main door, a question in her eyes as she looked over.

'I'm guessing that's her,' Lewis said to Annie. 'I can see the resemblance to Rab, even from that photo in the old newspaper.'

Rose gave them a short wave and pointed towards a narrow track leading round the back of the building, so following her directions Lewis drove his car in behind the shop, where he stopped and looked around. He guessed that what was now the farm shop had once been some kind of milking shed, and as he craned his neck, he saw that there were more buildings behind them, and then the road sloped up to a white two-storey farm-house.

The woman appeared from round the side of the shop build-ing, opened the car door and hurriedly climbed into the back seat.

'I hope to God you're Lewis Jackson,' she said with a half-smile. 'Or I've just made an idiot of myself.'

'He is, and I'm his sister, Annie.' Annie twisted around to look at Rose.

As she sat Lewis noted that her black hair, pulled back into a sleek ponytail, was damp. Seeing where his eyes went, Rose patted her head. 'Two or three times a week I go for a swim. There's a wee beach just tucked in under the headland there.' She pointed in a southerly direction. 'And I get it all to myself. No kids. No husband. Just me and the waves. Pure bliss.'

Despite her attempt at lightness her expression was tight, suggesting perhaps that she wasn't entirely comfortable talking to them. She had a slim, attractive face, large blue eyes and full lips.

'Nice to meet you, Rose,' Lewis said.

She nodded. 'I'm mibbe being a bit paranoid with all the cloak-and-dagger stuff, making you park back here, but folk round this way are terrible gossips.'

'Fair enough,' Lewis said. 'Would you prefer to go for a drive?'

'Nah,' she said as she looked around. 'This wee road only leads up to the farm, as you can see. Mrs Baird is in the shop, and her hubby is out in the fields somewhere with his beasts. No one else comes round here so we'll be safe from prying eyes.' She looked at Annie. 'So, you're the woman who found all those dead bodies up in the Highlands?'

'That's me.' Annie gave a little shrug.

'I don't know how that passed me by,' Rose said. 'It was Chrissie Fox that got me up to speed about you and your brother.' She looked out of the window, staring at nothing. 'I have to say, I avoid news of murder and dead bodies. Just cannae handle them. For obvious reasons...'

'Maybe that's a good place to start,' Lewis said. 'Can you tell us a bit about those reasons? If you're happy to.'

Rose looked at him then stared out of the window again, seeming to direct her words to someone outside. 'When someone you love just goes like that? The hole they've left consumes you. My mum has been tormented by it.' She turned her head and looked at Annie. 'She's even dragged me to psychics over the years, hoping for some sort of clue, you know? Not one of them helped, but she still felt driven to find answers. No one else was providing them. The authorities didn't give a shit.'

Rose cast her eyes around the buildings and fields, as if checking they remained unobserved, then tucked her chin down into the collar of her shirt.

'Well, hopefully by looking into all of this something will be thrown up,' Lewis said encouragingly. 'You sure you're okay talking to us?'

'Just nervous,' Rose replied, sinking down into her seat a little.

'You don't think you're putting yourself in any danger by talking to us, do you?' Annie asked.

'No, I ... I just don't want to be seen with strangers. That would set off the gossips. Look, I only have a few minutes before my shift starts. What do you need to know?'

'We'd like you to tell us about anything significant that happened around the time Rab died. Let's start with Craig Oldfield. How close were they?' Lewis asked.

'Close? That's an interesting word to use about Craig.'

'Why do you say that?'

'No one gets close to that dickhead.' She stopped, looking as if she was reluctant to elaborate, that she should choose her next words with care.

'And...?'

'If he knew I was talking to you he'd kill me.'

'You mean Craig Oldfield?' Lewis asked.

'Yes, Craig.' Her face was pale. Tight.

'Do you really think he's dangerous?' Annie said.

Rose bit her lip before answering. 'I'm pretty much convinced he was driving the car that killed Rab. And if you ask what that's based on, well, a bunch of stuff.' She sank even further down in her seat. 'And if he was capable of that as a kid, what kind of man has he turned into? You know my mum worked for his father, in his local office? Six months after Rab died, she was effectively sacked. Some made-up shit about missing client money. This is the woman who would blush if a police officer glanced in her direction.' She sighed. 'It was a "resign before we sack you" kinda thing. That's the action of a family that's hiding something.'

Lewis said nothing, thinking through what she said and how it matched with Steve Murphy's version. He merely nodded, wondering if bitterness at her brother's death had clouded her judgement in any way.

'So here's a bit about Rab,' she said, her eyes damp now. 'He was a perennial victim of bullies. Happened all through primary school and on into secondary. Dad was away with work a lot. I mean *a lot*, and he lacked any decent male role models. I stuck up for him a few times – I was the fighter in the family.' She smiled. 'But that didn't help. Then he made it into the football team – mostly as an unused substitute, but it got him into contact with the popular boys, you know? And one of them was Craig.' She looked away. 'Rab was one for making up stories – the more shocking the better. But this particular one he told me just days before he died had the ring of truth.'

Rose was silent for so long Annie said, 'If it makes you un-comfortable...'

'It's not that, it's just so long ago.' She wiped at a tear. 'And we're still no closer to the truth.'

Annie reached through between the seats and gave Rose's hand a little squeeze.

Rose sniffed and offered a weak smile. 'Sorry,' she said. 'There was going to be a big party up at the Oldfields', and as Rab tells it he was invited, which' – she made a face – 'was nonsense. Must have been. Those parties were infamous. Wild, apparently – drugs and sex, and all that. There's no way a kid like Rab was getting an invite. It was strictly adults only, and only those and such as those, if you know what I mean?' She pushed her nose into the air to demonstrate what she meant. 'But Rab was adamant he was invited and he was going to get the Oldfields back – and stiff Craig's old man for some cash at the same time.'

'What did he mean by that?' Lewis asked. 'Get them back?'

'He'd moaned *loads* of times before all this that Craig and he were pals until Damien came along. Then Craig began spending more time with Damien. Playing football. Listening to music. Going fishing. All that kind of stuff. I thought Damien was actually way more interested in the sister than Craig, but I think Rab felt jealous, or left out or whatever, and I also thought there was something else ... something ... sexual going on?'

'What made you think that?' Annie asked.

'The week before he died Rab had all this cash. All he would tell me was that Oldfield gave it to him, and when I tried to dig into why someone would give him money he clammed up. It was like he was ashamed, you know? Really ashamed. But it made me think ... *that* level of, I don't know, self-disgust in his eyes?' She scratched at the side of her face. 'I knew my brother well, and as much as it pains me to admit, he was borderline homophobic. For him to be showing that emotion it could only have been caused by something sexual with another boy.' Her expression tightened with confusion. 'Och, I don't know. I've gone over every conversation we ever had trying to uncover some sort of clue as to what Rab was up to before he died.' She looked out of the window, her eyes glazed over with memory and an ongoing loss. 'Whatever was going on, one thing I can swear on was that Rab told me, the day before he died, that he was going to get the Oldfields.'

'Really?' Lewis sat up.

'And whatever means he used to "get" the Oldfields, he was dead within hours.'

Chapter 39

Sylvia
1990

When Sylvia entered the dining room for lunch, Gwendaline was already a few glasses of port down, judging by the way she was slumped in her chair.

'Anything interesting, dear?'

'Nothing to write home about,' Sylvia replied breezily, looking at the buffet that had been placed in the middle of the large table. She helped herself to some salmon and potato salad before taking a seat.

'Ever regret giving up the child?' Gwendaline asked as Sylvia took her seat.

Sylvia remained quiet for a moment. Gwendaline knew all about it, of course. She'd arranged the visit to Switzerland.

'I ... haven't thought about it in an age,' Sylvia said at last.

'Don't lie, Sylvia, it's such a waste of time,' Gwendaline replied. 'Of course you have. But it was just as well, don't you think? Your grandmother didn't rate your potential as a mother. Too cold, she said.'

Sylvia stiffened at the old woman's cruelty.

'I had the same thing happen to me when I was fifteen,' Gwendaline continued. 'Never leaves you, does it? Then the father, the cad, went and married your grandmother, of all the people. Died in the war, so that served him right.' She paused. 'That was a joke. A bad one, I know.'

Another sip, more of a gulp. Then she drained her glass.

'Be a dear, dear,' she said. 'And fill my glass.' She pointed at the drinks trolley. 'In fact, just bring me the whole dang bottle.'

Sylvia rose and fetched the bottle, Gwendaline's eyes never leaving her.

'Maude and I had a complicated relationship as a result,'

Gwendaline said as she poured. 'We had a hate-love relationship, you could say. We hated that we loved each other.' She drank from her newly filled glass. 'Best friends against the world when we were girls at school. And then...'

'The salmon's lovely,' Sylvia said. 'You should, you know, actually eat some.'

'Very good,' Gwendaline nodded, and picked up her knife and fork. She cut off some salmon and chewed it slowly. 'Poison,' she said suddenly. 'That's how your mother died. Poison.'

'I know,' Sylvia said.

'And I have to confess I supplied it.'

This last part was news. 'Why are you telling me this?' Sylvia demanded.

'It was in a little glass bottle with its own green velvet bag.'

Sylvia's head shot up. Almonds, she thought. It smelled of almonds. Would it still be effective?

'Oh, you've seen it?' Gwendaline asked with a faint smile. 'I wondered where it had got to. The story of the plane crash was for the wider public. We all love a romance, don't we? As far as the family was concerned, they got the truth, or a version of it.' She studied Sylvia's face, waiting for her reaction. 'That it was some kind of tawdry suicide pact.'

'Yes?' Sylvia sat back, tilted her chin up, daring this wicked old woman to give her worst.

'I loved Georgia, your mother. Hated that she was Maude's. She should have been mine. The daughter I gave up.' Gwendaline pointed her knife at her chest. 'Instead I became this dead block of a woman.' Sylvia had never seen such a look of self-loathing on someone's face, and it occurred to her that this revelation explained so much. 'I was forced to abandon my child too. I was seventeen. *Seventeen*. Sent away to Switzerland. Same place as you. Then just a few months later, while I was away, George and Maude fell in love. Maude was a year or two older than me. Twenty when Georgia was born – a much more suitable age to have a baby. My baby.' The wattle under her chin trembled. 'Your mother came to me saying she wanted to kill your father because he was having an affair. I didn't realise she was going to give it to you both and take it herself. I thought I was doing her a kindness.'

'What, by giving her the tool to kill someone?'

Gwendaline ignored the question. 'I took great satisfaction in telling Maude all of this, but she refused to believe me.'

'You provided her daughter with the poison that she could use to kill her family,' Sylvia said. 'That wouldn't have been easy to hear.'

'Georgia should have been *my* daughter. Your grandmother took everything from me,' Gwendaline spat. Then shrank from her own words. 'I didn't think she would kill all of you. Just him.'

Sylvia shook her head. There was little wonder she'd turned out the way she had. 'Was there anything about my mother that suggested there was more than murder on her mind?' she asked.

'Hindsight provides clarity, Sylvia. I now see that your mother was damaged. Touched. Quite mad, actually. Your grandmother was on tenterhooks, worrying that you both might inherit that particular gene.'

Sylvia sat forward. 'Wait. You said *both*.'

The old woman's expression was bright with confusion. 'Yes, both. You and your twin sister?'

'I had a sister? A twin?'

'Why, yes,' she replied falteringly. 'Maude didn't tell you? She was stillborn, the poor mite.'

'I had a sister.'

Everything silenced around her. Light faded. There was nothing but that thought, her dry mouth and heavy pulse.

'I had a sister.'

And in the corner of her eye, movement. A shadow raising its hand.

Chapter 40

Sylvia

MAUDE'S JOURNAL

Sylvia, in these meagre pages, I hope to explain that which I couldn't during my lifetime.

You already know, thanks to the interference of your teacher, Phineas Dance, that your parents didn't die in a plane crash in Africa. I lied only to protect you, Sylvia. Knowing as a child that your parents killed themselves AND tried to kill you was a burden I was keen to shield you from.

Gwendaline tried to tell me that it was all your mother's idea. That she found her husband in bed with another woman, and that it was she who fed you and your father the poison. I do not accept this version. Your mother may have been disturbed, but she was not a cold-blooded killer.

The first I became aware of your mother's state of mind was when she was a teenager – around the time she had her first bleed. Until then she was a quiet child, liked to play on her own, mostly with a one-eyed, half-bald doll. A horrid thing, but it made her happy.

The first time it happened, her maid came running to me, worried that she couldn't get the child to stir. She was just sitting there on her bed. staring into space.

I went to Georgia's room and approached her, shook her, and received nothing. She simply stared at the wall. I slapped her, thinking that would bring her out of whatever funk she was in. I did it twice, as I recall. The second time she blinked, scowled at me and said something to the effect that she was trying to hear them. No explanation as to who 'they' might be. Just that she was trying to hear them – that she could hear whispers inside her head and couldn't make out what they were saying, that she needed to know. And then she screamed at me and her poor maid to leave her alone.

In those early days she did come out of this trance quite often, and ate and drank when prompted, but then, as the year progressed, her silences became longer and longer, and all she would say was that she had to know what the whispers were saying.

The medical establishment was worthless. I tried doctor after doctor and received no diagnosis and little in the way of prognosis. Stop panicking, I was told, she'd grow out of it. It was women's problems, one little squirt said when I reported it began after her first menstruation.

The length of her silences increased, to the extent that we would have to bathe her and force her to eat. She lost so much weight I feared for her safety. She was taken to hospital and electro-convulsive therapy was used. To no effect.

Gwendaline had heard through her extensive network that patients in the South of France were being treated for depressive illness with something called lithium, and it was having amazing results. So, we packed Georgia off to Marseille, and she returned six months later with strong French, a prescription to keep her going until the English doctors got on board, and a much more amenable persona. Georgia was then able to get on with her life, finish her education, and meet and fall in love with your father. All was well, or so we thought.

But the voices she heard – her 'torments', she called them – had only been muted by the lithium. They came back with a vengeance as soon as she stopped, which she did while she was pregnant with you and your sister. We were all so excited about the arrival of the twins. But sadly, your sister was stillborn, and I'm certain that loss was what pushed your mother over the edge.

Here, Sylvia paused in her reading. Why was it never mentioned that her mother gave birth to twins? It was as if that had been erased from her grandmother's mind. Perhaps it had been too painful to speak of. She could only write about it in this journal. She returned to the page.

> *The rest you know. The 'torments' became too much and she thought the only thing she could do was to end her life – and yours and your father's.*
>
> *Throughout your childhood I was on alert as far as you were concerned, to see if whatever afflicted Georgia might affect you, but I was gratified to see that this was not the case. You were an aloof child, and cold. Smart, I grant you. But not mad. Could have gone in to politics and run the country like that Thatcher woman.*
>
> *And that would have been that, had I not met Annabel Swift.*
>
> *As you know, I had enjoyed a seance or two. It began after your grandfather died; I was driven to try and speak to him beyond the grave. And then, after Georgia died, I made several attempts to speak to her. To no avail.*
>
> *And then Annabel Swift came to my attention. She was known to be a powerful medium, so I invited her to London.*
>
> *It was apparent from the start that Annabel was the real deal. No theatrics, no drama; she simply asked for a cold glass of water and an object belonging to the soul concerned.*
>
> *The only thing I could find was the horrid little doll Georgia played with as a child. It was hidden away in a box in the attic. When I handed Annabel the doll, she sat back in her chair as if an electric current ran through her. I shall replay her dialogue here, as best as I can recall it:*
>
> *'Whispering. Your daughter heard whispering. It made no sense. No sense at all.' At this she paused, and cocked her head as if she might hear them herself. 'They tormented her. Drove her mad, poor thing. Quite mad.*
>
> *'There were sisters. Both gifted, but they would have been thought of as witches in their time. Inseparable. Until a man,*

unwittingly, set one against the other. The women's love for one another curdled under the force of that competition and the witch hunts of the time. I see flames. The heat is incredible.

'*Oh, dear God, the pain.*

'*One sister accused the other and that poor woman and her children were burned at the stake.*

'*And so a curse was born. But the curse rebounded so that it affected both sides of the family.*

'*It is this curse that afflicted your daughter.*'

Having made this pronouncement she then looked at me, as if it were all my fault.

'*The torments,*' *I murmured.* '*She called the voices her torments.*'

'*Such cruelty among you and yours,*' *she said with a look of near disgust.* '*And it doesn't end there. There's another who has been twisted by the curse, and by the actions of those who should love her. You must change the direction of her life before more people die.*'

Chapter 41

Lewis

As they drove back up to the city, Lewis and Annie chatted through everything Rose had told them.

'So how might all this have affected Damien?' said Annie. 'From what Steve Murphy told you, Damien went off the rails around the time Rab Daniels died. Was that a guilty conscience?'

'Maybe his guilty conscience about that day bubbled up years later and he said something to Craig. Could that have been a good enough reason, in Craig's mind anyway, to make his old friend go away permanently?'

'Lewis...' Annie's tone carried a note of warning. 'We have to be careful we don't conjure up a narrative and then look for the evidence to suit it.'

'Fair point,' Lewis agreed. 'But just to carry the theory on a bit: Craig would know from his sister about Damien's habit of dis-appearing for days on end, and could bank on that being the official response from the police when his family reported him missing. Meaning he'd have plenty of time to hide any evidence of what he'd done to Damien.' He paused. 'But there's nothing here the police would see as actionable. A second-hand confession – from when Damien was high. Rab's sister's suspicions. We need some kind of concrete evidence, then we can go and have it out with Craig Oldfield.'

'We only do that in public, Lewis. The man's quite possibly a killer.'

Lewis decided to ignore that for the moment. 'And perhaps when we confront him, he loses it – enough to tell us the truth about what really happened to Damien.'

Lewis expected Annie to reply with a comment that would bring him back down to earth, but she was silent, her gaze fixed on a large house, on a hill just above a bend they were approaching.

'Annie?' he said.

'Mmmm,' she replied absently.

'What do you think about my plan?'

'Yeah,' she shook her head as if stumbling from a dream. 'Yeah,' she repeated. 'Craig Oldfield's worth the watching.'

Back home, Lewis checked his emails and social-media pages. There was a reply on Facebook from another of Damien and Craig's old friends – a Ryan Henderson.

Happy to talk, mate. Anything to help find my old mucker Damien, he wrote. *What do you want to know?*

I'd prefer to meet up, Lewis replied. *You free tomorrow?*

Meet me on my lunch hour if you want?

Ryan suggested they meet just outside a Costa coffee shop in the city centre.

Pleased that Ryan sounded keen, Lewis agreed, then closed his laptop and asked Annie if she wanted to join them.

'Yeah. Maybe,' she replied. 'Don't know.' She sounded as if she was half asleep, just as she'd seemed halfway through their journey home.

'Are you okay, Annie?'

'Why do you keep asking me that?' She rubbed at her eyes. 'I'm fine. Totally fine.'

Chapter 42

Annie

Annie fought to work out where she was. Who she was.

Utterly confused as to whether she was in her own bed or a dream bed, she pushed herself up onto her elbows and turned her head so that she could scan the gloom of the room.

Where was she?

Was she dreaming?

Too many times in the last few days she had been so deep in her dreamscape, she often struggled to distinguish it from real life.

The last she could recall from the real world was being in the car with Lewis on the way home from meeting Rose Daniels. Then everything became a bit foggy.

'She wants to meet you,' someone had said.

Dream impressions were a muddle and muffle in her head. There had been a woman, all in green. She was to be found in a room reached by two seemingly never-ending flights of stairs, Annie's thighs and lungs protesting when she eventually reached the top.

A voice. *Nothing without effort is truly worthwhile.*

Then:

You may enter.

A door appeared in front of her. A modest, wooden door, painted white. The handle turned smoothly as if it had been recently oiled. She entered to find the windows were draped with heavy curtains, the room dimmed to a permanent dusk, but with just enough light to see that it was almost entirely bare. No paintings on the walls, no carpets, no chairs, no bed.

There must be a chair. There. In the furthest corner. Because if there wasn't, the figure there was hovering in a seated position. A woman?

Yes, a woman. Annie could make out long hair, and that the skirt of her long dress folded on to the floor, a dress that was the green of moss and bracken.

Welcome.

The word sounded in Annie's mind as clearly as if the woman had spoken, but her lips didn't move.

Without shifting, without being aware of how, Annie found herself sitting cross-legged in front of the woman. Her face was hidden in shadow, but her eyes seemed to glow.

'Who are you?' Annie asked. She had been frightened when she entered the room, but now she felt strangely reassured. Part of her mind accepted this; another part wondered, idly, if she was being wrong-footed somehow, whether her mind was playing tricks on her. Her murmurs were strangely silent. Were they complicit in all of this? Was this a new kink in their bid to torment her?

The lassitude that seemed to have taken over her mind provided an answer – she found she didn't care.

The woman's long black hair shifted like fronds of kelp in deep water. While she wondered at this, and where the breeze came from, the woman's voice continued to sound in her mind's ear – part invitation, part siren.

A friend. Or foe? You have a choice to make soon, young Annie Jackson.

Chapter 43

Sylvia
1990

Sylvia watched Gwendaline Montague die.

She'd listened to the constant hints from the old woman, wishing her life to be over, and, her mind full of spite after the bombshell Gwendaline had dropped on her, Sylvia decided to grant her wish. And what a bombshell it was.

Sylvia almost had a sister.

A flicker of movement in the corner of her eye at this thought. She smiled. She'd always somehow known, hadn't she? Her shadow had always been there, watching over her.

Concerned that there would be a post mortem on Gwendaline's body once it was discovered by her staff, Sylvia changed her mind about giving her the same poison she'd fed her parents, and contrived to help the old dear to an overdose of insulin. There was already plenty of the stuff in Gwendaline's medicine cabinet, and Sylvia thought any coroner would reason that this forgetful old woman had simply given herself too much.

Once the old woman was dead she made her way home and phoned Phineas Dance to ask if she could visit him. Her heart always felt a little thrill when she heard his voice, and she hated herself for it. She recognised that it was just a pathetic attempt to please her teacher – something she'd never quite grown out of. And she hated herself for that as well.

'What's your concern?' he asked shortly after she'd arrived.

'These "torments" as they're known – if they are a curse that drove my mother out of her mind, I escaped it. And from what my grandmother said, it skips a few generations. Or it seems to. I'm concerned that my child – wherever he is – will go through this, or his children will.'

'Do you ever think of him?'

'No,' she replied.

'Liar,' he challenged. 'You know what to do, Sylvia.'

'What?'

'It seems to skip a few generations?' He steepled his fingers before him. 'Mmmm. That suggests this is an old and powerful magic.' Dance's eyes pierced hers and Sylvia felt a chill travel the length of her spine.

'You need to go back to the very beginning,' Dance continued. 'Track down the origin of this "torments" curse – the witch who set it. Try to uncover their motivations, and the magic involved.' His eyes narrowed as he spoke. 'Be aware, if this does go back a long way, as I suspect it does – your grandmother mentioned generations after all – families build, they split and diverge, and it's quite likely there are others out there similarly afflicted. If that is the case, they might well be the key. Find out everything you can about anyone else involved, and then work out how to break the curse. Or break them.'

Chapter 44

Lewis

When Lewis walked into his living room he found Annie full length on the sofa. He put the TV on. Breakfast news might wake her up a little. A man in a suit was talking about the latest atrocity in the Middle East.

He waited. Nothing from Annie. Then she simply pulled her quilt over her head. 'Turn that off, will you, Lewis. Who needs to hear this?'

'You okay?' he asked, for what now seemed the umpteenth time in the last couple of days.

She sat up in increments, groaning all the while, and rubbed at her forehead, her hair a matted nest on top of her head. 'Aye,' she replied. 'Fine.'

'I'm going to meet this guy in town later. Ryan Henderson. Want to come?'

'I think I need to shower for a few hours,' she replied. Yawned. 'Don't know why I feel so groggy.'

'Make it a few days, will you?' he joked, and wrinkled his nose. 'I can smell you from here.'

'Cheeky shite,' she replied, and threw a cushion at him. And then, as if that effort had worn her out, she slumped back down onto the sofa.

'Right, while you gather yourself together I'm off to the gym. Phone me if you want me to bring you along to the meeting, okay?'

But when he phoned her after his cross-fit session, she declined his offer.

'I'm feeling a little better. Don't know why I've been feeling so off. Maybe something I ate or drank? Think I need to rest a little more and I'll be back to my old self. You go ahead then report back, okay?'

Just as he ended his call with Annie, a message came through from Ryan.

You driving, mate? There's a multi-storey near Costa. Usually spots on the top floor.

Lewis made his way through the traffic, reminded of how busy Glasgow city centre could be and why he usually got the train, and found that Ryan was right – there were indeed a few spaces on the top floor of the multi-storey.

He tucked his car into a far corner then looked for the signs indicating the exit stairs and made his way over to them. Outside, the clouds were muddied a heavy grey, promising imminent rain, and as he walked he noted the Glasgow rooftops. He rarely got this view of the city – air-conditioning vents on top of hotels, the top floor of the Royal Concert Hall, and in the distance he could almost make out some of the tombs in the Necropolis.

He heard rapidly approaching footsteps behind him.

A shout: 'Mate, you dropped this.'

He turned round, patting his pockets to see what he'd lost, and saw a man approaching. His left hand was out in front of him. As if he was holding something. But there was nothing there.

'What…?'

The man rushed him.

Lewis automatically stepped back. Hair prickling with adrenaline. Fight. Flight. He raised his arms in the defensive manoeuvre he'd learned in Krav Maga.

But he was too slow.

The man's other hand swung round. He *was* holding something there. He whipped it across Lewis's face.

Lewis's forearms took some of the sting from the blow, but not enough. Pain bloomed across his jaw, the side of his head.

He was on the ground.

A barely remembered lesson: never fall to the ground. But he could do nothing to stop it.

Someone groaned. It was him.

A kick in the gut, and he raised his knees to protect his chest.

On to your feet. Get on to your feet.

But he couldn't. The command from his brain to his legs wasn't working.

His vision narrowed. Darkness beckoned.

He became aware of strong hands on his collar, lifting him off the ground, a face close to his. Too close. Lewis struggled to open his eyes. The pain seemed to be everywhere. Light created a silhouette around the man's head, his features blurred in black.

'He wanted me to end you,' the man said. 'But I'm not murdering for him. Stop asking questions or next time he'll send someone who will.'

Chapter 45

Sylvia
1990

A week after watching Gwendaline Montague die, Sylvia was with her grandmother's lawyer in his London office. The irony wasn't lost on her that here she was in a lawyer's office when she'd only recently murdered an old woman.

There hadn't been a moment since when the thought of her *almost* sister wasn't on her mind.

A flicker of movement in the corner of her eye earned a smile.

A cough from the old man in the grey suit in front of her brought her back to the present.

'I was the one your grandmother asked to look into these matters for her, but it was a long time ago, so forgive me if my recollection proves to be in any way inaccurate.' His name was Bernard Peters and he looked like he should have retired twenty-five years ago.

'I found my grandmother's journal just recently,' Sylvia said by way of reminding herself as much as him where they were in the conversation. 'In it she mentions a psychic who told her the family was cursed.' Sylvia recalled the psychic's warning – '*There's another who has been twisted by the curse, and by the actions of those who should love her. You must change the direction of her life before more people die*.' It had occurred to her straight away that the warning pertained to her. Did the psychic mean her work with the Order when referring to the direction of her life? And what of the warning that people would die? She had mused over these questions for no more than a moment. She didn't care. She was surrounded by sheep. She would do what was necessary to complete her work.

'Maude went on to say that she'd employed you to look into the family's history,' she said, once again pulling herself from her thoughts. 'To discover where that curse may have come from. But I couldn't find anything in her papers that might tell me what was found.'

Peters plucked a white handkerchief from the breast pocket of his suit jacket and dabbed at his right cheek, just under his eye. The eyelid had long since drooped, showing a stretch of blood-rich tissue that constantly leaked. 'Quite the thing,' he said, 'being asked to look into a family curse.' His smile revealed teeth that were almost as grey as his suit. 'I never found an actual curse, but I did discover a perfectly dreadful divide in your family going back centuries.'

Sylvia's heart gave a little flip of excitement. 'Oh?'

'It was one of my finest pieces of detective work,' Peters preened. 'Witch trials in the seventeenth century, my dear. It almost beggared belief.'

'Please continue.'

'Your side of the family weren't always wealthy, you know. That happened much more recently thanks to an intrepid soul going out to the colonies. There was even a hint of piracy in the eighteen hundreds.' Peters seemed to puff out his chest, pleased with his research.

Sylvia crossed her legs, keen that he just furnish her with the facts.

'You are directly descended from one Jean McLean, who was burned at the stake in 1707 in an area of the West Highlands called Ardnamurchan. Jean and her twins – a boy and a girl – were all found guilty of witchcraft, then worrit and burned.'

'Sorry. Worrit?'

'Apologies,' Peters said. 'At this point in history they weren't so savage as to burn these poor wretches alive. They strangled them first – or worrit as it was in old Scots – then fed their bodies to the flames.' He gave a little shiver. 'Dreadful, dreadful stuff.' He dabbed again at his eye. 'When I looked into Jean's family I found that she had another daughter and a sister.

'This daughter was protected by cousins and helped to found a new township in a more remote glen nearby. Jean's sister, Mary, her twin, I believe – lots of twins in your family – married the local laird. A Campbell.

'That was quite the difference in fortune, don't you think? One sister marries into relative wealth, and the other is burned at the stake for being a witch.'

'Were there any records of the judgement?' Sylvia asked. 'I presume they held some kind of trial?'

'Yes, trials of a sort were held. Although many of these poor people were tortured, or at the least sleep-deprived, so that they would confess. The records are patchy to say the least. But I was able to uncover a list of witnesses at Jean's trial. Not what they actually said, but their names, and on that list were Jean's sister, Mary, and her husband, John Campbell.'

'She testified against her own sister?'

'Indeed.' Peters head sagged low on his neck. 'One can only speculate as to how Mary might have assisted the prosecution, but I was able to see the birth certificates of Andra and Isobel, Jean's children, who also burned.' He paused, his look one of excitement, as if he was expectant of a shocked reaction. 'And they both showed John Campbell as the father.'

Chapter 46

Sylvia
1990

California was too warm, too busy, and the overbearing enthusiasm of its people was too, too much, on top of which Sylvia resented the timing. She had been sent by Phineas Dance to attend a series of lectures on legends of the British Isles by a Scottish academic, Dr Hetherington, at a second-rate American university. Her mind full of her meeting with the old lawyer, Peters, Sylvia would much rather be back home, researching her family.

But her mind was suddenly changed when she attended a lecture by Dr Hetherington about a creature from Scottish legend called the Baobhan Sith. There was something about this legend that captured Sylvia's imagination like nothing had since those first early lessons from Dance.

Sylvia could almost imagine herself as the legendary fey – appearing to lonely, desperate men in the hills of Scotland. She was beautiful, Hetherington said – a captivating, desirous woman that men could summon, who could satisfy any love or lust. But there was a catch: she had sharp teeth and under her long, green dress a pair of cloven hooves. The one who summoned her had to first intone the name of the Lord. If they didn't, instead of a night of carnal delights, she would tear open their necks and feast on their blood.

Later that very evening, full of excitement, Sylvia phoned Ben – because who else might she share this discovery with?

'It is said this being can read minds. Can you conceive of the power that would give you? We could catch great men with this – trap them with their lust – and then have them at our beck and call. Imagine what we could achieve? Imagine the power we would wield on behalf of the Order ... And the lecturer said that she'd found details of a ceremony that could raise her. How wonderful would that be? To bring a creature from legend to life?'

What she didn't add – because she thought it was none of Ben's business – was that it was quite possible, with such a creature as an ally, that she might have access to strong magic that could help her break her family curse. She had closed her heart off to the fact that she had a son, but even so, she felt a duty to protect him, should he be cursed by the torments that had so afflicted her mother.

'Right.' Ben sounded distinctly unconvinced.

'I've already gained the trust of this Dr Hetherington. She seems a gullible little woman. So I propose we simply steal her research. We won't have any issues. She thinks we're great friends already. I gather from her the ceremony to raise the creature can only take place every seven years, But we're young. We have time on our side,' she enthused.

'Wonderful,' Ben replied. His tone still didn't match his words, and Sylvia guessed it was because he was jealous she was the one on the glamorous overseas trip, and the one who would get the plaudits for thinking all of this up.

'Don't you get it, Ben?' she continued. 'This is it. This is why Phineas recruited me. This is what Phineas had in mind for me all along. This is the potential he saw in me. This is how I bring glory back to the Order.'

Ben sighed and Syliva could hear his frustration. But she had no time for it.

'What's wrong, little Ben?' she taunted. 'Are you annoyed you're back in Blighty, and not out here—'

'For goodness' sake, Sylvia,' Ben cut in angrily. 'You and your precious Phineas Dance. The potential he saw in you? Don't you get it? He's lied to you from day one. Pretending to be your friend, your mentor. Meanwhile he and your grandmother are in league, whispering behind your back. She was the one who got you into all of this.'

'Nonsense. You don't know what you're talking about.'

'Don't I?' Ben's voice was taunting now. 'Well, I know she came to him years ago, looking to learn how she could speak to your grandfather after he died. And I know they kept in touch through some crazy cousin of hers. Phineas told me himself. And that doll you made that killed the Montague girl? It was Dance your grandmother got the idea from. He wanted to see what you had in you.'

'Liar.' Sylvia felt a sweat bloom on her chest.

'He's been manipulating you even before you met.' Ben laughed now. 'And then there was the pregnancy. How unlucky it was to have sex that one time and fall pregnant.'

'It happens.'

'There are spells that can be used.'

'Oh, Ben!' Sylvia exclaimed. 'You really are nothing but a petty little boy.'

'The whole thing was him testing you, claiming power over you, enslaving you to his whims – to the Order.'

'Fool,' Sylvia snorted.

'Ask him,' Ben shot back. 'Next time you speak, ask him. He never outright lies, does he? He has a way of handling the truth that makes you wonder exactly what he's saying, but if you ask him straight, he has to tell you.'

'And what precisely do I ask?'

'Whether he cast a fertility spell on you, and when you fell pregnant, helped your grandmother to cast the child aside.'

Sylvia felt her face heat with anger now. She had phoned Ben to share her excitement, and now all of this was being thrown at her. It was too much. 'How dare you.'

'Right at the start he told us he would break us, and remake us. You've been his little project all along, Sylvia Lowry-Law. He wanted to see how far he could push you. And like his little puppet you keep coming back for more.'

Chapter 47

Annie

Annie drifted in and out of sleep. Every time she woke, she felt its pull again – and succumbed.

You've had a difficult life, Annie, a voice told her. *A traumatic one. But with help you will now enter a new existence. One where your gifts are treasured...*

Images bloomed in her mind.

A young man, chest crushed, slumped in his car, face a smear of blood.

An angry man at her door, finger pointing, mouth moving in a series of rapid insults.

A broken window. The paint on her door. A lifeless, long-eared bag of fur on her doorstep, its eyes staring out.

A series of faces, staring, fingers pointing, hands curved over mouths as they spoke hate.

Then a series of thoughts and emotions. Words and feelings settling across her heart and in her mind.

And then she felt a warmth spread from her heart to encompass every cell in her body. Followed by a chill that did the same. She shivered. She didn't quite know how to feel, or how to be in this moment, but did recognise an overarching sense of wellness.

This curse. These murmurs. They will plague you no longer, she heard.

Annie felt a surge of hope. 'Forever?' she heard herself say.

She almost wept with relief. To be without that chorus of madness in her mind. Never to see someone's face transform into a skull and hear how they would die. To be free of that would be wonderful.

Emotion bubbled from the tightness in her heart, up her throat, and sobbed from her open mouth.

And as she did so, it was as if someone wrapped her up in a cocoon of care and concern. And she let the tears flow. And how she wept. For the child she had been, the girl she had become, and the woman she was yet to be.

Chapter 48

Rose

Rose loved this little beach. It was a crescent of sand just beyond the main arterial route from Girvan to Stranraer, with rocks at either end. The beach was tucked under the cliff so drivers couldn't see it as they approached, and after, the road bent and rose onto the straight stretch that led to Ballantrae.

This little haven had all but saved her sanity a number of times. A dip in the cold water was enough for a mental reset, and if she went for more than a week without stripping off and diving in, it nagged at her like an itch.

Her parents had brought her and Rab here a number of times before he died. A distant cousin owned one of the houses in the little row just before you reached the beach. Other than those residents, pretty much no one else knew it existed.

She rediscovered it during the first Covid lockdown, after seeing lots of people posting on social media about going wild swimming. With a laugh she'd said to her husband, 'We used to just call it swimming.' Then she remembered the little bay and how she'd enjoyed swimming there. And a new habit was born.

Talking to Annie and Lewis Jackson had brought back a lot of pain. It had never really left her; it had always been there, like a shadow in the corner of her heart. But since talking to them in their car, all her old thoughts of Rab and his unspent future had returned. And they'd reminded her once again of the distress her parents had lived with every day since his death. The burden of their grief – which she'd always felt she had to carry.

It had lightened in recent years, she had to admit – since she'd provided her parents with grandchildren. Now they had somewhere else to focus their love, hope and attention.

Rose stripped down to her swimsuit, arranged her clothes and shoes in a neat pile, and strode towards the rocks. Once there, she'd clamber to the highest point and dive in. Then she'd swim breaststroke across to the rocks on the far side of the bay, and swim back again. The return journey was always front crawl. Her husband reckoned the bay was about thirty metres wide, and her record swim so far was back and forth twenty times.

Today however, she didn't feel up to breaking any records. All she wanted was the cold-water immersion, and the mental and emotional clarity that arrived after, every single time.

She heard a shout behind her. A deep, male voice. She ignored it. It wasn't completely unusual to have some company on her swims, but she rarely engaged in conversation out here, other than a polite hello.

The first rock she had to negotiate before she found her diving space was about hip height, and it was always an effort to climb it. And once that was navigated, the trip to the water was about fifteen metres across a stage of rock pools, razor-sharp barnacles, and the odd stretch of bladderwrack seaweed, like large, wet furry rugs discarded by the careless sea. She'd almost slipped on them a number of times.

Rose clambered onto the shelf of rock and began to pick her way across it.

Another shout.

She turned, and saw someone approaching. A man. He was waving.

What could he want? she wondered.

There was no one else around, so it had to be her whose attention he was trying to attract. She looked out to sea, in case there was something there she needed to be aware of, but she spotted nothing but lazy waves, some seagulls, and the silent, giant hump-backed rock of Ailsa Craig away in the distance.

The man shouted once more. Waved again. He was coming closer. Running and waving.

What on earth? Her instinct to help made her pause.

The man was clambering up onto the rocks now. He reached the top and stood up straight, and only then did Rose realise that she knew him.

Panic spiked her heart. He'd followed her out here. He must have. She spun round to escape. Slipped. Crashed down, feeling rock and barnacles tear at her flesh.

She managed to scramble to her feet.

His grin was a feral thing. A promise of bad tidings.

'Bitch,' he said. 'I should have ended you a long time ago.'

He leaped at her.

Chapter 49

Ben
2003

The first time they tried to summon the Baobhan Sith it was a failure.

Ben had been working in his new law practice in South Ayrshire for about three years, recently got married, and had just moved into a house above the town where he worked. The house was an extravagance he could barely afford at the time – one of a group spread out on a hill called High Dailly. The three-storey building stood at the highest point, overlooking Girvan, and it made Ben feel like landed gentry looking down on the peasants. To add to this, the house had a large and very useful basement.

His marriage was one of convenience – convenient to the Order that was. He needed to show himself to be an upstanding citizen. Unmarried men, in their view, could be regarded with suspicion, so a wife was chosen for him. She was an initiate herself, finding the organisation after a flirtation with the occult at university and subsequently using them to escape her overbearing parents. They wanted her to join them in a cult in Central America, and in an overly candid moment she admitted to Ben that she saw him as the least worrisome of her options at that time. Hardly a ringing endorsement. But what did he care? It was all about the charade.

For his part, as long as she fulfilled the role of wife, and possibly mother, that was fine with him. Expectations of romance and a deep connection were, to his mind, for the rest of the human sheep.

Ben's neighbours included the local GP; a musician who'd had a string of number-one hits in the charts but couldn't handle fame and had decided that living in comfortable obscurity was more his kind of thing; and a police detective attached to the nearby station, who, Ben judged, had to be bent. How else could someone on a policeman's wage afford a home up there. It was very handy that Ben had become fast friends with the detective – each of them, Ben thought, recognising the avaricious gleam in the other's eye.

Their first sacrifice to the Baobhan Sith was found by Sylvia. Ben was allowing her to do much of the work around the ceremonies. He had determined to himself that he would only take the glory once they were successful. He wanted the Order to see any failures as Sylvia's. She came across a young man, just off the ferry from Northern Ireland, and she brought him to Ben on the promise of a job on his land. He'd been a farm labourer, got the boss's wife pregnant and fled, knowing the farm-owner had connections to the old Ulster paramilitaries and would, at the very least, arranged to have him knee-capped.

Ben saw the man's soft hands and desperate eyes, and knew he was fleeing from something, that he'd never done a hard day's work in his life, and more importantly, if he died there was a solid chance no one would come looking for him.

The ceremony itself didn't work. Despite following Dr Hetherington's research to the letter. But what it did allow was for Ben and Sylvia to film the local worthies disgracing themselves in various ways. A carefully selected number of them had been invited to a party – chosen because of their prominence among the local citizens. The invites stated that the theme was mid-summer, the dress code white, and to expect to party until the sun came up the next day.

Hidden cameras were placed all around the property, including in the basement, where the real party would happen once the more obviously squeamish had been sent home.

The attendees were told that the people performing in the actual ceremony were all actors, the blood would be stage blood, nudity was permitted, and their only requirement was to let go and enjoy themselves. It would be difficult not to, once they'd taken a draught of the drink they were offered – the same concoction Sylvia and Ben had both consumed at the first ceremony they'd enjoyed with Phineas Dance.

The next man they used in the ceremony was walking the width of the country as a way of distracting himself from the death of his wife after a long illness. He was childless, and his disappearance would be marked only by ex-colleagues, who would probably assume he'd just fallen off a cliff somewhere.

That ceremony failed as well.

It didn't concern Ben that people were to die. Sacrifices had to be made if they were to succeed in their endeavours for the Order. Raising the Baobhan Sith would be his life's crowning achievement – what were the deaths of a few lost and wandering men compared against that?

Chapter 50

Lewis

'Hey.'

'Hey.'

'You alright, bud?'

Voices. Hands touching him. Prodding. Checking.

'Need a doctor?'

'Course he needs a doctor. Look at him. We need to call an ambulance.'

Lewis became aware he was lying on something hard. People were all around him. When he moved, the pain on the side of his head roared its reminder. He groaned. Tried to sit up.

A hand on his chest. 'Better you wait till the paramedics arrive, buddy.'

'No,' he groaned. Opened his eyes. Where was he? 'I'm okay. Honest, I'm okay.'

He tried to sit up.

His head spun. He wasn't okay. There was a heavy, dull feeling behind his eyes, and he felt sick.

He turned his head to the side just in time. Vomit surged up his gullet and out of his mouth, splattering the hard ground.

Everything came back to him. Arriving in the car park. Walking over to the stairwell as he admired the city around him. The man running at him. And then being struck, and a warning being delivered.

An elderly couple were standing over him. He was wearing a tweed jacket and a bow-tie, she had on a camel coat. They each mirrored their concern for him.

'Paramedics will be here in a minute, son,' the woman said.

'Aye,' the man echoed. 'They telt us they'd be here in five, so just you hang back there, squire. Nae need to move about until we know you're safe.'

Lewis managed to sit up, feeling foolish that this elderly couple were looking out for him.

'Here,' the man said, his eyes wide. 'Looks like someone hit you a fair old clatter. Was it a car? Can you mind?'

Sure, he could remember. It was no car. And he said as much.

Sirens. The squeal of tyres, as what Lewis guessed was the ambulance made its way towards him.

'Must be having a quiet day,' the woman said. 'Never known an ambulance to arrive that quickly.'

Lewis got to his feet, and then became aware of two people in green clothing rushing towards him. One man, one woman.

They took him by the arms, and sat him in the ambulance.

A number of tests later, including ascertaining his name, date of birth and address, and checking, Lewis presumed, the reaction of his pupils to light, and he was arguing with the paramedics about going to hospital, and whether he should report the attack to the police.

'I think they were just after my phone,' he lied. He wasn't about to fill them in about his investigation.

'Is there someone you can call to come and collect you, at least?' said the female paramedic. 'We're not letting you get back in your car.'

'I can't leave it here overnight. You seen the cost of parking?'

'Rather that than you kill yourself, and somebody else, if you get worse while you're driving.' She stared him down, raising an eyebrow.

'Okay. I'll phone my dad.'

She crossed her arms.

'While you watch, apparently,' Lewis added.

Mr Mac arrived thirty minutes later at the café opposite the multi-storey, where Lewis was sitting in the far corner, already tired of people looking at him as if he was some kind of miscreant.

Mr Mac took one look at his bruised and swollen face and winced. 'How does the other guy look?'

'Like an arsehole.'

Mr Mac nodded. And smiled, as if he was happy to see Lewis's reaction to the attack. 'That's the spirit.' He looked down at Lewis's drained mug. 'Want another, or do you just want me to take you home?'

'Let's just sit for a while,' Lewis replied. 'And if my vision doesn't go all blurry in the next hour and I don't fall asleep on you I'll go back up, collect my car and drive home.'

'You sure?'

Lewis nodded. And closed one eye against the resultant pain. He grimaced before saying, 'And while you're up at the counter, get me a doughnut.'

While Mr Mac was away, Lewis mulled over what happened again. It was clear to him that Ryan Henderson had essentially lured him up to that rooftop parking space in order to deliver a message from Craig Oldfield, and he was furious that he'd allowed himself to be sucked in.

As Mr Mac arrived back at the table with fresh coffee and cakes, his phone rang. He looked at the screen. Winked, and said, 'Trouble.' Then answered, and Lewis could hear Mandy's voice. Her husband looked over at Lewis. Winked again. 'He'll survive.' He handed the phone to Lewis. 'She wants to talk to you herself.'

'You okay, honey?' Mandy asked, sounding very worried indeed. 'Do you remember anything?'

Lewis went through it all again, trying to minimise the discomfort he was in.

She saw through him. 'If they called an ambulance for you that means you were way worse than you're letting on.'

'I'm fine. Honestly.'

'You're not fine. This whole thing is not fine. I wish Chrissie hadn't got you two mixed up in this. You've been attacked, Annie's spaced out and ... and...'

'Hey, what's up?' Lewis asked. Mandy sounded more panicked than she had a right to be. 'Has something else happened?'

Silence.

Then: 'It's Rose.'

It took a moment for Lewis to catch up. He recalled the woman he and Annie had met the other day. The way she'd had them hide out behind her workplace so they wouldn't be seen talking together. His heart surged with worry.

'Is she okay?'

Mandy sobbed. 'Oh, Lewis. This is bad. If Oldfield is capable of this, what else might he do?'

'What the hell's happened?' If he'd put this woman in danger, he'd never be able to forgive himself. His anger at Craig Oldfield simmered to rage. If he had...

'So far the police are thinking it's an accident. But—'

'Mandy,' Lewis interrupted. 'Just tell me.'

'She's dead, Lewis. Chrissie just phoned to tell me. Rose is dead.'

Chapter 51

Annie

Now Annie couldn't sleep.

Whatever had made her so dreamy and drowsy for the last few days had worn off, leaving her wide awake when she should be sleepy. Lying restless on the sofa while the rest of the world was snoring was lonely. And of course, while she lay there all she could think of was Rose Daniels being dead, and Lewis getting attacked in the middle of the city, in the middle of the day.

He'd walked back in the door with a sheepish look, one side of his face all puffy, the bruises beginning to bloom.

'Oh my God.' She'd jumped to her feet. 'What the hell happened? I wish I'd not let you go on your own to see that guy.' She rushed to his side.

'I'm fine. Alive. Which is more than...' He paused.

'More than what? More than who?' Annie's stomach twisted.

It was a shock to hear about Rose. The woman they'd spoken to just the day before was dead?

They found a news report on the BBC Scotland website. It said that a woman had slipped on some rocks, fallen into the sea and drowned. The working hypothesis so far was that she had hit her head then fallen into the water, where her ability to swim was impaired and she'd drowned. The report went on to say that the police were confident there were no suspicious circumstances.

This was no coincidence. A day after she spoke to them, she was dead?

Chrissie phoned them that evening. 'You've heard?' she asked.

Annie said that they had. 'Look, I might be reading too much into this, but do you think...?' Annie left her sentence unfinished.

'It happens,' Chrissie said. 'People do suffer terrible accidents. It doesn't have to be a ... something criminal, you know?'

But Annie could tell Chrissie was worried, that she didn't want them to come to any harm as a result of their investigation. Annie didn't have the heart to tell her about what had happened to Lewis. But reading between the lines as they continued their conversation, it was clear Chrissie didn't want them to stop their investigation.

Mandy was more unequivocal when she called.

'Coincidence? I don't think so. You've upset this guy. He's had someone attack Lewis, and then he's killed this poor woman. You have to stop this. Distance yourself from the search for Damien. It's too much, Annie. I'm really worried.' Annie could hear her start to cry. 'After what happened up in Mossgow – I can't go through the worry of you being in danger again.'

'Hey,' Annie said. 'I'm okay, I'm sure of it. And Lewis is a big boy. He can look after himself, what with all that Krav Maga and stuff he does.'

'It didn't help him this afternoon,' Mandy countered. 'Let me speak to him.'

'I'll put you on speaker,' Annie replied.

'Promise me, Lewis,' said Mandy. 'Promise me you'll speak to the police, tell them everything you know, and then step back from this.'

'But what about Chrissie and Damien?'

'You tried, Lewis. You both tried, but it's time to leave this to the professionals. It's become too dangerous.'

Chapter 52

Lewis

Next morning, eyes still sanded with lack of sleep, Lewis came to the decision that they were in way over their heads, and that it was quite likely their cack-handed attempts to investigate Damien's disappearance had led to Rose's death.

It was time to give up on his fledgling investigative career and get back to what he did best: compile peoples' accounts. Numbers didn't lie, vanish, or commit acts of physical violence. He was safe – and other people would also be safe – with lists of income and expenditure. His decision was confirmed when he saw the bruising and swelling down one side of his face when he looked in the mirror.

He was on his third coffee of the day when he received a text from Chrissie saying that Rose's mum wanted to talk to him and asking if it was okay if she passed his number on to her. Within ten minutes his phone rang.

'Is that Lewis?'

'Yes,' he replied.

'It's Kate. Rose's mum.' Her voice had little energy and it sounded to Lewis as if her throat was swollen. 'You don't mind me calling you, do you?'

'Not at all, Kate. I'm ... I'm so sorry about what happened to Rose.'

'She was a lovely girl. A great mum. I don't know how those kids will cope.'

And she started to cry. It went on for a long minute, Lewis simply listening.

Finally she sniffed. 'Sorry. You didn't answer the phone to listen to a woman you've never met cry.' She sniffed again.

'No need to apologise,' Lewis said. 'I can't imagine how difficult this is for you.' Losing one child must be bad enough, Lewis thought. Losing two must be a level of grief beyond coping.

'She phoned me the other day to say she'd met you two. Rose...'

She stopped for a moment, as if the mention of her daughter's name had stolen her capacity for words. 'It meant a lot to her that someone believed her. That Rab's death hadn't gone unnoticed after all these years. The two of them were good pals, you know. Rab was a wee shite at times, but he was a good kid at heart. He didn't deserve that. To be killed and then abandoned on the side of the road like...' She started to cry again.

Again Lewis waited.

'I just wanted to say thanks for looking into this. The law isn't interested, and the family really appreciates it, son.'

Lewis screwed his eyes shut. Didn't have the heart to say that he'd decided to back off – and was going to insist Annie did too.

'Those Oldfields,' Kate went on, bitterness in her voice now. 'You know they sacked me from their family business not long after Rab died? At the time, I thought I was unlucky. Money had gone missing and they had to make an example of someone. It was just a shame that someone was me, you know? But, as the years have gone by, I've started to wonder whether there was more to it. And Rose kept going on about it...' She managed a grim laugh. 'Boy, did she keep on about it. Dog wi' a bone at times, that lassie. Clever but. Could have been something if she'd stuck in at school, but Rab's dying messed her up. It wasn't just him that died that day, something in all of us did as well.'

'I'm so sorry, Kate.'

She sniffled loudly. 'They are a weird family; the Oldfields. I mean, most bosses would have been sympathetic to an employee going through what we were, but they were ... the best word I can think of is "distant". Even years later when I saw them, the mum and dad, out on the street, they'd just ignore me. Maybe they did think I was the thief, but even if that was true there were circumstances that should have made them a little more, I don't know, lenient? Know what I mean?'

'I do,' said Lewis, and despite his decision to stop investigating, he could feel his senses aroused by what she was telling him.

'I remember Craig when he was a kid,' Kate continued. 'He used to come into the office after school to wait on his dad. Just sit with a colouring-in pad or something, or when he got older just doing his homework, and I used to feel heart-sorry for him. His dad was so nasty with him, you know. Barely looked at him, and when he did it was like a bark. I wouldn't speak to our collie the way he spoke to his son. Just shows you: them that think they're better than everyone else often aren't. It's no wonder Craig turned out the way he did.'

'How did he turn out?'

'He has a bad reputation in the town. A drunk. Violent. Always pushing his weight around. Like he thinks the world owes him something, that he should be seen as a successful businessman. But he isn't a patch on his father in that sense. Pretty much wasted every chance life gave him. String of girlfriends, never settled down.

'Poor Rose,' she went on. 'She knew that area like the back of her hand. It beggars belief that she would...' A silence so profound followed that Lewis thought for a moment the line had been cut. Then a heavy breath. 'She practically grew up along that shoreline. I can't get an image out of my mind. I keep seeing her face down. Floating in that water. Blood around her head like seaweed...'

Chapter 53

Lewis

Next day, at first light, Annie knocked, pushed open his door and peered into his room.

'You up?' she asked.

'I am now.' He propped himself up on his elbows. 'What's going on?'

'I've been awake for ages,' Annie replied. 'Want to go back down to Ayrshire? See what we can dig up?'

'What about Mandy?' Lewis replied. 'I promised her we'd take a step back.'

'I didn't,' Annie replied with a shrug. 'C'mon. I'll fill a flask with coffee. You make yourself presentable and we'll hit the road.'

An hour or so later and they'd pulled into a little car park at a beach that was a best guess from what they could remember of Rose's description of the place she loved to go swimming.

Wind flattened the marram grass growing on the dunes. There was a sudden squall of rain, so they took a moment, settled into their seats, sipping at their coffee. The sky and sea were painted grey; a giant ink smudge from one side of the horizon to the other.

Lewis looked to the clouds and judged that this was as dry as the weather was going to get for the foreseeable. 'Coming?' he asked Annie, as he opened his door.

She nodded at the rain-misted windscreen and made a face. 'I'll just enjoy the view.'

On the beach he saw that rocks littered the sand, some the size of a football. Wind whipped the tall grass into a heavy lean, the surf to white peaks and the sand into his eyes. He squinted south, down the coast, and studied the beach as it curved and stretched towards the old harbour village of Ballantrae.

The wind was so strong it felt that it might always be a feature in this area; that it started somewhere out in the Atlantic and gathered strength as it neared the Scottish coast, driving the sea onto the beach.

He doubted this would be where Rose swam. The reports said she'd fallen into the sea from rocks. He turned and looked in the other direction, northwards, beyond a small row of homes. Here, the sand gave way to boulders. Fences limited access to the sea, and just under the headland he could make out a large cave.

Lewis started to walk in that direction, his feet sinking into the heavy sand, making each step an effort. Soon, over the sound of the wind, he could make out a snapping noise. A few more steps, and around a large boulder, he saw that waist-high poles stood up out of the sand, linked by blue-and-white tape, some of which had come loose and was being whipped in the air like frenzied snakes. This had to be where Rose was found.

Feeling a charge of sadness and an equal weight of guilt, he made his way round the cordon. Then sand made way for rock, and Lewis could see rock pools and stretches of seaweed.

'Excuse me,' Lewis heard. 'Excuse me.' Louder.

The last time someone had come up behind Lewis, it hadn't ended well, so he turned quickly and made ready to face whoever was approaching.

A young woman was walking towards him. Her dark-grey suit made her look out of place, her feet sinking into the deep, heavy sand as she quickly walked towards him. The strong breeze whipped her long blonde hair over her face. She pulled it away and tucked it behind an ear. She was pretty, Lewis happened to notice. And about his age.

'That area is – well it was – cordoned off, for a reason, sir. Please don't go any further,' she said.

Lewis held a hand up and walked towards her, both of them almost stumbling in the uneven sand. 'I'm guessing you're the police?'

'That's correct. Detective Corrigan. And your interest here is...?' She stopped. Cocked her head to the side. She held his gaze and something told him little would get past her.

'What's your name?' she asked.

He told her.

'The woman who died here?' he asked. 'You still treating it as an accident?'

'That's what the media are saying,' she replied. 'Why do you ask?'

'A guy I know – a family friend, Damien – went missing nearly two weeks ago. It was reported to you guys...' Lewis offered his best winning smile. No reaction. Not even a flicker.

'What has this got to do with the woman who died here?'

'We spoke to her the other day – the day before she died – asking her about a friend of hers and Damien's. A guy called Craig Oldfield.'

There. Something. A slight shift in expression before the shutters came down.

'We?'

'Me and my sister, Annie. She's back in the car.' He nodded in the direction of his vehicle. 'She didn't fancy being out in the rain. Which has stopped,' he added needlessly.

'What happened to your face?' she asked as she studied him. 'Looks nasty.'

Reading the expression on Corrigan's face, he realised that he needed to get himself off her suspect list as soon as possible.

'The day after we talked to her about Craig Oldfield, she died. That very same day, I was attacked, up in Glasgow. Two people who had been total strangers until days ago speak about an individual together and one of them dies, and the other gets...' He indicated the side of his face where the bruising bloomed.

'Malkied,' Corrigan said, a hint of a smile on her face.

'Aye,' Lewis replied. Grinned. He hadn't expected her to use such an expression.

'You are able to confirm that happened in Glasgow?'

'Some Good Samaritans helped me. Phoned an ambulance to come and sort me out. I didn't get the couple's name and address, but the paramedics will surely have a record. Why do you ask?'

'If you were in Glasgow, you weren't here.'

'Ah.'

She turned and started walking across the beach towards the houses, clearly expecting him to join her.

'So, Detective Corrigan, does that mean you are not considering Rose's death to be an accident?' he asked as he caught her up.

She stopped walking and faced him. 'Lewis, you seem like a nice fella. You asked me that already. Leave this to the professionals, eh? Or, if what you say has *any* basis in truth, the other side of your face might end up even worse.'

Chapter 54

Ben
2010

Each of the ceremonies they'd held over the years sadly failed. Ben was sure this was down to Sylvia. He had even, after the second failure, flown over to the States and attended one of Dr Hetherington's lectures himself to see if there was any detail Sylvia had missed. He went so far as taking the woman out to dinner to see if he could glean any more information, but during the meal he'd made the mistake of telling the good doctor that he and Sylvia were connected. Her warmth towards him cooled decidedly after that.

Sylvia was furious, of course, that he'd gone behind her back, but he had to check, hadn't he?

He had high hopes of the latest recruit, who he'd found himself. Perhaps, he reasoned with Sylvia, the previous attempts had failed because the sacrificial victims were so old?

'But he's a local,' Sylvia argued when they spoke about it over the phone. 'You know his family. His mother works for you. He will be missed.'

'And he'll be found,' he argued back. 'But with the blame deflected.'

'What plan are you working on now?' Sylvia asked.

'Two birds. One stone. That boy who's sniffing around my daughter – I can't get rid of him. So he's going to find himself in a very compromising situation. With blood on his hands. And I'll have him just where I want him.'

'Tell me no more,' Sylvia replied. 'Just make sure there's no blowback on us.'

Ben went out to his car, drove to the end of the drive and opened the door of his BMW to the lad who was standing there, waiting for him, hands in his pockets, shoulders back as if trying to look bigger, his chin raised defiantly. He was probably around five and a half feet, just recently started to shave and dressed as if he'd borrowed clothes from a taller, wealthier friend.

The boy climbed in and pulled the door closed. Now he was in an enclosed space with Ben he appeared less sure of himself. 'Awright?' he asked in that reedy voice of his.

'You told no one where you were going?'

'Nut,' the boy replied. 'It's naebuddy's business.'

'And you remember the party is this weekend?'

'Aye.' The boy grinned. 'Will there be birds there?'

'More women than you can shake your little stick at,' Ben replied, looking down at the boy's groin. 'But first, a trial. I need to check you've got the goods.'

'Cash first,' the boy said, his Adam's apple sliding up and down his throat as he swallowed.

Ben pointed to the pocket on the car door and a white envelope there. 'Fifty quid, as agreed,' he said.

The boy reached for it and slid it in the pocket of his jacket so quickly it was almost a blur. 'And just so you know,' the boy said. 'You do it to me. And that doesn't make me gay or nothin'.'

'Absolutely,' Ben replied, reaching across and squeezing the boy's leg, high up on the thigh. This wasn't about sex for him either. The Order and its needs were hugely important to Ben, but an added benefit for him was the thrill he got from playing with people. This exercise was to test how far he could push the lad. How much discomfort he would take before he started to push back. The ceremony demanded a certain amount of compliance before the drugs took effect and it would help to know where the boy's limits might be.

'And no one is to hear about the party after. No one. Understood?' he added.

The boy nodded fiercely in agreement, looking even younger than his sixteen years. Ben read the gleam in his eyes and was certain that if the boy got the chance he'd tell everyone he knew that he was at one of the famous parties up at High Dailly.

For a moment, Ben allowed himself to imagine the ceremony – they'd found a new site, one with terrible links to the past. In the cathedral-like space of that cave, he could almost see the boy's naked body laid out on the altar stone, the blade glinting in the candlelight as it hung poised over the heart.

'This remains our secret. If I hear that after the party you tell anyone, I will not be happy. Am I understood?' he asked, thinking that for Rab Daniels there would be no 'after'.

Chapter 55

Annie

From her vantage point in the car Annie could see Lewis talking to someone. A woman. A young, attractive woman in a dark suit. She had 'police officer' written all over her. Who else would be standing on an Ayrshire beach near the site of a recent death, wearing such formal clothing?

As she watched her brother talk, part of her registered the muffled noise of her murmurs. They had been mostly silent since she'd been feeling off-key – whatever had caused that was a mystery – but she was grateful that her curse had been offline for a while. She patted the stone stowed in the cup of her bra and sent it a little note of thanks.

Lewis made his way back to the car and sat inside with a huff. 'Well, that's me told.'

'Police, I'm guessing?'

'The long arm of the law looks prettier down here than in Glasgow,' he grinned.

'What did she want?'

'Me to fuck off.'

'Is that what she said?'

'Not in so many words.'

'The locals circling the wagons?' Annie asked.

'Nah,' Lewis replied, eyes on the police officer as she made her way back to her own car. 'It had the feel of the professional telling the amateur to back off.'

'And is that what we're going to do?'

'Is that what you want to do?' Lewis's eyes studied hers.

'Nah,' she replied. 'Let's find somewhere to eat and meet some more locals. See what we can stir up.'

'Great. I'll admit, I was about to give it up. But after chatting to her' – he nodded towards the other car – 'it's clear there's a lot more to find out.'

Annie nodded. 'We can't stop now.'

Lewis rubbed his hands together. 'That's my girl.' He plucked his phone from his pocket. 'What do you fancy eating?'

'It's still early,' Annie replied, and then smacked her lips. 'What about a full Scottish?'

Ten minutes later they were sitting by a window in the restaurant of a hotel with a view down the coast.

Annie let her pinkie finger just touch her little stone. Her murmurs had picked up a little since she entered the low-ceilinged building. Thankfully there weren't many people around, but, still, she had studiously avoided looking anyone in the face as she threaded her way through the chairs and tables.

She had been unable to avoid one old man. His seat was directly in her path and he'd smiled as she approached. Annie couldn't not smile back and as her eyes met his, her murmurs sang a note of impending death – a note threaded through with a dread diagnosis.

Heart attack. And the old man would be dead before he hit the ground.

She bit her lip, swallowed her nausea, and carried on to their table.

By the time their food arrived, Annie's nausea had waned and her appetite returned, so she managed to clear her plate. Just as she was finishing off her last mouthful, she became aware of movement behind her, and Lewis smiled at someone over her shoulder.

'Detective Corrigan,' he said. Then, eliciting a quiet groan from Annie, he asked, 'Do you come here often?'

'Mind if I join you?' she asked, as she sat down on the chair between them.

Annie smiled. 'The cooked breakfast is delicious,' she said, wondering what she might want.

Corrigan smiled back, her eyes searching Annie's as if trying to place her. She then turned to Lewis. 'I was passing and saw your car in the car park.'

'This is Annie,' Lewis said. 'Annie, meet Detective Corrigan.'

Annie nodded at the other woman.

'Can I get you a drink or something?' Lewis made to get up.

'That's okay,' she replied. 'I won't be long.'

Lewis leaned forward. 'Should I be concerned? Have I done something wrong?'

'Guilty conscience?' she asked, deadpan.

'Listen, I get a red face going through the "nothing to declare" section at the airport so don't read into anything I say.' He smiled.

'So,' Corrigan looked from Annie then back to Lewis. 'I was just wondering why you're so interested in Damien. It is a bit of a coincidence, as you mentioned earlier, that Rose dies, then you're attacked the very next day. Can you tell me anything more about what happened?'

Annie could see Lewis bristle at her mention of the attack. She knew he'd hated the feeling of helplessness he'd experienced as he lay on the ground while the man kicked him.

'I don't remember much,' he said. 'But I do remember that he said something to me before he ran off: that "he"' – Lewis made air quotes – 'wanted me dead. But the guy who attacked me wouldn't kill for whoever "he" was. And that I should stop asking questions or the next guy would, you know, do the deed.'

Corrigan narrowed her eyes. Assessing. 'Right.'

'What?'

'Okay, I can tell you that we *are* looking into Damien's dis-appearance. I can't say too much, obviously. What I'd like to know is what you think Craig Oldfield might have do with all of this.'

'So you're taking us seriously?' Annie asked.

'Us?' Corrigan raised an eyebrow. 'You guys are a team?' Corrigan paused. 'Let me tell you what I told your brother, Annie. Please leave this to the professionals.' She turned to Lewis. 'Tell me everything you know, and we'll take it from there. How about that?' Her expression gave nothing away.

Lewis glanced at Annie, and she gave him a tiny nod. 'We'll need more coffees for this, I think,' she said.

Lewis ordered them, and then between them, he and Annie detailed everything they'd learned so far. About Rab having cash before he died and Rose's guess that Craig had paid Rab for some sort of sex, Rab's assertions he was going "to get Oldfield", every-thing Steve Jenkins had told Lewis about the hit and run, and then now, all these years later, Damien's disappearance.

'And then the day after she tells me about Rab, poor Rose ends up dead on that beach. Can't be a coincidence,' Lewis said.

'Okay,' Corrigan leaned back, elbows resting on the arms of the chair, hands clasped in front of her. 'Let's say all of that is true. Why now? Why, all these years later, act to cover things up and get rid of anyone who can point the finger?'

'That,' Lewis took a sip of coffee, 'is what I aim to find out.'

Corrigan raised her eyebrows. 'This is a police matter, Mr Jackson. I don't think you should be aiming to find anything out.'

'How far have you got investigating Damien's disappearance?' Annie interjected.

Corrigan narrowed her eyes at Annie, as if wondering how much to say. 'We have just spoken with his mother. And I can tell you we haven't uncovered anything questionable yet, but our enquiries do show that he hasn't used his phone or his bank cards for over a week now. And *that* is something of a red flag.'

Her mobile rang. She pulled it out and answered. 'Clare Corrigan.'

Annie could hear a tinny voice speaking, loud enough for her to know the speaker was excited about something.

'It's his car?' Corrigan asked. 'Confirmed?' She looked at Lewis and Annie. 'Right. Give me twenty minutes.' She cut the connection.

They both looked at her expectantly.

She shook her head. 'I don't think it would be breaking any protocols to tell you. We've found Damien's car. It was abandoned. His clothes, wallet and phone were all placed neatly on the front seat.' She grimaced. 'But he's nowhere to be found.'

Chapter 56

Sylvia
2017

After years of renting homes near to where Ben lived with his wife, the house she eventually chose was perfect. It was just outside a village – close enough to civilisation when it was required, but distant enough for no one to know exactly what was going on within its walls.

She'd returned to the UK from the USA full of the zeal she'd left with, but now it had a different purpose. The revelation that she'd been a mere pawn in Dance's games didn't come as a complete surprise, but that he had been so dark in his machinations raised levels of resentment that she couldn't contain.

So, thoughts of finding the cure to her family curse were put on hold while she worked to get closer to Dr Hetherington, in order that she, Sylvia, would become the expert in the Baobhan Sith. What a perfect creature it would be to raise – one who preyed on the male.

From her spineless father, to Boney Ben, to Phineas Dance, and the countless men who'd touched her up on public transport, wolf-whistled at her on the street, talked down to her when she bought a car, or ignored her when she made valid points in university faculty meetings, she had had enough. If she could bring the Baobhan Sith to life, she would use her powers to get rich and destroy as many men as possible.

Dr Hetherington was a gentle fool. More than happy to share her research and point Sylvia to where she might find more. She only worked out what Sylvia planned when it was too late, when she'd found the ancient text that detailed the ceremony.

When it became clear what Sylvia intended, Hetherington reported her to anyone who might listen, but no one would. It was too fanciful for words. Bring a *what* to life? So, Hetherington was discarded as easily as Sylvia picked her up. 'Do your worst, lady,' Sylvia told her. 'You're a crank. No one believes you.'

Ben, on the other hand, was still useful. He'd built himself a little enclave of like minds just outside a small Scottish town, and caught so many of the local worthies in uncompromising positions that he'd become practically bullet-proof. Which could be a double-edged sword. The man was so full of his own importance and so willing to feed his impulses, he could yet become a liability.

Phineas Dance, she conceded, had to be dealt with.

Time was passing too quickly. Although she felt as vigorous as ever, she had to admit she was getting old, and now, she only had a limited number of ceremonies available to her before she died.

They had seven years until the next ceremony could be performed. Seven years to probe every aspect of the spell after the most recent abject failure. And that meant coldly assessing what hadn't worked on previous occasions and why.

Perhaps, she considered, one of the reasons the magic had failed when it came to the ceremony was that her mind and soul weren't completely clear. They were clouded by the conflict in her mind. The love and reverence she felt for Dance, and her chafing resentment over how she had been nothing but a puppet to him for most of her life.

She had determined when she uncovered his machinations that Dance would have to pay, but that she would do it at a time when he least expected. When he would be sure she had forgiven and forgotten. Which was really just an excuse to do nothing.

Time for honesty, Sylvia, she told herself. You have avoided this issue for far too long.

The spell's future success could well depend on resolving it.

She orchestrated a visit to Dance's quarters at a home run by the Order in Cornwall – saying she had uncovered some new research on the Baobhan Sith that he simply had to see for himself. Besides, wouldn't it be nice to visit? Talk over old times? Dance wasn't normally given to sentiment, but he had agreed, making Sylvia wonder if he'd grown soft in his dotage.

The home itself was a Tudor manor house just outside Newquay, and Dance had the run of the ground floor of the west wing. Which would make what came next much easier for Sylvia.

When she arrived he was sitting in a large, leather wing-backed chair by an inglenook fireplace. His gaze was just as stern and uncompromising as she remembered, but she noticed a tremor in his right hand as it rested on the arm of the chair. His face was heavily lined, and wisps of white hair clung to his liver-spotted scalp.

'You haven't changed,' he said. His body may have weakened but from the clarity of his intent look she judged his mind was as sharp as ever.

'You've grown old,' she said as she took a seat beside him.

'Coffee?' He smiled in amusement at her honesty. 'Or are you still drinking your herbs?'

'Coffee,' Sylvia replied, and felt a little frisson of worry at his mention of herbs. Had he guessed what she was up to? Dance rarely wasted a word – there was usually something else layered into his dialogue. He rang a little bell, and moments later a young man appeared bearing a tray of drinks. He served up, they sipped.

'So, what do you have for me?' Dance asked.

'This.' Sylvia handed him a brown envelope. He took it, lifted the flap and pulled out a sheaf of paper. As she watched him touch the paper Sylvia's heart gave a twist – her little shadow was there, almost in sight, shimmering with anticipation. On the paper was a copy of the ritual Dr Hetherington had discovered years earlier.

'I've taken Hetherington's work,' she said willing her pulse to slow, 'and cross-referenced it with rituals used for similar types of legendary creatures from around the world. The Inuit and the Mayans have some fascinating insights—'

'Will it take long?' Dance interrupted.

'Excuse me?' Sylvia asked, noting that he was slowly, deliberately, rubbing the thumb of his right hand together with his forefingers.

Dance looked up from his study of his digits. 'I presume the paper has been coated in some kind of neurotoxin?' He coughed. Blinked. Swallowed. 'Will it take long?'

'No.' Sylvia sat back. Of course he would have worked out what she was up to.

'Will it be painful?'

'Of course.' To her surprise Sylvia found that she gave this answer with little satisfaction. Now, in the moment of her revenge, she felt flat. No. Disappointed. For she suddenly realised that, even at the last, Dance was manipulating her. He'd not only known what she was up to – he'd expected it. This was what he wanted her to do all along.

'The best one can hope for,' he said. Licked his lips. Screwed his eyes up against a shot of pain. 'Is to choose the hour of one's own death.' He twisted in his seat. 'I didn't quite manage that, but this is satisfyingly close.' Sweat burst out in beads across his forehead. 'Will you sit with me?' he asked.

Sylvia climbed to her feet.

'Go to hell, Phineas.'

She left without a backward glance.

Chapter 57

Clare

Clare Corrigan slipped her phone into a pocket and leaned forward.

'Lewis, Annie, you both need to go back up to Glasgow, stay there and leave the investigating to the police.'

'Right. Okay,' Lewis said. Eyes anywhere but on her. 'I'm heading back up home right after this.'

She shook her head. He did seem like a nice guy, but he was a lousy liar. 'Good, because if you don't I might have to arrest you for interfering with a police investigation.'

'Really?'

'Really.'

'What about Damien's mum? What are you going to tell her? *When* are you going to tell her?'

Clare opened her mouth to reply but he carried on:

'Because I speak to her, or to my mum – her sister – regularly. So I need to know what to say.'

He looked genuinely worried for his mum and aunt, more than he had for Damien, Clare thought. This guy had a certain charm, she had to admit. She bit down on a smile.

'Our officers should already be speaking to Damien's mother. I wouldn't have told you what we'd discovered otherwise.'

'Of course,' Lewis replied, smiling a little at her now.

'Go back to Glasgow, Lewis,' she said, got to her feet and walked away.

Clare followed the directions her colleague back at the office had texted her. After the long stretch of road at Lendalfoot and before the Bennane headland, there was a turn to the right and a holiday park. A low, long, cream-coloured building and neat ranks of caravans occupied a thin stretch of land under the brow of the hill, edging onto a rock-strewn beach.

A sign pointed towards the reception and a visitor car park, and as Clare lined up her car in one of the spaces, a door in the building to her left opened and a woman in a black suit and white blouse walked out. She had sleek black hair to her shoulders, and her thin face was shaped with concern.

'You the police?' she asked. Then without waiting for an answer, carried on talking nervously. 'We spotted the car the other day. Thought it was someone who had a friend who was a resident, you know? But then we realised it hadn't moved for nearly a week, which is unusual. There's lots to see round about here, you know? People tend to go out driving. Maybe go along to Culzean or something?'

Clare felt a spot of rain spark on her forehead. The sky directly above her was getting darker. She looked out to sea, towards Ailsa Craig and beyond, to the hills of Arran, and round the sweep of sea to the right, where the horizon was slung with the low hills of north Ayrshire. In that direction the sun held an amber glow that was growing through the clouds.

'Sunsets must be amazing here.' She smiled at the woman, trying to relax her.

'Spectacular,' she agreed.

'Is there somewhere we can talk before the rain hits?' Clare asked. 'I'll try to get out of your hair as soon as I can.'

A nod. 'My name's Amy, by the way. I'm the duty manager.' She seemed to be more in control now. 'If you just come with me.' She turned and walked back inside, holding the door open for Clare to follow her.

If the little office she showed Clare into was a sign of the workings of the establishment, the whole place had to be sparkling clean. A large brown corner desk sat to the right of a window looking out onto the beach, and the walls had large wooden bookcases filled with large folders. Everything regimented and in its place.

'Can I get you a coffee or a tea?' Amy asked.

'No, thank you. Just had one.'

Amy pointed to the spare seat at the desk, and they both sat.

'Who discovered the car?' Clare asked.

Amy nodded. Hands in her lap, fingers entwined. 'Gary Sheils. He's our odd-job man – jack of all trades, kinda guy.'

'Can I speak to him?'

'He's gone for today.' Amy's face fell. 'Sorry, should I have asked him to stay? I'm so sorry. We thought the details he gave to the uniformed guys would be enough.'

'Not to worry,' Clare replied. 'I just need to dot the i's and cross the t's. Give me his details and I'll get in touch later. In the meantime, if you could give me the broad strokes. How long the car was here. When it was noticed. What you found, that kind of thing. And then if I could have a look at the car itself?'

'Right. As I say, it was Gary who noticed it first. Asked if anyone knew whose car it was. Then when it hadn't moved for a couple of days he asked again. None of them knew anything. So we discreetly asked a couple of our regulars. Then it got kind of busy around here – holiday weekends and stuff tend to bring lots of people out. After the weekend was over, the car was still there, same place. So we decided we needed to do something about it. Gary had a look, saw that there was a pile of clothes in the front seat and the car keys were sitting on top of them.' Her face lengthened. 'We thought, uh-oh, this can't be good. We wondered if it was suicide.' She tugged at a strand of hair, tucking it behind her ear. 'There's a cave round the headland, and a bit of a local legend about a family of cannibals, you know? It attracts all kinds of strange people.'

'I am a local,' Clare nodded. 'So I'm aware of that.'

'Aye,' Amy nodded. 'Sawney Bean. I don't buy into the whole cannibal thing. Piece of nonsense.' She shook her head. 'But there is a strange energy down there,' she said, then, raising a well-shaped eyebrow: 'I'm sensitive to that kind of thing. How and ever, what folk don't realise is when there's a mention of the cave in the press – a new book, or a true-crime documentary, whatever – it tends to bring the nutters out. They want to find the cave and ... do whatever nutters do. There *have* been a few suicides over the years. They usually throw themselves off the top of the cliff.' She said it matter-of-factly. 'But some of them get in through our car park, go along the beach, and climb into the cave where they do whatever it is they feel they need to do.' She shuddered. 'Sometimes the tide carries them off, depending how far into the cave they go, like, and they're washed down the coast.'

'Did Gary go and check the cave, just in case?'

Amy nodded. 'Thankfully for him there was nothing, or no one, there.'

Clare stood up. 'Can you take me to the car?'

The two women left the office, and walked round the back of the building to where a silver Volkswagen Golf sat on its own. As Clare walked she noted a couple of CCTV cameras lodged just under the building's guttering.

She pointed at them. 'I'll need to see the film from those.'

'Ah,' Amy said before biting her lip.

'What's the problem? No film in them?'

'No, no, no. The car was sitting round the front of the building. The camera will just show Gary driving it round here. He thought, when he found the keys, it would be better for the punters if it wasn't on view, so he moved it round here for you guys to have a look at.'

Clare hid her disappointment. 'Means will need to take Gary's fingerprints.'

Amy's mouth was a little 'o' of surprise. 'We didn't...'

'Any other cameras around the site that might be of interest to us?'

'Doubt it. We have to be careful only to have them pointed at public areas. The few we have are trained on the doors into the communal spaces.'

'Nothing at the main gate?'

Amy shook her head. 'Sorry.'

Clare pulled a pair of blue gloves from her jacket pocket and approached the car, pulling open the driver's door. The car was filthy and the inside was almost as dirty as the outside. In the foot-well of the passenger seat she could see some rubbish, signs perhaps of the owner's last supper.

Moving to open the back door she spotted a child's booster seat, and to the side of that a couple of toys – the kind you got with a child's meal at a fast-food place. There was also a little book, a toy car, a dinosaur and some chocolate wrappers.

Back to the front seat, and among the neat pile of clothes Clare spotted a navy Harrington jacket, a white T-shirt, a pair of dark jeans, still with the belt in the loops, and in the footwell a pair of Adidas Samba trainers with a pair of black ankle socks tucked inside.

Which prompted the question: did the guy walk out of here naked and shoeless? Clare looked along the waterline and noted the rock-strewn sand. It couldn't have been easy to negotiate that with bare feet. Maybe he was past caring?

Back to the car and she noted that the way the clothes were so neat and ordered was at odds with the refuse dotted about the car's inside. There was more rubbish in the front passenger foot-well than in the back, as if the driver regularly ate while driving, throwing the packaging to the floor as he went.

There were two empty plastic water bottles, a couple of apple cores, a banana peel, clear plastic packaging for roast beef slices, and a little empty tub of Greek yoghurt. Clare cast around and spotted a spoon under the middle console. Eating in the car must be the driver's habit. She picked up the empty meat packet. It displayed a discount sticker. And a sell-by date of ten days earlier.

Clare already had a picture of someone. They were untidy and on a budget – but also deliberate in the choice of food they ate. And it didn't seem to her like this was someone eating their last supper. Who on earth would eat healthy, natural – and discounted – food before they completely stripped off, walked into the sea and killed themselves?

Chapter 58

Sylvia
January 2024

For a time, life was good for Sylvia, on the surface at least. She remained disappointed by several failed attempts at raising the Baobhan Sith, but the discarded bodies of several young men didn't bother her. What did was the fact that as she grew older, her shadow seemed to go missing from her life for months, sometimes years, at a time, and when she did reappear she would give off a dark, hateful energy, as if her invisible mouth moved in what felt to Sylvia like silent imprecations.

'What are you saying?' Sylvia would demand, but her shadow sister flitted away without response. Sylvia found that she missed her when she was gone, but was unsettled when she came back. Indeed, she was beginning to think of her shadow less as her long-lost sister, and more like her own private haunting. The word 'torments' crossed her mind more than once, but she shied away from it every time.

Her interest in dealing with her family curse was reignited by, of all people, Ben.

He called. 'Sylvia,' he said in that slow, affected, pompous voice of his, and she had to resist the urge to hang up.

'Yes.'

'Have you been watching the news lately?'

'You know I don't have a TV, Ben.'

'You do have a laptop. You've not completely abdicated from the modern age.'

'If you could get to the point, Benjamin...'

'The Bodies in the Glen case that's been all over the news? The trashier news stations are reporting that the young woman who found the bodies has some kind of psychic gift, that she's under some sort of family curse.'

Sylvia sat up. 'Oh.'

'If I remember correctly' – there was no 'if' about it, Ben had a faultless memory – 'your grandmother's journal mentioned a place up north, on the Ardnamurchan peninsula?'

'Right?' Sylvia felt a surge of expectancy.

'Well, the young woman connected to the case found the bodies in that area, and apparently that's where she was brought up. Might it be related to your own family curse?'

'What was her name?' Sylvia asked.

'Here's where it gets strange – or convenient, if you want to follow this up.'

'Ben,' she said, biting down on her impatience. 'Get on with it.'

'It appears she's a relative – a cousin or something – of that useless piece of shit who got my daughter pregnant. Damien Fox.'

'Really?' That was useful, Sylvia thought. 'Now, Ben, are you going to get on with it and tell me who she is?'

'Her name,' he replied, after a suitable pause, '...is Annie Jackson.'

Chapter 59

Lewis

From several cars behind, Lewis watched as Corrigan turned into a holiday park at the far end of the Bennane headland.

'X marks the spot,' Annie said, turning her head to keep her eyes on Corrigan's car as they passed by the holiday-park entrance.

'Strange,' Lewis said. 'Who would go into a holiday park to abandon their car?' Wouldn't you choose somewhere with less people about?'

'Exactly what I was thinking,' Annie replied.

'There was a sign a way back for a parking spot near a war memorial. Let's go there and wait a wee while.' His thinking was that they'd give it an hour then make their way to the holiday park and see who would be happy to talk to them.

Once they'd parked up, Lewis pulled out his phone and searched for the holiday park that Corrigan had driven into. The website was pretty slick, promised quality accommodation and spa facilities, and proudly offered access to a private beach that led to the famous cave where the legendary cannibal Sawney Bean once lodged with his multiple offspring.

'Hey, did you know Sawney Bean, the cannibal, lived down there?' he said to Annie.

His next search was for the cannibal family itself, and that delivered a tale straight from a horror movie. The article was sketchy on the dates, suggesting Bean was alive sometime in the fifteenth century. He and his wife, charmingly known as Black Agnes, relocated to the south-west coast of Scotland from the Lothians, and here he found a hideaway that allowed him access to passing travellers. Who he killed, pillaged, and then ate their flesh. By the time the Beans were caught – twenty-five years later – he and Agnes had reputedly bred eight sons and six daughters. And those children had grandchildren of their own – eighteen grandsons and fourteen granddaughters.

The dangerous brood took on one too many victims and were discovered, and the king ordered they be rounded up and brought to Edinburgh for execution. The men were gelded, their hands and feet cut off, and allowed to slowly bleed to death before their corpses were thrown on a huge pyre. The women were forced to watch all of this before they themselves were fed to the flames.

Lewis looked up from his phone and along the coast. All of that supposedly happened in a sea cave just along the coast from where they sat?

'God, that's grim,' Annie said when he'd finished reading the article to her. 'I need some fresh air after that.' And she got out of the car.

Lewis joined her and they both leaned against the bonnet, taking in lungfuls of the salted air. They looked over at the memorial and beyond, to the galleon clouds breezing across the sky, the distant hills of Arran, and then closer, at the waves approaching the coastline. As they watched a fat seal hauled itself out of the water and onto a table-topped rock, completely uncaring that a human was within throwing distance.

The sound of a car braking, the crack and pop of tyres on the gravel, and he turned half expecting – or perhaps, hoping – it to be Detective Corrigan. But it was a black BMW, a man in dark glasses behind the steering wheel.

Craig Oldfield.

Lewis stepped away from his car, bunching his keys in his fist, with the longest one poking out from between two knuckles. Last time, Craig's lackey took him by surprise. Now he was prepared, and willing to give as good as he got. In fact, a large part of him hoped something did kick off, because he relished the idea of giving Craig some of his own medicine.

'Lewis,' Annie muttered. 'There's a police officer just up the road. Don't be getting caught up in anything stupid.'

'The man had me attacked the other day, Annie.' Lewis set his jaw. 'He'll not find me such an easy target this time.'

Craig Oldfield parked his car beside Lewis's, leisurely reversing into the space as if sending a message: you mean nothing to me. He got out of his car, looked over at Lewis and smiled. All teeth and bravado.

'Hey, prick,' he said as he marched over. 'You fucking stupid or something?' He was walking like the school-playground bully, arms wide, chest puffed out.

'I don't know what you mean.' Lewis paused. 'Craig, isn't it? We haven't been properly introduced.' Lewis held his hand out for a handshake he knew wasn't coming. He felt a surge of adrenaline, noted a swirl in his gut.

'You were told to keep your big nose out of things that didn't concern you.' Craig's face knuckled into a fist.

'Where's Damien?' Lewis asked, taking a step closer to him.

Craig stepped back. Blinked, bit his lip. Then, as if he remembered the part he was playing, he puffed his chest up. 'How the fuck should I know?'

'Did you knock him out and push him into the sea like you did with Rose Russell?'

'What the fuck are you talking about, dickhead? Rose who?' He bared his teeth. 'The woman who washed up on the beach down the road? For the record, I don't hit women.'

He looked off to the side, and something flashed in his eyes. He knew something, Lewis was sure of it.

Then Craig smiled. 'But nosey arseholes like you are fair game as far as I'm concerned.'

'I thought you got your mates to do your dirty work for you.'

Craig looked at the side of Lewis's face. 'You should get that seen to, mate. Looks nasty.'

'What are you scared of, Craig?' Lewis asked.

'I'm not scared of anything, mate.' Craig seemed slightly discomfited by the fact that Lewis didn't appear to be cowed by him.

'We're all scared of something, Craig,' he said. 'You followed me and my sister out of town the last time we were here. You had someone attack me in Glasgow...'

'Don't know what you're talking about.' Grin. And another glance at the bruises on Lewis's face.

'You were scared what Rose might have told me. Is that why

you got rid of Damien? Did he threaten to go to the police about what you did back in the day?'

If it was possible, Craig Oldfield's expression darkened further. 'You'd better watch what accusations you throw around, mate.'

'Why, what are you worried about?'

'Told you,' Craig snarled. 'I'm not worried about anything.'

'Then why are you here? Why follow us into this car park?'

'Just take my advice, prick. Stop asking questions and get the hell out of this town.'

Lewis laughed. 'Is this when you walk away into the nearest saloon and slug a shot of whisky while the wee guy plays piano in the corner?'

'You're fucking addled, mate.' Craig pointed at his temple with an index finger. 'Something's wrong with you.'

'You're a murderer, Craig Oldfield, and I'm going to prove it.'

'Fuck off.'

'Maybe I'll take a drive back into town. Go see that sister of yours and ask her what she knows about you and Rab Daniels joyriding all those years ago.'

'You go near my sister...' Craig was in Lewis's face, grabbing his collar, his breath a stale mix of garlic and mint, voice tuned to a low growl. 'And I'll fucking end you.'

Lewis tensed, moved to strike, but before he could connect, he felt someone pull at him.

It was Clare Corrigan. He'd not even heard her car pull up.

She stepped in closer, put a hand on each of their shoulders and pushed. 'What's going on?'

'I was just minding my own business, and this guy goes mental,' Craig said.

'That's not true, Detective Corrigan,' Annie piped up. 'This guy followed us in here, looking for a fight.'

'Yeah. I was just standing here, admiring the view,' Lewis added.

'Craig.' Clare tilted her head to him. 'Leave.' Her voice was soft and deliberately low in energy. 'Lewis – I recommend you do the same.'

Craig spat on the ground. Pointed at Lewis, his finger only inches from his face, hate large in his eyes. Then without another word, he walked away, got in his car and drove off. The powerful vehicle surged away so quickly the air was sprayed with pebbles.

Lewis became aware how fast his heart was pumping. His muscles were shaking with the release of adrenaline.

'Well?' Clare demanded, eyebrows high. 'I thought I told you guys to go home?'

It appeared to Lewis that there was a familiarity in the way Corrigan spoke to Craig Oldfield. 'How do you know him?' he asked.

She paused for a beat, as if debating whether or not to answer. 'Our paths have crossed.'

Lewis breathed slowly, deeply, trying to get back to some sense of self. He felt the breeze on his face. The ground under his feet. Breathed again.

Then something snagged in his mind. The moment he accused Craig of pushing Rose into the sea a strange look had filled the man's eyes.

His mind whirred, and before he knew it he was asking, 'Craig reported seeing the body. Rose. He said he found her, didn't he?'

The reaction was blindingly fast, and Lewis almost missed it, but there was a flash in Clare's eyes, an assessment as she set her jaw. 'I can't tell you that.'

'He did.' Lewis stepped away. Turned. 'The brass neck on that guy.' He shook his head. 'That fucker pushed her in and then called the cops.'

'We don't know anything of the sort,' Corrigan said. 'You can't go throwing accusations around like that.'

Annie came to stand beside Lewis. 'You have your suspicions as well, though, don't you?'

Clare looked at Annie. Her expression blank. 'Time to go home, folks.'

Lewis smiled, trying to inject some warmth and charm into his voice. 'You going to escort me out of the area?'

Clare crossed her arms. 'Let me see if I've got this right.' She squinted her eyes at him. 'You saw me go into the holiday park from your spot three cars behind me. So you thought you'd drive here, give it an hour or so, and then go to the holiday park yourselves and quiz the staff. How am I doing?'

'Well...' Shit. She'd read him like a book.

'Go home,' Clare said. 'The both of you.'

Chapter 60

Sylvia
February 2024

The phone call about Annie Jackson set Sylvia back on her heels. She'd all but put thoughts of the family curse – or whatever it was that contributed to her mother's torments – from her mind. Her energies, mental and physical, had all gone into learning about the Baobhan Sith and fine-tuning the ancient ceremony so that she could put the creature to her own use.

She put all that aside for the moment and read everything she could find about Annie: how she had fallen for a pastor, how he'd enticed her up into the hills, and how she'd fought him off when he attacked her, resulting in his death. Then the authorities found a number of buried bodies within the ruins in those hills that they were able to link to the pastor's father.

Looking at the images of Annie in the press, Sylvia saw that she was a pretty and unconventional-looking young woman who dressed with no real thought to the fashions of the day. Perhaps that's what happened when you regularly received premonitions of people dying.

Frustratingly, Sylvia could find little on the nature of Annie's curse, but one podcaster had been a good deal more diligent about her work than the national press. This site looked like it had little traffic, and was possibly more of a hobby for the woman who ran it. She was clearly obsessed with true crime, and the episode covering the Bodies in the Glen case detailed how, as a girl, Annie had warned one of the victims not to go for a ride in a red car. As to how the curse might otherwise have affected Annie, it made no mention, but this article more than any convinced Sylvia that she needed to investigate Annie Jackson further.

This was more than a coincidence, surely. Annie had this strange gift; Sylvia herself had a suggestion of otherworldly events in her family; and they both had historical links to the same geographical area of Scotland. She could feel with a certainty stronger than any she'd felt before that this meant something. Years before she had researched her own family history through Bernard Peters. He'd surely have retired or died by now. Might he have an able replacement?

A short phone call to his old offices and she was put through to another Bernard Peters – the old man's grandson. She quickly outlined what she was looking for, and he said he would need a couple of weeks to investigate.

A fortnight later and he duly called her back. 'A fascinating case, Ms Lowry-Law,' Bernard began. 'My researchers here at the practice were delighted to get away from the usual boring legal projects about—'

'Please, Mr Peters,' Sylvia cut him off. 'What did you find?'

'Having the previous research helped enormously. It quickly became apparent that your family lines do indeed converge with those of this young woman, Annie Jackson. The family split a long time ago. A very long time ago. You will recall – indeed it would be hard to forget – that there were sisters, one of whom – Jean McLean – was found guilty of being a witch? That is the side of the family you come from, as you know.' He paused. 'Annie and her family are direct descendants of her sister, Mary who married the local laird, John Campbell.'

Sylvia's heart gave a charge of excitement. She knew it.

'As far as evidence of a curse is concerned, that is harder to quantify, but we did discover that a number of women in Annie's family were confined.'

'Confined?'

'To hospital, Ms Lowry-Law. For their own safety. Nowadays it would be couched in much more friendly terms, but more than a few of them were considered to be quite mad.'

'The torments...' Sylvia muttered under her breath – and looked to the side where a small figure was wearing a light in her eyes and a smile that hinted at what that madness might look like.

When she first reached out to Annie, her aim was to explain how they had ancestors in common and a curse that looked like it affected both sides of the family. She wrote several letters to her, explaining what she'd learned and how she would like to meet with Annie to discuss it all.

None of her letters were acknowledged.

Feeling the injustice of that keenly – how could someone with such a link to her ignore what she'd written? – she decided to write one more letter and deliver it herself.

Aware of the little cottage by the loch, but unsure exactly where it was, she rented a house in the Mossgow area, and took several long walks in the area, hoping to bump into Annie. She engineered conversations with the locals about the young woman, but they all remained tight-lipped, especially when mention was made of the bodies in the hidden glen.

So she decided on a new approach. She knew that the family of the teenage girl who Annie had begged not to get into a car ran a local hotel – the Lodge on the Loch. She booked a night's stay, and while being served at the bar by the owner, she spun a lie. Told him that she was sure one of her relatives was also a victim of the local serial killer.

His eyes became moist and coloured with pain. 'I'm so sorry,' he said.

Sylvia dabbed at an eye. 'It drove my parents mad.' She read his name badge. 'It was the not knowing, Mr Burns, you understand?'

He nodded slowly. He understood. 'Please, call me James.'

With that reply she knew he was on her side.

'But that young woman? Annie something? What an amazing story.'

He straightened his back. 'She may not thank me for saying it, but she's a saint. To hold all that fear and pain in her head and not crack up?'

'What do you mean?'

'She has this gift. She calls it a curse...' At that word Sylvia's heart gave a little trill. 'She has premonitions of people dying. She warned our Jennie not to go in that car all those years ago. And she somehow knew where her body was. Can you imagine walking around with all of that stuff going on in your mind?'

'I think I'd hide from people if that was me,' Sylvia replied. 'Reduce the risk of, you know, coming across someone who's about to die, knowing you can't stop it, and knowing they won't listen if you try to tell them.'

He nodded. 'That's exactly what she does. Gets all kinds of nutters seeking her out. And the mail she gets? Mountains of the stuff.' He leaned forward. 'You'll have heard about the glen where the bodies were, and the old ruins. She has a cottage not far from there. In the middle of nowhere.'

'Wise woman.'

'She's not a total recluse, though. She has a job in a wee café over at Lochaline a couple of mornings a week.'

'The bills have to be paid somehow, I suppose.' Sylvia vowed to find the little café. There couldn't be too many in a small place like this. Then she'd wait until Annie had a break, hand over her letter and introduce herself.

Her chance came just two days later. Walking into the little café in Lochaline, Sylvia spotted Annie straight away.

Chapter 61

Clare

Clare made her way back to the office in Girvan, mind full of her encounters with Lewis and Annie Jackson, and Craig Oldfield. As she drove she put her phone on speaker and dialled Damien's mother. Officers had called on her earlier in the day, as she'd told Lewis, but it might be useful, and supportive, if Chrissie received a call from the investigating detective.

'Yes, they told me about the holiday park,' Chrissie said. 'It's the one just along from the Sawney Bean cave, isn't it?'

'Yes.'

Chrissie started to cry and in a voice punctuated by sobs she said, 'I've known people to go into the sea there. Oh my God, Damien. What have you done?' But then she rallied. 'No. I'm not buying it. No way did he kill himself. He had Bodie to live for. The wee man is his heart and soul.'

'At this point, Chrissie,' Clare said, 'we aren't able to come to any conclusions, but we will be investigating this further.'

'You really will? The other officers said that, but I wasn't sure to believe them.'

'Yes, really,' Clare said. Then left a small pause. 'There's something I'd like to ask you: I met a young man today. Lewis Jackson. He says you're paying him to investigate Damien's disappearance?'

'Well, not paying, as such. Him and Annie are my sister Mandy's kids.'

'Oh yes, Annie was there too. Although Lewis did most of the talking.'

'So you met Annie?'

'Well, yes, I did. She was there,' Clare replied, frowning a little.

'You didn't recognise her?'

'Should I have done?'

'She's *the* Annie Jackson – the psychic girl who found all those dead girls up in Ardnamurchan last year?'

'Ah. Right.' Of course she remembered that. 'So that's Lewis's sister?'

No wonder she was quiet, Clare thought. That must have been a real test of her character.

Then something turned in Clare's mind. 'So ... you're thinking that this gift Annie has will help you find Damien?'

'I'm desperate, Detective Corrigan. Desperate.' Chrissie's voice was full of emotion. The sound of sniffing came over the phone.

A thought occurred to Clare. 'Can I ask: Lewis said it was you who put him in touch with Rose Russell?'

'Oh, and the poor lassie ends up deid the very next day. Another tragedy for that family. How you come back from that as a parent is anybody's guess.' Then, as if remembering her own situation, Chrissie began to cry once more. 'Sorry....'

'No need to apologise,' Clare replied, 'But if I could ask you what Rose said to you when you contacted her? From Lewis's account she was very keen to talk to him.'

'Aye,' Chrissie said, urgency in her tone. 'She was all like, "everyone needs to know what that bastard did to our Rab".'

'That bastard being Craig Oldfield?'

'Aye.'

'Do you know if she based this on anything other than suspicion? Did she know anything concrete?'

'I'm not sure, hen,' Chrissie replied. 'I don't know any of the details. You'll need to talk to Lewis about that. But one thing's for sure, she was absolutely convinced that the Oldfield boy ran over her brother all those years ago, and she was desperate for justice to be served at last.' Chrissie sniffed again. 'I can't believe she died just a day or so after she talked to me. Poor lassie.'

A few minutes after ending the call, Clare reached the office. She parked her car, and as she walked towards the door she heard footsteps approaching and a loud, insistent voice calling her:

'Detective Corrigan?'

She turned to see a small man with a lined face and a bristle of white hair march towards her, elbows out, fists pumping as if he was on a mission. He was wearing light-grey trousers and a navy Pringle jumper stretched across his wide ball of a stomach. He was waving at her as if demanding her immediate attention. One look at his face was enough. She knew who this was.

'Detective Corrigan, a word,' he said when he reached her.

'Mr Oldfield.' Clare nodded. Whenever she saw this man, she had to fight the urge to take him down a peg or two, but knew she would never hear the end of it. Her bosses would be all over her after one phone call from this guy. Just listen to the man and walk away, she told herself.

'You're new to the office here,' he said, looking her up and down. 'How long have you been here? A year or so? But you're a local, so I suppose you might be given a little leeway.'

She held herself in check, didn't react to his little power game – letting her know he knew who she was and that his voice held a lot of sway in the area.

'It has come to my attention that someone is spreading scurrilous rumours about my son, Craig. Those rumours will not be tolerated, Detective Corrigan. Am I understood?'

She felt herself heat at this. Pompous arse. Before she knew it her mouth had taken over.

'Mr Oldfield, let me remind you that you are no longer a working lawyer. That you are an ordinary member of the public and as such it doesn't matter to me...' she paused meaningfully '... what connections you have, or who you play golf with.'

'Well, I never...' He puffed his chest out and reached up to his full five foot two inches. He took a deep breath as if to launch into a tirade, but before he could speak Clare did. But she kept her tone level, respectful.

'However, I don't listen to rumour. I follow the evidence. Much as you would have done yourself during your successful career.'

'I ... ehm ... well.' It was as if the combination of her defiance and respectful words discombobulated him.

But it didn't last long. Whatever this man was, whoever he had been, there was a sharp mind in there bent on self- and family preservation. She knew his type; small towns like this were full of them. Men and women who saw themselves as shining lights, demanding respect and constant acknowledgement of their position.

His eyes narrowed, as if his intellect was back online. 'I am reassured to hear you say that, Detective. Nevertheless, let me put this as clearly as I possibly can: me and mine are off limits. Understood?' He stared at her. His cold eyes demanding her obeisance.

'Mr Oldfield, it seems that we are in agreement,' Clare said in her agreeable tone, the one she used when she was facing down a truculent defence lawyer in court. 'We agree that rumour has no place in any investigation, but that I will go where the evidence leads.' She nodded down at him, feeling more than a little pleased at the five or so inches she had over the man. 'Pleasure to see you, Mr Oldfield,' she smiled. Gave him a nod. 'Your reputation is well earned, sir.'

When she got inside, a long-serving sergeant called Fraser Duncan was at the reception desk. He was sharp as a tack, knew everyone in the area, and was a real boon to Clare when she first accepted the position down here.

He was on the phone, nodding, saying yes repeatedly, and when he saw Clare he rolled his eyes. 'I'm noting that down, Doctor,' he said. 'Yup. Yes. If anything comes of it we'll be in touch.' He hung up. Shook his head. 'That woman just won't give up. Man!'

'Who was it?' Clare asked.

'You've never spoke to her?' Fraser asked in disbelief. 'She must phone at least once a month about your man Oldfield, there.'

'Really?'

'Says he's in a cult and he's looking to raise an ancient demon kinda thing.' He made a dismissive face. 'That him and his followers murder someone every seven years and use their blood in a ceremony.'

'Wow.' Clare chuckled.

'And the next seven-year event occurs this Halloween. So we're to watch out – another body is going to wash up on the coastline.'

'You've never charged her with wasting police time?'

'If we did that, Clare, we'd never be out of court, with all the head-bangers and complaint artists that get in touch.'

'True.'

'Thing is – you must have heard the rumours about Oldfield and his cronies up in High Dailly?'

'Of course I have. Gets on my nerves, to be honest. It's just jealousy. People like to fixate on those who have more than them.'

'I saw you getting cornered by the man himself.' Fraser nodded in the direction of the car park. 'Wasn't his boy, Craig, the good citizen who called in the discovery of Rose Russell's body?' Clare nodded. 'What did the old arse want?'

'To make sure no one impugned him or his family.'

Fraser's well-creased face shifted into a toothy grin. 'And judging by your self-satisfied demeanour, I'd say you put him in his place?'

Clare returned his smile. 'I was polite and professional.'

'Good lass,' Fraser laughed. 'Wish I could have been there to hear it. That old bastard made my life a misery when he was still on the job.'

She was about to walk on through to her desk, when she stopped, Oldfield Senior and the respect he demanded from the locals playing on her mind. 'What gives, though?' she asked Fraser. 'He's not on the job anymore.'

'What do you mean?'

'He's been retired a few years, right? Why do people still kowtow to him?'

Fraser crossed his arms. 'Who knows, lass.' He winked. 'Mibbe the raising a demon thing isn't utter nonsense, after all. Or mibbe Oldfield knows where all the bodies are buried.'

Chapter 62

Lewis

Lewis aimed his car north, towards Turnberry and the snaking line of the A77. Golf courses, hotels, and beaches with hills and pasture on one side and the silvery-grey deep of the Firth of Clyde on the other, all sliding past his car windows.

A sign read *Kirkronald*.

As he drove through this village he was surprised by the cultivated feel it had. The buildings were old, but sharply maintained. Mostly. On the way in, a hotel that sang out its link to Robert Burns and his poetry, and on the way out, a whisky shop. Scottish tourism in miniature.

The sound of deep and even breathing came from his side, and he turned to see that Annie was fast asleep, head slumped to the side, almost touching her shoulder. Must be exhausted, he thought. She'd said she barely slept last night.

His phone sounded an alert. But his phone was in the pocket of his jacket, which was draped along the backseat.

Looking ahead, he saw a lay-by just in front of a little shop. The shop front was covered in dark-grey shiplap cladding, with a pair of hanging baskets either side of the glass door. He pulled in and parked, and climbed out of the car to go into the backseat and get his phone.

Annie stirred. 'What you doing?'

'Go back to sleep. I'm just checking my phone.'

Just as he opened the back door of the car, an old woman walked past trailing a lumbering yellow Lab. She was wearing a long, waxed overcoat and the blue, patterned silk scarf covering her head was tucked in tight under her chin.

'Hurry up, Bob,' she cajoled, and with a wag the old dog upped its pace. The woman switched her attention to Lewis. Cocked her head. 'Do ah ken you, son?' she asked. 'You're awfy familiar.'

'Sorry,' Lewis replied. 'Just passing through.'

'Aye,' she said. 'But naw, you're no.' She narrowed her gaze. 'Be seeing you, son. Don't be a stranger.' And she carried on, the dog now at her heel.

Lewis smiled to himself and reached into the car for his jacket. Plucked the phone out of his pocket and checked the screen. There was a voicemail alert and a missed call from Chrissie. Apparently he had no signal here, so couldn't call her back.

He looked up and saw that the shop had its *Open* sign up, so went inside, thinking a bottle of water, and a protein bar would be in order, and he could ask about phone reception in the area.

A slim, middle-aged woman with shoulder-length grey hair was standing behind the counter. 'I see you've met our local worthy,' she smiled. 'Don't mind Ina. She's harmless.'

'Aye,' he agreed, smiling too. 'Adds a little bit of colour to the village, I imagine?'

'For sure,' the woman said fondly. 'She's a good age. Well into her eighties, and walks the dog twice a day, rain or shine.'

Lewis scanned the shop for what he wanted, carried it over to the counter. He was tempted by the scones under the glass bell jars, thinking he should buy one for Annie.

As he paid, he asked the shopkeeper about the phone signal.

'Most of the village is fine, to be fair,' she answered. 'It's just this wee bitty dip at the shop. Don't know why it causes an issue. Which way are you heading?'

'Back up to Glasgow.'

'Right. You could walk twenty yards in either direction and you'll be fine. Or, if you want to get back on the road, there's a lay-by just outside the village, before you see the big house up on the hill over to the right. The signal should be better there.'

He thanked the shopkeeper, jumped back in the car, and drove along to the lay-by, as she'd suggested.

Chrissie answered straight away. 'You've heard?' she asked.

'About Damien's car?'

'Aye,' she replied. Her voice was so soft Lewis could barely hear her. 'I think they've written him off, son,' she said. 'They think he's dumped his car and gone for a too-long swim.'

'Is that what they said?' he asked.

'As good as,' Chrissie replied. 'They were very...' She paused as if collecting her thoughts. 'Non-committal. As if they didn't want to offer me too much hope. They'll just be waiting for his body to wash back onto shore...'

'That wasn't the impression I got, Chrissie. I spoke to the detective who's looking into it, and she seemed pretty open-minded.'

'Maybe to your face, Lewis, but a mother can read these things. They think he's killed himself. But I'm no' buying it. My boy's too in love wi' his own wee boy to be doing something that drastic. I just wish ah knew where he was.' She sighed. 'You're no' going to give up on me, son, are you?'

'No, I'm not,' Lewis replied, thinking he had been on the verge of doing just that only a day ago.

After they said their goodbyes he cut the connection, then saw that he'd received an email.

He read the name of the sender with a lurch of surprise.

Excuse my presumption in contacting you in this way, Mr Jackson. The name possibly rings a bell? I am Craig Oldfield's father. It has come to my attention that you've been in town asking questions about Damien, Rose Russell and Robert Daniels. I share your concern over all three. Robert's death was a terrible event that has marked this town for years, and one can only imagine the pain his family is going through now that Rose has also recently met an untimely death.

With regards to Damien, I've known the lad for years, and as the erstwhile partner of my daughter, and the father of my grandson, he has been, frankly, a great disappointment. Despite that, I too want him found. A boy should know his father. To that end I would like us to combine our resources. I understand Christine, Damien's mother, has engaged you to look into Damien's whereabouts. I seriously doubt any money has been exchanged for your services, so let me remedy that. I will pay you £250 per day, including time spent. I'll also meet any expenses you may have, receipts pending. I'm sure you will find this generous, having worked as an accountant. But first we need to meet. My address will follow. Please be there tomorrow at ten am. And prepare to discuss tactics.

Yours,
Ben Oldfield.

Chapter 63

Lewis

Lewis read the email again, trying not to be irritated by the arrogant tone. The cash would be welcome, if the offer was genuine. But the reference to Lewis's profession was no doubt a signal: Oldfield had done his due diligence. The fact he'd also tracked down Lewis's email address told him that this was a man to watch.

Lewis got back in his car, woke up Annie and showed her the email.

'How did he get your email address?' she asked, rubbing her eyes.

'No idea.'

'And he wants to meet? Do you think that's a good idea? This is a man whose son you as good as accused of murder. And had someone beat you up. And here he's offering you a job?'

'I could just go and meet the guy and get a sense of what he's up to?'

'You're not going on your own, Lewis. This whole thing is a set-up. Oldfield Senior wants to know what we know, before he does whatever he can to protect his family name.'

Lewis read Annie's expression. If he was going to meet Oldfield, so was she.

'Okay. Is there any point in driving back up to the city, only to jump in the car first thing and come back down here?'

'What are you thinking?' Annie asked. 'We get a B&B for the night?'

'Why not?' He grinned. 'Oldfield did mention expenses.'

'And Turnberry Hotel is just back down the road a wee bit...' Annie raised her eyebrows.

'That's too cheeky even for me. Let's go back down to the wee shop and see if the owner can set us up with some digs.'

The woman in the shop smiled at them as they walked in. 'It's you again, dear,' she said to Annie. 'Back down to look at that big house?'

Lewis frowned at Annie. But she ignored him. 'Ah. Yes,' she replied. 'It is lovely.'

The shopkeeper then looked to Lewis. 'Did you get a signal for your phone okay?' she asked.

'Yes, thanks. Worked well,' he answered, still wondering about Annie looking at a big house.

'And what can I do for you now?' the shopkeeper asked.

Lewis explained what they were after. 'Ensuite, if possible. And if they do an evening meal and a giant cooked breakfast, even better.'

'I can think of a couple of places.' The woman pursed her lips in thought. 'The house you pulled up alongside at that lay-by? The one the young lady was interested in?' Lewis sent Annie another searching look. Again she ignored him. 'She sometimes takes in paying guests. It's called Summerhill Hall. She does prefer women – she often runs female-only retreats.' She shrugged. 'But my impression is that she's struggling and might not want to turn down paying guests, regardless of their chromosomes. And then there's one at the other end of town. A farmer that converted his barn into guest accommodation.' She tapped the side of her nose with her index finger. 'Let me make some calls. Can I ask your name?'

'Lewis and Annie Jackson.'

'Husband and wife?' she asked.

'Brother and sister,' Annie replied. 'Twins, actually.'

'How nice. Twins.' She clapped her hands. I'm Jo, as you know, Annie. Just give me a moment. We'll try Summerhill Hall first. You've already almost been down there so that will be easier for you.' She plucked a landline phone from its docking station on a shelf behind her. Then pushed a few buttons.

'Thanks, Jo,' Lewis replied. 'It would be cool to see inside the place. From the road it looks pretty special.'

Jo cut the connection. 'Answerphone, I'm afraid. No point in leaving a message,' she explained. 'By the time they got back to me I might have shut the shop. I close at six. I'll try Kirk Farm. See how we get on there.'

The phone rang, and rang, and also went to answerphone.

Jo hung up with a smile of commiseration. 'Turnberry's just

back there. We could try them, if you can afford it?' Her phone rang out. 'Oh. Excuse me, guys. Let me just get this.' She answered with a businesslike voice: 'Kirkronald stores, how can I help you?'

Lewis could make out a female voice speaking on the other end.

'Yes, it was me,' Jo replied. Looked at Lewis. 'I have a young man and his sister in a bit of a bind, looking for some accommodation for a night.' She listened, then she looked at them both. 'It's Kirk Farm. Would a twin room do or would you prefer to be separate?'

'Whatever they can manage,' Annie replied.

Jo relayed this, then her face brightened and she replied, 'Lovely. That's wonderful. Their names are Lewis and Annie Jackson and they'll be with you in five minutes.'

They left the shop with directions to their room for the night, jumped in the car and as Annie put her seatbelt on, Lewis asked, 'What's this about you visiting that big house, Annie?'

'What?' she asked as if distracted, but Lewis guessed she was playing for time. There was something she didn't want him to know about.

'The big house that the shopkeeper mentioned. Why were you looking at a house near here, and when did you even have the chance to do that?'

'Exactly,' Annie replied her face a mask. 'The woman's clearly got me confused with someone else. I have no idea what she's talking about.' She yawned. 'Let's get to the digs. I'm starving and I think I need an early night – we've got a big meeting tomorrow.'

Chapter 64

Lewis

Next morning, after a fitful night's sleep, Lewis was woken by Annie moving about in their shared room. He looked at his watch. It was 6:48 am.

'Why are you up so early?' he asked. 'It's not even light outside.' Annie was dressed, ready to go out.

'Couldn't sleep,' she replied. 'You know how I've been. Couldn't stay awake for days, and now I'm wide awake all night. I'm off for a walk before breakfast.'

'I'll come with.' Lewis sat up then got out of bed. 'But let me have a coffee first, eh?'

Half an hour later they were ambling through the picturesque village. As they were returning to the entrance to the farmhouse, Lewis spotted a newly familiar figure and her dog walking down the path of a little cottage that sat just back from the road.

The old woman was wearing the same scarf on her head that she'd worn the day before and the same waxed raincoat.

She beckoned them over.

'You'll be needing some tea,' she said, nodding a hello to them both.

'Ehm, we're staying at Kirk Farm. We're just going back for breakfast,' Annie replied.

'We can fit in a cup of tea first, though,' Lewis then said with a smile. He recalled the shopkeeper telling him the old woman's name. 'Ina, isn't it?'

She smiled in reply and then stepped closer to Annie, an unreadable expression on her face. 'Didn't expect to see you here again, dear.'

'You must have me confused with someone else,' Annie replied, her face drawn.

'Don't stand there gawking, guys,' Ina said, then turned and started to walk back up the path. 'This way.' The dog looked up at her, and with a resigned almost human sigh, as if well used to his owner's eccentricities, followed her up to the cottage.

'That's two people hereabouts that have mistaken you for someone else,' Lewis said to Annie under his breath. 'What's going on?'

'I think we should just go back to the farm for breakfast,' Annie replied. 'We don't have that much time before we go to meet Oldfield.'

'Annie,' Lewis insisted. 'What's going on with you? When did you meet Ina and ask about the big house? And why is it all such a secret?'

'The kettle's not long on,' Ina shouted back up the path to them.

'Some other time, maybe,' Annie replied to Ina, taking a step back. 'We really should be going.'

'Coming,' Lewis shouted in his turn. Then raised his eyebrows to Annie and whispered, 'If you won't tell me, then I'll have to find out from her what this is all about, won't I?' And he strode up the path, leaving Annie little option but to do likewise.

Lewis, with Annie trailing him, followed Ina into the house, through a door off the hall and into a little sitting room. Its small window faced the road, and there was a large fireplace on one wall, crowded by two dark-green leather armchairs and a matching sofa. A dark wooden dresser was stationed at the back wall, its shelves tight with books, fronted by rows and rows of skulls in all shapes, sizes and colours, a couple even studded with rhinestones.

The dog circled on the rug in front of the unlit fireplace and lay down, his eyes never leaving his owner.

'Tea,' Ina announced. 'Bob. Stay.' The dog stared from Lewis to Annie as Ina left the room.

Weak light came in the small window, reflecting off a gilded mirror above the fireplace. As he looked around, Lewis saw that every space in the room held some sort of framed image. Lewis wondered if any of them were the little woman's ancestors – black-and-white and sepia photographs of people with formal, dark clothing, stiff smiles and stiffer backs. Not one of them, that he could see, held a resemblance to her. There was one in an oval frame: a man with a tall black hat, sharp cheekbones and a white handlebar moustache. In another, a woman sat in a dark dress with a high white collar; for some reason she was holding a small goat under one arm, while she held a knife in her free hand. There were also sketches and paintings of ruined castles, sea caves, and kirkyards stubbled by graves, and between the pictures, protruded ornate sconces, each of them holding a melted candle.

As he turned, surveying the room, he studied the books on the dresser. From the spines on show the books looked to be a mix of the antique and the modern. Titles shone out like warnings – *The Dark Side of History*, *Encyclopaedia of Occult Murder*, *Scottish Ghosts* – and a few of them had the same author. He peered closer to read the name a little better.

'Can we just go...?' Annie hissed at him.

'Hang on,' he said as he bent forward and read. 'Dr T. Hetherington's been busy.'

'Lewis,' Annie hissed again. 'Let's go.' But it was too late. Ina returned, bearing a tray.

She had divested herself of her coat and scarf and was wearing a blue tartan skirt and had a navy wool shawl over her shoulders. She placed the tray with two cups of tea on it down on top of a low table. 'Sit down, you two,' she said. 'And drink up.'

Lewis looked down at the cups, suddenly unsure; why had he just blithely followed this strange woman into her house? They had no idea who she was, or what she wanted.

'Don't worry,' Ina said, reading where his eyes had gone. '*I'm* not going to poison you.'

The way she stressed the words 'I'm' gave Lewis a moment's pause. What had he gotten them both into? The woman in the room was very different to the one they'd met out on the street. Gone was the bowed back and the distracted manner, and in its place a pair of stern, clear eyes and a fixed jaw. 'What do you—?' he began.

'Why did you invite us in here?' Annie interrupted.

Ina studied Annie. 'Didn't I tell you before that there was nothing here for you?'

Annie shot Lewis a look, and he could see in her eyes that she knew now that she'd been caught out. But what was she hiding from him?

Ina took a seat in an armchair – it took her a while to lower herself into it – then she gestured to the sofa and they both sat down.

Lewis picked up a cup and sipped at the tea uncertainly.

'You've seen some strange things, or heard some strange things, eh?' Ina leaned back into her chair as she looked at him. 'There's more in this world than our senses tell us about, Lewis. But you know that already, don't you?' Now she was looking deep into Annie's eyes. 'You both know that.'

'How do you know my name?' Lewis asked.

'There's no jiggery-pokery there,' she replied. 'I asked Jo in the shop if she knew you.' A dry, rattly laugh sounded in her throat. She shook her head, then held Lewis's gaze for a long moment. 'Whatever I say you're not going to believe. It's as clear as that confused look on your face, son. But, nonetheless I feel I must try.'

She then stared at Annie again.

'You have the gift, lass,' she said, her eyes heavy with empathy. 'That's not some kind of divination, by the way. I recognise you from the news this last year. And if you're Annie Jackson...' She looked to Lewis. 'You must be her brother, Lewis Jackson.' Her smile was soft now, like a condolence. 'Your gift, Annie. It's a terrible thing.' She paused a beat. 'I'm not sure I can offer you any advice. I'm sure you've long since discovered that the best lessons are the ones we learn for ourselves.'

She closed her eyes for a long moment – so long that the silence became uncomfortable.

'There's things I know,' she began. 'Things that would make you despair of human nature. Things that if I told you them, you'd be phoning the men with the white coats and the straitjacket.'

She pushed herself to her feet with a groan. And even in the dim light Lewis could see there was something swimming across the film of her eyes. A very real fear Lewis had not seen there before, and again Lewis regretted accepting her invitation. This had all become just so very strange. And he still wasn't sure why Annie seemed to have been here before.

Ina looked at Lewis now, her eyes piercing his. In response he felt a shot of fear as if she had somehow transferred the emotion to him. 'I brought you both in here,' she said, 'to talk to you. To deliver a warning that you would have dismissed as nonsense if I had talked to you out there. Here...' she looked around herself, arms by her side, hands up '...you can see that I'm a serious person.'

She drew herself up to her full, modest height. Her back as straight as a poker.

'You are both in very real danger. You need to leave this place and never come back. And you need to leave now.'

Lewis had no doubt she fully believed what she was saying. Her hands dropped to her sides and her face was wreathed in shadow, the weak light in her eyes hinting at a complicity in something that would haunt her for the rest of her life.

Chapter 65

Annie

After they left Ina's house, neither of them spoke until they were back on the road and nearly at Kirk Farm.

'Well, that was intense,' Lewis said.

Annie gave him a little punch. 'What were you thinking, Lewis? That was mental.'

'I was thinking,' he retorted, 'that you were hiding something from me, and going in to Ina's might force you to tell me what was going on.'

'I don't know what to make of it at all,' Annie said, carefully not answering the question in his comments.

He shook his head. 'I'm not sure either. I can't decide whether she's a deluded old woman or we should take what she said seriously. I'm sorry I forced you in there. It could have turned out a lot worse.' They'd reached the gate to the farm, and he stopped and turned to face her. 'But you still haven't told me how both the shopkeeper and Ina came to meet you.'

Annie closed her eyes for a moment, still unsure why she was so reluctant to tell Lewis anything about the house, or indeed the dreams she'd been having. Maybe it was because she still hadn't made any sense of it all, or because she was sure she'd sound just as strange to Lewis as the old woman they'd just left.

'You know I tell you everything, Lew...' she began.

'Eventually.' His tone was one of resignation.

She smiled. Nodded. 'I knew you'd understand. I just need to work out what's happening – and then I'll tell you what you need to know,' she said. 'Okay?' She wasn't sure she could trust what was happening to her with anyone – not even Lewis.

The drive from Ina's village to the Oldfield house had only taken twenty minutes or so, the scenery along the coast now becoming familiar to Annie, but once they turned off the main route and drove up a long hill, the surroundings became a little more rarified. There were high, trimmed hedges, ancient trees, and here and there eight-foot-tall gates, suggesting the houses behind them were large and grand. At one bend, when Lewis slowed to allow a tractor through, Annie spotted a tall, crow-stepped turret.

'Very posh,' Annie said. 'Do you think this is where the rich folks live?' Her question was answered by the sight of a dark-blue Bentley approaching them from the opposite direction.

'This is different,' Lewis said when they finally coasted up a long drive to the Oldfield home.

The house looked like a student architect had brainstormed the brief 'create a big house that looks like a wedding cake'. The three-tiered construction was not what Annie expected Oldfield Senior to live in. The walls were all white, and the tiers, each a little smaller than the one below, was topped off by a wraparound walkway with a dark-green balustrade. As Annie stepped out of the car and surveyed the surroundings she thought the architect had been spot on by giving the inhabitants a 360-degree view. The house sat on top of a hill, like a castle might have once upon a time, with panoramas down and along the coast, and inland to the hills of South Ayrshire and beyond.

Lewis parked and turned in his seat to face his sister.

'So how do you want to play this?' Annie asked, saying it before he did.

'I'm pretty sure the old man has invited me here on a fishing expedition – he wants to know what I know about Damien and Craig so he can do some sort of damage-limitation exercise.'

'That's presuming we're right about what has actually happened,' Annie warned.

Lewis nodded. 'Fair enough,' he replied. 'No assumptions. We keep open minds, and we give nothing away about what we know.' He looked up at the building. 'Let's go.'

The front entrance was an oak double door with a portico and weathered stone lions on either side. They didn't match the white walls of the house, and she thought they said a lot about the ego they might find inside.

Oldfield was standing at the front door in a pair of lime-green golf trousers and a white, short-sleeved polo shirt, its tightness showing how out of shape the little man was. The massive head of a gold designer watch weighed down his wrist.

As Annie took the man's measure – and instantly disliked what she saw – she realised the assessment was being returned. Going by the raised eyebrow and thin, tight line of Oldfield's mouth, she and Lewis were being just as harshly judged.

'You'll be the famous Annie Jackson?' Oldfield gave Annie a little nod.

Annie tried to see a resemblance between father and son, and could only think that the father had twice the attitude and double the inflated ego.

'Lewis,' Oldfield then said. No question in the statement. He'd clearly done his research and knew what Annie and Lewis looked like. 'This way.' He turned and walked inside.

They followed him through a short passageway and another set of double doors, into a square hallway, the floor covered in black and white tiles, the walls lined to shoulder height with oak panelling, and a staircase in the far corner that led up to a wraparound balcony. She looked up and saw that this was repeated on the floor above; so there were wraparound walkways on the inside and the outside of the house.

'This is very ... grand,' Annie said. It was too much for her. Would likely give her a headache staying here for a day, but she could see how it fitted with the character of the owner.

Oldfield took them through another set of double doors into a bookcase-lined study. A large desk faced the doors, and beyond that a wide window flooded the room with light. It occurred to Annie that it was odd that someone would sit with their back to the view, but then she realised the desk was positioned to create maximum effect when someone entered the room: this was the seat of power.

As if reading her thoughts, Oldfield took up position behind the expanse of the desk in a green, highbacked leather chair. He motioned for Lewis and Annie to sit on the more modest seats facing him.

The desk top had an inlay of green leather with a gold filigree border, a laptop sat off to one side, on the opposite corner an old phone on a cradle, and a gold-framed photograph of a woman and child that Annie recognised as Oldfield's daughter, Alison, and her little boy, Bodie. She noted that the photo was angled towards the visitor seats rather than at Oldfield.

Annie opened her mouth to comment on the view, but Oldfield held up a hand, index finger pointing up. 'Tea or coffee? One might as well observe the niceties.'

'Coffee.' Lewis didn't bother with a 'please', presumably matching the older man's briskness.

'Tea,' Annie said.

Oldfield reached for the desk phone, dialled and barked, 'Two coffees. Cream for mine. And a tea.' Then he hung up. 'You found the place, okay?' He sat back in his seat, hands curved over his capacious stomach, fingertips barely touching.

'It's quite the house,' Lewis replied. 'Visible from miles around.'

'It was an Italian designer,' Oldfield said. 'The man who built it used to own a chain of furniture stores. He went bankrupt during the last banking crisis and we got the house for a steal.'

'One man's misfortune...' Lewis said, matching the other man's stance.

Oldfield studied him, as if trying to decide if there was an insult couched in Lewis's comment. He then gave a little shake of his head, and to Annie's mind that meant Oldfield didn't care either way.

'Quite,' he replied. Then he turned his gaze to Annie, and after just two seconds Annie felt the need to take a bath.

'I followed your case closely, Annie,' he said. 'That must have been some experience.'

'It was,' Annie replied.

The door opened behind them, and Annie heard someone enter.

'The drinks have arrived.'

Annie turned and to her surprise saw that it was the man's son, Craig.

'Lewis. You two have met, I believe?' Oldfield Senior said.

Craig leaned past Lewis and Annie and placed the tray of drinks on the desk.

Lewis shot Annie a look of surprise over Craig's back.

'Help yourself, Lewis,' Oldfield said when his son stepped away. 'Annie. Here you go.' He pushed a cup towards her. She picked it up and sipped. And was reminded of the cup of tea she had at Alison Oldfield's, made by her mother. And, it suddenly occurred to her, when she'd had this tea at Summerhill Hall. It *was* tea, but there were notes of earth, ginger, and honey, and something she struggled to name. Mushroom?

Oldfield nodded to his son, 'Sit.' Then he looked at Lewis and Annie. 'You have mobile phones?'

They nodded.

'Then please put them on the desk. I'd like to see that you are not using them to record this conversation.'

Annie pulled out her phone, wishing they'd been experienced enough to think of doing just that. She switched it off and sat it on the desk in front of her; Lewis did likewise.

'Craig owes Lewis an apology,' Oldfield said.

'I do?' Craig asked. He looked cowed and unhappy, rather than just his usual aggressive self.

'You most assuredly do.'

Annie could see Craig's jaw muscles working, his right knee jackhammering up and down. 'Sorry.' He flicked his eyes to the side, then looked to the floor.

'Once more, with feeling?' Lewis said, biting down on a smile of satisfaction.

Craig glared a *fuck you* at him.

'What exactly,' Lewis asked, 'are you apologising for? Chasing me out of town? Having your friend attack me in Glasgow?'

Craig jumped forward in his seat as if preparing to launch

himself at Lewis. But a bark from his father had him slouch back, and he did it so readily Annie wondered if he was just playing a part. What was going on here?

'Lewis,' Oldfield Senior said with calm assurance, 'I would like this meeting to go smoothly, and I think you would too. Your comments are frankly slanderous and could see you in court. Now...' He looked from Lewis to Annie and back again. 'Why are you both here?'

'You invited us,' Lewis replied.

'And you accepted. Why? You have a dim view of my son, and an exaggerated idea of what he's capable of; so why would you come into the lion's den?'

Annie sat up, something about the cool, detached way the man spoke sending her signals of alarm. Were they in danger here? She looked from the father to the son and noted the urbane, relaxed demeanour of the older man and the blanched, for now, aggression of the younger. She tried to home in on her murmurs – but they were silent. What she did feel was a strange thirst. She picked up her cup and drank some more.

'My cousin is missing,' Lewis was explaining. 'My contacts tell me they – Craig and Damien – have a past. I want to know if Craig has anything to do with Damien vanishing.'

The father looked to the son. 'Did you have anything to do with Damien going missing?'

'Did I fuck.'

'Honestly, if bluntly, put,' Oldfield said, his hands clasped before him. Annie had an image of him in court, in complete control of his milieu.

'That's hardly conclusive.' Lewis turned to Craig. 'When did you last see Damien?'

Craig shrugged. 'Maybe six months ago, at the wee man's birthday.'

'But you spend a lot of time at your sister's, I assume?' Annie said.

'I do. What of it?' Craig demanded.

'Damien was down there every weekend, so it's hard to believe, given you were good pals at one point, that your paths didn't cross more often.'

'Asked and answered,' his father said.

Annie saw Lewis bristle at the old man's dismissiveness. 'We're hardly in a court of law, mate,' Lewis said, and Annie guessed that Lewis's tone was designed to annoy Senior, but what she didn't expect was to see his son smirk in response.

Interesting. The two of them weren't exactly on the same page.

'What did you both talk about when you met?' Lewis asked Craig.

'This and that,' Craig answered. 'The football. Bodie. Who we were shagging, that kind of stuff.'

Annie heard Oldfield chastise his son for his uncouth language, but the words weren't clear. Her head was suddenly feeling thick and foggy, and she was struggling to focus. Lewis was speaking now; she tried to tune in to what he was saying.

'...and a short while later Rab gets killed in a hit and run.'

A look passed between the father and the son. It was a fleeting moment, but Annie did manage to note it through her mental fog. And then thought perhaps she'd imagined it. There was a little mist at the edges of her vision.

Lewis was still talking. She understood scraps. 'Whatever passed between Craig and Rab is lost to us ... the one person who could have told us Rose Russell ... meets with us decades later ... is too frightened to tell us ... next day she drowns on a swim she routinely took.'

Lewis raised his voice, making Annie snap to: 'And guess who phoned the police to report the body?' He nodded over at Craig. 'This fella here. Hell of a coincidence.'

Craig looked about ready to burst. Annie was sure if the old man wasn't here that Craig would have attacked Lewis by now. But then she caught a glare Craig aimed at his father in a moment when he was sure the old man wasn't looking at him. Interesting. It was clear father and son were at odds with each other. Oldfield Senior was confident that Craig was under his control, but Craig looked like he was straining against that leash.

Another glance, another glare by Craig; one that was full of hate, and it occurred to her that it wasn't Lewis Craig wanted to attack – it was his father.

As she studied the Oldfields, trying to work them out, her head swam. The feeling of fatigue increased. She reached for her cup again, and paused. Could there be something in it?

Her murmurs sounded. A weak noise at first, but the cackles built until they dominated her mind. She felt nausea, and that tell-tale tightness in a band across her forehead. Someone in the room would die, she knew. She saw a knife, a face so distorted in pain that it was unrecognisable, and a spray of blood.

Oldfield. But which one? She looked from one to the other. Both their faces were shimmering, skin and muscle shrinking back to bone.

'You okay, Annie?' She was aware that Lewis was talking to her. She ignored him and tried to focus in on what her curse was trying to tell her. But then it faded. All of it – the pain in her head, the murmurs, and the sense of violence.

Which of these men was going to die? She looked from one to the other again and received no sign. Perhaps, she thought, decisions were yet to be made, actions leading to reactions yet to unfold. But she felt sure the life of one of these men was in the balance.

Oldfield Senior was talking now: 'None of what you just said is actionable, Lewis. It's all easily refuted.' He relaxed into his chair, his gaze fixed over Annie's shoulder.

Lewis turned to her, and through a blur she could see his face was worried. 'Annie? You okay...? Annie?'

A shadow passed across Annie's line of sight. There was

someone else in the room. When had they come in? A hand came down. Landed on the back of Lewis's neck. Metal glinted in the light, and he jumped as if shocked.

The room swam, the light narrowed, Annie's pulse raced. She thought she might be sick, but she needed to sleep.

And then, before dark descended she heard Craig demand, 'Mum, what have you done?'

Chapter 66

Lewis

Lewis heard a shout in his mind. 'Lewis!' He stirred, confused, mind a muddle, and he woke to the smell of burning, and the worst headache he'd ever experienced.

He groaned, rubbed at his forehead. Water. He needed water.

The smell of burning asserted itself. Something was on fire. Where was he?

Information arrived in pieces. The cushioned seat. The steering wheel under his fingertips.

Heat, and smoke.

Flame.

Groggy. Everything in slow motion.

'Lewis. Move.'

Lewis looked to the passenger seat. It was empty. He turned. Slowly. Very slowly. The backseat was empty too. But she'd sounded so real. As if she was right there. How could Annie be here, but not here?

'Get out of the car.'

Smoke billowed from the bonnet. Flames licked up from under the console. The heat on Lewis's legs was building.

Finally, the gravity of his situation impressed itself into his mind. Adrenaline surged. His mind cleared. Smoke in his lungs.

He coughed, and as he coughed, he tried to bring his right hand up to his mouth, but he couldn't. Confused, he looked down and saw it was fastened fast to the steering wheel by a heavy-duty, black plastic grip tie.

Shit.

He pulled.

Nothing.

He pulled again.

The plastic dug into the soft flesh of his wrist. It was painful, and the tie wouldn't give way.

The flames grew. Smoke built. He coughed, a long fit, his lungs squeezing and wrenching from the noxious fumes. With his free hand he pulled up the neck of his T-shirt and covered his mouth. The coughing wouldn't stop. His throat was sore, lungs aching, eyes stinging. He banged on the steering wheel in panicked frustration. Pressed the horn.

Screamed, 'Help.'

'Help!' he shouted. 'Help!'

But there was no one there. He was on his own, and he was going to die. Sweet Jesus. He didn't want to die. No, no, no, no, no.

Desperately he tugged at the steering wheel, then he began to rock it back and forth as hard as he could. He wasn't going to die. Not here. Not now.

It was becoming increasingly difficult to see, to breathe, to think. Heat was building. The noise of the flames a warning to every cell in his body. How long did he have? Minutes? Seconds?

Panic was all. Fear surging. He rocked the steering wheel hard. Harder. Nothing was happening.

The window. He needed to break the window. Get some air in. But it was his right arm that was restrained. He swivelled, pulled up his legs and with all of his might kicked out at the passenger window. He was wearing solid shoes and it quickly cracked. He kicked again. It cracked some more.

Another harsh, lung-rending coughing fit. Pain sharp across

his head. Eyes clenched tight, he kicked again, this time it broke, and sweet oxygen leaked into the car. But it wasn't nearly enough to displace the smoke streaming in from the engine.

He was aware only of the heat, the flames, his brain screaming danger. His lungs spasmed again, continuously coughing, gasping for air the moment the coughing ceased, but nothing was coming in apart from more smoke.

How long did he have? He couldn't think. Lack of air was shutting him down. He could barely move his arms.

Weak. So very weak.

Annie. Where was Annie?

Pinioned fast.

He was so tired he could barely lift his arm.

Everything was closing down to a pinprick of light, and a long, slow, shuddering wheeze as he fought for one last breath.

Chapter 67

Lewis

Darkness hung over him like a sodden blanket.

Annie, Lewis thought. Where are you, Annie?

If only he knew where she was and if she was okay.

Then.

Movement at his side.

The door wrenched open. Hands reached in. Cut the plastic, grabbed his arm and pulled him, pulled him, pulled him out of the car and onto the grass.

Pulling him further away from the car; from danger.

'Jesus, you're heavy,' someone said, struggling, panting. 'C'mon, man, got to get you out of here.' Lewis became aware of hands gripping his wrists; his back, his buttocks, his calves and heels being dragged across rock and earth.

He was released and he turned over, made it onto his knees, coughing, gasping, breathing, eyes stinging, vision blurred.

A hand on his back, thumping. 'Get some air in there, man.'

Lewis looked up to thank his saviour. Eyes screwed against the sting of smoke, he could make out a male figure outlined against the daylight, indistinguishable through his streaming eyes. In between coughs he gulped at the air; sweet oxygen.

'I'm so sorry, man,' his rescuer was saying. 'I'm so fucking sorry.'

He looked up to say, *you just saved me, why are you apologising?* when he finally made out the identity of his Good Samaritan.

'Craig?' he croaked.

Chapter 68

Lewis

Lewis stared at Craig in disbelief. Acutely aware of how close he had come to dying.

'What the fuck?' he croaked. 'How did I end up in that car?'

'I'll tell you everything, but first we need to get you to a hospital. Your lungs could be permanently scarred or something. There was a hell of a lot of smoke.'

'I'm not going anywhere until you tell me what's going on...' Lewis blinked several times, trying to clear his eyes.

Last he remembered, he was in the Oldfield house. In the office with Annie. He turned around, looking for her. Had she been in the car with him? Panic tightened his chest. Pain pulsed throughout his body.

'Where's Annie?' he asked. He coughed. Hard. 'Annie?' he repeated and this forced another bout of coughing. He held a hand to his head.

'Annie's fine, dude. She's fine.'

Lewis looked at Craig, and was reassured to read nothing but honesty in his face and was filled with relief. 'How did I end up in...?' He coughed some more. His lungs and his head felt as if they were filled with shards of broken glass. 'Got any water?' he managed once the pain abated a little.

'Here,' Craig pulled him to his feet. 'There's a wee stream over there. Maybe having a drink and washing your eyes out will help.'

Lewis allowed Craig to guide him over a small fence, past a thicket of trees, down a small slope to a river bank, where Lewis got to his knees and sluiced water over his face. Finally, the stinging stopped. Lewis caught some water in his palms and fed it to his mouth, swirled it around and spat it out, then swallowed some, feeling the blessed relief of a clean mouth and clear eyes. He had another coughing fit.

'We need to get you to the hospital, dude.'

Lewis slumped onto the grass and lay back. There was a light fall of rain – a smirr, as Mandy used to call it – and he enjoyed the touch of it on his face.

And being alive. He breathed deeply and slowly. He could have died. He thought of the flames. He could have died in agony.

'You're going to go from nearly frying to having a cold,' Craig insisted. 'Let's at least get inside my car.'

Lewis looked at him, feeling a surge of gratitude. Craig, who he'd thought of as one of the worst examples of manhood he'd ever come across, had just risked his own life and pulled him out of a burning car. Another thought suggested itself to him: that he'd probably been involved in setting fire to the car in the first place. He shook his head, and pain burst through again.

'Fuck,' he massaged his forehead. 'My head is killing me.'

'Hospital, man. Now,' Craig said, and pulled him to his feet.

'Wait a minute. I can't make sense of this. You clearly...' A fresh bout of coughing disturbed what he was about to say. 'You and your dad tried to kill me. Then you save me? What the fuck is going on?'

'In the car, dude. And I'll tell you everything that I can.'

Once inside Craig's BMW, Lewis sank into the plush cushion of the seat and looked over at his own car. As they'd walked past it, the heat was incredible, and the noxious fumes made him start coughing all over again. Once more he thought about how close he'd come to dying. A sob bubbled up his throat and out of his mouth.

Craig cast him a glance. 'Jesus, you're not going to start crying on me.' A raised eyebrow and a half-smile suggesting he was relieved to be able to inject the moment with humour.

'Fuck off,' Lewis aimed a punch at his arm and turned to look out of his window as he fought to get control of himself. He coughed. Cleared his throat. And felt that he was going to be coughing and clearing his throat for the rest of his life.

'Fair enough,' Craig said. 'That must have been absolutely fucking terrifying.'

'Aye,' Lewis said simply. And thought of his ancestors, some of whom, he'd not long learned, had been burnt at the stake in the belief that they were witches.

Lewis turned back to see what he thought was a look of shame on Craig's face. And he noticed his hands were shaking as they gripped the steering wheel.

'If I could have got to you sooner, I would have,' Craig said, and clearly meant it. 'But ... there was stuff I had to do first.'

Lewis's heart lurched in his chest. 'Where's Annie?' he asked again.

'She's fine. Dad thought that if he got you out of the way, he wouldn't have to worry about her. He thought she'd back down if' – his eyes definitely had a haunted, guilt-ridden look now – 'something terrible happened to you.'

'Where is she? She wasn't looking well...'

'She passed out. Dad said he took her to a friend's house to recover. He told me they got into her phone and phoned one of her regular contacts to come and collect her.'

'Regular contacts?' Lewis wondered how they'd managed to get beyond her phone's security. 'Who was it?'

'There were a number of calls between Annie and somebody – a Mrs Mac? So Dad said he got Mum to get in touch with her.'

'Mrs Mac,' Lewis said. 'They do talk to each other all the time,' he said with a rush of gratitude. He managed to relax a little. 'And where's my phone?' he asked.

'Fucked if I know, mate. There was too much going on to be worried about phones.'

'You said you would have got here sooner. Not that I'm ungrateful, but what could be more important than saving someone's life?'

Craig's expression seemed to shut down, as if protecting himself from thoughts of his own dark deeds. 'Stuff,' Craig replied in a way that told Lewis that was all he was going to get.

Soon they were winding down the hill towards the coast and the town of Girvan. Initially, Lewis forced himself to sit in silence, afraid that talking would set off the pain in his head and another bout of coughing. But the questions racing through his mind didn't keep him quiet for long.

Again, he mentally replayed his last memory before waking up in the burning car. He and Annie in the Oldfield home, sipping their hot drinks. Questioning Craig. The old man behind the desk, relaxed in his chair. Too relaxed. As if everything was playing out just as he hoped.

Lewis recalled hearing Annie asking something. Her voice sounded slurred. He turned to her and saw that her expression had slumped. Wondering if she was okay? Had she reacted to something? Her tea? Then he had become aware of someone behind him. A sharp pain in his neck, and Craig's shout of 'Mum' before he blanked out.

'That was your mum behind me, aye?'

Craig nodded.

Lewis thought about the moment when he'd faded out of consciousness. 'What was it she injected me with? Roofie?'

'Think so.'

He was momentarily back in the burning car. Frightened for his life. Certain he was going to burn to death. He felt sweat bead on his forehead, and fear was a tremor in every cell of his body. He retreated from the thought. Hastily.

He recalled instead a point in their conversation back at the house. Something shifted in Craig when Lewis spouted his theory about what had happened at the time of Rab's death. Something cast itself over his eyes, just for a flash. Lewis had expected to see guilt, or perhaps even a note of pleasure that he'd got away with something for so long. But it wasn't that. It was resentment. Deep, deep anger and resentment.

'Tell me, Craig – explain to me like I'm an idiot.' The rest of his question was obliterated by a fit of coughing.

'What is going on?' he continued once he was able to talk again. Questions crowded his mind. 'Where's Damien? And why does your old man want me dead?'

Craig looked out of his side window, but Lewis could see the muscles of his jaw tighten and loosen and tighten again as if Craig was trying to work out exactly what to tell him.

'How did I end up in that car?' Lewis persisted.

'Mum injected you. Then me and Dad carried you out to the car, took you up to that spot in the hills, and … well, you know the rest.' Craig said all of this without once looking at him. Staring at the road, the verge, other cars, eyes anywhere but on Lewis's face.

'What made you come back for me?' Lewis asked, his voice softer now.

Silence ticked by. Craig seemed to mull his reply for a long minute.

'You have to realise something, mate.' Craig took his eyes momentarily from the road to look at Lewis. 'I fucking hate that man. Being his son has been like a curse,' he spat. 'It's a wonder I'm not in the looney bin after being brought up by him.' He lifted his hand from the steering wheel to rub at his chin, and Lewis noted that it was trembling. 'If Alison hadn't been there for me over the years I think I'd have topped myself long ago.' He stopped talking, and slowed as they reached the next bend.

He didn't start talking again when they hit the straight, but Lewis realised that he was close to a moment of revelation so he kept quiet.

'*That* at the house was the last straw.' Craig's voice shook with the force of his emotion. 'When Mum injected you? It became clear to me that his plan all along was to get you out of the way, perhaps even kill you. They told me they'd invited you guys to the house to find out what you knew. That was it. But when Mum appeared with that needle – and Annie collapsed with whatever Mum had put in her tea – I couldn't have another death on my conscience. I just couldn't.'

'Another death?' Lewis asked. 'What ... who are you talking about?' He thought about Craig calling the police to report Rose's body. 'Rose?' He recalled Oldfield Senior's calm demeanour back at the house and it occurred to him that her death might not have been the first Oldfield had been involved with. It took cold calculation to plan a murder.

'He's done it before, hasn't he? Killed someone,' Lewis said as the thought unspooled. 'However your father explained it to you, you suspected that Rose's death wasn't an accident, didn't you?'

Craig nodded. 'Dad had the farmer Rose worked for report back to him, so he knew you and Annie had been down to speak to her.' At that Lewis felt a shot of guilt. 'The way Dad tells it is this: the day she died he phoned the farmer to see if she was at work. He wanted to warn her to say nothing more to you. The farmer told him she was at her usual swimming spot, so he said he went just to talk to her. He said he caught her on the rocks before she was about to dive in. They talked. She shouted at him, and then actually went for him. He tried to defend himself, and she tumbled into the water, hitting her head on the way down.'

'That sounds like a crock of shit,' Lewis said.

'I believed him. At first. But as I said, when it became clear he was going to kill you? He was acting so matter of fact, you know? Nobody should be that callous. And that's when I realised he must have done it before, and that he must have killed Rose.'

'And if he did kill Rose,' Lewis said. 'It would have been to silence her. To protect an earlier crime?'

'Aye,' Craig said.

'Rab,' Lewis said simply.

Craig kept his eyes fixed ahead, the set of his jaw tense. Lewis wondered if he would never find peace – because of the actions of his family, and the abrasive power of his own sins.

'Go on then,' Lewis encouraged. 'Might as well tell me everything. Now that you've saved me, you and your family won't ever be speaking again.'

Craig bit his lip and Lewis detected a note of fear.

'Wait ... Do you think you're in danger from your own old man?'

Craig didn't answer, didn't move his eyes from the road.

'Surely he wouldn't do anything to you?'

'You know, there's been a rumour going around the town that he's not my father at all. So...' His laugh was full of bitterness.

'If you think you're in danger you need to go to the police.'

'You're kidding, right? He's got the police in his back pocket.' Craig's face darkened. He thumped the steering wheel with the heel of his hand and shouted, 'Fuck!'

'What is it, Craig?' Lewis knew he was getting through to him now. 'Talk to me. Did your dad kill Rab all those years ago? And how the hell does Damien fit in to all of this? And where the fuck is he?'

Craig braked so hard, Lewis's head jerked six inches forward.

'What the hell?'

'We were kids,' Craig began, both hands on the steering wheel, his face a stretch of guilt and anguish. 'Dad had one of his parties. We were never allowed near them. God forbid, you know. But this time he gave me and Damien some stuff, saying it was time we expanded our horizons. No idea what it was, but all I remember was feeling great – I mean fucking *wonderful*. Then freaking out. Seeing all of this weird shit in my head. It was cool at first – naked women and stuff. Then it was monsters and demons. Giant fuckers. And people were all around us, fucking and fighting and screaming. I had to fight off one big, hairy, naked dude. Don't know what he wanted to do to me. Don't even know if he was real. At one point my heart was beating so hard I thought I was having an actual heart attack. It was terrifying and amazing at the same time...'

He paused for a long moment, as if preparing himself to relive what happened next.

'When I came to, next morning, we were in this little garden room Dad has in one of the corners of the garden. And Rab was ... There was blood everywhere.' He swallowed. 'His throat was cut, and Damien was conked out beside him with this huge knife in his hand.'

Chapter 69

Lewis

Lewis watched Craig as he spoke, and realised this had been the defining moment of the man's life – something he'd never fully recovered from.

'I was screaming,' Craig said. 'Damien woke up and he was screaming too. And we were both covered in blood.'

The tears trickled down Craig's face now, and Lewis wondered if he'd ever even talked about this before.

'Then Dad appeared and he was yelling at Damien – "What the hell have you done?" It was bedlam. And there was this dead boy at his feet.' He shook his head. 'I'll never forget the look on

Rab's face for as long as I live.' He exhaled. 'The empty look in his eyes.'

'What happened next?' Even as he asked the question Lewis was able to paint the picture in his mind: someone must have got a car, staged an accident and then got rid of the vehicle, leaving Rab's body looking like he had been the victim of a hit and run. 'And how did your dad manage to make a stab victim look like a road-traffic accident?'

'I don't remember everything. Most of it is just a blur. I was so grateful that I wasn't going to prison for being an accomplice to murder or something.' Craig looked at Lewis, his eyes framed with hate and self-loathing. 'Dad coached us how to get rid of...' he swallowed '...the body and made sure his friends in the police didn't question the narrative – and I guess that would include paying off whoever did the post mortem.'

'Jesus,' Lewis said. He stared out of the window for a moment. 'Were you guys really that out of it that Damien would have killed someone?'

'I'm just telling you what fucking happened, man,' Craig shot back.

'So, piecing all this together now – with the benefit of hindsight – do you think your dad wanted to silence Rose, and me, to protect you from future charges?'

Again Craig sat in silence.

'Or do you think he's protecting himself? His reputation?'

Craig looked at Lewis. 'He doesn't give a fuck about me. It's himself he's thinking of.'

'And did you and Damien ever talk about it? Try and make some sort of sense?'

'Did we fuck. If he wasn't crazy in love with my sister I don't think I'd have ever even seen him again.'

'What happened next?'

Craig shrugged. 'We got on with our lives. Tried to pretend it didn't happen. But, man, it fucked us up. It would have almost been better if we'd been caught and gone to prison. The guilt has been...' He shook his head. His chin was wobbling, and he took a couple of large breaths. 'So now you know,' he finished.

He started the car and they moved off again, in silence now, both of them lost in the enormity of Craig's confession.

When they approached the community hospital Craig slowed to a stop. He exclaimed as something attracted his attention. 'Fuck.'

Two women at the entrance to the police station next door. One of them was Clare Corrigan. The other was...

'Mum. Shit. What's she doing here?' Craig said.

As if they heard his exclamation, both women turned to face the car at the same time. Craig's mother took a step towards them, her face a mask of rage.

'Fuck. Fuck.' Craig thrust the car into reverse and spun the car around in a tight circle.

'Craig!' Lewis shouted. 'What's going on? You have to let me out.'

'In a minute,' Craig shouted back. 'In a minute.' His car shot out of the hospital car park and back the way they'd come, across the roundabout then one hundred yards down a quiet country road, where Craig braked so suddenly Lewis shot up from his seat and almost hit his head on the windscreen.

'Right. Out,' Craig said.

'What, here?'

'Just get fucking out, Lewis.'

'But...'

'Get out.'

'Right. Okay. Jesus,' Lewis said. 'What the hell's going on?'

'I can't tell you any more, Lewis. You have to trust me on this. Now will you get out my fucking car?'

'I'm going. I'm going.' Lewis opened his door, and released his seatbelt. 'But before I do, what about Damien? Where is he? What the hell has happened to him?'

Chapter 70

Lewis

Lewis watched Craig Oldfield drive away, his car revving hard, tyres kicking up stones. Then he turned and walked back towards the hospital and the community centre, where he knew the local police station was also situated. As he walked, he was aware of how tired he was, ridiculously tired, as if even this slight exertion meant insufficient oxygen reached his lungs. He coughed. Coughed some more, feeling a raking pain in his chest.

So tired.

He guessed that Craig had driven about a kilometre before practically pushing him out of the car. A kilometre. Might as well have been fifty for all the strength he had. Looking ahead, then back the way he came, he hoped that a car would appear, and soon.

As he trudged forward, concentrating on putting one foot in front of the other, he recalled Craig's answer to his question about Damien.

'Genuinely, I don't know, mate, but...' He paused and his expression darkened. 'Don't hold out too much hope. Now, fuck off and get those lungs seen to.' With that he had driven away.

A little white Volkswagen Polo zipped towards him. Lewis held a hand out with a thumbs-up. It sped up and drove past. He realised he probably looked a mess – smoke-stained, possibly bruised and walking with the energy of a reanimated corpse.

Another car. Coming from behind him this time. He turned. And got the exact same result.

Lewis walked five more minutes and thought he might have to find a seat, he was so breathless. But then the sound of another car had him look along the road, and as the car drew nearer he recognised it. And the driver.

It stopped. The window scrolled down.

'I thought that was you,' Clare Corrigan said as she ducked down to look across the car and out of the window at him. 'Wait.' Her mouth fell open. 'Man, you look dreadful. Are you okay? You look like you should be in hospital.' She studied the road ahead, and then looked back to him. 'How did you get here? Didn't I see you in Craig Oldfield's car?'

'If you take me to the hospital I'll tell you everything I know,' Lewis managed.

'Get in,' Clare said. 'Jesus, are you okay?'

Lewis pulled open the passenger door and sank into the seat with a loud sigh of relief, which set off another harsh bout of coughing.

'What the hell happened? You smell like ... like you've been in a fire.'

Lewis nodded. Sucked in some oxygen. Coughed. 'And then some.'

Clare executed a three-point turn and raced back towards the community hospital. As she drove, Lewis told her, as best as he could, about what had happened that day.

'Right. Hang on. I need to call this in.'

After she alerted her colleagues to her recent sighting of one Craig Oldfield she turned to him.

'Lewis,' she scolded. 'I warned you.'

'Yes, and you were right. When you find Craig just bear in mind that he saved my life.'

'Aye, after he tried to turn you into a human torch.' She paused. 'Did he say where he was going?'

'No. Just raced out of that car park in the hospital when he saw you talking to his mum, and then practically threw me out of the car.'

Lewis looked across at her and saw that she was chewing on the inside of her lip. He found it endearing. And despite the mess everything was in, he thought he could feel some kind of connection forming.

As if she felt his gaze on her, she turned to him for a second before focusing back on the road ahead. 'What?'

'Nothing,' he replied, and noted he was feeling slightly better. His lungs were grateful for the rest. Or maybe it was the company. 'My sister. Craig said that she'd been picked up by Mrs Mac – our adoptive mother – can you check in with her and make sure she's okay?'

'Let's get you seen to first, eh?'

'Alright,' he replied with reluctance. He would feel much better once he actually spoke with Annie.

'You should know,' Clare said, 'that the uniforms and an ambulance are heading up to the Oldfields' house right now. Craig's mother said Craig attacked them, but she managed to escape, ran out of the house, and came straight to the police station to report him, and to ask that we send an ambulance up to check on her husband.' She paused, her expression grim. 'It already sounded a bit off to my mind, but what you just told me...' She chewed on her lip again. 'Thing is, Oldfield is fiercely protective. If we throw any accusations at him we need them to be airtight.'

'Well, there's more,' Lewis said. 'A lot more.' And he related the story Craig had just told him about him, Rab and Damien.

Her eyes were large. 'Wow. That really does cast a different light on things.' She narrowed her eyes, thinking. Then shook her head. 'If it's true, it's going to be mighty hard to prove after all these years.'

'But maybe that's why Damien has gone missing? Perhaps he threatened to confess, so the family cleaned up? I tried to get Craig to tell me, but he chucked me out of his car before I could get an answer.'

They'd reached a roundabout – the hospital just ahead. 'I'll drop you off and make sure you see somebody. Those lungs of yours don't sound too good. But I can't wait with you. I need to get up to the Oldfield house.' They reached the hospital, and she parked up. 'You're going to be okay,' she said, and lightly, briefly, patted his knee. 'I'll take you inside, and that'll be the full extent of my caring side.'

As Lewis climbed out, he looked through the glass front doors into the waiting area of the adjoining police station, and recognised Mrs Oldfield. She was looking worried. Very worried.

'What's she still doing here?' he said over his shoulder. 'Attempted murder is probably the least of her crimes.'

'Now, Lewis,' Clare said. 'Leave her to me.'

Lewis kept his eyes on the woman inside, and as they took the steps to the hospital entrance, he saw her spot them then come charging out of the doors. It wasn't an emotional response – Lewis was sure he'd seen her make a decision to go on the attack; a tactic she'd probably learned from her husband.

'I hope you're locking that young man up,' she shouted at Clare, her arm out, finger extended like a dagger. 'Him and my son are in cahoots. Craig stole every last pound out of our safe, and then the two of them disappeared, leaving my poor husband...' Here she paused, marshalling her emotions, releasing an anguished sob '...bleeding on the floor of my kitchen.'

Lewis looked at Clare. 'You're not buying this, are you?'

Clare gave him a brief shake of her head and a frown. 'Mrs Oldfield, officers will be at your house already, and we'll take a statement from you too. For the moment this young man has smoke damage to his lungs and needs urgent care.'

'Doesn't look too urgent to me.' She gave Lewis a look of poison, as if she'd already convinced herself of his culpability. 'Have you searched him?' She approached Lewis at pace. 'Where's my money?'

Clare came between them. 'That's enough.'

'What are you talking about?' Lewis shouted. Then gave in to a bout of coughing. Once he got his breathing under control, he demanded, 'Do you inject all your visitors with drugs, you psycho?'

'Lewis,' Clare said. 'Get inside.' She turned to Mrs Oldfield. 'I'll in touch, Mrs Oldfield. There are some more questions I need to ask you.'

'What about my husband? Is he okay?' And now she was every inch the worried wife, her eyes glittering with suppressed tears, arms crossed, her fist clenched at her throat. 'Is he even still alive?'

Chapter 71

Clare

Early on in her career, Clare Corrigan had learned not to judge, but the moment she looked up at the Oldfield home, she matched the wedding-cake house with Oldfield's grandiose self-importance. She could barely stand the guy before; now her dislike was changing to disdain.

Climbing out of her car, Clare saw the spread of the town fringing the sea, and it occurred to her that the house managed to do two things: it was out of sight of most people, but the owner could see everything – lording it over all those below.

The houses up here in High Dailly, and their inhabitants, had been a constant source of gossip when Clare was a young girl. The properties wouldn't offer much change from a million pounds each. And the residents were reputed to include a family who owned a chain of hotels in the region, a surgeon who flew in and out in his helicopter, a reclusive retired movie star, a couple of town councillors, and, of course, the Oldfields.

She'd heard tales of all kinds of wild parties and strange goings-on; mostly hearsay to Clare's mind. There was even a rumour, reported to Clare by her Great-Aunt Phemie, that people 'up there' were investigated for ritual child abuse around the same time as the satanic abuse trials in Orkney, which was, of course, found to be all in the imagination of an overzealous social worker.

Phemie had gathered the folds of her cardigan around her and said, 'But, mark my words, them folks up at High Dailly are up to something.'

The door opened as she approached, and two paramedics in green jumpsuits stepped out. One of them was Charlie Frith, a woman she often encountered in her work.

'He okay?' Clare asked, nodding in the direction of the house.

Charlie made a face, and mouthed, 'Arsehole.' Then said, 'Mr Oldfield Senior has nothing more than a bloody nose. No breakages. Apart from his pride,' she winked. 'He was complaining that his son had all but tried to murder him. If he did, he didn't try very hard. Looked like one punch and done to me.'

'Why he couldn't have taken himself down to the community hospital like a normal person would, I have no idea,' her colleague added.

'You guys are finished with him?' Clare asked, resisting the opportunity to discuss the man's ego.

'He's all yours,' Charlie winked. 'Just follow the sound of the moaning and you'll find him.'

Clare walked past the pair of stone lions at the door, through into the vestibule, and from there across what felt like an internal courtyard in black and white tiles and into a large kitchen and lounge, where she saw Mr Oldfield lying on a sofa, one hand over his eyes and another over his heart.

On hearing her footsteps he sat up, groaning as he did so.

'Ah, Detective Corrigan. If you've come to protect me, you're too late. And if you're looking for my son, I have no idea where he is.'

Clare nodded at the uniformed cop – Chris Hall, a newbie who looked like he was shitting himself at having to be on point duty for such a man of importance locally. 'Give us a minute?' she sent him a wink, and he gratefully exited the room. She looked around the kitchen, at the double Belfast sink, the large, black range with gold handles, the expansive windows that gave a view out onto the town of Girvan and the sea beyond.

Oldfield's eyes seem to glitter with satisfaction as he watched her take it all in.

'Perhaps you could tell me what happened, Mr Oldfield?'

'My wife has gone down to the police station to give a statement.'

'And I'm here asking you for yours.'

He stared at her. 'I've already talked to one of your colleagues.' He then mentioned the name of the regional inspector. Someone, Clare suspected, that Ben Oldfield played golf with regularly.

'And now we do the formal part,' she offered him a smile. 'But if this is an inconvenience, I can ask you to come down to the police station tomorrow, if the swelling has gone down sufficiently, that is.' She looked pointedly at his face.

'It doesn't look much now,' Oldfield said. 'But my son did threaten to kill me before rushing off to God knows where.' He sniffed. 'You should be out there looking for him instead of in here quizzing me.'

Clare ignored this and pointed to a chair beside the sofa. 'Mind if I sit?'

He shrugged.

She sat and pulled out her notebook and a pen. 'Right. What happened?'

Oldfield outlined his son's attack, and as Clare made notes, she wondered how heavily he was editing it.

'So.' Clare looked up from her notebook. 'You had words about how little work Craig does; he became furious, lashed out, and left?'

'Correct.'

'Any idea where your son might be now?'

'I have no idea, Detective Corrigan.' He held both hands to his nose, carefully pressing on either side as if to judge whether or not it was broken.

'This is a rather large house,' Clare said as she looked around. 'Any chance he could be hiding out here?'

'What – doubling back and hiding where we might least expect to find him? He's not that smart, Corrigan.'

'Any of his favourite haunts you could tell me about?'

He shook his head. Very slowly, as if to protect himself against any pain. 'Do you have children?' he asked.

'No. I haven't been blessed as yet.'

The side of his mouth lifted in an ironic half-smile. 'Then you'll find that when you are thus *blessed* that your children tell you nothing.'

'So you have no idea where your son might have gone?'

'Asked and answered, Detective.'

She put her notebook away, satisfied that the pitiful amount of information Oldfield had given her was all he would divulge. She stood, walked to the door, and turned.

'One other thing ... Lewis Jackson said that your wife injected him with Rohypnol and then you and Craig drove him out into the hills, where you set his car on fire with him still in it. Unconscious and tied to the steering wheel.'

'Fanciful nonsense,' Oldfield said, his expression flat, his eyes giving nothing away. 'I should sue that boy for slander.'

'Mind if I look through the house and just check that Craig isn't actually hiding out somewhere within these walls?'

'Yes, I do mind.' Anger flashed across his eyes. 'Your duties have been carried out as well as could be expected of an officer with your...' he paused '...experience. I'll be sure to let your boss know how adequate you were.' Then as if all that talking was too much, he lay back on the sofa. 'Now please leave.'

'Of course. Thank you,' Clare replied, trying, unsuccessfully, not to bristle. 'If I could just use your toilet before I go?'

He stuck a hand in the air and waved it in a vague direction. 'The door on the right before you leave the main door.'

Clare retraced her steps and found the toilet by the entrance. She didn't need to use it, but waited a moment, flushed, then turned the tap on. She notice the soap on the sink was unused –

wrapped in cellophane with a little sticker in the middle proudly proclaiming it was made from beeswax from somewhere called Summerhill Hall. She ensured the toilet door closed silently, then stopped in the hallway and listened for any movement from the kitchen area. Nothing.

She scanned the hall, then pushed open the door facing her and saw a cloakroom, holding a range of wellington boots and waterproof coats. There was another door off the hall, away to her right. She made her way there on soft feet and opened it. It was a sitting room with two large white, leather sofas swamped with cushions.

There was a door further into the house, nearer the kitchen, and one step closer to detection. Intriguingly, it had a key in the lock. She opened it to reveal a bookcase-lined study, with a large landscape window and a pine desk with green leather inlay. It was just as Lewis Jackson had described it. So he had definitely been here.

Her eyes ranged across the book titles; they were mainly legal tomes, with the odd celebrity biography. She walked into the room, feet sinking into the deep pile of the carpet, and stopped at the near side of the desk. A photograph of a child and a young woman faced her. Clare picked it up, and as she did so the glass front fell off, landed on one of its corners and shattered on the desk top.

'Shit.'

She reached for it, to try and put everything back together, and as she did so a piece of paper fell out from behind the black cardboard backing. She picked it up.

On first glance it looked like a page that had been torn out of an old book. The words were in an antiquated script and the page itself was yellowing around the edges. As she read, Clare felt the air around her cool:

'These are very powerful magiks. You must follow the instruction to the letter, else the spirit you conjure turns against you.'

What on earth had she just found? She read some more. There were phrases in a language she didn't recognise, then she came to another line in English:

'Deceit is Her middle name, but with diligence on your part,
She will make you the richest man in the world.'

Chapter 72

Lewis

Lewis was assessed quickly by the medics, given an x-ray, shown to a bed and put on oxygen. As he lay there, the straps of the oxygen mask biting into his cheeks, he thought through the last few hours; the sting of the needle on the back of his neck, his certainty he was about to die, and then his rescue.

A nurse approached his bed, care in her eyes. 'You okay, son?' She reminded him of Mandy: same height, build and hair colour, the same benevolent air.

Lewis could only nod, emotion bubbling in every cell. He clasped his hands tight, trying to minimise the shaking.

'You've been through a lot,' the nurse said.

Lewis nodded again in reply. Now that he was actually in a position of safety, he found he had no control of his emotions, and was just as likely to laugh as he was to cry.

'I'll sit with you for a wee while, eh?' she asked. 'Any family we should get in touch with to let them know you're here?'

He shook his head.

'You poor thing,' she replied. 'You must have someone.'

Lewis pulled the mask away from his face. 'Don't want to worry them,' he replied. He wondered about Annie, hoped she was okay. As soon as he was able he would get himself to a phone and call Mrs Mac to speak to her.

The nurse patted his hand. 'Maybe get a good night's sleep and then we speak to them in the morning, eh?'

He sat forward, alarmed. 'I can't stay here tonight. I need to—'

Gently, but firmly she pushed him back down. 'You're going nowhere, young man. We need to be sure your lungs aren't damaged by the smoke. Take a telling.' She raised an eyebrow.

'I need to talk to my sister,' he said. 'Make sure she's okay.'

'I think she can wait until morning, son. You need to sleep. Not talk.'

Surprisingly, he did sleep, but it was fractured, full of flame and fear, barking dogs and crouching lions, and underscored by a sense of disquiet for Annie.

When the weak light of a new day filtered through the blinds in his room, he sat up in bed to assess his situation.

He was in a small room on his own, the walls painted an institutional cream. A solid wooden door faced him, he assumed leading to the bathroom, and to his right stood the door to the corridor. The only pieces of furniture in the room, besides his bed, were two chairs, and a small, blond pine cabinet.

A quick inventory of his physical condition had him thankful for his lucky escape. No burns, and the ache in his lungs was much lighter than the night before. He slipped out from under his sheets and found his belongings had been stowed in the cabinet.

He sniffed at his jeans and noted the strong smell of smoke. Thinking they would have to do for now, he fished in his pocket and found his wallet.

He checked the time on the little clock above the door. 6:45 am.

The rhythmic squeak of a soft soled shoe warned of someone's approach. A different nurse from the one the day before entered his room. She was taller, younger, long blonde hair tied at the nape of her neck.

'You're up?' she asked. She was wearing the same kindly expression as yesterday's nurse. 'Want some tea and toast?'

'Don't go to any bother...' Speaking set off a coughing fit.

'No bother at all, mate,' she said, her eyes tightening at the sound of Lewis coughing. 'You can't start your day without tea and toast, eh?'

'Well...' he began, once his coughing had subsided.

'C'mon,' she bustled over and helped Lewis back onto the bed. 'Let's get you some pillows so you can sit up nice and comfy, and someone will fetch you your breakfast.'

'When will I be able to leave?' he asked.

'Want rid of us so soon?' she grinned. 'The doc will be on her rounds in a bit – why don't we wait and see what she has to say, mmm?'

Lewis was duly delivered his tea and toast and settled in to wait for the doctor to sign off his discharge. But two hours went by and no one had been to see him. Another hour, and he was about to get up and go, when his door opened, and Clare Corrigan walked in. She was wearing jeans and a light-blue padded jacket, and her eyes looked weighed down by whatever had happened to her since he last saw her.

'How's the patient?' she asked.

'More's the point: how's the detective? You look like you found a fiver and lost a winning lottery ticket,' he said. And coughed.

Her face screwed itself to a pained expression. 'That doesn't sound so good.'

Lewis managed a wave. Another cough. 'I'll ... survive.'

'Hope so.' She winked. 'Key witness and all that.'

Clare walked over to one of the chairs and sat. She looked at him as if debating something. 'Do you know if the hospital staff took a blood or urine sample from you?'

Lewis shook his head slowly. 'I'm not aware of any urine sample being taken, and I was pretty out of it later, so they might have taken some bloods without me being aware.'

'That'll be a no then,' she said. 'I'm pretty sure you'd have noticed a needle being stuck in you.' She grimaced. 'I did ask them to, you know.'

'Why? What's up?'

'The Oldfields are denying they injected you with anything, and sticking to their story that you and Craig were in cahoots to rob them.'

'So did your lot find the old man covered in blood and lying in their kitchen, like his wife said?'

'A bloody nose is all,' Clare replied. 'Mrs Oldfield made it sound like Craig had beaten his father to within an inch of his life.' She sat. And looked like she was stewing over something.

Lewis frowned. Clare had been more forthcoming in the last five minutes than in any time since they'd met. He waited a beat and then asked, 'What are you not telling me? And why are you here like it's dress-down Friday?'

'What? A girl can't wear her casual stuff without raising questions?' She was trying to make light of things, but Lewis could sense a simmering anger. Clare sighed, forcing herself to relax. 'Let's just say the Oldfields have friends in high places.' She raised both eyebrows, her mouth a tight line of dissatisfaction. 'Mrs Oldfield complained that I had been seen fraternising with the man who was a suspect in the theft from her house.'

'Fraternising?' Lewis was incredulous. 'You were driving an injured man to hospital.'

'Exactly. In any case, you can imagine my delight when I had the divisional commander on the phone at midnight last night telling me I was off the case and to take a month off.'

'The divisional commander? Really?'

'Really.'

'If you're off the case and on holiday, why are you here?'

The door opened behind them, and a woman in a white coat entered. She had short, dark hair, a sharp nose, and walked in as if she had two hours' worth of work to do in two minutes.

'Dr Menzies,' she announced. 'Do you mind if I have some time alone with the patient?' she asked Clare.

Clare got to her feet. 'Detective Corrigan,' she introduced herself. 'This man is a possible victim of a crime. I requested that blood and urine samples be taken when he was admitted last night. Can you confirm if this was done or not?'

'I ... er...' Dr Menzies looked down at the clipboard she was holding. 'I can't see...'

Clare offered a smile and continued: 'I understand you guys are short-staffed, doctor, but if you could see to those samples that would be such a help.'

Dr Menzies nodded as she looked Clare up and down. 'I'll see that is done, but first I have to examine Mr Jackson. Make sure his lungs aren't too damaged by what he has just been through.'

Clare left the room, with a quick nod aimed at Lewis, and the moment the door closed Dr Menzies had him lift his shirt so she could listen to him breathe through her stethoscope. He took the breaths as directed while she placed a cold, steel rim at several points on his chest and back.

'Mmm,' was all she said after she'd directed him to rearrange his clothing.

'How am I?' Lewis asked. 'Can you tell if there's been any lasting damage?'

'Time will tell, Mr Jackson,' she replied. 'You're a lucky young man. It could have been a lot worse.' She offered a smile of encouragement. 'The x-ray we took last night showed a little damage, which with time and care will, I'm sure, heal up. You know how to use facial steam baths? And we'll give you a steroid spray. Use it. And it's important you listen to your body. Don't rush back into exercise just yet.'

'Thank you, doctor. And the tests?'

'I'll get a nurse to come right in.'

As she left. Clare returned.

'And?' she asked.

As Lewis was telling her what the doctor had said, a nurse

entered with a small tray that held a syringe and a small empty sample tube.

Twenty minutes later, both samples taken, Lewis was fully dressed and ready to leave.

'You got a phone?' he asked Clare.

'Who do you need to call?'

'Need to make sure Annie's okay. She'll be out of her mind with worry about me.'

Clare fished in her pocket for her phone. Handed it to Lewis. 'Can you even remember her number?'

He paused, the screen of the phone facing him. 'Good point. Actually, no. But I remember the Macs' house telephone number. I'll call that.'

It rang out then went to answerphone.

'It's Lewis here,' he said. 'Just checking in. Everything is okay at my end. Hope all is well with you guys. Get Annie to give me a call when you get in. I've ... er ... misplaced my phone. The number to get me on is...' he looked at Clare, and in response she plucked a small purse from her pocket, released a business card and handed it to Lewis. He read out the number before hanging up.

'Where are we going now?' he asked her.

'Since when did this become a "we" thing?'

'The minute you walked in here after being suspended.'

'I wasn't suspended.'

'As good as.' He paused. 'How long until we get the results of the tests, do you think?'

'As long as the proverbial piece of string,' she replied.

'In the meantime, I need to hire myself a car, seeing as mine is a burnt-out wreck.'

'Or I could drop you off at the nearest train station and you make your way back up to Glasgow. You heard the doctor, Lewis. You need to look after yourself to make sure there's no permanent damage.'

'You were listening in?' He grinned. 'You care.'

She shook her head.

'Okay. Take me to the train station and I'll make my way home.'

Clare studied him for a moment. 'Is that code for "I'll pretend to get on a train and hire a car from the first place I can find"?'

'Maybe.'

'Jesus. You've got a one-track mind.'

'Says the woman who's on leave.'

'Fair enough.' Clare sighed. 'Let's go get you a proper feed and we can discuss what happens next.'

A half-hour drive down the coast back in the direction of Ayr saw them sitting in a café eating a full Scottish breakfast. They were by a large window, at either side of a table covered in a red, checked tablecloth. Outside the waves were high, flecked with white, the sky a haze of greys.

'Penny for them?' Clare asked as she speared the last piece of sausage.

Lewis looked down at her plate, now empty apart from a smear of tomato sauce and egg yolk. 'I like a woman with an appetite.' He smiled. Coughed.

'Shut up, you.' She barked out a laugh, and he felt a warmth at her reaction. He'd like to make her laugh more. 'Don't think I've eaten for two days,' she said. Then put her knife and fork down and picked up her cup. 'Now ... Craig Oldfield. Did he say where he was going?'

'No. He just did his hero thing, and then dropped me off in a panic when he saw his mother at the police station.'

'What do you think was going on in his head?'

Once again, Lewis brought to mind the moment in Benjamin Oldfield's office when Craig had swallowed, flicked his eyes towards Lewis and then to the floor.

'A dog that's kicked too often will eventually turn on his

attacker. I think his father has bullied him all his life, and up until they tried to kill me...' He paused at that, thinking it was a collection of words that when spoken sounded utterly surreal. He could understand now what Annie had gone through with Chris Jenkins. 'Until then, he had been completely cowed all his life. But being there at the moment of attempted murder was the last straw, and helped him see through his father's lies.'

'Do you think it was actually Benjamin Oldfield who killed Rab all those years ago?'

'After yesterday I could believe anything of him.'

Clare chewed on that for a moment. 'What about Rab's sister, Rose? Craig was the one who alerted the police that her body was in the water. What's your view on what happened there?'

'Oh, aye,' he said as he remembered what Craig said as they drove to the hospital. 'Craig said his dad told him he was there on the beach, trying to speak to Rose just before she died. And that she tried to attack him, and when he defended himself, she stumbled, hit her head and fell into the water.'

'And he didn't think to try and save her?' Clare asked, outrage in her voice. 'And what about Mrs Oldfield? What do you think her part was in all this?'

Lewis shuddered as he remembered looking over his shoulder and seeing the expression of calm and ruthless concentration on Mrs Oldfield's face as she drove the needle into his neck.

'Who knows?' He pushed his plate away and sank back in his chair. 'One thing that's nagging at me – why have Craig report the body? What would they get out of that?'

Clare raised her eyebrows. 'He didn't just report the body. He waded into the sea, fully clothed, and pulled her out.'

'Oh. I didn't know that bit.' Lewis thought that through. 'Which means he was in the vicinity when his father was talking to Rose. Wonder if he was in the car while they talked. Then the father asked him to fish out the body and call it in...'

Clare shrugged and shook her head sadly.

'Why draw attention to yourself like that?' Lewis looked out to sea and watched the waves for a moment. 'Unless ... they were sending me a message. Or rather, old man Oldfield was. He didn't want poor Rose to wash out to sea. Who knows how long it might take for the tide to bring her back in, or where. He wanted to tell me what he's capable of.'

A phone rang out.

'That's me,' Clare said, and answered. Lewis could hear the rumble of a male voice, but not what was being said. Clare listened. Nodded. Said, 'Text me that address, will you?' She nodded some more. 'And when you get the address for that four-by-four, text me that as well, please?' Then she hung up. 'That was the office. Someone from the holiday park down in Lendalfoot phoned in some suspicious activity.' She stood up.

'They don't know you're off duty?' Lewis asked as he got to his feet too.

'It's five minutes back up the road,' Clare said, ignoring his question.

Her phone rang again. She answered, then said:

'It's Mandy McEvoy.' And she handed him the phone.

'Lewis, son, where are you?' Mandy's voice was strained. 'I've been calling your mobile.'

'Sorry,' he said. Coughed. 'I was in hospital—'

'Oh my God. You were where? What's wrong? What happened?'

'I'm fine. Honestly, I'm fine. There was...' He wondered how to tell her everything that had gone on without getting her more worried. 'There was an incident, but I'm fine. They just kept me in to keep an eye on me.'

'What do you mean, an incident? What happened?' Throughout their teen years and into adulthood Mrs McEvoy had always been calm and unflappable. But she wasn't now. 'How's Annie? Let me talk to her,' she asked.

'What do you mean?' His heart lurched. 'I was told she was with you.'

'With me?' Mandy's voice went up an octave. 'What do you mean you were told she was with me? You've been damned near killed and now you don't know where Annie is?'

Lewis shot a look at Clare. 'She felt unwell. Passed out. I was told she was taken to some house to recover and you'd been phoned to come and collect her.'

'Nobody phoned me, Lewis,' she replied. Indignant. 'What the hell is going on?'

Lewis exhaled, looked again at Clare, a hot feeling of panic rushing up his throat as he said, 'Where's Annie?'

Chapter 73

Annie

Annie became aware she was in bed – but slowly, her brain providing her with the information in increments: the soft pillow under her head. The slight weight of fabric covering her. The mattress under her back.

Where was she?

Pain thumped in a band across her forehead with each beat of her pulse, her mouth was dry, and when she lifted her head from the pillow the room spun. Had she been drinking? She couldn't remember doing that, but this was exactly how a hangover felt.

There was little light in the room, but she could make out a metal framework at the far end of the bed, a free-standing wardrobe facing her and a padded chair to the side of the door.

Recent memory filled her mind.

Being in the Oldfield house. Benjamin Oldfield across the desk from her, his face so full of self-satisfaction, she wanted to take a scourer to it.

She'd been drinking some kind of tea. What on earth was in

it? She was dizzy. Nauseous. Desperately trying to keep tabs on the conversation. Lewis looked like he was in control, and yet Oldfield was sitting there like he'd won the lottery.

Then ... what?

Nothing.

Until now. In this bed. No longer feeling nauseous, but aware of a heaviness in her limbs and unsure if her legs could take her weight should she try to stand.

Where the hell was she? And where was Lewis?

Worried for him now, she swung her feet over the side of the bed and slowly stood up. And promptly fell back down again. She was as weak as a kitten. And hungry. As if she hadn't eaten for days. How long had she been here? Wherever *here* was. She made another attempt to get to her feet, and putting her hand on the bedside cabinet to aid her balance, managed it.

She looked down to see what she was wearing. A cotton night-gown that reached the floor. Where were her clothes?

Where was her phone?

It would help if there was more light in the room, so she carefully made her way across to the windows and moved the heavy drapes aside, just enough to see out.

Beyond the glass, as far as she could see, clouds dark with the promise of rain dimmed the world, and as if her thoughts didn't quite yet belong to her, Annie tried to work out if it was morning or evening.

Annie was in bed. Lying on her back. Had she been dreaming? Hadn't she just walked to the window? Mind a scatter of confusion, not sure she was in the world, or even of it, she pulled the quilt aside and pushed herself out of bed. She made for the window – a journey of a few steps that seemed to take an age – and pulled open the curtains.

Where was she?

Even from this vantage point she recognised the view, and the curve of the drive, and the main road beyond that swept round the corner, before vanishing behind a blockade of trees.

Movement behind her.

'You shouldn't be out of bed, dear. You haven't been well.' That voice. She'd heard it before. Soft, yet commanding. Drenched in the enunciation of the well educated.

Annie turned. Tried to see who she was talking to. Fought for focus. 'If I could just get my clothes...' She stumbled.

The woman caught her and guided her back to bed. A swab of something on the back of her hand, and she felt sleepy. And warm. And comfortable, and as if she was where she should be.

'Rest, my dear,' the woman said, her hand smooth against Annie's forehead.

Something dropped onto the corner of her mouth, some kind of liquid. Instinctively she licked it, and within moments felt a surge of emotion. Love and acceptance and surety. Somehow she knew she was loved. She was appreciated. She was seen and heard. She belonged. All of that knowledge washed over and through her, and she had never felt more grateful for anything in her life.

Still, part of her mind questioned, where was this coming from? There was a sense of fuzziness that suggested she'd been drugged, but she found she didn't care. Because the weaker part of her – the greedy, needy, shameless part – revelled in it. Warmth filled her chest and grew until it softened her edges. She never wanted to leave. And this, she was certain, was where she should stay forevermore.

Chapter 74

Lewis

'Car. Now,' Clare said, standing up, before Lewis had got more than two words out.

He followed her out of the café and they made their way to the car, Clare holding up a finger for silence when Lewis tried to protest. His mind was in turmoil. Annie had now been missing for more than twenty-four hours. He felt sick with worry.

Once inside the vehicle, Lewis swung round to talk to Clare. 'Why did we have to come out here? Why couldn't we talk inside?'

'We don't know who has links back to Benjamin Oldfield. They could be anywhere. And I've been warned off by my boss's boss's boss, Lewis.'

Lewis nodded his head; he understood. 'I'm really, really, worried about Annie now...'

'Remind me what Craig said when you asked him about her.'

'Like I said to Mandy on the phone – he said Annie passed out, so they took her somewhere – someone's house, to recover. And that they'd accessed Annie's phone, picked Mrs Mac's number because there were so many phone calls and messages between them, called her and asked her to come and collect Annie.'

'Did he specifically say it was Mrs Mac they called?'

Lewis thought that through. 'Yes. He did. Jesus, I'm such an idiot. Trusting him.' Anxiety surged. 'What does that mean? Is Craig in cahoots with them after all? But why would he set me and my car on fire and then save me?'

Clare tapped the steering wheel. 'Maybe the parents never really trusted Craig with any of this and fobbed him off with an explanation that would set his mind at ease.' She looked at Lewis, narrowed her eyes in thought. 'Do you think they injected Annie with Rohypnol as well?'

Lewis slowly shook his head. 'I was out of it pretty quickly. They could have...' He played through the events of that morning, hardly believing it was just yesterday. 'Before I conked out, she did look tired and kind of unwell. And she was looking at her cup as if ... They put something in her tea, I'm sure of it!'

'They didn't put her in the car along with you, so that means they don't want her dead.'

'Is that supposed to make me feel better?'

Clare didn't reply.

Lewis stared out of the window. 'If they don't want Annie dead, what do they want with her?' He was silent for a moment as he tried to batten down his concern. Annie was going to be fine. Of course she was. Whatever was going on she was able to handle it. She was the strongest person he knew.

He exhaled sharply. Crossed his arms. 'I asked Craig about Damien, and he was adamant that he had nothing to do with his disappearance.'

'Do you believe him?'

Lewis thought back to the moment and the man's look of incredulity. He nodded. 'I do. And I also believed him when he said Annie had been taken somewhere to recover. So, either he's a consummate liar, and I'm a gullible fool. Or he believes what he was told and he's the gullible fool. In either case, the last people we know of that were in touch with Annie were Mr and Mrs Oldfield.' He stared at Clare.

'I don't like that look, Lewis.'

'You've been warned off and you've been benched. If you do anything here you could lose your job. I don't give a fuck what they do to me. I have to find Annie.'

'I get that, Lewis, but—'

'Drive me to the nearest police station, please. I'll make a complaint. Tell them what I know and they'll have to look into it.'

'The nearest station is Girvan. Where I work.' She grimaced. 'Or used to, and Oldfield clearly has his contacts there. The minute, the second you walk in there you'll be arrested.'

'We can't just let them get away with it.'

'Agreed, but we have to be smart. You being locked up in a jail cell won't help Annie. I'm surprised you even got away from the hospital without being wheeled through to be questioned.'

Lewis sat. Simmered. 'The Oldfields have got Annie,' he stated, hating how helpless he felt.

'I believe you, Lewis. The Oldfields have as good as abducted her. And I don't give a toss about friends in high places. Bad people need to pay for their bad shit.'

'That's like a Clint Eastwood line.'

Clare offered a sympathetic smile. 'Do you often hide your worries behind daft wee quips?' She reached for his hand and gave it a squeeze. 'We'll find her, Lewis.'

Emotion tightened his throat, and he could only nod, then coughed.

'That phone call I had before Mandy got you?' Clare said. 'There's something the folk at the holiday park want me to see. Let's pop in there first.'

'Won't you get in trouble if you bring a civilian with you?'

'We'll be discreet. By discreet, I mean you say nothing while I talk.' She drove off. 'In any case, at this point I'm so pissed off with them I don't give a shit what the bosses say.'

Minutes later they were at the far side of the town of Girvan, driving into the entrance of the holiday park. They parked and as they got out of the car a woman in a black suit appeared at the main door.

'Thanks for calling this in, Amy,' Clare said to the woman as they approached.

'No bother at all,' the woman replied. Lewis read her badge and saw she was the manager. She paused as if waiting for Clare to introduce him, but instead Clare asked, 'What have you got for me?'

Amy opened the door. 'This way, please.'

They were guided into an office with a large window looking out to the sea. Amy walked behind her desk and pushed the screen of her computer around so that Clare and Lewis could see.

'After you were last here, Clare,' Amy began, 'when that car was found, we've been much more diligent at looking at any strange vehicles coming into the park.' She glanced at Lewis. 'Most of our customers are long-termers, coming down every weekend and holidays and such, so, if we're looking, it's fairly easy to spot a newbie.' She pointed to the screen. 'We have a CCTV camera at the entrance to the park and it picked this car up last night.'

The image was in black and white and showed the front view of a dark-coloured Range Rover. An older model, as far as Lewis could make out. The image wasn't clear enough to make out the driver or the passenger, but the shape of the head and the hair suggested they might be both female.

'I looked back on our CCTV library to see if it had been here before. We only keep the film for a month or so before it's scrubbed.' Amy made a face of apology. 'In any case...' she brought up another image. 'Here it is again.'

'Right,' Clare said.

'Look at the date and time,' Amy pointed at the lower left-hand corner, where a series of numbers were on show. 'That's 23:25. A week before we called in the empty car on our lot.'

'Can you print that off for me, please?'

Amy moved to a printer at the side of her desk and plucked a piece of paper from a tray. 'Already done that,' she said proudly.

'Excellent,' Clare said as she accepted the sheet of paper. 'Good work, Amy. Thank you.'

They walked towards the door, but before they left, Lewis turned.

Ignoring Clare's stare and her earlier admonition to keep quiet, he asked, 'If someone comes in here and they're not staying in one of your lodges, where would they be going?'

'The cave,' Amy said simply. 'We don't advertise there's a way through, or we'd be overrun, but at the far end of the park there's a beach, and at low tide, if you walk along there, you come to Sawney Bean's cave. The cannibal cave.' She crossed her arms. Gave a little shudder.

Back in the car Clare said, 'I thought I said to say nothing?'

'You don't think the cannibal cave thing might be significant?'

'Oh, c'mon, Lewis. Why would someone want to go there in the middle of the night?'

'When else would someone with dark motives go to a legendary cave once inhabited by an infamous cannibal?'

Clare looked at him. 'When Damien's car was found, a couple of my guys checked the cave, and along the coast, but didn't find anything.'

'Might it be a coincidence?' Lewis asked. 'That other car being here just a short time before Damien's car was found?'

Clare looked at him as she pulled her phone out of her pocket. 'Just going to call one of the guys back at the office.' As soon as it was answered she said, 'Look this registration up for me asap, will you, and text me the address?'

She hung up.

'Now what?'

'Give it a minute.'

A moment later her phone sounded a text alert. She read it. Looked at Lewis.

'The Range Rover is registered to a Gaia Jones of Summerhill Hall...'

'I think I know it,' Lewis said. 'It's near to a village I stayed in with Annie – Kirkronald?'

Clare started the engine. 'And you know what else?' she said.

'What?' Lewis demanded.

'I had a little poke around at the Oldfields earlier. Used their facilities. There was a soap from Summerhill Hall in their guest bathroom...'

'Coincidence?'

'It may well be that he or his wife bought the soap in a local shop, but it needs looking into. When it comes to missing people and suspicious deaths, Lewis, there's no such thing as coincidence. Only connections.'

Chapter 75

Clare

Clare left the holiday park and drove down to the spot where Lewis had his run-in with Craig Oldfield.

As they arrived her phone rang. She recognised the number. 'It's Fraser. I'll put it on speaker. But you need to be quiet. Okay? I don't want to compromise Fraser any more than I need to.' She pressed accept and a deep voice came online.

'CC,' Fraser said. 'You okay?'

Clare felt a shot of pleasure at hearing her friend's voice. Until that moment she hadn't realised how difficult it was to be removed from her usual position in life. 'Been better, Fraz.'

'It has been reported that one Lewis Jackson was last seen leaving the hospital in your car, Clare. I hope you know what you're doing.'

'Do you trust me, Fraser?'

'Course I do,' he answered immediately. 'He still with you?' he asked. Then, after a pause: 'Hello, Lewis.'

'Hi,' Lewis replied, sending Clare a look, and feeling sheepish.

'Bloods were taken before Lewis was discharged. Any update on them?' Clare asked.

'Nope. I did call in and say there was a rush on them. But the lassie I spoke to on the phone got all awkward, so I think somebody's given her a talking-to.'

'Benjamin Oldfield. Or one of his minions,' Clare said. 'I'll be surprised if those results don't somehow get lost.'

'What have you got yourself mixed up in, lass? These are serious people we're dealing with. I've never known a regional boss to get involved in a case down here. Lost blood tests might be the least of your problems.'

The silence that followed was so long and so deep that Clare asked, 'You still there, Fraz?'

'Aye,' he replied. 'I'm wondering what Oldfield's up to, and what he has on the big boss to make him stamp down with his size tens.'

'Are you aware of any previous connection between the two? Other than the usual golfing and drinking thing?'

'Och, there's just the usual gossip about them that lives up in High Dailly. Fur coats, nae knickers and seances. My predecessor used to refer to Oldfield as Mr Teflon, saying there had been a few strange accusations about him over the years, but not only did nothing stick, he came out acting peeved, threatening to sue every-body.'

'Did this guy give any details about these accusations?' Clare asked.

'Matter of fact, he didn't. As if he was afraid to.' Pause. 'But the night he retired, him and me had a lock-in with his favourite whisky, and he hinted at Benjamin Oldfield and the "black arts" as he put it.'

'Black arts?' Lewis and Clare looked at one another. And Clare was reminded of the piece of paper she'd found in the Oldfield house. It clearly referred to the occult.

'Aye. A weird choice of words, but what he meant by them he refused to explain, as if he was afraid we would be overheard, even though we were the only people in the room.'

'And were you never tempted to look into these accusations, or these so-called black arts, yourself?' Clare asked.

'In actual fact, I did, Clare – just a cursory look, to be honest, cos I had plenty of live cases to be dealing with. There was nothing on record. At least, nothing I could easily put my hands on.' There was the sound of someone talking in the background. 'Right, got to go, guys,' Fraser said quietly. 'Keep your heads down, eh?'

Black arts. Something unspooled, then clicked in Clare's mind. A connection made.

'Just one more thing, Fraser. A few days back, that time you saw me and Oldfield talking in the car park, remember? You mentioned someone who regularly called in to complain about him.'

A pause. 'Oh, aye – old Dr Hetherington. She's as fruity as an orchard. You don't want to be paying her any attention. She called again this morning.'

'Saying what?'

'About some seven-year anniversary coming up, and it being near time for Ben Oldfield and his cult members to raise their favourite demon.' He snorted in disbelief.

'What if she's right?' asked Clare, feeling excitement stir in her gut. 'Not about the actual demon – that's bullshit, clearly – but about the ceremony? There have been rumours about Oldfield and his cronies going about, even when I was a kid. What if there's actual truth in them? Did anyone ever investigate this Dr Hetherington to see what she had against Oldfield Senior?'

'Not that I'm aware of.'

'How far back do her complaints go?' Clare asked.

'Och, it will be years.'

'Any way of finding out?'

'You're not asking me to root around in the old paper files?'

'Please, Sarge?' Clare looked to Lewis and raised her eyebrows.

'I'm only ever Sarge if you want something from me, Corrigan.'

'I have a feeling about this, Fraser. Oldfield has clearly been up to something for years. You guys might have just ignored these complaints from Hetherington – and for good reason; it all sounds crazy – but a whole load of new information has come to light. I won't go into it on the phone, but trust me, maybe it's time to pay closer attention to what this Dr Hetherington has been saying.' She paused. 'Can you trust me on this, Fraz? You know I wouldn't ask if I wasn't convinced.'

Fraser didn't answer for a moment. Then he sighed and said, 'Right. Okay. But I'm not promising anything.' He hung up.

They sat in silence for a moment, digesting what they'd just been discussing.

'What now?' Lewis asked. 'We can't just sit here and do nothing. I have to try and find Annie.'

'I say we go and visit Gaia Jones at Summerhill Hall.'

Chapter 76

Annie

Annie found herself tramping across farmland, down to a river. Once there she strode out along the river bank, enjoying the vigour she was feeling in her thighs, and the air whooshing in and out of her lungs. The effort was all, and it felt good to be young and vital and full of purpose. The world was cast in a golden glow, and Annie felt a sense of belonging so strong she almost wept.

Across the river sat some thick woodland, and beyond that moorland stretching up to a rounded hill. At the top of the hill she could see a monument of some sort. The curve of the hill stopped abruptly as if sliced by a giant's sword, and beyond it Annie saw a stretch of sea before the horizon introduced a swathe of light-blue sky with a scattering of spun-sugar cloud.

All this beauty. Annie felt emotion build. She wanted to shout into the world how much everything meant to her. How much she would treasure this experience.

'Thank you.' The words came out in a near whisper. 'Thank you.'

But there, in the near distance, her murmurs gathered, like a crowd of crows speckling the naked branches of a tall, dead tree, flapping their wings, sharp beaks opened wide in a raucous concert of mockery.

Chapter 77

Lewis

Clare and Lewis stepped out of the car and stood looking up at the big house. Lewis felt a wave of fatigue. He put a hand on the roof of the car for support and reminded himself that just yesterday someone had tried to set him on fire.

'You okay?' Clare asked.

He forced an answering smile, dredging up strength from somewhere. No matter how exhausted he was, his sister was missing. He could rest later.

A bird flew overhead. Trees shifted in the breeze. Late-afternoon sunlight glinted off the large windows.

'There's something about this place,' he said to Clare.

'Sorry?'

'When I drove by here with Annie, it was like she was, I dunno, hypnotised or something.' He recalled the strange, dreamlike state she'd fallen into. And then he realised he'd missed something. Annie had been holding something back from him about the village. She'd been to Kirkronald before – alone. Met Ina, and the woman from the shop, Jo ... Then it clicked: Jo asked Annie if she'd come to look at 'the big house' again. Annie had pretended Jo was mistaken.

Clare's eyes were flat, one eyebrow raised, waiting. 'And?'

'She had that weird reaction. And when we were in the village, I found out she'd been there recently. Was interested in a big house. And then we're led here, to *this* big house. Don't you think that's spooky?'

'I'm a cop, Lewis. I don't do spooky. I do facts.'

Lewis let his gaze roam across the building's frontage, searching the windows for movement. 'Okay then. The facts: my sister got all weird looking up at this building. Then I discover she'd been down here looking at it alone. And now I find myself here looking for *her*. You don't think that's important?'

'She liked the house. Maybe she liked to imagine living here. I do that kind of shit all the time.'

He sighed and marched towards the stairs.

'Lewis, wait,' Clare said, and quickly followed. She reached him just as he raised a hand to lift the brass doorknob. She put a hand on his forearm. 'I know you're worried about Annie, but we have a process to follow. Facts to ascertain.'

'You do,' Lewis replied. Knocked. 'I have a gut feeling.' He knocked again. 'Benjamin Oldfield told Craig that Annie was at some friend's house. You find soap from this place in his bathroom. This house is it. I just know it is.' He stepped back, suddenly impatient. Hands on his hips. He shouted: 'Hello.'

His voice bounced back off the cold stone walls and unblinking windows.

'Lewis,' Clare said, and her tone made him turn to her. There was a forced calm there and a warning. 'We can't jump to conclusions.'

'A conclusion is where the coincidence led, no?' He turned back to the door and tried to turn the handle. It was locked fast.

'What are you doing? You're just going to walk in?'

'We're in the world of Annie Jackson now. That world doesn't follow the usual rules. Either you accept that, or you drive off and leave me here.'

The longer he stood here the harder his certainty that this house would provide answers to the disappearance of Annie – and of Damien too. He stepped to the side and walked up to one of the windows.

'Lewis,' Clare said, 'try to force that window and I'll arrest you.'

Lewis put his hands up. 'I'm simply looking inside. Enquiring of the residents of this fine house if they might know the whereabouts of my sister.'

Clare studied him for a beat, her eyes drilling into his. 'The minute, the *minute* you go too far, I'm pulling you away from here. Understood?'

Lewis jumped down the steps, turned and faced the building. 'Annie,' he shouted. 'Annie!'

Nothing but a quickly dissipating echo.

'Hello. Anybody there?'

A spark of rain on his forehead. The wind pushed at his cheek, and he noticed the clouds were heavier. Rain began to fall in a steady pattern.

'What about cars?' he said. Head hunched down into his neck, he walked over to the far right of the building. 'Where's the Range Rover we saw in that CCTV image?'

The chipped drive continued beyond the house into a little courtyard area bordered by what he assumed at one time had been a stable block built from the same blond sandstone as the main house and topped by crow-stepped brickwork. Two sets of large doors faced him. He tried to run to the first set, but his feet were slowed by the gravel. He reached for the handle, and pulled. It was stuck fast.

Clare walked to the other set and pulled. They were also locked.

'Big enough to hide a Range Rover, eh?'

Clare nodded. She looked around. 'It's very quiet. Where is everyone?'

Lewis spotted a door at the far end of the courtyard, tucked into a corner where the main house connected to the stable block. 'Kitchen?' he pointed.

'We're getting soaked. We should go back to the car,' Clare said.

This door was wide, painted dark green, with six panes of glass in the upper portion. A heavy net curtain prevented Lewis seeing what was inside.

So he knocked.

The sound reverberated in the stone cavern of the courtyard.

'There's no one here,' Clare said.

'Unless they're all cowering out of sight.' He exhaled in frustration. He was so sure this place would provide answers.

He knocked again. Hard. And felt a pane of glass rattle in its frame. 'Where is everyone?'

'Look, let's get out of this rain, and come back around dinner time? We'll probably have more luck then.'

Lewis nodded, reluctantly. If Clare hadn't been with him, he would have been breaking one of those panes of glass to see if there was a way to unlock the door from the inside. He shoved his hands into his pockets as if stopping himself.

'Okay,' he said. 'But I'm coming back. Whether you're with me or not.' He walked back around the building towards the car, still looking back up at the windows.

As Clare clipped her seatbelt on, her phone rang.

'Fraser,' she said, and put it on speaker.

'Right,' Fraser began. 'You fucking owe me, Corrigan.' He sounded wary.

'What have you found?'

A sudden squall of rain drummed on the roof of the car, drowning out Fraser's voice.

Clare reached for the volume control. 'Can you say that again, Fraz?'

He cleared his throat. 'Don't know if you two will have even been born when this happened...'

Chapter 78

Annie

Annie was in a kitchen. In a white nightgown. The house rang with quiet. But there had been shouting. Just then. And knocking. Wasn't there?

She was sure she'd heard her name. Had she? Her mind felt like it had been fragmented – sensory imprints coming at her in a muddle – colour was sound, sound had a taste. She rubbed at her forehead. Tried to slap her cheek. And missed.

'Wake up,' she told herself.

It was dark. Rain rattled the windows. Wind surged, and the house shifted and moaned around her.

She should go. Find her way out.

A funnel of light burst across the room, like headlights.

A car.

'Help,' she squeaked. She tried again. 'Help!' This time she managed more volume, and as she shouted she shuffled towards the front of the house, using the walls as her guide and support. A car was there. It was too dim for her to make out anything other than the lights, and that there may have been two people in it.

And then, sweeping the road with light, the car was gone.

No. Please. No.

She stopped at the staircase, hand on the post to give her some support. She was so tired. All she wanted to do now was sleep. She looked up towards the bedrooms, but instinct told her not to go there. She might not get back down.

Then, with fright, she realised if there was someone else in the house they'd hear her moving around. She stood statue still. Listened. Waited. Muscles tense: ready to run. But there was nothing – the way the quiet rang in her ear made her feel sure she was on her own. For now. But whoever brought her here would surely be back.

But where was *here*?

She forced three slow deep breaths, and concentrated on her feet, solid, on the floor. Her mind cleared a little. She felt a little less fatigue, a little less fog slowing her thoughts. Whatever they'd been feeding her was surely wearing off. A flash of recognition as she looked around herself. She'd been here before. She'd knocked on the door and that woman let her in. This was the house on the hill she'd felt herself drawn to. The house she'd dreamed about.

But who'd brought her back here, and why? The last memory she had – the last proper memory she could trust – was when she and Lewis were at the Oldfield house. She'd been sipping tea, started to feel groggy and then that woman had been behind Lewis. Her hand was on the back of his neck.

Lewis? How was he? Where was he?

She needed to act, but she was fearful of any movement in case she was caught. She didn't yet quite trust her limbs to do as they were told. She tested them, lifting her knees, walking on the spot. Feeling weirdly foolish, she stopped.

More deep breaths. Okay. Enough. Time to get out of here. She listened again, alert for the presence of anyone else.

Silence was an echoing song in her ear. Shadows flitted and danced. Rain drummed on windows. The house creaked in the wind.

Do something.

She made her way back into the kitchen. Finding the sink she turned on the tap and sluiced some cold water into her mouth with her hands. She realised how thirsty she was and drank too much, too fast. She choked; coughing loudly.

A noise. A knocking noise.

Shit. She froze.

More knocking. It sounded like it was coming from below her. 'Hello,' Annie ventured. 'Hello?'

Knuckle on wood. A door being rattled. A voice hoarse with frustration and anger. Then sobbing. A male voice.

Annie stood still. Breath on hold. Fear a shiver under her skin.

Then silence settled around her, like a world dampened to quiet after a heavy fall of snow. As if it never happened.

Had she imagined it? No. The fog in her mind was definitely retreating. She was sure the knocking was real.

Then. A sustained burst of sound. More knocking. A kick. And another kick. A flurry of shouts for help. A voice shrill with desperation. It was coming from under her feet she now realised. Was there a cellar there? Was someone else being held in the house?

She should just get the hell out of here while she could. She doubted she had the strength to help herself, never mind someone else. But the desperation in the man's voice spoke to her. There was just no way she could ignore that.

There must be a cellar. She looked around and tried to see through the dimness. She didn't want to turn on the light in case that alerted whoever had brought her here.

There were a couple of doors in the far wall. She shuffled there and pulled one open – to find a pantry. She reached for the handle on the other door. Feeling the cool, smooth, roundness of the handle in her palm, she held still for a moment, licked her lips. Did she want to know what was on the other side?

Annie twisted the handle, pulled the door open and looked down into blackness.

'Hello?' she heard, and noted the fear and desperation in those two simple syllables. 'Anybody there?'

Chapter 79

Sylvia
April 2024

She remembered walking into that café in Lochaline, and meeting Annie for the first time. How excited and nervous she had been. That hadn't happened since she'd been at school, for goodness' sake.

Perhaps that was why she reacted so poorly to what happened next. Sylvia had never been treated so badly. People had died for less.

She'd never forget Annie Jackson's reaction to her. The lack of interest – no, the outright irritation and anger. 'Jesus,' Annie had said. 'Leave me alone.' Then she'd barged against Sylvia so that she fell onto a table, before screaming, 'Just give up will you.' Then stormed out of the café.

At her side, Sylvia was aware her little shadow's mouth was open wide, her throat pulsing in silent, mocking laughter.

'What in the seven hells...?' Sylvia managed to hold it together until she got back in her car. 'How dare she?' She battered the steering wheel with the heels of her hands. She screamed. How dare Annie Jackson treat her with such contempt?

She tried to calm herself. Worked hard to still her emotions. Stared out of the windscreen and into the distance for a long time, her mind busy all the while.

Finally she pulled out her phone and rang Ben.

'How's your wild-goose chase?' he asked in that mocking tone of his as soon as he'd answered.

'For once, shut up and listen, Ben,' she snapped.

'Lovely to talk to you too, Sylvia, or Gaia, or whatever bloody name works for you today,' he snapped back. 'Oh, by the way, that Hetherington woman is at it again. Stirring up the natives.'

'Just ignore her, Ben. She's an old crank. No one takes her seriously,' she said.

'It's easy for you to say. I'm the one she's always complaining about.'

'Well, you shouldn't have drawn yourself to her attention all those years ago, should you.'

'Probably because I'm the more prominent citizen,' Ben said haughtily, as if Sylvia hadn't spoken. 'That's why she gives my name to the police time after time.'

'Oh, do be quiet, Ben,' she urged. Her mind was too full of Annie to worry about Hetherington. She could still see that irritated, uninterested look in Annie's eyes. No one dismissed Sylvia Lowry-Law in that manner.

'You sound even more dyspeptic than normal, Sylvia. What's happening?'

'The next ceremony...' she began.

'Right. About that. I'm tired, Sylvia.' His voice was strangely flat. 'I've had enough. It doesn't work. Won't ever work. Whatever we've been doing wrong over the years—'

'We've been using male victims,' Sylvia interrupted. 'Thinking that's who the Baobhan Sith preys on. But what if that only applies when she's incarnate once more? *That's* where we've gone wrong all these years. It needs a female sacrifice. Of course it does. After all, why should this ceremony be different from anything else in this bloody world.'

'Please,' Ben said stiffly, 'save me from the feminist rant.'

'I have someone,' she said, feeling a stir of excitement at the possibilities. 'Someone powerful.' She inhaled deeply. 'You mentioned the father of your grandchild?'

'Right?'

'He's a burden on you?'

'What are you suggesting?'

She could hear a note of interest in his voice now. 'We can't simply kidnap this young woman. She's too well known. She's hidden herself away in the highlands for a reason. So we ... I' – she corrected herself – 'need to entice her to this area on some pretext. I'm hearing she gets all kinds of requests for help, but refuses them. If this person is a member of her family, and he goes missing...'

'Go on.'

'...I think she'll find it more difficult to refuse. So what I want you to do is get your goons to make sure this guy goes missing. I don't care what you do with him – dump him in my basement for all I care. Just make sure it's in our neck of the woods. I'm certain her family will ask her to try and find him, and that will bring her down there. I'll work out how to slip her a glamour of some sort to make her feel the pull of Summerhill Hall. Once she comes, I'll keep her there and prepare her for the ceremony, which we can perform on All Hallows' Eve.'

'Excellent,' Ben replied, and she could see him in her mind's eye, nodding as he thought her idea through. 'I thought I had the lad where I wanted him years ago. And then I tried to pay him off when he came out of prison. Apparently, he developed a conscience while he was inside and now thinks he's father of the year. So this is a much more satisfactory plan.'

'I don't care about him, Ben. This is about the ceremony. The young woman I'm talking about has a gift. And she is connected to me by blood.'

Sylvia felt Sarah's stare: her judgement. She turned round. Snapped. 'What?' But she had shimmered out of view.

Sarah was beginning to be too much. For most of Sylvia's life she'd been a sporadic but mostly positive presence. But gradually over the last few years she'd become a dark influence, giving off waves of spite and malice. This had worsened considerably over the last few months, and in recent weeks, ever since she'd tried to deal with Annie Jackson, in fact, her shadow – Sarah – had become almost permanent. And her silence was beginning to terrorise Sylvia. Who would have thought that quiet could be so unnerving. So tormenting.

'Go,' she shouted at the wing mirror of the car.

'Who are you talking to, Sylvia?' Ben asked. 'Are you with someone?'

'Of course not,' she replied. 'I'm talking to you.' She fought to marshal her thoughts, to relegate Sarah to the back of her mind and return to the subject of her conversation with Ben.

She was on the right track. She was sure of it.

Two birds. One powerful cast of a weighty stone.

As a young woman with otherworldly gifts, Annie's blood would offer a potent contribution to the magic. Powerful enough, she was certain, to raise a demon.

Her lawyer had assured Sylvia that Annie was the last female of her line – the last female descendant of the Campbell who had treated her ancestor so sorely. Therefore, Annie's death as a blood sacrifice would surely satisfy the spirits who maintained the curse – thereby breaking it once and for all. Sylvia would just have to make sure that every last drop of her blood was spilled.

She thought of Annie's reaction to her once more. An insult too much to bear. Anger simmered in her heart. 'This is a sacrifice with real power behind it, Ben. What we've been missing, what we've been waiting for all these years, I'm fast becoming certain, is Annie Jackson.'

She hung up without another word, aware of the burn of attention at her side.

'Leave me alone.'

But the shadow thickened, pulsed with spite, and Sylvia could feel Sarah's eyes bore into the side of her head, and into her brain, with a malignancy darker than any demon she'd ever encountered.

Chapter 80

Annie

As her eyes adjusted, she noted a set of stairs descending into the dark. The gradient was steep and seemed to go on forever. The ceiling was so low she had to duck her head. Placing her hand on the handrail, smooth with use, she took the first step. The staircase made a little creak. She took another couple of steps, her pulse a hammer in her neck, her breath coming in short bursts.

'Hello,' she spoke down into the darkness, her voice flattened by the dead air below. 'Hello.'

Annie held her breath. Lowered her foot onto the next step. 'Hello?'

'Who's there?' A cracked voice, muted from behind a door somewhere, still panicked. 'Hello.' The owner of the voice dredged up some strength from somewhere. 'Help. You've got to help me.'

Annie held a hand over her heart, alarm a siren in her mind. She stopped. Should she go back? Might she be in danger if she went any further? Her head felt completely clear now. Adrenaline awakening every part of her body.

'Help me, please. They've locked me up. I've been...' A long pause. 'I've been stabbed.' The sound of a door being rattled in its frame. 'I've lost ...there's so much blood. Too much...'

'Wait. Wait,' Annie urged, and hurried down the rest of the stairs.

She reached a short passageway. Something slight hit her forehead. She reached for it; realised it was a light cord, and pulled. Weak light from a naked bulb helped her see where she was. Solid, narrow, light-coloured walls – and facing her, a black door.

'You have to be quiet,' she said as she reached it. She tested the handle. It was firmly locked.

'Who are you?' the man asked. He sounded fairly young. And familiar. 'Tell Dad I'm sorry. Tell him I won't say anything.'

'You need to be quiet,' Annie said as she reached the door. She pressed the side of her head against the wood. 'Are you okay?'

'No.' His voice cracked. 'I've been here ... I don't know how long. Lost track. There's another ... There's someone else in here. Too dark to tell.' He started crying. 'I think he's dead.' At this his voice grew louder. 'You have to get me out. You have to get me out.'

A key? There had to be a key somewhere. Annie reached up with both hands and traced the width of the lintel in case a key had been placed there. It was almost too tall for her, but on tip-toes she managed. From one side to the next she checked, but there was nothing.

He rattled the door once more. Hard. A fury of wood on wood. Then silence, and Annie could hear sobbing.

'Hey,' Annie said. 'You need to trust me. I'm doing the best I can. I've been held here too, but I'm going to get you out. Get *us* out.' The door shook in its frame as if the man had fallen against it. Then she heard the swish of clothing down the wood as he collapsed to the floor.

'You don't have a key? Please. I need to get out of here.'

'What's your name? My name's Annie,' she said in an attempt to reassure him that help was on its way.

'Annie?' he asked after a pause. 'Annie Jackson?'

Annie's mouth dropped open. She replayed his voice in her mind's ear and felt a spark of recognition.

'Craig?'

'They told me you were...' He stopped. 'And why should that have been true when everything else is a lie, Annie?' he added in a rush. 'It's Craig. Craig Oldfield. I saved your brother's life. I saved Lewis.'

'What?' Annie cried. 'Saved him from what...?'

'He's safe now, Annie,' he said desperately. 'He's safe. And now you need to help us both.' Annie heard the sound of sobbing. 'I'm so tired. I think I've lost too much...' His voice faded. 'Too much blood,' he cried. 'I'm going to die here, aren't I?'

'Craig. Craig, stop...' Annie said. 'I'll find a key and get you out of here, but you need to stay calm while I go and hunt for it, okay?' She fought to inject a comforting note into her voice.

'My dad had me attacked and dumped here. Can you believe that? It's what they do – they just leave people here to die. Your cousin's here.' He paused. Sniffed. It sounded like he was crying. 'Damien. He was alive when I arrived. Just. But he hasn't spoken for ages. I think they locked him up and just let him starve.' His sobbing became loud, constant. 'I don't want to die.'

Annie took in his distress and tried to separate fact from fiction. What had really happened? Was he telling the truth? The last she saw, this guy he was in his father's study wearing a sneer and acting hateful towards her and Lewis.

She did remember picking up some kind of tension between father and son. Was everything not what it seemed? And here he was, on the other side of a locked door, in the basement of a house she'd also been confined in, sounding like he was in a huge deal of pain.

'Annie?' he begged. 'You still there?'

'I'll find a key, Craig. I'll get help.'

Chapter 81

Clare

'From what I can see the first complaint was just a few years after the Orkney Satanic Abuse scandal,' Fraser began. 'The authorities made such a monumental cock-up there, I'm guessing it threw a lot of doubt on this, and quite possibly other allegations.'

'What happened?' Clare demanded, impatient to know.

'There was a complaint about some residents of High Dailly: Oldfield and his wife, Evelyn. It came from one Dr Thomasina Hetherington, Emeritus Professor of the Occult and Modern Art at Chapman University in California.'

'She's travelled far,' Clare said.

'That name rings a bell,' Lewis muttered.

'The Oldfields were actually interviewed under caution. And their house was searched, but the case was dismissed,' Fraser said.

'Oh,' Clare responded, unable to hide her disappointment. 'What did the allegation consist of?'

'Hetherington alleged that a contact of Oldfield's had attended her course and took some of her research into Highland legends and demons way too seriously. This contact, she claimed, intended to try and raise one of these demons using ritual human sacrifice. Hetherington said this woman had joined forces with Oldfield. She was certain that if the police looked closely they would find there had been people missing around that time.'

'Did they ever manage to cross-reference this with any suspicious deaths or missing people?' Lewis asked.

'Not that I can find,' Fraser replied.

'Want to know who signed off and closed the case?' Fraser asked, and Clare noted his voice rose in pitch. 'One Detective Brian Ward.'

'Oh,' Clare said, and looked at Lewis.

'Who?' Lewis asked.

'That's the man who went on to be the regional super, and who just put me on leave.'

'Then, it looks like every seven years for the next twenty-one, Dr Hetherington has repeated her allegations. But on subsequent occasions the complaints were merely noted, and filed away without action,' Fraser continued. 'Interestingly, her more recent ones were sent in from a local address.'

'Dr Hetherington moved to Scotland to keep tabs on Oldfield?'

'That's dedication to the cause, eh?' Fraser said.

'I do know her,' Lewis exclaimed. 'I've been in her house. With Annie.'

Clare looked at Lewis, trying to juggle what he was saying with the information relayed by her colleague.

'And when we popped into her house she warned us.' Lewis's mouth formed a narrow O. 'She tried to warn us, and we wouldn't listen.'

'What are you talking about, Lewis?' Clare asked.

'This woman, Dr Hetherington. I've been in her house. It has to be the same woman.' He exhaled sharply. 'Annie. Oh God.' He swivelled in his seat to face Clare. 'Why kidnap Annie ... unless they want to ... to *use* her in some way?' He bit his lip, tucked his hands under his arms.

Clare noted how pale Lewis had grown and placed a hand on his forearm. He shrugged it off as if he couldn't bear the contact.

'Every seven years, you said?' Lewis asked, his face creased in thought. 'Rab Daniels died in what, 2010? That's fourteen years ago. Counting back, that meets the "every seven years" criteria. He could have been one of the sacrifices.' Lewis chewed on that for a moment. 'I have my doubts about Craig's story. Not that he doesn't believe it himself, but that it happened in the way he described. What if Rab *had* been a ritual sacrifice? And the Oldfields get Damien so out of his head that he's convinced he killed him. Impressionable teenager and all that.'

'That's cold. Involving their own son,' Clare said.

'Damien and Alison were in love. If the Oldfields got Damien to believe he killed Rab, not only did they have a way to get rid of the body but they had something they could hold over Damien forevermore. Win-win.'

Clare thought that through. 'And Craig? He was, what, collateral damage?'

'If they're calculating enough to kill a kid and frame his pal, who knows what they're capable of – and by the way, Craig's not even sure the old man is his old man.'

Fraser jumped in. 'I'm aware of that rumour as well – that Craig isn't Benjamin's actual son. The Oldfields had a brief split years ago, as I recall, and when the missus came back she was pregnant.'

'She could have come back *because* she was pregnant,' Clare argued.

'Or to hide the fact the baby wasn't his?'

Clare and Lewis exchanged a look.

'Can you text me the address of Dr Hetherington, please, Fraser?' Clare asked.

'No need,' Lewis interrupted. 'I know exactly where she is.'

Chapter 82

Lewis

Kirkronald village was becoming very familiar to Lewis, and as he looked at the houses they drove past through a rain-slicked windscreen he realised what season it was.

'God, I'd forgotten it was Halloween.' He nodded in the direction of a house that had a collection of three pumpkin lanterns on its doorstep. The next house had a witch's broom on theirs and cobwebs draped over the inside of their living-room window.

'Poor kids,' Clare said as she switched the windscreen wipers to a faster setting. 'There's not going to be any trick-or-treating going on on a night like this.' She drove further along the main street. 'You were here before, you said?' Clare asked. 'Can you see the right house?'

Lewis peered through the rain and the waning light, and spotted the cottage he and Annie had so recently visited. He pointed. 'It's this one.'

As they'd driven up from Girvan he'd filled Clare in on how they'd passed through the village when they first started looking into Damien's disappearance – and how both had separately, and then together, bumped into a strange old woman called Ina.

'So Ina must be short for Thomasina,' Clare said now, giving a series of slow nods. 'Could this case get any stranger?'

As she parked, Lewis plucked his phone from his pocket. 'Dr Thomasina Hetherington,' he said as he thumbed out some letters. 'Let's see what's online about her.' He paused. And then read out loud: '"Dr Thomasina Hetherington, a leader in her field, lectures on the historical importance of spiritualism, mysticism and folklore to examine how the unknown became a pivotal metaphor for the purpose of expanding and remaking the tangible."'

Lewis exhaled. 'I have no clue what any of that means.' And now even more in a hurry to find out who Ina really was and what she knew, he climbed out of the car and stepped onto the path leading to the little white cottage. He heard a bark of welcome from the old Labrador, Bob, and as he neared the door, he could hear the dog huffing on the other side of the wood.

Clare joined him as the door opened and Ina peered out, Bob's head by her knee.

Ina studied him for a moment. 'Lewis,' she said, 'didn't I warn you to stay away? Where's Annie?'

'Dr Hetherington,' Clare said before Lewis could reply. 'My name is Detective Clare Corrigan. May we come in?'

'May I ask why?'

'Benjamin Oldfield,' Clare answered simply. 'It's better if we come in. Is that okay?'

Ina nodded, turned and shuffled into the house, leaving the door open for them. They followed her into the gloom of the sitting room. She pointed towards the sofa and they sat side by side.

Ina lowered herself into her chair, her expression unreadable. The dog sat by her feet.

'Dr Hetherington—' Clare began.

'It's been a long time since anyone called me that,' Ina interrupted.

Clare nodded in acknowledgement. 'I understand from our records that you've made a series of allegations about Benjamin Oldfield over the years.'

'All of which your colleagues ignored.'

Rain drummed against the window, and wind whistled down the chimney.

'New information has come to light suggesting we take a closer look at this particular individual.'

'Oh my.' Ina sat forward, eyes wide, relief softening her features. 'After all these years somebody is paying attention. What sort of information, may I ask?'

'We are not at liberty to say,' Clare replied.

A thought seemed to cloud Ina's eyes and she looked to Lewis. 'Why's Annie not with you?' she asked.

'If we could ascertain how and why you know the Oldfields, Dr Hetherington?' Clare said before Lewis could reply.

'I met Annie before I met you, Lewis,' Ina said as if Clare hadn't spoken.

'I guessed as much. But she tried to hide it from me. Any idea why?' he replied.

'She was in my wee local shop talking to Jo, the owner. I overheard her asking about Summerhill Hall.'

Lewis sent Clare a look. That house. He *knew* Annie had some kind of interest in the place.

'She spun some tale about her and her brother looking for somewhere to turn into a hotel. I contrived to bump into her outside the shop,' Ina said. 'To try and warn her off.'

'Warn her off what...?' Clare asked.

'Summerhill Hall is not a place for a lovely young woman like her.' Ina frowned. 'You're with the police, but I'm thinking this isn't an official investigation...' She turned to Lewis. 'Where is Annie?' she asked again. 'Is she missing? Is that why you're with...' she looked Clare up and down, assessing her clothing '...an off-duty detective?'

Lewis simply stared at the old woman. She might be old, her body weakened, but her mind was sharp. She missed nothing.

The wind whistled down the chimney again. The old dog looked up, whined a little and moved closer to his owner.

Ina looked to Clare now. 'You say you're not at liberty to tell me what new information you have about Ben Oldfield, but I've been warning your people about him and his cronies for years. I think I'm owed something, officer, don't you?'

Lewis could see that Clare was reluctant to give too much away, but he sensed that to get Ina to open up they needed to tell her what they knew. 'After seeing you a couple of days ago, we went to the Oldfields' house.' Lewis paused. 'They tried to kill me and I think they have Annie somewhere.'

Ina gasped. 'Oh, son,' she said, clutching at her collar.

'What?' said Lewis, sitting forward. 'Is Annie in danger?'

'Lewis, I don't think—' Clare began.

Lewis was aware that Clare wanted him to shut up, but he carried on regardless. He may have been unsure of Ina when he first met her, but to his mind she was clearly on their side. 'I'm also certain he killed a boy called Rab Daniels, quite possibly his sister, and he's somehow done away with my cousin, Damien. Does that mean they might have done something to Annie—?'

'I've been fighting to alert the authorities to their activities for years,' Ina interrupted looked accusingly at Clare for a moment. 'Are you new to the area?'

Clare shot Lewis a stern look before replying. 'I grew up in Girvan, but yes, only recently came down to this neck of the woods for work. In the last year or so.'

'Tell me, Ina. Is Annie in danger?' Lewis urged.

'The literature always suggests that it is male victims that are required.' Ina tilted her head to the side. 'At least as far as this ceremony is concerned.' She paused as if assessing that fact anew.

'Let's take a moment,' Clare said. 'Exactly what are we dealing with here? What literature, and what ceremony? And how did you even come across the Oldfields?'

'I was giving a series of lectures in a university in California, back in the eighties. A woman called Sylvia Lowry-Law came along.' Ina stared into the fire for a moment. 'One topic seemed to particularly intrigue her. That of an ancient fey creature of Scottish legend called the Baobhan Sith. I'd recently found a piece of text that suggested there was an occult ceremony one could use to give this creature life.

'Sylvia and I became sort of friends. She was very interested in my studies. Plied me with compliments. Took me out to expensive restaurants. Then, a man came over to visit. Ben.' Ina stopped talking and looked from Clare to Lewis. 'He's a danger. All the more so because he's a man of influence. He has friends in some very high places. So, whenever I called the police I concentrated on him, thinking he'd be the better one to stop.

'But, make no mistake, Sylvia is no bit-part player. You really need to be wary of her. She is a zealot.' Ina played with the top button of her blouse with thin, trembling fingers. 'It took a while for me to realise it. I can normally tell the deranged and disturbed from a hundred paces, but she was very convincing. I was delighted to have found a like mind. If I'd thought for a moment that she would put my research to actual use...' Her face slumped

with shame. 'I have the death of several young men on my conscience.'

'You really believe that they have killed a number of people?'
asked Clare.

Ina nodded slowly, looking again into the fire.

'When you contacted the police, making these allegations –
were you never afraid for your own safety?' Clare asked. 'Have
they ever threatened you?'

Ina shook her head. 'I've hidden in plain sight. They think I'm
a harmless old biddy, easily dismissed. But I've kept chipping away
at them, and the authorities. Always ready to expose them the
moment they make a mistake.'

'Do you have any idea why they might want Annie? It's
Halloween,' Lewis added, panic rising. 'Don't these kind of people
believe this is a date of significance?'

Ina nodded, and in that nod Lewis read a great deal of dread.

'Let's be clear,' Clare said. 'We're talking about Benjamin
Oldfield, the lawyer?'

'Yes. Sylvia and Ben. They've known each other since they were
small children. When you see them together they're like cousins,
or brother and sister. I doubt they've ever been lovers, but you
never know with people who chase the occult.' She exhaled.
'Benjamin Oldfield comes from old money. Privately educated.
And he has the arrogance of his class – thinking his connections
will always save him from any consequences. Sylvia is a different
cauldron of fish altogether. And I use the word cauldron advisedly.
She is a genuine witch. Versed in some very dark magic indeed.'

'You believe she's actually using magic?' Clare asked.

'It doesn't matter what I believe, dear,' Ina replied. 'It's what she
believes that's important – and she's as devout as they come. As I
said: she's a zealot.'

'And where is this Sylvia woman? Is she going to be hard to
track down?' Lewis asked.

Ina allowed herself a slight smile of satisfaction. 'She changed her name when she bought Summerhill Hall.' Lewis sat up. 'Nowadays she pretends to provide a retreat for vulnerable young women. A charitable refuge of sorts. But it's a front – to hide what she's really up to. And she calls herself Gaia Jones.'

Chapter 83

Annie

With the shocking thought that Damien might have been alive while she was also in the house, Annie clambered up the stairs and into the kitchen to hunt for a key to the basement room, adrenaline having burnt off the last of her fatigue and mental fog.

'Please find that key, Annie. I don't have much...' Craig's voice followed her.

As she rummaged and searched, she thought about the door. It was old, heavy wood, well set within the lintel. The keyhole was carved into the wood, rather than a circle of brass that might take a Yale key – would that mean a key on the end of a long leg?

'Annie,' Craig shouted. 'You still there?'

She made her way around the kitchen, looking in every drawer and cupboard, checking every space for a key; even lifting the lids on the pots in case it was being hidden there. Then she went around everything one more time.

A noise at the front of the house. She froze.

Waited.

Everything was still.

Mouth dry, she wanted to scream with frustration. How was she going to save them both? Could she kick the door in? It was too solid. Maybe Craig could.

Back down in the cellar, mouth at the door, she said: 'Sorry Craig, I searched the kitchen for a key, but there's nothing. Can you kick the door in?'

'It opens inwards, Annie.' Craig coughed. 'Even if I had the strength all I would do is break my foot.'

He was sounding weaker than when she'd last spoken to him. Annie rattled the door, feeling for any give in the wood or in the hinges.

'Annie?' Craig said.

'I'm so sorry,' she replied, fighting back tears of frustration. 'I don't know how...'

Silence. Then:

'Save yourself, Annie. Get away from here and get the police. People might not believe—'

'I can't just leave you,' Annie protested.

Craig tapped on the door. It was a weak sound. A gesture of acceptance. 'I'm sorry for my part in any of this,' he croaked. Sniffed. 'Go, Annie, go. There's no point in the two of us getting stuck here.'

'Do you have an idea what they gave me?' Annie asked. 'And what they want from me?'

'Annie,' Craig said, and even through the thickness of the wood Annie could hear how adamant he was. 'Go.'

She put a hand to the wood, rested a palm against the cool, un-yielding surface, and was reminded of the day she'd been in the Oldfield house. Both Benjamin's and Craig's faces had blurred into skulls, and her murmurs had sung of their death: a chorus of violence. She'd seen a knife, a spray of blood, a face contorted with agony. But then both faces had resolved themselves, the murmurs stopped, her usual headache abated and she'd thought that whatever might lead to that outcome was yet to be resolved. Decisions were yet to be made. She hadn't been able to tell whether it was the father or the son, or both, who would die. But now she had her answer.

'Okay,' she said, reluctance a weight on her mind and body. Once again she was thrust into a situation where her gift, her knowledge, was useless. Someone would die and she could do nothing to stop it. With a heavy, resigned heart she turned to face the stairwell.

The little light bulb flickered, the air cooled, and Annie's murmurs burst into contemptuous song.

A woman stood there. Cast in an unearthly light by the weak light from the bulb. Her hair dark as a void, the skin of her forehead, nose and cheeks a cold sparkle. She moved closer, and her features were softened. Annie recognised her now. She'd met her when she first came here. Gaia. Her murmurs cackled, but Annie was reassured by the expression on her face.

'How did you get into my house?' the woman asked. 'And why are you down here? Are you okay?'

A thump sounded from the other side of the door. Craig in a high pitch of panic – it sounded like he was saying, *Get away, get away*.

With an expression of shock Gaia asked, 'Is there someone in there?'

'Yes,' Annie relaxed. She was safe. Hope surging in her heart. 'He's been locked in. Said his father had him attacked. He said he's lost a lot of blood. I've been trying to find the key. Do you have it?'

'How did...?' The woman shook her head. Then she seemed to make an effort to gather her wits about her. 'His father? Oh my word,' the woman said. 'The key. Gosh, I haven't seen it. Why don't you go upstairs and ... Oh my word. I've been away, you know. I gave him the key while I was...'

The woman was rambling. Annie wanted to give her a shake.

'The key,' Annie said, mustering calm. 'Where's the key?'

'I keep it in the tallboy by the back door. In the little drawer on the right. Why don't you go up and get it, and I'll talk to Craig and keep him calm.'

As she moved to the side to let Annie pass, two facts presented themselves to Annie's mind.

The woman knew exactly who was behind that door – she'd used his name.

And she'd had one hand behind her back the entire time they'd been talking.

Annie surged forward, but she was too slow, too late. A hand came over and down and she felt a sharp pain at the back of her neck.

Then all became smoke, and silence.

Chapter 84

Clare

Lewis jumped to his feet. 'We need to go back to Summerhill Hall,' he told Clare.

Ina looked at them both. 'You've been?'

'Yes, just,' Clare replied. 'And we will go back, but armed with as much knowledge as possible. It's pointless trying those doors again.'

Lewis sat down and turned to Ina again. 'What you said earlier about Annie asking about Summerhill Hall – Annie and I drove past it when we were down here looking into Damien's disappearance. And she got a bit weird when we passed it.'

'In what way, weird?' Ina asked.

'She became all kind of dreamy and kind of stared at it with this look of longing.' He shook his head. 'The more I think about it, the stranger it feels. And even after we were long past it she was in a kind of trance.' Lewis looked at Clare. 'The day I was attacked in Glasgow – Annie told me she'd spent the afternoon out driving. She must've been down here.' He turned back to Ina. 'That must have been when she met you and Jo for the first time. You said she was asking Jo about the house. Why was she so attracted to it...?'

Ina shook her head. 'If I'm not mistaken she'll have been subject to a glamour,' said Ina. 'It's a charm or a spell. Sylvia, or

Gaia as she now is, could have attracted her to the house with one.'

'Whatever these people are up to,' said Clare, 'it looks like they've convinced themselves they need Annie. And you two played into their hands by going to the Oldfield house.'

Lewis crossed his arms. 'God, I was such an idiot.'

'Right.' Ina clapped her hands loudly, and looked at Lewis. 'To help you both make sense of what might be going on...' She pushed herself out of her chair and walked over to the bookshelf where she reached up and pulled out a book. She showed the cover to them.

'*Highland Folklore and Legends* by Dr T. A. Hetherington,' Clare read, then looked across to the old woman. 'You wrote this.'

Ina nodded. 'A long time ago. So long ago that it almost feels as if it was written by someone else.' She opened it up, picking a certain page and turned it so they could both see.

An artist's rendering of a woman with long, dark hair took up half a page on the left. Her eyes were staring, her teeth bare and pointed. She was wearing a long dress that was green, but looked as if that green came from moss, leaves and grass rather than some kind of dye. And just visible under the hem of her dress was a cloven hoof. There was a heading: 'Succubus – Banshee – Faerie Vampire, the Baobhan Sith'.

Clare took the book from Ina and read the first line: '"She has watched over and preyed on the inhabitants of this cloud- and mist-covered land for an age – before the Norse, before even the armies of Rome."'

Clare carried on reading silently for a few moments. 'That's the reason behind the Oldfields' cult, or whatever it is?' she asked.

Ina looked from Clare to Lewis and back down to the page. 'There are things I learned while researching and writing that section that didn't make it into the book. The detail I left out,' Ina began, 'but that I shared with Sylvia.' She paused. Clare could see her chin wobble, and she knew that it was fear for Annie. 'Dear

Lord,' Ina gasped, eyes wide as if she had just made a connection. '*That's* why they want Annie.'

'Why?' Lewis demanded.

'There's a ritual, a black mass if you like, to awaken the Baobhan Sith. They've been trying the ceremony, and failing, for years. But I think they would have interpreted the literature to mean that the ritual required young men. I'm worried they think it's time to try something new.'

Clare exchanged a look with Lewis – she could see in his eyes he was thinking of his sister.

'What's so special about Annie?' Clare asked.

'Annie's rare. Someone with a genuine form of otherworldly power. Her blood would be seen as being very potent indeed.'

Clare felt a very real shot of fear herself now. Lewis was so tense she thought he might explode.

'But how?' Lewis asked. 'What would they want with her?'

'The black mass,' Ina answered with a grim, forbidding expression. 'The ritual needs freshly harvested blood. And lots of it.'

Chapter 85

Ben
NOW

The rain was so heavy they could barely see more than two feet in front of them as they tried to load the near-somnolent young woman into the car. As he watched, a gust of wind plucked at Sylvia's coat, drove her hair over her face, and in the time it took for Evelyn and Sylvia to guide the woman into the backseat of the Range Rover, he was soaked.

A shout came at him from Evelyn but the wind gusted the sound away. From the clenched expression on her face he could see she wasn't happy with him. Too bad. It was a poor idea from beginning to end. He didn't want to be here, and if the two women hadn't badgered him, he'd be cosied up in his study with an expensive single malt.

Ben made his way to the car and climbed into the front passenger seat. When Sylvia sat beside him he asked, 'Is someone going to explain why in the blazes we're not waiting for better weather?'

'Shut up. Shut up. Shut up,' Sylvia shouted. But when Ben turned to snap back at her, she was turned slightly to the side as if addressing someone just out of his sight.

'Who are you telling to shut up?' Ben demanded. She'd been increasingly strange over the last few weeks.

'No one,' Sylvia replied. She blinked. Smiled. And looked as if she was back in control.

Her hand was on the strap of the seatbelt when she turned to him. 'Stop bitching, Ben. We've been over this,' she said as if the shouting interlude hadn't happened.

'Yes, Ben,' Evelyn said from the backseat. 'A million times.' Ben wondered just when she had become a devotee of Sylvia and her plans. For much of their marriage she'd complained about their relationship, seeing it as a threat.

Sylvia looked across at him. 'Put your seatbelt on.' She sat forward in her seat and tried to study the sky through the rain-lashed windscreen. 'There's going to be an opening in the weather and we have to get there before the storm closes in again or we'll never manage to walk from the car park to the cave.'

'I just think it would be better to wait. Hecate is the mother of magic and sorcery. Her day is the end of November. The weather might be better then...'

Sylvia ignored him. They reached the main road. And without waiting to see if any cars were coming, Sylvia took the turn south.

'Bugger of hell,' Ben exclaimed, holding on to the handle inside the door. 'You'll get us all killed.'

'You're perfectly safe,' Sylvia said, staring straight ahead, her eyes gleaming. '*She* won't let anything happen to us. We are the blessed ones who will help her be reborn. She'll make sure everything goes without a hitch.'

'It has to be tonight,' Evelyn added, and Ben was aware of her hard eyes on him. He turned to face her.

'You alright, dearest?'

Her mouth was a sour line as she replied, 'Never better, *dearest*.'

'There's truth in every cliché,' Sylvia said slowly, her eyes on Ben. 'Humanity has long been aware that there is power in this night. When the world shifts and the land of the dead and the land of the living come into contact with one another—'

'Save me the lecture, Sylvia,' Ben interrupted. 'I've been studying this for as long as you have.'

'Seems like you've forgotten most of what you learned.'

'What's that supposed to mean?'

'Death is a sacred event. It has to have meaning or the bloodshed spoils the earth. Sours the magic,' Sylvia said.

'What the hell are you talking about?' Ben demanded.

'Did you have to kill him, Ben?' Evelyn asked.

Ben thought of Damien languishing in the cellar these last weeks. 'I ... The boy was in the way. He could have spoiled everything we've worked for,' he replied. He studied Evelyn's face in the mirror. Really looked at it, and realised for the first time in all the years they'd been together that his wife was a total stranger to him. 'I thought you would understand that.'

'I see you, Benjamin Oldfield,' she replied. 'The veil has lifted and I see every part of you.'

'What in the blazes has got into you?'

'I saw what I wanted to see, and that is on me,' Evelyn said. 'When I met you the Order was everything in my life, but the wheel turns, Benjamin Oldfield, and eventually, so does the worm.'

'What on earth are you talking about? The Order never really recovered from the death of Phineas Dance, and you think to mention it now?'

Evelyn stared out of her window as if he hadn't spoken, a solitary tear gleaming on the silvered pale of her cheek. 'It's thanks to Sylvia I have a new direction in life.'

'All hail Sylvia, or Gaia or whatever you call yourself these days,' Ben humphed, wondering what had become of the placid woman who'd all but bowed to him every day they'd been together. He stole a look at Sylvia. 'What have you been saying to my wife?' he demanded, worried now that Evelyn might not have meant Damien when she asked why he'd killed him.

Sylvia's expression was inscrutable as she guided the car towards their destination.

Did Evelyn know about Craig?

Had Sylvia told her?

No, he decided, Sylvia wouldn't dare. He was still the senior partner in this endeavour. And besides, Craig had to go. He'd despised the boy on first sight. It was clear, even in the crib, that Phineas Dance was his father, and that this was Dance's last effort to place one more torment in his way. But by the time the baby was born it was too late: disowning him and his mother would have cast a huge shadow over his work and reputation.

No, he decided, glancing back at his wife again. If she thought he'd harmed a hair on her precious boy's head he'd be propped up on pillows fighting a slow death by arsenic right now. Everything was fine, he relaxed. Everything was just as it should be.

'Look at you, all in white.' Evelyn was addressing their captive, slumped on the seat beside her. She gently guided the young woman's head on to her lap, and as solicitous as a new mother she drew her hair to either side of her face and lightly stroked her cheek, then her neck, along the line where the blade would soon part the flesh.

Chapter 86

Lewis

Lewis jumped up. Started pacing. The dog rose to his feet, sounding a low growl of concern.

'They've been trying this ritual for years. And failing. They now think Annie is the key,' he summarised, fighting to keep his fear for her under control. She needed the calm and logical brother to step forward here, or she would die. 'Where is she? There's no one at Summerhill Hall. Where would they take her to do this – ritual?'

'Lewis,' Ina said quietly. 'Please sit down. I can't think when you're charging about.'

He sat. But stood straight back up again. He looked at the walls, at the images there. The one he'd seen before, when Annie was with him, of the woman holding the goat, gave him chills. He imagined the poor animal being sacrificed shortly after the photo was taken. 'Where would they take her to do something like this?' he repeated.

He walked round the sofa and as he paced, he thought through everything he'd learned, everywhere they'd been since he and Annie first drove down to this part of the world. 'A ritual like this,' he looked from the walls to Ina. 'What do they require? What do they believe makes the magic work?'

'They have the ceremony. They have the sacrificial...' she paused and Lewis knew it was before she said the word 'victim'. 'And there's no getting away from it – today is an auspicious one for people with this set of beliefs.'

'Putting ourselves in their heads for a moment,' Clare said, and Lewis could see her detective's mind working, 'they'd want somewhere private where they won't be disturbed. Somewhere they don't have to spend time cleaning if they ... make a mess.' Lewis heard a wince in her voice. He closed his eyes against the thought.

He stopped walking, and when he opened his eyes again his attention was snagged by a woodcut image at eye level on the wall. It showed a man and a woman on a horse surrounded by what Lewis guessed might be witches, men and female, all of them reaching towards the couple atop the horse. The female was depicted in the act of falling off, eager hands below grasping, and her partner was wielding a sword. All around the borders of the image were leafless trees, and beyond the endangered couple, top centre, was the suggestion of a cave – a high, narrow slit on a wall of rock.

'Hang on,' Lewis said. 'I've seen this before.'

'It's a bit of local history,' said Ina. 'This is the moment that lead to the capture of the cannibal Sawney Bean and his clan.'

'But I've seen this exact image before,' Lewis said, as a memory burst into his mind. 'Benjamin Oldfield. He has the very same one on the wall behind his desk.'

'He does?' Ina looked up at him.

'Coincidence?' Lewis asked.

'Coincidence is only ever guidance from higher beings, Lewis,' Ina replied.

Clare stood up to take a closer look at the picture. 'Ina's right. It shows the moment when things started to go wrong for the cannibals.'

'You know about the legend?' Lewis asked.

'I grew up in this area, Lewis. It's impossible not to be aware of the legend of Sawney Bean round here.' She paused, face screwed up, as if trying to connect dots. 'As the legend goes, on this night' – she pointed at the woodcut – 'Sawney and his gang attacked a couple on a horse on their way home to Ballantrae from visiting relatives inland. The man fought them off with his sword. His wife fell to the crowd and was disembowelled before his eyes. He ran off, told the local law, or whatever stood for law in the sixteenth century, and the king sent five hundred soldiers to root them out once and for all. The entire clan was shipped across to Edinburgh, where they were all executed.'

The wind picked up. Rain battered the window.

Lewis turned away from the image, and stared out of the window, trying to ground himself in the real world, away from talk of cannibals and magic rituals. 'I thought I was done with this shit. Last year when Annie was out in the wilds with that pastor, I was beside myself. If something happens to her...' The window was rocked by a particularly strong blast of wind.

'The cave,' Ina said. 'That's it. That's what we're missing.' She pushed herself to her feet and came to stand beside Lewis, looking up at the image. 'The cannibal thing is likely nonsense, but the cave is real.' She looked at Lewis, her eyes full of certainty, and concern. 'Clare will be able to tell you – it regularly attracts all kinds of weirdos, anything from camp-outs, to weddings, to suicides.' She held a hand to her mouth. 'Why didn't I see it before? Of course! This is a place of power, of dark energy. This' – she stabbed at the image with a bent, trembling finger – 'is where it is going to happen.'

'Dark power? Dark energy? Really?' Clare raised her eyebrows.

'It's your job to be cynical, dear,' Ina answered. 'But it has been known for millennia that there are sites where energy converges – and for whatever reason, people are drawn to them.'

Lewis stared into her eyes. 'I've heard too many mentions of Sawney's cave in the last few days. Maybe you're right, and coincidence is really guidance from an otherworldly source.'

'And it was near there that Damien's car was found,' Clare said reluctantly. 'But the cannibal's cave is entered from the beach. That image makes it look like it's in the middle of a wood.'

Lewis chewed on that for a moment, an idea for action forming in his mind. 'What's that look on your face?' Clare said, looking concerned.

'Annie's there.' He turned to look out of the window into the bluster of the wind and rain. 'And I need to go right now.'

Chapter 87

Annie

Sensory impressions flicked through Annie's brain, like a pack of cards scattered in the air. A car door slamming shut. The screech of tyres. Squeal of brakes. Tired and heavy limbs as her feet sank into sand. Stumbling over a rock. A gull screaming imprecations into the night sky. A firm hand on her arm as she was corrected before she fell.

There was rain. Then there wasn't. And wind shifting from a hefty push to a silky kiss in seconds. Salt in the air, brine teasing her nostrils to a sneeze. More walking, shuffling, stumbling. Uncaring hands and daggered fingers pushing, probing, guiding.

Her sight came and went, feeling like it arrived on the whim of a capricious god, gifting her images of a silvered seascape, exhausted waves limping onto a storm-strewn beach; small trees and giant logs being rejected by the oceans and spewed back onto land.

If she could just sit on one, gather her thoughts, make sense of now ... but hands pushed, fingers poked and she was back on her feet, and there before her a cliff face sundered by a jagged, lightning-shaped opening.

Huffing breath at her ear, and a voice: 'Nearly there.'

Nearly where?

She was removed from sense and reason. Part of her was too exhausted, too worn down to care. She was nought but a speck on a mote of dust. A cluster of cells that belonged nowhere. A motherless child. So worthless even her father killed himself rather than be with her. Hated by her neighbours. A guileless girl, so obtuse her boyfriend lured her to a killing site. A woman tormented by a curse and a concert of murmuring with no purpose behind it other than to permanently unmoor her from sanity.

'Here,' someone said. A female voice. A strong hand on her

shoulder. Something warm at her bottom lip. She opened her mouth purely by reflex. 'Sip.' She did, and swallowed.

'Not too much,' someone else said. 'She needs to be more awake.'

Then, a sense of being held, consoled, reassured about who she was and her place in the world – for she would be rebuilt, re-moulded, would have a life full of wonder and joy and power.

Then

Nothing.

Then

Cold.

Cold stone under her. Cold, rough stone, abrading her tender flesh when she moved.

Cold. So very cold.

Annie tried to sit up, but it felt like there was a weight on her, holding her down.

And it was dark, so very dark. The only light in the space was flickering away to her far left. A candle. No, bigger than a candle. Some kind of open fire, or flaming torch?

A memory of being in the passageway down in the cellar, face pressed against the door of the room in which Craig had been held. She couldn't help but imagine the two men inside – Craig, and the recently deceased Damien Fox, both of them lying there like a shuffle of bones.

Then silence.

A world of silence so profound it rang its echo in her ear.

And now here she was, splayed out on this rock. The thought almost stopped there before she could finish ... splayed out like a sacrifice.

The thought was enough to provide a surge of energy. Just enough for Annie to lift her head and look around. But her torso and legs felt like lead, as if they were moulded to the rock below her.

Light flickered, cold seeped up from the rough stone, slowly numbing every cell of her body. Wind elbowed its way through the long gap in the cliff face, whistling an urgent song of death and hunger, and Annie tasted salt on its wings. She became aware of shadows reaching up the walls. Where was she? In a cave? Light grew and flickered, and she became aware of people.

'What are you doing?' she mumbled, aware that her words were weak, incomprehensible even to her: 'Whatyoudoin?'

Her defiance in that moment was a feeble thing. A dandelion seed cast in the face of a gust of wind. A mouse baring its teeth to the lion.

'Help,' Annie managed. 'Help.'

Annie fought to move her arms and legs, but the impulses wouldn't arrive at the nerve endings, and her limbs felt as if they were stuck to the surface on which they lay. Move, dammit.

In the next moment, Annie felt her awareness grow. She was above herself, looking down. And she saw people arranged along the cave wall. Some of their identities were revealed to her slowly, like pages of a book being pulled back. Gaia. Benjamin Oldfield, and his wife, Evelyn. Then a face that sparked recognition – she was famous, but for what? And then a tall man in his fifties, already with white hair. She wouldn't have been surprised if he'd been a policeman. Another couple of men she didn't know.

Words were being cast into the air above them. Strange, guttural syllables from a language that made no sense. A phrase repeated. Like a prayer or a hymn. No. Not a prayer. A spell.

Annie knew a deep and terrible fear. This was where she would die. In this cold, dark, strange place. This entrance to a hell no one knew existed.

Someone came near, her face formed out of darkness, and kissed her forehead.

'We break the curse tonight,' Gaia said softly. 'Your family and mine have shared it for centuries. These torments have plagued our lives. But no longer. Their end will be your end too. And your blood, your wonderfully rich blood will help us *finally* raise a she-devil.' She stroked Annie's cheek. 'And all you need to do is lie there and embrace death.'

Chapter 88

Lewis

The headlights of Clare's car pierced the thick dark ahead of them. Lewis drummed his feet on the floor, certain that something terrible was about to happen to Annie. He'd never resorted to prayer, but his need to find her safe was a long, uncut string of words in his mind – let her be okay, let her be okay, let her be okay – aimed at whatever higher power might be paying attention.

'You alright?' Clare asked.

Fear and worry were twin twists in his stomach, a catch in his throat. Making sound in that moment was beyond him and he could only nod. He replied with a growl.

'I'm sure Ina's exaggerating,' Clare said. 'This is all just some kind of collection of coincidences.'

Lewis coughed. 'You said there was no such thing as coincidence when it came to crimes being committed. That everything had to be checked.'

'I did say that, yes.' The low sweep of her car lights showed a gap in the road, a turn to the right. 'We're here...'

As soon as she stopped Lewis was out of the car. Clare joined him and squinted against the driving wind and rain.

'Do you know where we're going?' he shouted into her ear.

'This way.' Hunched against the wind she walked towards the shore line. 'Just ... watch ... slippy.' Every other word was torn from her mouth, like rags cast into the fierce wind.

Lewis knew nothing but the need to move. Annie was near, and in imminent danger. So as fast as the uncertain surfaces and poor visibility would allow, hunched against the wind and rain and spray from the sea, he followed Clare and picked his way around rock pools and the shoulders of barnacled boulders, swathes of bladderwrack, and more sticks and branches thrown up by the still-churning sea.

Lewis stumbled. Bumped into something. Clare. At that moment there was a break in the clouds, and the moon shone through, just enough for them to get their bearings.

'It's here. Just ahead.' Clare pointed.

And then they were standing in front of a high split in the cliff face, the sea behind them suddenly quieter now, sounding a lazy roll against rock and sand, the salted breeze chilling their skin.

A shout came from within the gap. A cry for help. Without hesitating Lewis ran inside, Clare following. They stumbled over pebble and rock until moments later, breath harsh, they both halted as if they'd ran into a glass panel.

Lewis looked around, his eyes moving from one image to another, his brain trying to keep up and make sense. Everything was wreathed in shadow or camouflaged by a stuttering light. Little equated with his long-established view of the world.

His nose filled with the scent of sea and earth, and something long dead. Somewhere in the vast hall a drip echoed; like the metronome of a diseased heart. There were people here, how many he couldn't tell, but he could hear them breathing fast, as if on the verge of a group panic.

And then a strange chant began to rise from them, like aural dust. Something flew past Lewis's head. He ducked. Stumbled, and when he managed to correct himself, he saw Annie. She was supine on a flat rock. An altar.

'Lewis,' she called. 'Help me.' He'd never heard such desperation in her voice.

He caught movement to his right, and he watched as someone,

a woman, reached towards Annie, something long and glinting in her hand.

Chapter 89

Annie

'Lewis,' Annie shouted. 'Lewis.'

She knew he was near. She could feel it. But could he even hear her? See her? Voices built in the chill air of the cave; thin, discordant, but holding a rhythm that was suggestive of another place in time. The noise grated, verging on the painful, and Annie wanted to shout desperately at everyone to stop. She looked towards the singers and saw them all, in a line, eyes closed, mouths working on a chant.

Fatigue pulled at her eyes. Tired. So tired. What had they given her? It felt like she hadn't been properly awake for days. Living in a world where dream and reality wove through and in and out of the other. She was unable to discern the difference. If only she could pick a sense that was based on real life and tether herself to that.

The roar of wood on flame, the anguished screams of dying women fed to the fire for someone else's sins. Head forward, hair covering her face, falling to the earth, she cried, too much. It was too much.

No more. The sin was not hers, and she would not be tormented by it for another moment.

Where had that thought come from?

Pick a sense. Tether to that. Use that as a rope to pull you into the here and now.

Her murmurs. They were the only thing she knew was real. She homed in on that hum. Welcomed them as they built to a cackle.

I feel your hate, she told them, and I welcome it because that's where real life is.

She was now able to lift her head from the rock table, and as she watched, Lewis ran to her. But his path was blocked by one of the men. The cop. They grappled. Lewis swung at the man's head.

Another man joined him and they wrestled with Lewis. Held him tight. He struggled against them, his mouth working on a shout.

Clare Corrigan appeared and joined the fray. She was pushed off, fell back. Hit her head on a rock. She scrambled back up to her feet.

Annie tried to sit up. She may have been awake now, but her body wasn't yet obeying the commands from her mind.

A woman was over her, a large knife in her hand – Gaia.

Please no, Annie thought. No.

Evelyn joined Gaia. 'Let me,' she shouted over the chanting, and with the knife now in her possession she kissed the blade.

Annie fought to catch her gaze. 'No. please, Evelyn, no,' she begged.

'The cup,' Evelyn shouted. 'For the blood. Bring it to me, Ben,' she insisted.

Annie was aware of movement by her side. Ben collecting the cup, and the knife was poised over her heart once more.

'No,' Annie urged. She tried to sit up. 'No,' she begged. 'Please, no.'

Gaia moved to stand by her head, her hands pressing down on Annie's shoulders, holding her in place.

'No. Don't do this,' Annie shouted, and struggled, and fought with everything she had.

Ben reached his wife's side, and Annie was aware of him moving her hand and placing it over the cup.

Lewis broke free. Clare picked up a rock and threw it at the other man. But they were too far away. Evelyn lifted her hand high.

The knife dropped. Evelyn twisted as she brought it down, and buried it into her husband's chest.

Chapter 90

Annie
Four weeks later

Dark soil was heaped up on one side of the grave. Sound was deadened by a rain so thick and constant it felt that the air was pure moisture. The minister was hunched against the elements, his voice thin but unwavering as he went through a ceremony he'd doubtless performed hundreds of times.

He looked up through his sodden fringe. His eyes catching Annie and Lewis. A note of appreciation in his eyes.

'Thank you for coming. It looks like everyone else has deserted this poor soul.' He looked sideways. 'Apart from that solitary ghoul from the press.'

Annie had spotted the photographer the moment she stepped out of Lewis's car, but ignored the shouted request for a quote about the funeral they were about to attend. She was surprised there was only one. But then the story the media had gone with was that Craig Oldfield had only been a bit-part player in the whole saga – the 'Sawney Bean Murders', as the media nicknamed the affair.

It was a month since they'd all staggered from that cave into a rising tide and wind and rain. Shivering and exhausted, they'd managed to make it to the office on the caravan park, knocked on the door until the night watchman let them in. He gave them blankets and warm drinks, while Clare called her colleagues at the local police station.

Why she felt the urge to attend his funeral, Annie couldn't quite explain. She'd been to Damien's, but not Benjamin

Oldfield's, of course, or those of any of the faceless, nameless bodies that had been covered with lime in that terrible cellar at Summerhill Hall.

Ben Oldfield had garnered all the headlines, of course. The prominent citizen and lawyer who had spent his life protecting people's rights while at the same time studying the occult, had a string of sacrifices and dead bodies behind him. What a delicious irony, the hacks sang in countless newspaper and online articles, that he had his just desserts when his wife of nearly three decades stabbed him in the heart. Evelyn then tried to turn the knife on herself, but Clare Corrigan rushed over and disarmed her.

Everything dissolved into chaos then. People running for the exit, no doubt trying to put as much distance as possible between them and a dead body – the corpse of the very man who had no doubt forced their attendance at the ceremony.

And that was the moment the other architect of all of this, Gaia – or Sylvia Lowry-Law – disappeared. From her place on the plinth, Annie turned her head and watched the woman as she ran from the cave, under cover of all the confusion and shouting. She had since vanished.

During the investigation that followed, each of the others at the ceremony, noteworthy residents all, pointed the finger at Ben Oldfield, alleging he'd bribed them to appear, and they had no idea what they were really involved in. The authorities refused to accept these explanations and a series of trials was scheduled over the next year. The wheels of justice turned slowly but determinedly, and Annie was pleased that each and every one of them would be tried in court.

Oldfield's most likely critic, Evelyn, was in police custody and was saying nothing, however. She had offered no explanation for her part in the crimes over the years, or why she had finally turned on her husband, although Annie didn't need that explanation, given the man had arranged the murder of her beloved son, Craig.

Annie couldn't entirely explain the empathy she felt for Craig Oldfield. Being part of such a family wouldn't have been easy for him, and that explained his carapace of arrogance, and his anti-social behaviour. When she spoke with his sister, Alison, she said she had no idea what had been going on under her nose. She had been at an utter loss to explain to Annie – and the police – how all of this had happened without her being aware. The only thing she could think of was how protective her mother had been.

'All my life,' she said, her eyes pleading with Annie to believe her, 'my mother rarely let me out of her sight. She all but rushed me to hospital every time I got a bruise or a cut as a kid.' She paused. 'And when I think of Dad?' She shuddered, no doubt at the thought of the horrors the man had unleashed. 'It was as if I barely existed. As if he and Mum had a silent agreement that I was hers to care for, you know?'

Her assertions seemed genuine to Annie, and she understood why Alison wasn't here now. But Annie felt that someone had to be here to mark Craig's passing. After all, he had turned on his parents to save Lewis's life.

After attending the funeral, Annie and Lewis were invited to a late lunch, at Ina Hetherington's. They were sitting at Ina's kitchen table with Clare, each of them holding a spoon before a bowl of lentil and bacon soup, steam curling like a promise.

'How are you getting on? I saw you again on the news the other night.' Ina looked at Annie, her eyebrows knitted with concern.

Annie reached across the table for Ina's hand and gave it a squeeze of thanks. 'The locals might still be scared of me, but they like the media even less, so no one has gotten wind of my where-abouts – yet. I've been left, largely, to my own devices.' As she finished speaking, she caught a wince and raised eyebrow from her brother.

'Largely?' he asked.

Dead bodies being found in the infamous cave ensured a frenzy in the press, and once again the media were all over Annie – the psychic and survivor of the murderer on Ardnamurchan, who was once more embroiled in murder and mayhem. Her name and face had rarely been out of the news these last few weeks. It meant that she was once again all but locked in her little cottage. Which was fine with her: the building was once again wind- and water-tight, and her old boss at the café in Lochaline's waterfront regularly came by with her shopping.

This meeting at Ina's was a rare day out, one Annie had only undertaken after she'd worked on the disguise of a baseball cap and a pair of sunglasses.

'Have you found out what they were feeding me yet, Clare?' Annie looked across the table to the young cop who was fast becoming a friend. She and Lewis were spending a lot of time together, and Annie couldn't have been happier for them.

'The lab reports haven't all come back yet, but our technicians found all kinds of strange herbs and plants in the garden at Summerhill Hall. One of the guys said he'd never seen anything like it outside of a Victorian poison garden he'd once visited.' Clare made a face. 'You're a lucky girl. By all accounts Lowry-Law was an expert in growing and ministering them. Some of the stuff in her garden was so lethal the technicians blow-torched it.'

'Clearly the plan was to use the herbs, or whatever, to keep me docile and hidden long enough that they could do the ceremony on Halloween.' She shook her head, thinking how close she had been to death. Again. 'It's only over the last few days that I've managed to piece it all together. She came up to see me in Lochaline. I'm not sure if she fed me anything then, but...' Annie looked to Lewis. 'Remember the Inn in Ardgour? When that relative of poor Lachlan had a go at me? Sylvia was there that day. She pushed past me and I felt something wet on the back of my hand. She must have followed us down from the cottage. Wonder what kind of hallucinogen she gave me then. I was certainly spaced out for a couple of days after that. And then the tea I had at

Alison's gave me the same disorientation as the stuff Evelyn fed me at the Oldfields.'

'What about Sylvia?' Ina asked Clare. 'I'd hate to see her get away with all of this.'

'There have been reported sightings all over the place. The public doing its usual good job in confusing matters for us, but now that I'm back at work I'm confident we'll catch her. Her luck is bound to run out eventually,' Clare replied.

Annie was gratified and relieved to see the determination in Clare's face. Sylvia had got to her with ease, and she was more than a little worried that she was still at large – with who knew what kind of devilish plans in her head.

'She's a clever, cunning woman,' Ina said. 'But arrogant, and hopefully that arrogance will be her undoing.' As if the dog sensed her agitation he gave a little bark and Ina stretched down to pat him on the head. 'I'm just so happy that you two are okay, and that Oldfield and Lowry-Law's days are over,' Ina added.

'And well done you,' Lewis said. 'Keeping an eye on those two for all these years.'

Ina gave Lewis a little nod of thanks. Then Annie saw her face drop. She realised why: people had died, despite Ina's best efforts.

'Anyway,' Ina said, looking up. 'What now for Annie Jackson?'

Annie raised an eyebrow, held a hand over her heart, allowed the thought that if Benjamin Oldfield hadn't killed the young man he raised as his son, his mother wouldn't have turned on her husband, and she'd be in that grave she'd just visited. And she felt profound gratitude for the wholeness she felt under her fingers, and the distant, accusatory hum in her mind.

She returned Ina's smile. 'What now indeed?'

Epilogue

Sylvia Lowry-Law burned with hate. It seethed in every cell of her body. She was glowing like a hot coal.

That stupid, stupid Oldfield woman. She was supposed to stab her husband, and then give the knife to Sylvia so she could finish Annie Jackson. That was what they agreed when she'd told her what Ben had done to her son. And surely that would have been enough blood – enough of a sacrifice that the Baobhan Sith would finally make an appearance.

It was pleasing, that Ben died. He got just what he deserved. He was too cowardly to kill Craig himself, so he'd paid someone to do it. They had chickened out, hadn't finished the job, so they'd had to dump him in the basement at Summerhill Hall along with Damien Fox, and let nature take its course.

And what a deliciously cruel irony that was. Killing his own son. It was Sylvia who'd planted the seed that Phineas Dance was the boy's father. Dance couldn't deny it because by then he was dead; and Ben was so twisted by Dance's ministrations over the years that he easily believed the lie, no matter how often and vociferously Evelyn protested that he *was* the father.

As for Annie Jackson, that she survived was too much. Distant cousin or not, she deserved to die. And she would. Justice would be served in that regard. It would just have to wait for now. One thing the young Ms Jackson would learn to her cost was that Sylvia Lowry-Law forgot nothing.

When everything went wrong in that cave Sylvia had slipped out among the noise and confusion and hid just along the coast in another cave. The authorities wouldn't consider that she might seek refuge so close to the scene of the crime.

It had been bone-snappingly cold, and she was hungry, but she was used to testing herself. She'd waited there for a couple of days and then made her way down to the village of Ballantrae, where she'd hitched a lift from a passing lorry driver. He'd dropped her off just down the hill from the Oldfield house. The initial search and investigation would find little up there in High Dailly, while at Summerhill Hall they'd find a number of bodies. How it saddened her that her home was now lost to her forever.

Ben had given her a spare key long ago, in case of any trouble, so she'd let herself in and had a long shower, fed herself and dressed in Evelyn's clothes. They were almost the same size so that saved her looking too strange. Surely, Sylvia thought, as she studied herself in the mirror, if the authorities were looking for a dangerous criminal, as they had described her in one news bulletin, they would never suspect someone dressed in a lavender twin-set and pearls. Evelyn always did have a deeply old fashioned sense of style.

Fortune had continued to shine on her: she found Evelyn's driving licence in the glovebox of her car and saw that the vehicle had an almost full tank of petrol.

Waiting out the authorities for another couple of days, she phoned a national crime helpline and reported sighting one Sylvia Lowry-Law in a motorway service station on the M74. Then she phoned again a day later to report a sighting outside of Hull – suggesting she was aiming for a ferry to the continent. She had then called around some of the friends she made over the years, and sightings of her began to pop up across Europe, from Paris to Berlin.

Where she was heading now was probably the most obvious route out of Ayrshire – but knowing human nature as she did, the obvious would already have been checked first and by now discounted. She was going to Cairnryan, where she would hop on a ferry to Belfast and head south from there. She had a couple of old associates from the Order who lived in the Republic of Ireland. They would put her up for a few months, until the coast was well and truly clear. That would give her time to arrange a new identity and work on a new plan.

A quick spell before she left – seeking safety and favour – one that included an apology to her ancestors that she hadn't yet managed to cancel the curse, to end the torments. But that would come in good time, she was sure, with the eventual death of Annie Jackson.

At that her little shadow shimmered in silent judgement.

'Say something, dammit,' she shouted to her side. She felt a scream build, but fought to contain it. She would not give the little demon the satisfaction. But the resentment that she should be so cursed by this presence smouldered on. 'Leave me be,' she snapped. 'You and your quiet condemnation. We used to be friends...' She stopped. Biting down on her frustration. Then she took a long, slow breath, determined to return to her spell and fighting with every ounce of her will against the agitation she was being pushed towards.

In truth, she was terrified that she was one scream away from losing it altogether. No. She would not end up like other women in her and Annie's family line – on strong medication, drooling onto a straitjacket.

If that little horror – she looked quickly to the side – would just leave her alone.

Her last spell before she left the house – and the country – also included a beseechment to the Baobhan Sith. Be patient, she prayed. Her time would surely come, for she refused to give up on that purpose. She was woman. She was power – in the final reckoning, the Baobhan Sith would help Sylvia gain revenge on her enemies.

The drive to Cairnryan was uneventful, the road at this time of day fairly quiet, the weather calm after the storms that had raged over Halloween and the following days. She left Evelyn's car in the far reaches of the car park at the ferry terminal. Abandoning it was not her favourite part of the plan, but it would make her more easily identifiable. She had enough cash to get to Belfast, and from there to Dublin, where she could arrange to be collected.

The wait in the terminal for the nod to go onboard was excruciating. Made worse by the gangs of football supporters who were drunk and singing stupid football songs at the top of their lungs. What she would have given to have some of her herbal solutions on her – send a few of them to sleep – but she would have to make do with stern looks and whispered curses.

Finally, the announcement was made that they could board, so inserting herself among a group of fans, she made her way along the corridor to the gate for the boat.

Everything slowed when they reached a final security check. There were three officers there – two men and one woman, each of them luminous in oversized waterproof jackets. The men were carefully checking tickets while the woman was scanning the crowd. This unsettled Sylvia. Might she be looking for her? No, that was ridiculous. Besides, everything she had done was in service of the Baobhan Sith. Surely she would protect her.

The closer she got to the front of the queue, though, the more nervous she became. Her heart racing. She was close. So very close to a new life.

Her shadow mocked from the sidelines.

'Go away,' she hissed.

They edged closer, and feeling relief that she was near to boarding, Sylvia allowed herself to relax a little, especially when she saw that there were only two security staff at the gate now.

In the periphery of her vision she saw her shadow and felt her hard stare.

'Leave me alone,' she barked.

Someone turned to her. A man. 'You alright, missus?'

She stared him down.

Edging forward.

All eyes ahead now. Everyone with their ticket and ID in their hand.

Edging forward.

And Sylvia felt a tap on her shoulder.

'Excuse me.'

Sylvia turned, ready to give whoever it was a sharp piece of her mind.

'What do you ...?' she began, and saw a young woman in a luminous oversized jacket, clear-eyed and determined.

'Sylvia Lowry-Law, my name's Detective Clare Corrigan, and you're under arrest.'

'No, no, no,' Sylvia shouted, struggled against the hand on her forearm.

But her shadow was there, right there, eyes hard, face up against hers, lips peeled back in a smile, and Sylvia screamed, and screamed. And as she succumbed to her screams, part of her mind – perhaps the last part not given over to madness – realised that the shadow she'd taken for her sister was in fact the family curse come home to roost.

And she would be there every day for the rest of Sylvia's life, harassing, scalding, searing her every breath and thought in a plague of quiet torments.

Acknowledgements

Dear Readers, welcome back to the world of Annie Jackson!

It was with some trepidation that I made, with *The Murmurs*, a change of direction with my writing, but your willingness to take Annie so enthusiastically into your hearts repaid all of that worry and hard work in spades.

As ever, to get the words from my head and into the stack of pages you hold in your hands has taken a group effort. Huge thanks must go to the editorial team who have saved my blushes countless times in this manuscript: Karen Sullivan, your support and belief during a testing time for publishers and authors is immense. West Camel – do you have any hair left? Thank you so much for your patience and diligence; this book is a much better read for your efforts. I also send my appreciation to Amanda Sedaka and Rachel Sargeant for their work on the book.

Thanks also to the extended Team Orenda – Cole Sullivan, Anne Cater, Mary P, Danielle Price, Mark Swan et al.

Then there's the crime-scene crew – helping keep me sane over the years, and providing laughs and distractions and helping to spread the word. Thanks to all the authors, booksellers, bloggers, reviewers, book-festival organisers, and particularly readers. We are a truly special community of like minds. Book people really are the best people!